Praise for
The Strange Adventures of Rangergirl

"Tim Pratt's *The Strange Adventures of Rangergirl* is a two-fisted meta-fiction of Old West mythos and modern day—sharp writing, cool characters, fascinating ideas, and the courage to have fun. Readers of comics and classics and both will enjoy this novel."
 —Jeffrey Ford, author of *The Portrait of Mrs. Charbuque*

"*Rangergirl* is a fine blend of imaginative and engaging—a tale well-told."
 —Cory Doctorow, co-editor of *Boing Boing* and author of *Someone Comes to Town, Someone Leaves Town*

The Strange Adventures of Rangergirl

TIM PRATT

BANTAM BOOKS

THE STRANGE ADVENTURES OF RANGERGIRL
A Bantam Spectra Book / December 2005

Published by
Bantam Dell
A Division of Random House, Inc.
New York, New York

Bantam Books, the rooster colophon, Spectra, and the portrayal of a
boxed "s" are trademarks of Random House, Inc.

Library of Congress Cataloging-in-Publication Data
Pratt, Tim, 1976–
The strange adventures of Rangergirl/Tim Pratt
p. cm.
ISBN-10: 0-553-38338-8
ISBN-13: 978-0-553-38338-6
I. Title.
PS3616.R385 S73 2005   2005048227
813/.6 22

Printed in the United States of America
Published simultaneously in Canada

www.bantamdell.com

For Heather,
who brought water to my desert.

The
Strange
Adventures of
Rangergirl

Skull Cracker

MARZI LEANED ON THE counter and watched, with dread twisting in her belly like a knot of rattlesnakes, as Beej trudged up the stairs. The worst of the morning rush was over and Hendrix was in the back watching his thirteen-inch portable TV, so Marzi would have to wait on Beej herself. He was talking to himself in a dreamily pleasant tone, which was somehow worse than mere ranting, and Marzi heard her own name several times in his otherwise incomprehensible monologue. Beej had always been a slob, but his hygiene and dress sense had deteriorated completely over the past few weeks. His carrot orange hair hung in greasy clumps around his face, and his ever-present black leather jacket—which must have been stifling in this heat—was smeared with mud and bits of grass. Marzi wondered if he'd lost his apartment or something; if he was sleeping outside.

Beej still came into the café every day, and Lindsay said he was still attending art classes, but clearly *something* had come catastrophically loose in his life. Marzi had seen heroin addiction in action, and it looked something like this, but she didn't think drugs were Beej's problem. Something in his eyes, the way they seemed to roll around loose lately, made her think he was having problems inside his *head*.

Beej clumped up to the counter, grinning at her, showing teeth that had gone too long without cleaning. He dropped a handful of coins, a few bottle caps, a beer can pull tab, and several pieces of a shredded photograph onto the counter.

"Lemon tea, Beej?" she said lightly.

"No. A mocha." He gripped the edge of the counter, his hands visibly shaking. "I found the shrine of the earthquake," he said. "I followed the path that leads to waste and hardpan. The god of the earthquake has accepted my devotions."

"Uh-huh," Marzi said, turning to the espresso machine to start his drink. "How have you been sleeping? You don't look so good." He didn't smell good, either; like mud, and ashes, and old carpets.

"I don't need to sleep anymore," he said. "My god gives me strength. But Marzi . . ." He frowned, then shook his head.

"What?" she asked, wondering why he'd been saying her name on the steps, if she should be worried. He often flirted with her, awkwardly, and she had a fondness for him despite his social deficiencies—he was always polite, and a talented collage artist and photographer—but she questioned if he was becoming obsessed.

"Nothing," he said, not meeting her eyes, taking his drink and heading for the Cloud Room. Beej liked that room the best. He said the castles in the mist—certainly the most soothing of the several room-spanning murals in the café—made him feel peaceful.

Marzi was about to drop his coins into the register when she noticed there was an Indian head penny and a buffalo nickel in the mix, in addition to a Sacagawea dollar coin. She pocketed those, making up the difference with cash from her own pockets. She didn't collect coins, but that mix of change had a distinctly Old West feel. She'd never thought much before about the way icons of the West appeared on currency. Maybe there was a story in that—something about counterfeiting, or magically transforming natural resources into cold cash. It seemed like more of an Aaron Burr story than an Outlaw one, but that could be good—she hadn't done much with Burr in the past few issues of her comic.

A scream, raw with shock and pain, erupted from the Cloud Room. Marzi came around the counter fast, holding a knife she didn't even remember picking up, and ran toward the sound, her heart pounding. She raced through the front room, bumping a little table with her hip and almost toppling it, and reached the Cloud Room just in time to see someone dash into the Teatime Room. She only caught a glimpse of him, but he was a striking figure: eagle feathers woven into his black hair, flesh the color of pale sand, the skin on his shirtless back oddly tattooed to resemble cracked earth. She didn't go after him—there was no other door out of the Teatime Room anyway, and Beej was lying on the floor beside an overturned chair, in need of more immediate attention.

Marzi knelt by Beej, keeping one eye on the empty doorway to the Teatime Room. "Are you okay?" she asked. "Did that guy hurt you?"

Beej opened his eyes and looked up at her dreamily. Then he giggled. Marzi flinched. If he'd wept, or whimpered, that would have been all right, something she could deal with, but the giggle was strange and terrible. "He wanted to see my brain," Beej said. "To compare the wrinkles in my head to a map of the canyons and gullies, to see if my mental terrain matches the texture of his territories. To touch me more deeply, to write his name with a knife in the folds of my mind . . ." He trailed off, then sat up, rubbing his fingers across his hairline, frowning. "Something . . ." He mumbled words she couldn't understand.

How could you tell if someone had just had a seizure? Maybe Beej was just having a fit of some kind, and the tattooed guy didn't have anything to do with it. "Beej—" she began.

The room shook—more, the *world* shook, and Marzi fell against a table. *Earthquake,* she thought, and almost as soon as she thought it, the quake was over. It was a fairly strong quake, nothing like the Loma Prieta disaster of 1989, but no tiny trembler, either. Marzi's stomach kept lurching even after the quake stopped, some part of her backbrain still insisting the ground beneath her was unsafe. Beej tried to stand up, and Marzi turned her attention to him, grateful to have something to set her attention on after the chaos of the last few moments. "Hold on," she said. "There might be aftershocks."

"No aftershocks," he said, rising. "That was a *fore*shock. Just a hint of things to come. I knew the earthquake was coming. The god gives me wisdom."

Marzi frowned and, after a moment, rose to her feet. Beej seemed fine—physically, anyway—so she stepped toward the Teatime Room, still holding her knife. She ducked her head inside, and there was no one there, just empty tables watched over by the painted gods on the walls. The man must have slipped out while she was distracted by the quake. "That man, with the tattoos—"

"No tattoos," Beej said. "His flesh is broken stone."

"What—" she began, but then the day manager, Hendrix, called her from the other room.

"Marzi! Get in here! That quake knocked three bottles of syrup off the shelf! It's going to smell like Irish Cream in here for years!"

"You're sure you're okay?" she asked.

"Never better," Beej said, picking up his overturned chair. "I'm going now. Things to do, people to be. See you later." He waved cheerfully before leaving.

He should get some help, Marzi thought, but that was as far as it went. Beej wasn't her responsibility, after all, but cleaning up the mess in the other room was.

LATER. WHEN THE quake clutter was cleared away and things had slowed to the usual late-afternoon lull, Marzi sat staring for a while out the big bay window onto Ash Street, watching bicycles and cars pass by. In Santa Cruz there were only two seasons—rainy winter and sunny summer—and winter was a long way off. The café was nearly deserted, and it looked a little shabby with so few inhabitants: a threadbare couch, scrounged chairs, mismatched tables, worn and scratched wooden floors. Only Garamond Ray's enormous murals set Genius Loci apart from all the other cafés in town, and up here in front the only painting was a space-scape, all cold white stars and shadow-occulted planets, not the loveliest of the murals. Still, the air smelled of coffee, there was a good Two Dollar Pistols disc on the stereo, and the morning madness was behind her.

She spotted Denis, the most regular of the café's regulars, looking dour as always on the couch, leafing through a book about modern art. His muddy boots were propped on the battle-scarred coffee table, making a mess, but Marzi didn't have the energy to tell him to put his feet down. An older woman Marzi didn't know sat drinking orange spice tea in the Ocean Room, tapping her pen rhythmically against the table, looking down at a spiral-bound notebook. A few tourists were talking loudly out on the deck, the usual background noise to Marzi's workdays. Hendrix, pale and improbably dreadlocked, sat on a stool in the kitchen, watching his tiny black-and-white television. He was the only person who'd been working at Genius Loci longer than Marzi had, and the only employee who'd been personally hired by the mysterious owners.

Marzi was on the verge of striking up a conversation with Denis, in the vague hope that his condescension and affected world-weariness would annoy her enough to keep her awake, when Lindsay came through the door like a glittering whirlwind. "Marzipan!" she said. "To what do we owe this honor? Shouldn't you be sleeping, or hunched over the drawing board?"

Marzi grinned. "Tina called in sick, so Hendrix asked me to cover her shift. I've got to work during the day tomorrow, too, but then I'll be back to my usual nocturnal ways." Marzi was normally the night manager—which was good, since that way she almost never had to see Hendrix, who managed during the day.

Lindsay leaned on the counter, looked around, and whispered conspiratorially: "Have you met the new boy yet? The one who moved into the Pigeonhole?"

"What's it to you?" Marzi said, taking down a pint glass to draw Lindsay her usual Guinness. "I thought you'd sworn off boys."

"Not for *me*," she said, rolling her eyes. "I'm interested for *you*. So you haven't met him?"

"Nope. He's still a man of mystery."

"Well, *I've* met him," Lindsay said. "Yesterday."

"Oh? What's the verdict?"

"Yummy. Speaking from a strictly consulting position, of course, since I've sworn off boys."

"What's he like?"

"Sort of an art-house Kafka-reader type, non-smoker but if he smoked they'd be black Czech cigarettes, makes jeans and a black shirt look like a black trenchcoat and dark glasses, butter-wouldn't-melt kind of cool. You know?"

It was actually a fairly succinct and comprehensible description, for Lindsay. At least she hadn't compared the new boy to some long-dead German artist, or worse yet, a figure from an obscure painting.

"He have a name?" Marzi asked, not sure if she was interested, or even interested in *being* interested.

"Jonathan. He's getting his master's in art history from some school in North Carolina. He's out here for the summer doing research."

Another academic artsy type. Ah, well. He'd come to the

right place, with Lindsay, Beej, and Denis already in more or less continuous residence. "What's he here to study?"

Lindsay spread her arms wide. "This."

Marzi frowned. "This what?"

"The murals. The last works of Garamond Ray."

"Ahhh," Marzi said. "That explains why he agreed to live in the Pigeonhole."

"It's about the only thing that *would* explain it," Lindsay agreed. "I'm sure he'll be around. He lives right upstairs. Where else would he go for coffee?"

"I'll wait with bated breath," Marzi said.

"Speaking of you and the men who love you," Lindsay said, "I hear Beej flipped out this morning."

Marzi nodded, though the details were fuzzy in her memory—the little quake loomed larger in her mind than anything else. "He was acting really weird when he came in," she said.

"How could you tell?" Denis interrupted from his place on the couch. "Beej is *always* weird."

"Yeah, so what's his deal?" Lindsay said. "He still comes to classes, but it's like having a wild animal in the studio, he's always wandering around and knocking stuff over, talking to himself. Is he okay?"

"How should I know?" Denis said. "I'm not his keeper." Beej and Denis had a strange relationship—like Pigpen meets the Boy Who Couldn't Stop Washing His Hands, Marzi sometimes thought. They argued about art and metaphysics, conversations that Marzi could barely follow, and which usually ended with Denis storming off and Beej looking sheepish. What if Beej was having a nervous breakdown or something? But what could Marzi do? She wasn't his keeper, either—just the barista who served him coffee, the woman he had a crush on, maybe. He wasn't her responsibility.

"Anyway," Marzi said. "He seemed kind of out of it, and a few minutes after he sat down, he started screaming. I ran in to see if he was okay, and he was on the floor babbling, basically, about gods and stuff. Then the earthquake hit, and he left shortly after. He *did* say he could sense the earthquake coming, though." She didn't bother to mention the tattooed man. He probably didn't have anything to do with it anyway. Still, thinking about him made her weirdly anxious.

"Wonderful," Denis said. "Beej thinks he's a Richter scale, now. As if he weren't delusional enough."

Lindsay turned and made a great show of looking Denis up and down. "Apparently you're under the delusion that you're part of this conversation." Lindsay was normally sweetness and light, but she seldom bothered to be civil to Denis; it was wasted effort, as he took kindness and scorn with equal disinterest.

"I'm crushed by your rejection," Denis said. He packed up his things and walked out, leaving muddy bootprints on the floor.

"See, it's guys like him that made me swear off boys," Lindsay said.

Marzi laughed. "He does give the gender a bad name."

Lindsay leaned over and kissed her cheek. "I've got to go study, Marzipan. Say bye-bye when you leave—I'm in for the long haul tonight. If you're working tomorrow, I'll see you then. And if the new boy is around, I'll introduce you."

"My heart goes pitter-pat. But I'm not sure I want to date anyone right now, you know?"

"You just say that because your years in the service industry have made you misanthropic," Lindsay said. "They're not all like Denis."

"If they were all like Denis, there'd be no trouble with overpopulation in the world," Marzi said.

"Stop being witty," Lindsay said, picking up her beer. "I've got work to do." She winked and went toward the Ocean Room.

Faced with further hours of relative boredom, Marzi went to the little shelf of secondhand books they kept for customers and picked up a copy of Louis L'Amour's *Hondo*. She'd read it before—she'd read all L'Amour's Westerns—but not for years. L'Amour—Love. Maybe she could have L'Amour, or a thinly disguised version of him, appear as a character in the next issue of *The Strange Adventures of Rangergirl*. Maybe he could be Rangergirl's love interest. She'd never done a love story before.

Scratching Gravel

THE NEXT DAY, MARZI met Jonathan.

She was busing tables in the Circus Room, whistling along to "Daboo Dabay" by Lutch Crawford and His Gone Geese, from a good old jazz disc she'd been playing during a lot of her shifts lately. Marzi carried her bus tray past a pale, dark-haired young man sitting at a small table under Harlequin's gaze. He whistled "Daboo Dabay" too, and for a moment their whistles synched perfectly. A sketchbook lay on the table before him, and he held a pen in his hand. He nodded to her and said, "Great music." He was cute, in a too-thin kind of way, but Marzi wasn't in a flirting mood. She'd had nightmares about a sand-colored Indian in a feathered headdress the night before, and the lingering aftereffects had bothered her all day.

"Sure is," Marzi said, glancing at his sketchbook as she passed. The page was covered with harsh cross-hatching, as if he'd scratched out every drawing he'd begun, and she wondered what he was trying to create. She went to the kitchen with the bus tray, took her disc out of the stereo, and said good night to Bobby-O. It was two o'clock, and she was done for the day, having come in at five A.M. to open. She had the night off—a rarity—and since she didn't have to work tomorrow, it was practically a vacation, given her usual work schedule. The guy with the sketchbook was bent over his work, drawing furiously, and she paused, thinking of talking to him—she suspected he might be interesting. But no. If he turned out to be a regular, she could be friendly later. Right now she just wanted to get to her drafting table and sketch the sandstone savage, get him out of her head and into the pages of her comic. He could be a minor villain in the next issue, or maybe a mysterious figure with an undisclosed agenda of his own—her comic was full of such shadowy characters, some of them with intentions so ambiguous even Marzi could not have said with certainty whether they were villains, heroes, or something else entirely. Marzi walked out the front door.

Lindsay was coming up the stairs as Marzi went down. "No, no, don't go," she said. "I have to tell you what happened in class today."

"Oh, joy. Tales from the ivory tower of academia."

Lindsay stuck out her tongue. "I get just as much paint on my clothes as you do, working girl. You'll want to hear this, believe me. Save me a seat," she said, pointing to the mostly full patio.

Marzi thought longingly of her pencils, her paper, and her drafting table, but she nodded. She and Lindsay had trouble synching their schedules and getting together during the school year; Lindsay was still on academic time, while Marzi had been a civilian for two years and had a somewhat erratic work schedule to boot. Marzi expected to be at home alone all evening anyway, so she could be social now. Her sandstone savage would wait.

Lindsay returned a few minutes later with a pint of Guinness and a cup of tea, and set the latter ceremoniously before Marzi. "So you met Jonathan," she said.

"Who?"

Lindsay rolled her eyes. "The new *boy*. The one who's getting Pigeonholed. I wouldn't mind if he pigeonholed *me*. But boys just lead to trouble."

"Oh! You mean the guy in the Circus Room? With the black hair and the sorta sunken eyes?"

"Sunken? They're dark and mysterious and haunted, hinting at a dangerous past, Marzipan."

Marzi sipped her tea. "Duly noted. So I met him. Glad we got past that awkward first step. So what's the story you have to tell? The sordid tale of a pop quiz gone wrong?"

Lindsay shook her head. "I was in class this afternoon, the class I have with Beej? We were all working, painting with oils—I hate oils—and Beej just flipped *out*. He fell off his stool and put his arms over his head and started yelling 'Earthquake!' And we all stopped, you know, Dr. Payne, too, and sorta paid attention to the world around us for a few seconds, and there was no earthquake, but Beej kept yelling. Dr. Payne threw him out of class, and Beej went stumbling out of the room like he was drunk or something, like the ground really was shaking under him." She shook her head. "Creepy. And he smells weird lately, too—weirder than usual—like ashes and old garbage and stuff. You saw him yesterday, you know how he is, right? I worry about his mental health. Maybe he should drop out of school for a while, get some help—" She stopped talking and winced. "Sorry, Marzi. I wasn't thinking."

"It's cool," Marzi said, dredging up a smile. "It was a long time ago. Taking the withdrawal was good for me. I needed to do it."

"I kinda wish you'd come back to school afterward," Lindsay said, looking down into her beer.

Marzi just nodded. They'd had this conversation before, and it never went anywhere new. For Lindsay, school was important: She needed the structure, and enjoyed the instruction. But Marzi tended to think that the only reason to get an art degree was to get a job teaching art—welcome to the closed loop of the humanities. Lindsay, obviously, disagreed.

"Anyway," Marzi said. "That thing with Beej yesterday."

Lindsay nodded. "Yeah, you said he was screaming? But there really was an earthquake, that time."

"Only *after* he was screaming, by coincidence." Marzi sighed. "Maybe next time I see Beej, I'll suggest he see a counselor at school or something."

"Me, too," Lindsay said. "We'll be concerned members of the community. He's a talented guy—I hate to see him fall apart." She sipped her Guinness. "So anyway. I told Jonathan to come out and join us once he finished drawing." She grinned, impish.

"Matchmaker, matchmaker. Why don't *you* hit on the new boy? And don't tell me you've sworn off boys—I saw you making out with Michael Baker just two weeks ago."

"A drunken fling," Lindsay said with a wave of her hand. "Too much red wine and too little discernment. No more than a grope in a corner. It only served to confirm my all-girl resolve. Besides, I don't *need* romance in my life. I've got someone."

"Oh?"

"Alice Belle," Lindsay said.

Marzi widened her eyes. "*Alice?*" Alice was a semiregular at Genius Loci, one of the bikers who frequented the place, mostly on weekends. She wore leather and kept her hair cropped short, and she had a tattoo of one of Edward Gorey's Gashlycrumb Tinies on her forearm.

"I am being fully initiated into the mysteries of Sapphic love," Lindsay said, deadpan, and Marzi burst out laughing. "I've never been all *that* experienced with girls," Lindsay went on. "Just a little making out here and there. But Alice . . . Wow. Just, wow. She's a fire-dancer, did you know? She practiced in her backyard last night, and I watched. It was amazing; she's so graceful, so all-in-control—and not just when she's dancing. I had so much fun with her, I thought about you, and how much fun you're *not* having. When was the last time you did more than sleep in bed?"

"A lady has her secrets," Marzi said. It had been a long time, actually, and the last time hadn't been very good, a romp with an old lover who was better in her memory than he was in her bed. "But I can sleep with Hendrix any time I want."

Lindsay giggled.

Jonathan appeared in the doorway, carrying a black messenger bag over his shoulder and a coffee cup in his hand. *So much for working,* she thought, but the conversation was pretty effectively purging her mind of bad dreams, so it was okay.

Jonathan came down the stairs to their table, putting down his cup and pulling up a chair. Lindsay put her elbows on the table and set her chin in her hands, blinking at Jonathan prettily.

I bet she'll flirt with the doctor on her deathbed, Marzi thought, with something like admiration.

Jonathan held out his hand to Marzi, and in the process knocked over Lindsay's half-full pint glass. Guinness splattered everywhere, and Lindsay leapt back to keep from being soaked. Jonathan grimaced, said, "Shit, I'm sorry," and wiped at the spill with a napkin. Marzi caught Lindsay's eye and silently mouthed "Cool, huh?" Lindsay shrugged expressively. She could shrug like no one else; her shrugs had nuances. This shrug meant, roughly, "Sure, but what do I know?"

Jonathan sopped up the rest of the spill. "Shit. I'm a klutz. I'll buy you another one."

"Deal," Lindsay said. "But don't expect me to put out afterward."

Jonathan just laughed. So he was at least *that* cool. If Lindsay had said something like that to Beej or Denis, they would have blushed at the least, and possibly run away. Jonathan went back into the café.

"So now you've met him twice," Lindsay said. "Not much of a first impression, I guess, and an even worse second impression, but they say the third time's the charm."

"Don't hold your breath, Lindsay love."

"He's just nervous because he's into you," she said. "You know how guys get around pretty girls. You make him all fumble-fingered."

"Then why doesn't he knock stuff over when he talks to

you alone? Or is that a facet of your relationship you haven't told me about?"

"No, he's cool around me, but I'm not *pretty*."

"Lindsay—"

"I'm not being down on myself. It's true. I'm not pretty. I'm *cute*. I have round cheeks. I'd look good in gingham. I could do television commercials, hold puppies and tell people to buy things, but I'm not *pretty*, just cute. I'm the best-friend-girl, the one guys talk to about the women they're in love with." She shrugged with an air of gracious resignation. "I'm used to it. Though it's been a while since any guys have come mooning to me about *you*. Maybe I miss the second-hand attention, did you ever think of that? Even if I have sworn off boys." She grinned, then glanced at the stairs. "Where's my beer? I tell you, the service in this place . . ."

"Whoa, what's that?" Marzi said, pointing toward the street. A car had just pulled into one of the metered parallel spaces in front of the café. It was a hatchback, but Marzi couldn't determine the make, model, or even color, as the car was covered entirely in thick mud, except for a rough oval of mostly clear glass on the windshield. "Did they drive through a monsoon or something to get here?"

"A monsoon would've been cleaner," Lindsay said. "It looks more like they drove through the middle of a mud-slide."

The car door opened, and the driver climbed out, just as mud-spattered as the car. Marzi couldn't even tell if she was wearing clothes; only the shape of hips and breasts identified her as a woman.

"Maybe she's some kind of performance artist," Marzi

said. The woman was disturbingly familiar—she reminded Marzi of a minor character from her comic. In that story line, the rainmaker Charles Hatfield nearly destroyed San Diego with a rainstorm—something that had actually happened, historically, though Marzi had her doubts that Hatfield was really responsible for the storm. One of the women who died in the flood became a ghost, and in her desperate wish for flesh and substance she fashioned a body for herself out of mud. Bits of the mud-ghost kept sloughing off, or drying up and flaking away, and she was eventually dissolved in the Colorado River, where she remained, becoming a sardonic, disembodied oracle of sorts—as well as one of Rangergirl's only friends.

But that was a comic book, and this was real life. This was no ghost, but an actual woman, walking around covered in mud. Her face was daubed with white clay, making her resemble a figure from some African tribal ceremony—she had the face of a skull.

"That's Jane," Lindsay said. "Holy shit."

Of course. Lindsay knew everybody. "Who?"

"Jane Canarray. She was the TA in my psych class last semester. She's *brilliant*."

"Does she often cover herself in mud?"

"Marzi, I've never even seen this woman with split ends or ragged fingernails. This . . . I can't believe it. She used to go out with Denis, I heard. Do you think Mr. Clean Freak would go out with somebody who covers herself in mud?" Lindsay spoke quietly, watching Jane. For her part, Jane seemed content to stand by her open car door and gaze down the length of the street.

"Maybe she's performing a psychological experiment."

"Maybe," Lindsay said doubtfully. "I know there's an Abnormal Psych teacher who makes his students do publicly deviant things to, like, teach them about cultural prejudices. But the students usually just talk really loud in elevators or stand on corners yelling about flying saucers. This is above and beyond."

Jonathan appeared, beer in hand. "Huh," he said, looking at the mud-covered woman. "That's unusual."

"Welcome to Santa Cruz," Lindsay said, and then the mud-covered woman started yelling.

"HERE!" she shouted, flinging out her arm to point at the café. "This is the seat of her power! This is the place of her imprisonment! She must be released!" Jane's eyes scanned the deck; everyone was staring at her now. Her gaze locked on Lindsay, Marzi, and Jonathan.

"Hey, Jane," Lindsay said. "Are you protesting something?"

"Imprisonment," Jane spat, mud flying from her lips. She stalked around the front of her car, dropping off bits of mud as she came. "My goddess is here, trapped."

"This isn't about boycotting Brazilian coffee, is it?" Lindsay said. "Because Genius Loci complied with that, like, ages ago."

"You," Jane said, pointing at Marzi. "You stand before the door to her prison. You prevent the goddess from bestowing her blessings upon the world." Jane came up the steps, still pointing unerringly at Marzi. "Why, sister? Why don't you embrace the dark goddess of the earth?"

"I'm an atheist, sorry," Marzi said, backing away. Jane's

hands were curled into muddy claws. "I'm going to have to ask you to leave. You're tracking mud all over the deck, and I'm the one who has to clean it up."

"It will all be mud, soon. Buried in mud." Jane swung her head balefully, her gaze resting at last on Jonathan. She smiled, and there was mud on her teeth. "Mud in your heart, boy. You'll piss mud, shit mud, and spurt mud when you come." She flicked her fingers at him, getting a spatter of mud on his shirt. He looked down at the smudge, then back up at Jane, meeting her eyes, and Marzi felt a nasty crackle of tension between them, sort of the opposite of good chemistry, and she wondered if Jonathan was going to do something violent.

Instead, he picked up a napkin and dabbed slowly at his shirt, never taking his eyes from Jane's, not flinching when she took a step closer and thrust her face close to his. The way he stared at her, Jane might have been an insect—one with a stinger, perhaps, but nothing to worry much about. Marzi was impressed; her own heart was beating in 6/8 time. Jane began to hiss like a teakettle just hitting its boil.

"That's enough!" Marzi said. "I'm not asking, Jane. I'm telling you. *Leave.*" She hesitated. The next thing she wanted to say wasn't strictly within her authority, but Hendrix would back her up. "You're banned from Genius Loci. For life."

Jane pulled back from Jonathan and looked at Marzi. "For my life, or your life? Because your life . . ." She laughed, a rich, liquid sound. "That's nearly over now." Jane lunged at her, fingers hooked and clawlike.

Marzi crouched and brought up her hands defensively. Jane crashed into Marzi's arms and reached for her throat, trying to strangle her. Marzi knocked Jane's arms aside, then put both of her own hands flat on Jane's chest to shove her away.

Marzi's hands sank into mud up to the wrists, deeper than should have been possible, and she didn't feel flesh underneath. She tried to pull away, but her hands wouldn't come loose—if anything, she felt as if her hands were being *pulled in,* absorbed by Jane's body. Lindsay and Jonathan grabbed Jane's shoulders and tried to pull her away, but all they got for their trouble were hands full of mud. Jonathan frowned, as if doing a tricky bit of math in his head, and threw a short, vicious punch at Jane's shoulder. Bits of mud flew off on impact, but Jane didn't seem to notice at all, grinning into Marzi's face, her teeth like tiny white tombstones. She reached for Marzi's throat again.

Fuck, Marzi thought, and threw herself backward, away from Jane. Her hands still didn't come free, so she pulled Jane with her, twisting Jane against her hip and smashing her into the table. Jane hit the tabletop and shouted—it sounded more like surprise than pain. Marzi wrenched her hands out of Jane's chest, then pushed the table over, thankful Hendrix had settled for chaining the tables to the railing rather than bolting them down. The table fell against the railing and Jane rolled off the surface, over the rail, and fell a few feet, landing facedown on the sidewalk.

Jane scrambled to her feet, snarling, face twisted in fury. Marzi picked up Lindsay's untouched pint of Guinness and threw it, glass and all, into Jane's face. Jane shrieked and batted the glass away, where it broke on the sidewalk. The beer streaked Jane's face, and the mud ran, but it didn't expose her skin—just more, and darker, mud. "I *said,* you're banned for life," Marzi said. She picked up a napkin and began to wipe Jane's mud from her hands.

Jane looked at her for a long moment, then turned her gaze to Jonathan, and to Lindsay, as if marking them. "I'll be back. The goddess—"

"Shut up!" someone shouted from the deck. A couple of other people took up the catcall, and then everyone was shouting "Piss off!" or "Get lost!" or, funnily, "Go back to the commune, hippie!" Everyone except Marzi, Lindsay, and Jonathan, who looked at one another, bemused. Jane jerked her head around, flinching as the people shouted at her. She got back into her filthy car without another word. The people on the deck began clapping. Someone threw half a muffin at Jane's car, and it stuck in the mud on the roof, looking like a fine detail in a surrealist painting. Jane drove off, weaving a little in her lane, and took a sharp right onto Sandalwood Street and out of sight.

"Should we call the cops or something?" Jonathan asked.

Marzi hesitated, then shook her head. Talking to cops was a lot of trouble, and they had a way of making her feel guilty, even if she'd done nothing wrong. "I'm not hurt or anything. And I already banned her for life, right? If she comes back, I'll call them." She turned to Lindsay. "I guess it's my turn to buy you a beer now."

"I could use one," she said. "Let's have it inside, though. That way, the crazy people will have to come all the way up the stairs in order to attack us."

Down in His Boots

DENIS REARDON WOKE in his clean white bed and looked at his smooth ceiling. His jaw hurt from grinding his teeth all night, and he had half-moons in his palms from clenching his fists and digging his fingernails in while he slept. He'd had the same dream he always had, lately: the dream of the machine that grinds.

He sat up in bed, scowling at the alarm clock. It was already two o'clock in the afternoon. Denis had stayed up all night, hoping a disruption in his sleep schedule would knock loose whatever had gotten stuck in his head, the needle in the repetitive groove that made him dream again and again of a smooth chrome machine rolling over the landscape, grinding every obstruction down to glassy nothing...

But it hadn't worked. Nothing had, not even sleeping pills. He had no choice but to live with the dream.

He could not possibly live with the dream.

Denis's boots were still by the door, still muddy. He'd gone on wearing the filthy boots since Jane died, trying to forget they were dirty, sometimes almost succeeding. To clean the boots would be tantamount to an admission of wrongdoing. Denis Reardon did not have muddy boots. Denis Reardon did not do the sorts of things that *led* to muddy boots.

But he had done such things, and now Jane was dead. He was even—if one interpreted events in a certain light—somewhat responsible for her death. He was certainly responsible for keeping that death a secret.

Denis went into the kitchen to make a cup of tea, but his hands shook so badly that he couldn't fill the pot. He put the heels of his hands against his forehead and breathed slowly in and out nine times. The number nine always seemed to soothe him—counting to it, or repeating actions nine times.

Denis was mildly obsessive compulsive, of course, and knew it—he was neither sheltered nor stupid. He counted, and he found deep comfort in routines, and tiny imperfections distracted him, which was why he kept his apartment so austere. The compulsivity was a point of secret pride for him, in fact: He was *careful*, he was a *perfectionist*, he did things right. He was self-aware. He didn't—

But he had.

He thought back to the night—just two days before!—when he'd last seen Jane. They hadn't been on a date in weeks, having broken up after a particularly vicious disagreement over the role of the Dadaists in the development of contemporary art. It was a stupid misunderstanding, really—Jane mistook Denis's admiration for certain qualities in Duchamp's and Rauschenberg's works for a wholehearted endorsement of their artistic philosophies. She should have known better than that, and Denis told her so, and it only went downhill from there. The discussion had gone from the philosophical to the personal, and they'd parted after exchanging heated, or, in Denis's case, terribly cold, words.

Jane had returned two nights ago bearing a bottle of passable white wine and an apology, wearing a short white dress, thigh-high stockings, and no panties. "I brought a peace offering," she said, and laughed. "A piece of ass offering, you might say."

Denis thought puns were the lowest form of humor, but he refrained from saying so, eager to make up—and make out—with Jane.

Jane's vaguely goddess-related quasi-spiritual posturings gave her a taste for sex in the outdoors, so they took her Datsun hatchback and drove into the hills. Jane took a winding back road and finally parked beside a steep, muddy slope, concealed from the road by a stand of young redwood trees. They spread a blanket on the ground and drank wine from plastic cups, talking together, laughing. Jane had also brought a loaf of French bread and a wedge of brie. Denis picked up the butcher knife and frowned. "You don't have a bread knife? This is going to destroy the bread."

"It's the only knife my housemate had. You know we don't cook." She picked up the loaf of bread and tore off a hunk with her hands, offering it to him. "There, is that better?"

After a moment's hesitation, reassuring himself that Jane's fingernails were generally quite clean, he took the bread and ate. They made themselves comfortable, sipped wine, and after a while Jane stripped off her dress, reclining on the blanket, wearing nothing but her stockings. She smiled at him fetchingly. Denis admired her body, her smooth, almost entirely unblemished skin, the long lines of her limbs. Jane was not perfect—in his fantasies, Denis coupled with seamless, wrinkle-free women, with flesh more like water than meat, and orgasm came with no spurts or convulsions—but she was the closest he'd ever found.

Denis went down on her, and she made a small sound of pleasure. He'd studied the techniques of cunnilingus since he was a teenager. Erections were unpredictable things, and he never wanted a too-early orgasm or an uncooperative member to keep him from satisfying a sexual partner—it wouldn't do to have people say he was a bad lover. He'd heard from mutual friends that Jane considered him the best lover she'd ever had, and Denis took pride in that, as well.

Besides, if his mind wandered when he was going down on a woman, it wasn't obvious—he could let his tongue work on autopilot while he thought about abstract geometries, or the sculptural possibilities inherent in PVC, latex, and Lucite, and his lovers wouldn't notice, since they couldn't see the faraway look on his face.

After a while, Jane touched Denis on the top of his head. He looked up, and she smiled devilishly. "I've got an idea," she said, and inclined her head toward the steep slope of the hill. There had been an unseasonable rain shower the week before, triggering a minor mudslide, and raw, still-wet earth glistened at the base of the hill. "Have you ever made love in the mud?" she asked.

"No," he said, cautiously.

She sat up. "I have, at an arts festival, a few years ago. We painted one another with mud, and then . . ." Another smile. "It was amazing, so cool and sensual—I've never felt anything like it, all that squishy goodness against my skin. I felt so connected to the earth, to the natural rhythms of the world—I swear, the goddess moved *through* me that day."

"It sounds like a breeding ground for infection," Denis said, mostly to keep himself from making an acid comment about her absurd quasi-paganism.

Jane rolled her eyes, an insufferable habit of hers. "You're so dramatic. Come on." She grabbed his hand and stood up, pulling him to his feet. He protested, and she kissed him, putting her talented tongue into his mouth. Her hands went to the buttons on his clothes, and she began stripping and fondling him with gusto.

Denis was astonished. She really wanted him to fuck her in the *mud*. She didn't know him at all; that, or she was being willfully stupid, choosing to be blind. Much like the way she'd accused him of being a closet Dadaist—anyone who knew Denis at *all* would have recognized the idiocy inherent in such an assertion.

But she *had* come to him and apologized, had made the first gesture of reconciliation. Perhaps she was simply demanding a sacrifice of his in return, as a way of maintaining balance in their relationship. Could she be doing so unconsciously, or was it a deliberate act? Jane was a student of psychology, and should thus recognize her own mechanisms, but Denis knew that not everyone possessed his own degree of self-knowledge.

She stripped off her stockings and led him to the mud, stepping into the patch of wet earth and digging in her toes. Denis thought about putting his feet in there, about the filth that would get in under his toenails where he'd never be able to clean it, and he returned to the blanket. He put on his socks and boots and returned to the mud, knowing he looked ridiculous in just his shoes, preferring that to filthiness.

Jane laughed. "You don't know what you're missing. The connection to the earth, the feel of it between your toes; it's remarkable, it's like the goddess is singing just to me."

Denis shook his head.

She held out her arms. "Come on, cowboy. Fuck me with your boots on, then."

They weren't cowboy boots, only hiking boots, but Denis appreciated the general sentiment behind her words, and he didn't correct her.

The mud wasn't so bad at first, really—it was surprisingly smooth, not rocky as he'd expected, and it *did* feel good against his skin, as long as Jane kept him distracted from the fact that he was, basically, rolling in wet dirt. She drew patterns on his chest, runes and circles and stars. She cajoled him into painting her, and Denis actually became fairly interested in drawing certain patterns on her back. He'd never considered mud as an artistic medium before, for obvious reasons. Finally she demanded that he mount her, and Denis moved to oblige. The mud on his body was drying uncomfortably, starting to itch, and he wanted to get this over with. Jane was on all fours in the mud, looking back at him over her shoulder coyly. Denis knew he could penetrate her and finish in a few thrusts, and tell her later that the whole mud-covered experience had gotten him so hot he couldn't contain himself for a more respectable duration. She'd be more flattered than annoyed, and all would be well.

Just as he entered her, his knees deep in the mud, he saw something come crawling out of the dirt just a foot away from Jane. It was a large beetle, disgusting, caked with mud.

Denis could clearly discern the beetle's antennae. They were filthy.

Denis suddenly realized, deeply and all the way through, that he was in a repulsive situation. This was filth; this was the lowest rung on the ladder of degradation. There were *insects* in the mud, bugs crawling past his knees, crawling over Jane's hands and feet, spreading filth and disease—which was taking coals to Newcastle in this case, taking silicon to San José, because this was a *sea* of filth, a *citadel* of filth.

His erection wilted, and he withdrew, shuddering.

Jane looked over her shoulder, her expression dangerous and displeased. "What?"

He shook his head and backed out of the mud. "I'm sorry. I can't."

She stood up, crossing her arms over her breasts. "This is so fucking *typical,*" she spat. "I come to you, swallow my pride, and take you back even though you behaved like a spoiled child, but when I ask you to do something for *me,* to help me connect with the spirit of the earth, to transform our lovemaking into something spiritually significant—oh, no, that's too much to ask, that's *imposing* on you." She stalked toward him, looking lethal as a jungle cat, horribly primal with the mud smeared on her body. The sight of her sparked some deep, almost archetypal terror in Denis—this was Woman, in a dangerous way.

"Fuck *you,* Denis Reardon," she continued, standing with her feet planted in the mud. "You can *walk* your selfish ass back to town." She stalked past him.

Denis grabbed her arm, but she wrenched free, shooting him a murderous glare. She stooped and snatched up his clothes, her clothes, and the blanket, running for the car, leaving behind the remains of the bread and cheese, and the knife. Denis had a momentary vision, absolutely clear, of himself snatching up the knife and running her down before she could get in the car. He would drive the blade between her shoulder blades.

He would stab her, nine times, and leave her dead in the mud.

Denis shook it off, shocked at his own thoughts. He was not a murderer, despite occasional bright flashes of temper, and he ran after her without the knife. He grabbed her shoulder, pulling her up short, and tore his clothes away from her grasp. She swung at him with her fist, and he stepped back, having rescued his belongings. "You bitch," he said, surprised by his own fury. Denis usually kept his anger under better control than this. He thought of stabbing her again, and this time even turned his head and looked at the knife on the ground.

She stood by her open car door. "I hope your dick falls off, Denis. It's not doing you any good anyway, though I have to admit, I like it better than having you slobber all over my cunt." She got into her car and started the engine.

A great rumble filled the air, and Denis stumbled. The earth had moved, as if someone had shoved the firmament. An earthquake. Not a big one, but—

The hillside was moving. Already loosened from the recent mudslide, and now jostled by the quake, it began to slide down.

The earth was falling. That shouldn't happen. The ground should be trustworthy, dependable—something you could count on.

Denis ran away from the slope.

Jane's car started to back up, but she'd parked on a patch of mud, and the back wheels just spun. Once Denis was a good distance from the hillside, he turned and watched as the mud came down.

The mudslide buried the car completely.

Denis could hear Jane screaming. It was muffled and very far away. *She shouldn't scream like that,* he thought, shock lending him a comfortable detachment. *She'll use up all her air.*

No one else would hear her, he knew. They were far from any houses, far from anything but occasional passing cars.

Denis had a cell phone in his coat pocket; the coat was draped over his arm. He could call the police, give them directions. They could bring earth-moving equipment, even a crew of men working with shovels and buckets. The car wasn't buried deeply. The top of the mudslide couldn't be more than a foot above the roof. Jane could still be saved. She had enough air to last a while. The windows had been closed, and since he could still hear her screaming, he could assume the windows hadn't been broken by the mudslide. She wasn't suffocated, or crushed, just . . . entombed.

If she'd gotten into the car with my clothes, she'd be doomed, he thought. *I wouldn't have my cell phone.*

Denis thought about that for a long while. Her screams went on, more quietly, with longer pauses in between bursts.

Jane was . . . messy. She would be trouble in his life, he knew, even if he took steps to save her. She would not be grateful; being saved by Denis would infuriate and offend her. She would spread stories about him to her friends, ruin his reputation, become a nuisance. Jane was opinionated and loud. He didn't know what he'd ever seen in her, truly, apart from her modest physical charms.

She stopped screaming. *Must have gotten tired,* Denis thought. She still had a fair bit of air, probably.

Denis remembered his fantasy of stabbing Jane, gouging her out of his life with swift penetrations. That was no good. That was *messy.*

This was better. Seamless. Clean, in its way, despite the mud.

Besides, it wasn't *his* fault. She'd tried to steal his clothes, his phone. If she had succeeded, she would have been doomed just the same. "Far be it from me to interfere with your choices," he said aloud. "I won't impose my patriarchal paradigm on you. A man rescuing a woman is such an antiquated notion anyway, isn't it?" He dressed methodically, brushed dirt from his jeans, and began the long walk back down the hill to town. She'd told him to walk back, hadn't she? He was only doing what she wanted.

Two days after leaving his lover to die, Denis sat down on the tile of his kitchen floor, leaning back against the white refrigerator. He wondered if Jane was dead. He wondered how he could have done such a thing to her—but in a way, he didn't regret it. He hadn't taken the knife, after all, hadn't stabbed her in the back, hadn't given in to his homicidal urges. If he was guilty of anything, he told himself, it was simple negligence.

His cell phone probably wouldn't have worked anyway. Wireless service was spotty in the hills. It didn't matter that he hadn't tried to make the call, did it? Not really.

Denis got up from the floor and went into his living room.

He looked at his reproduction of Rauschenberg's famous 1951 *White Painting,* the triptych of blank white panels. Rauschenberg had been making a statement about content in art, but Denis just liked the idea that something so clean and simple and unadorned—indeed, *anti*-adorned—could hang in museums, be reproduced in art books, be talked about by critics for decades. He disliked most of Rauschenberg's other work, especially the horrendous goat-with-a-tire sculpture, but this one . . . this was something special.

Normally, looking at the triptych soothed him, as much as counting to nine did.

Not tonight. It reminded him, in a melodramatic way, of Jane's pale skin.

He suddenly remembered that he'd left the knife, the blanket, and their trash in the hills, so close to Jane's tomb. What if the police found those things, and suspected foul play, and somehow traced it back to him? He couldn't let a loose end like that dangle.

Denis sighed. He would have to go back. Take his car up into the hills, to the site of the mudslide, the site of Jane's burial alive. Not just to get the things he'd left behind, but to stand by the mud and think. That might provide closure for him. It was such a painful cliché, returning to the scene of a crime—but he hadn't actually committed a crime, he reminded himself, not in any *real* way. So it would be more like . . . visiting a grave.

And he could try his cell phone, just to prove to himself that it wouldn't have worked anyway, even if he'd tried.

Denis got his coat, put on his muddy boots, and headed for the hills.

Fireguard

MARZI SAT AT HER drafting table and worked on inking the next issue of her comic. She was winding up a major story arc in this issue: Rangergirl had finally found the rattlesnake sphinx, and now she was faced with its peculiar riddles, which would give her the key to stopping the Outlaw's latest assault on reality.

But Marzi couldn't concentrate. She kept thinking of Jane, covered in mud, reaching for her with clawed hands. She'd washed her hands in the bathroom at Genius Loci, and showered when she got home, but she still felt dirty. And afraid, which was worse. Being afraid had caused her serious problems in the past. She found it too easy to hunker down and hide from the fear, rather than go out into the world and face it. When she managed to stop thinking about Jane, she found herself thinking about Jonathan, which was almost as uncomfortable, for entirely different reasons. It wasn't even *him,* particularly—it was the very possibility of closeness.

Marzi sighed and pushed herself back from the table. Maybe she could go out . . . though it was cozy at home, too. She lived in a small apartment on Rosewood Street, just a couple of blocks from Genius Loci and the downtown core of Santa Cruz. She liked living downtown; she hardly ever had to drive anywhere, since her job, grocery stores, bookstores, and bars were all within easy walking distance. Marzi had lived in the apartment for four years, since her sophomore year in college. The landlord lived down in Florida somewhere, and was apparently unaware of the way rents in Santa Cruz had skyrocketed in recent years. Marzi hoped he never got clued in. The cheap rent was the only way she could afford to live by herself and have a job that paid as little as managing the coffee shop did.

The apartment was cluttered and jumbled, caught between coziness and chaos, with a blue thrift-store couch, a cedar chest, and brightly painted bookshelves filled with trade paperback and hardcover comics: almost everything by Alan Moore, the whole run of *Preacher*, Tomine's *Optic Nerve*, McCloud's illustrated nonfiction, *Sandman*, some Frank Miller, Will Eisner, R. Crumb, Dori Seda, Art Spiegelman's *Maus*, Richard Moore's *Far West*, and scores more, shelved and stacked in most of the available space. Her single issues of comics were boxed and stacked under the long dinner table she'd gotten for a steal at Goodwill. Most of her noncomic books were Westerns by Louis L'Amour, Zane Grey, and Joe Lansdale, along with a formidable collection of nonfiction about the West. Most of the reference was piled around her drafting table, so she could reach it easily when working.

She did her drawing in the living room, at a drafting table that faced away from the windows, to keep her from staring into the world outside when she should be working. If there were windows, she would look out of them. Sitting at the table, though, with nothing before her but the walls, forced her to open the windows in her head, and look out on stranger vistas. A land of tumbleweeds, painted deserts, wagon trains, dusty-robed necromancers, rainmakers, gullies filled with gold, treachery, cowardice, and heroism. The world of her comic, *The Strange Adventures of Rangergirl*.

Marzi rose from her place at the table and went to the windowsill, looking at her prickly garden, a dozen cacti in terra-cotta pots. Marzi laughed. *She* was the cactus girl, right? Keeping everybody at a distance, even Lindsay, being prickly to protect the soft stuff inside. Why was she so resistant to Lindsay's matchmaking attempts with Jonathan? Admittedly, there had been no blazing flash of light when their eyes met, no string music playing in the background, but he was cute, and seemed nice enough, and they had some interests in common . . . so why was her immediate reaction so negative? Had she just been out of the game for so long that it would be easier to avoid playing at all?

She touched the spine of one of her cacti, pricking her finger, but not breaking the skin. It was so tempting to stay here, safe, to avoid the possibility of seeing Jane, to avoid the pleasanter possibilities that Jonathan represented. But did she want to live that way, safe, locked away?

Maybe tomorrow she'd talk to Jonathan. See if she liked him. He and Lindsay had gone out drinking tonight, and they'd wanted Marzi to come along, but she'd declined, thinking she wanted time alone. Maybe she still did, but the more she thought about it, the more she didn't want to spend time alone *here*. She could feel the creeping edge of agoraphobia as she contemplated going out, a manifestation of her old anxiety that she hadn't experienced in months. She looked at her closed front door and shuddered. How could she *know* what was on the other side of the door? How could she be *sure*—

Marzi shook her head and went to put on her shoes. She was stir-crazy, and shaken up from her encounter with Jane, but that didn't mean she was having a relapse. She decided to go for a walk. Through sheer force of will, she didn't hesitate when it came time to open the door; she just grasped the doorknob, turned it, and stepped into the perfectly ordinary night. No strange vistas loomed behind the door, no monsters, no alien landscapes. No whatever-it-was that she'd once feared so much.

She stepped outside, onto the sidewalk. The weather was lovely; May in Santa Cruz was perhaps her favorite time and place. The sun stayed out until quite late, and the afternoons were warm, turning cool in the evening. She carried her leather bookbag slung over her shoulder, filled by a notebook and an oversized sketch pad. She was seldom overcome by an urgent need to draw *right now,* but she was fairly certain that if she ever left her bag at home, she would be struck by a powerful and transitory inspiration that would disappear before she could find a pen and paper.

Maybe she thought too much. The curse of the artist: too much introspection. But that wasn't always true. Lindsay had a pretty happy and carefree life, and she painted almost as diligently as Marzi drew. Lindsay took every day as an adventure, every problem as a challenge, every surprise as an opportunity. Why couldn't Marzi be more like her? That would certainly simplify her feelings toward Jonathan, who at best embodied an intriguing set of possibilities at this point.

Then again, Lindsay had never suffered a nervous breakdown. Maybe Marzi was right to be careful, to analyze her reactions and behaviors. She had to watch herself.

Marzi went down Rosewood Street, crossing Ash. Genius Loci was still open, with Bobby-O and Caroline running the counter, and Hendrix probably lurking in the back somewhere. He hated working evening shifts, but Marzi refused to work every night. It wasn't like Hendrix had a family or something to go home to—as far as Marzi knew, he just sat up naked at night watching pornos on a thirteen-inch television, eating peanut butter straight from the jar. Not that he'd ever said so; it was just the image that sprang to mind.

She continued toward Pacific Avenue, the main street downtown that had all the best shops, the good restaurants, and the wonderful bookstores, then changed her mind and turned back. She didn't want to walk downtown tonight. The street performers, the tourists, the students—they would be too much. She didn't want the crush of humanity around her.

There was a little park a few blocks away, and Marzi decided to go there, sit on the grass, and maybe have a cigarette. She'd stopped smoking regularly a couple of years ago, but she still carried a pack of cigarettes with her, and every once in a while, when she needed to calm her nerves, she had one. And after that altercation with Jane, surely she had a good excuse to calm her nerves?

Thinking of Jane made her glance around at the street, looking for Jane's mud-covered hatchback. Lindsay insisted that Jane was usually a nice, unassuming girl, but for Marzi,

Jane was only and always savage and mud-streaked, like some totemic monstrosity. For the first time, Marzi wondered if they should have called the cops. They'd just laughed off Jane's assault and had a beer. For Marzi, the cops had always been something bad that *happened* to you, busting up parties, giving out tickets, being high-handed bastards. The cops weren't something you turned to for help. But surely they'd be interested in a madwoman who assaulted people in the middle of downtown? Was it too late to call them? Probably.

Marzi turned a corner and went toward the park. There was someone else there, standing in the shadows beneath a tree, nothing visible but the general human shape and the glowing ember of a cigarette hovering near the mouth.

Marzi hesitated. Could it be Jane? But Jane probably wouldn't smoke; Lindsay said she was a super-healthy activist type. Then again, Lindsay also said it was unlike Jane to coat herself in mud and try to kill people. Probably it was just someone else out for a walk, like Marzi herself. The park was pretty safe, even at night. Insofar as Santa Cruz had a "bad part" of town, this wasn't it—that was down by the beach, maybe, where you could buy drugs and whatever else you wanted. You could buy that stuff downtown, too, but you had to know where to look. Closer to the beach, that stuff knew how to find *you.*

The figure approached, tossing the cigarette into the grass. At first Marzi thought it was a man, but then she recognized Alice Belle, Lindsay's new love interest.

"Hey, Marzi," Alice said. She was six feet tall, three inches taller than Marzi, with close-cropped blond hair and clear blue eyes, her features a bit too strong to be conventionally pretty. Marzi had never really looked before, but now that Lindsay had mentioned it, she saw that Alice *was* in great shape—her biceps clearly defined, her stomach taut beneath her tight white T-shirt. She didn't have any breasts to speak of—or else she kept them taped down—but she had nice hips and long legs. Marzi didn't feel any particular sexual attraction—girls sometimes turned her on, but it was a once-in-a-blue-moon sort of thing—but she could certainly see what Lindsay saw in this woman, physically, anyway.

"Hey, Alice. How you doing?"

Alice frowned, then shook her head. "I don't know, to tell you the truth. I'm all sort of scrambled up in the head. Just taking a walk, trying to figure things out."

"What's wrong? Is it . . . about Lindsay?"

Alice looked startled, then laughed. "She said she was going to tell you about us—I guess she did. She didn't want to make too big a deal out of it." Alice shrugged. "I don't know if it is a big deal. We have a lot of fun together, but who knows where it'll go? I feel like a cradle robber, truth be told. I'm turning thirty next month."

"It's only six years' difference," Marzi said.

"I feel like I'm a long way from being in college, though, you know? Even if she is in grad school. No . . . it's not Lindsay. Things are good with her. I don't know what it is."

"You want to talk?"

"You don't even know me. It's not your problem."

Marzi shrugged. "Lindsay's my best friend, and you're important to her, so . . ."

Alice nodded and sat down on a nearby bench. Marzi sat with her. They looked out at the grass for a while, then Alice said suddenly, "I used to start fires, when I was a kid."

"Yeah?" Marzi tried to sound neutral.

Alice laughed. "My dad was a firefighter. I guess I did it to piss him off. I'd burn napkins, piles of leaves in the yard . . . Once I burned a bunch of Barbie dolls he gave me. I doused them in lighter fluid and put them on the grill. It drove him nuts. He was sure I'd burn the house down some day."

Another long silence. "Did you?" Marzi asked at last. "Burn the house down, I mean?"

"No. I never did. I think I used to like the destruction, but now, I just think fire's beautiful. I do fire-dancing, you know?"

"Lindsay said."

Alice smiled at that. "And there are lots of candles at my house, and hurricane lamps, shit like that. Having flames around relaxes me. It's not like I'm a pyromaniac or anything. But lately . . ." She took a pack of cigarettes from her pocket, offered one to Marzi, took one for herself. She flipped open a filigreed silver Zippo and lit both cigarettes. They puffed for a moment, quietly. Marzi enjoyed the rush of nicotine, like having a balm rubbed on from the inside. Soothing.

Talking to Alice is a lot different from talking to Lindsay, Marzi thought. Lindsay was an onrushing torrent, while Alice . . . well, it wasn't exactly like pulling teeth. More like waiting for molasses to run downhill. Steady, but slow.

"I was riding my bike up in Oakland a few years ago," Alice said. "During wildfire season. And there was a fire, a bad one. I saw it from the road. The flames came jumping up the hillside, crackling, like something alive . . . it was beautiful, but dangerous. Like a tiger." She half-smiled. "Like a motorcycle. I sat on my bike and looked at the flames for a long time. Way *too* long. Wildfires are tricky. They can cross roads, catch the wind right, and go flying over a pretty good distance. I could've been trapped, burned. I should have hauled ass out of there, but I couldn't seem to get motivated. I just watched the flames turning the dry grass into ashes, spreading, so fierce and wild and alive. I finally snapped out of it and rode away, didn't get trapped, didn't get hurt. People died in that fire. Not me, though. I was lucky." She took a long drag.

Marzi wasn't sure what to say, whether she should say anything.

"You know those signs up by the university, that say 'Chance of Wildfire Today,' and then 'Low' or 'Moderate' or 'High'?"

"Yeah."

"When I see it on 'High,' I think, 'Maybe this'll be the day. Maybe this'll be the day I get caught in another fire.' " She glanced at Marzi. "Fucked up, huh?"

"I think people have always been fascinated by fire," Marzi said slowly. "From our earliest myths, even. Prometheus stole fire from the gods. So did Raven, according to some Native Americans. It's dangerous and powerful stuff."

Alice seemed to visibly relax. "So you don't think I'm obsessed?"

Marzi laughed. "I don't see any reason to think that, no." *And I would know,* she thought. *I know about obsession.*

"The last time I was fire-dancing, I thought about swinging my firepots faster and faster, like a sling, and then just letting them fly, flinging them up into a tree and letting them burn everything. That freaked me out, a little—I could *see* myself doing that."

"But you didn't do it."

"No. I guess you're right. I didn't."

"So you're okay."

"Yeah," Alice said. "Everybody thinks about weird shit, right? You're only in trouble when you *do* something about it."

"That's the way it seems to me," Marzi said.

"I'm glad I ran into you tonight." Alice stood, then held out her hand for Marzi to shake. Alice's hand was callused and firm—Marzi wondered, briefly, how it would feel to have those hands pass over her skin, touch her belly, her breasts. She wondered if Lindsay liked the feeling, if Alice touched her gently or roughly or both.

When Alice Belle gets me horny, I know it's been too long, Marzi thought. "I'll see you around. Give Lindsay my love, if you see her before I do."

"Sure thing," Alice said. She walked toward the tree where she'd been standing when Marzi first saw her. She picked up something long and dark—a chain, with metal, spherical cages affixed to either end. Her firepots. She slung the chains over her shoulder, and waved good-bye.

Marzi waved back, then dropped the remains of her cigarette and ground it out under her heel.

Smoke Out

BEEJ HURRIED ALONG the sidewalk on a street a few blocks from the heart of downtown Santa Cruz, past boutiques and small restaurants, most of them already closed for the night. Beej didn't care about the stores, though—he wasn't out shopping, he wasn't hungry, and human habitations in general didn't hold much interest for him lately. He hadn't been home in days. He'd been living outside, sleeping in parks and alleys, getting closer to the god.

Beej carried a large black plastic garbage bag slung over his right shoulder. He'd spent most of the day gathering its contents: driftwood, pebbles, blue and green glass bottles with the labels meticulously picked off, the shiny circle of metal from the top of a tuna can, a sandal with duct tape mending a torn strap, hair swiped from the floor of the barber shop on Front Street, the skins of popped balloons, several flowers pulled up by the roots, and a tarnished brass cowbell rescued from the gutter. Beej inventoried the objects in his head, trying to decide if he'd left anything out, if there were any other elements essential for the ritual. It wasn't like the movies, where people had magical books to consult, or where some wise shaman came along and told you what to do. Beej was operating from his inner resources, with no guidance other than what he could glean from his own mental tremors. He tried to *sense* the contents of the bag, their gestalt, and feel for gaps.

He found one.

Beej stopped, staring blankly at the concrete sidewalk before him. He couldn't go to the altar yet, then—there was one offering still to acquire. Beej looked around, and saw what he needed right away: a potted palm near a wine shop. He whooped with delight, walked over to the plant, and set his bag down. Looking around to make sure no one was watching, he scooped out a handful of soil from the pot and piled it neatly on the sidewalk. He unzipped his pants, took out his dick, and looked at the sky, humming a swing tune. After a while his bladder relaxed—he always had trouble pissing in public—and a stream of yellow urine poured out, soaking the soil. After a while, he switched to pissing in the potted plant, so as not to supersaturate the dirt on the sidewalk. He finished and zipped up, then knelt and scooped a double handful of dirt from the sidewalk. It was damp and thick, now, transformed into mud by the water from his body. He opened the plastic bag, dropped in the mud, and wiped his hands unself-consciously on his pants.

That took care of the mud, but he still needed fire. He walked a few blocks to the drugstore, going the long way to avoid the crowds on Pacific Avenue, wincing as he entered the well-lit parking lot. This was a night for shadows, not artificial lights. Beej went through the automatic doors into the store, and someone started yelling at him. "Hey! You can't come in here!"

Beej looked up, startled. "Are you closed?"

The teenager, dressed in an ugly green vest with a name tag, hesitated. "No, we're open. But . . . you can't come in here to sleep, or just hang around. It's only for customers."

"I am a customer," Beej said. "Why would I want to sleep here? It's too bright."

"Ah," the kid said. "Sorry. I thought . . . sorry." He nodded toward the plastic bag. "You have to, um, check your bag, though."

Beej clutched the bag to his chest, the bottles and driftwood clanking. "You *will* watch it carefully?" he said. "It took me a long time to get it just right, and if anything happened . . ."

"Sure thing," the kid said, backing off, stepping behind the protection of his cash register. "No worries."

Beej handed over the bag reluctantly. As soon as the cashier took it from his hands, Beej raced for the back of the store. He snatched up a can of lighter fluid and a box of kitchen matches, then ran back to the register. After dumping his purchases on the counter, he reached across and snatched his bag back from the boy's grasp. Everything was still there, still potency-in-waiting, and Beej breathed a long sigh.

"Your bag smells like pee," the boy said.

"Still waters run deep," Beej said, grinning, and nodded toward the lighter fluid and matches. The kid rang up the purchases and Beej grubbed around in the pocket of his leather jacket until he came up with a few coins and bills. The boy took the money, wrinkling his nose. Beej saw that he'd accidentally given the kid a wad of gum wrappers along with the money. Except it *wasn't* an accident—it was all part of the god working through him. Beej was an instrument of the lord of wreckage now, and everywhere he went, chaos and detritus would follow.

The boy picked the wrappers out of his hand and threw them into the trash, then made Beej's change. "Paper or plastic?" he asked.

Beej grinned. "I've got a bag, thanks." He dropped the matches and the lighter fluid into his garbage bag, then left the store.

The moon was up and full, leering like an albino jack-o'lantern. Beej went the long way around Pacific again, and this time he walked all the way to the altar.

The altar was in a hole in an empty lot surrounded by a fence, with a clothing boutique on one side and a parking garage on the other. Once there had been a building on this lot, but that was before the 1989 earthquake. Loma Prieta. That was the last major quake to hit the area, and it had leveled much of Santa Cruz. The heart of town, as it stood now, bore little resemblance to the town's layout before Loma Prieta. Beej hadn't lived here then, he'd still been in Indiana, but he'd seen pictures of the old town, and the wreckage, at the Museum of Art and History. In typical California fashion, the residents had started rebuilding right after the disaster, reinventing the town. There was a time when Beej had respected that impulse to rebuild and re-create, had found it wonderful—humankind uniting in the face of adversity, taking back the world from the elements. But he knew better, now. His eyes had been opened.

Humans were stupid filthy persistent insects. The world

slapped them with an earthquake, and they came back for more! The earthquake was a message from the god itself, and they disregarded it. How much clearer did the god have to be? What part of "I don't want you here" didn't they understand? They had pride sufficient to offend the god.

Next time, there would be no rebuilding. The destruction would be utter, the ground scoured of life, no stone left on a stone.

For the first time in his life, Beej felt in total harmony with nature. So *this* was what all those pagans at school were talking about! He'd thought it was airy-fairy shit, all about trees and fields and the moon, but it was really about the raw brute force of nature. Titanic earth forces. The ground itself making its will known, throwing off the parasites that lived and thrived on its surface.

For whatever reason, this empty lot hadn't been rebuilt after the quake, despite its prime location adjacent to downtown. This patch of ground was unchanged since the day after the earthquake, except for the rubble that had been hauled away, and the fence, and the grass growing up inside. It still bore the mark of the god's fury.

Beej squeezed in through a hole in the fence and stood on the edge of his temple, the altar of the earthquake. Whatever building had once stood here had had a basement, and there was still a large hole with partially broken concrete walls shoring up the earth. Tumbled chunks of concrete filled the pit, with bits of rebar sticking out. Beej skidded down the steep slope into the hole, his bag over his shoulder. Several of the concrete blocks had tumbled together and formed something like a table, with a flat block across the top. The first time Beej saw that, he knew it wasn't coincidental, not just a random pile of wreckage—it was a sign. It was an altar.

Beej worked happily, the moon providing his light. He took out the contents of his bag and piled them on the altar, arranging them until the configuration pleased him, in much the same intuitive way he constructed collages. The last thing he took from the bag was a stack of comic books, tattered and well read, the whole run of Marzi's comic, *The Strange Adventures of Rangergirl*. Beej wasn't sure why the god wanted those, but he knew Marzi was tangled up in this somehow. He fanned out the comics on the altar stone, looking at their covers, remembering the stories—the rainmaker, the mud woman, the rattlesnake sphinx, Aaron Burr, and the box canyon. He'd never liked Westerns, but that wasn't what Marzi's comics were about. He hated to burn them, but consoled himself with the thought that these were only reading copies; he still had mint duplicates bagged at home.

Once the objects were arranged to his liking, he smeared mud on the stone, imagining for a moment it was actually blood. Then he sat cross-legged on the ground, closed his eyes, and waited for a revelation. The god's communications were usually subtle: whisperings in the night, partial words written in dust, voices hidden in the creak of bedsprings. Granted, the emissary that came to him yesterday in Genius Loci had been pretty dramatic, skin like cracked rock, black hair woven with feathers, a scalping knife in its hand. When it touched his head, Beej had felt a shifting of the plates in his skull, and had understood immediately what the god was doing. It had reconfigured the bones in his head so that they exactly matched the earth's continental plates. His skull was a geological map now. That delighted him—there must be a vast sympathetic magic there! Marzi had tried to help him, he realized, by rushing in with a knife and driving the emissary away. That had been a mistake, but how could she know? It must have looked awful to her, like Beej was being attacked. He thought of Marzi, perishing under a pile of rubble, and felt a twinge. Maybe there was a way . . . but no. Marzi would die with everyone else, unless by some miracle the earthquake god chose her to be an acolyte, too. Perhaps Beej could initiate her into the church of the earthquake . . .

Fire.

The word hit Beej's brain like lightning. More than just the word—the *vision*. Flames dancing on the altar. Very well, he would make it so. He squirted lighter fluid over the trash and the comics, then struck a match and tossed it onto the altar. The fluid ignited silently, and the trash—symbolic, Beej knew, of all the wreckage that the earthquake god would create on Earth—began to burn. The smell was unpleasant, but that was part of the deal. Destruction wasn't pretty.

The fire didn't interest Beej much, and neither did the mud. They were side effects, he knew. The heaving of the earth would trigger mud slides, and fires would start when the gas lines broke. They would aid the destruction, but that was all they were: handmaidens. The earthquake itself was preeminent, the first cause. The earthquake was god.

Something appeared in the flames. Beej leaned forward, staring at the shape in the fire. It was the emissary from the coffee shop, the sand-colored Indian! The figure was small at first, a gray form in the flames, but it gradually grew to human size. It stepped off the altar and stood before Beej, holding a large bowie knife casually in its left hand, feet hovering just off the ground. "Beej," it said, voice smoky and distant. Indeed, everything about the figure was vague and attenuated, its body now made of smoke, not solid sandstone-colored flesh as before. Was the earthquake god weakening?

"I'm too far from my epicenter," the Indian said, and Beej realized with a thrill that this wasn't an emissary at all, but the god itself. Indeed, why would a being so powerful have need of messengers? It could be anywhere, everywhere—wherever there were fault lines, the earthquake god held sway. "I'm trapped," it said, "locked behind a door, and by *pushing* and *pushing* I've managed to open it a crack, enough to reach out to you this way. But I'm still trapped, Beej." The god wavered, its face blurring. "You have to let me out. You will have assistance from other worshippers, acolytes of mud and fire. But you are my favorite. Remember. My chosen one."

"Yes," Beej said. "Yes, oh yes. Where are you trapped? What can I do?"

"I'll show you," the god said, and raised its knife.

Beej sat calmly as the god sliced into his scalp. There was not much pain—the knife was very sharp. The god touched the bones of Beej's head and tugged, and the plates parted. The sensation sent a shiver through Beej's body. It was better than orgasm. It was an earthquake in his flesh.

With the tip of the knife, the god began writing on the surface of Beej's brain.

Knowledge filled him. He knew where the god was imprisoned. He knew about the artist, Garamond Ray, and how the god had been changed and trapped—and he knew what Marzi had done, what she was still doing. Beej whimpered as the god's mind brushed against his own. Even at this distance, with the god only reaching through the crack in the door of his prison, Beej sensed its enormity, its inhumanity, its unrelenting purpose.

Its message conveyed, the god retreated, putting the bones in Beej's head back together. A breeze blew in through the fence, swirling the god apart, wisping its transitory body into nothingness. Beej touched his head tenderly and found it unharmed. He smoothed down his hair, feeling grubby and human again.

The things on the altar were smoking lumps, blackened by fire, and Marzi's comics were now ashes. Beej touched the warm altar stone for a moment, then trudged up out of the hole.

The sense of total understanding was fading, had begun to fade the moment the god stopped touching him, but Beej remembered enough. He knew what he had to do first.

He had to break into Genius Loci, and open a door.

Misty Beyond

DENIS REACHED THE site of Jane's inhumation shortly after nightfall. He pulled his car off the road and drove into the trees, parking well away from the hillside. He searched halfheartedly for a flashlight in the glove compartment, but he hadn't brought one. That was stupid, but he was under a lot of stress. Denis considered moving his car closer to the mound and letting his headlights illuminate the area, but that would bring him entirely too close to possible entombment. The way Jane had died . . . that wasn't for him.

Denis got out of his car, wrapping his overcoat around him against the evening chill. It was noticeably cooler here in the hills than it was downtown. Denis squinted in the darkness as he approached the mound. The moon was silvery bright, but its light was pale and filtered through the redwoods overhead. Denis stumbled and cursed as he walked, but when he saw the tire tracks running through the mud, he stopped. He hadn't thought about it before, but Jane had left a trail, driving here through the soft earth. Would someone notice the tracks, and follow them to the mound of mud? Jane had pulled off the road, but she hadn't gone *that* far from the beaten path, just a few dozen yards.

Someone would find her eventually, Denis supposed. There'd be no evidence of his involvement, though. Not once he picked up the knife, and the other remains of the picnic. There were his footprints in the mud, but his boots were not an unusual brand, and by the time the car was discovered, his prints would likely be washed away. Maybe he would scuff away the bootprints when he left. No one had seen him with Jane that night, Denis reminded himself. As far as anyone knew, they had broken up and were no longer speaking. He was safe. There was nothing to fear from Jane now but bad memories and bad dreams—but even dreams of Jane would be a relief from his usual nightmares about the machine that grinds.

Denis followed the tire tracks . . . and then found another, much fresher, pair of tracks crossing the original set. Denis crouched and touched the new tracks, bewildered. The old tracks were dried on the edges, while the new ones were still damp. Someone had driven out of here recently, today, by the look of it.

With a sinking feeling, a sort of disbelieving dread, Denis followed the new tracks toward their inevitable starting place.

The mound of mud was still there, but it looked more like a broken volcano now, hollowed out and caved in. A hole gaped in the side of the mound, and the sides and top had fallen into the hollow center. Somehow, impossibly, Jane had driven out of the mudslide. But how could that be? Surely the weight of the mud would prevent any escape, the slickness beneath the wheels would make traction impossible—but he was faced with the refutation of those assumptions. This mound of mud, and no car, and tire tracks leading out and away.

"Oh, *fuck me*." Jane was alive. And she knew that he'd left her here to die. What would she do to him? Tell the police? Or come after him herself, attack him, talk to him, try to blackmail him? He tried to figure out which approach her personality would dictate. Could he . . . take care of her himself? Actually kill her, to keep her quiet, to keep his secret? He didn't think so. The past two days had been hellish, edged with hysteria and denial, and then he'd been guilty only of negligent homicide, at worst. Denis was a creature of habit, and premeditated murder would catastrophically break his routine. To actually murder Jane would probably unhinge him. But there had to be some way to contain this situation.

His mind refused to function properly. Every time he attempted to think in a rigorous line, he imagined Jane's car driving out of the mudslide and bearing down on him, running him over, crushing his body into the mud.

When headlights appeared behind him, throwing the mound of mud into sharp relief, Denis screamed.

He sucked in a breath and squeezed his hands into fists. Screaming wouldn't help. Perhaps this was just a random passerby, someone looking for a make-out spot, or even a police officer who'd seen Denis's car parked off the road. There was no cause for panic yet.

The car rolled toward him slowly, headlights blinding

Denis to any details of the vehicle's make, model, or provenance.

The engine sputtered like an arrhythmic heart. Denis thought about walking up to the car, to see what they wanted, but why should he? He'd been here first. The fact that the driver could see him while Denis himself couldn't see anything but the glare of headlights annoyed him, however, so he shaded his eyes and walked toward the driver's side.

The driver's door opened, and someone stepped out, just a person-shaped blob in Denis's still-dazzled vision. He blinked, waiting for his pupils to dilate so he could see in the dimness.

"Denis?" the person said. Denis recognized the voice. It was Jane. Absolutely, no doubt about it, Jane. He took a step back, and she rushed at him.

Denis threw up his hands defensively, and it took a moment for him to realize that he was being embraced, not attacked. Jane wrapped her arms around him and hugged him tightly. She sobbed into his shoulder.

What *was* this? Didn't she understand what he'd done, what had happened?

"Shh, baby, it's okay," Denis said, patting her shoulder. Cool mud smeared under his hands, and he realized she was wholly covered in filth. She'd gotten somewhat muddy during her wish-fulfillment fantasy with him, but her clothes shouldn't have been so streaked, and the layer of mud on her body shouldn't feel so *thick*. Why was she dirty, if she'd *driven* out? It wasn't as if she'd crawled bodily through the mud. The car should be filthy, yes—and he saw now that it was, that her white hatchback had been turned brown by mud, the filth covering everything but a wiper-scraped semi-circle on the windshield. Jane must have gotten down and rolled in the mud for some reason. That was the only explanation that made sense.

Not that any of this really made sense.

"I woke up in the dark, Denis," she said into his shoulder. "I was so afraid. I don't understand what happened. After I woke up I got into the car and drove out of this muddy mess, looking for you, but I couldn't get to your apartment. Every time I started driving I wound up on Ash Street, by that coffee shop you like so much. I felt like there was something inside the place, *pulling* me. Do you remember when I told you about the goddess?"

"Yes," Denis said, trying to hug her as lightly as possible. She clung to him like a barnacle on a hull, smearing dirt into his clothes, his coat. He took deep breaths to calm himself, to overcome his total revulsion, but even breathing deeply didn't help—Jane smelled of earth and wet and mold, and revolted him.

"I think the goddess is trapped in the coffee shop," Jane said. "I have to help her escape."

She's gone insane, Denis thought. Being trapped in her car had driven her crazy—or else she'd run short of oxygen and sustained brain damage. Believing in some primal Earth Mother was one thing, but thinking the goddess dwelt in an espresso machine was something else altogether.

"Let's get you home," Denis said. "Get you cleaned up." Then he thought of Jane's housemate. Denis didn't want anyone to see Jane in this state—it could only reflect badly on him, lead to questions. "Better yet, come to my place."

"You'll stay with me? You'll help?" Her voice was husky and frightened. Denis had never heard her speak this way before, so vulnerably.

"You can stay with me."

She looked into his eyes. Her face was ghost-pale in the moonlight. "Will you help me set the goddess free?"

Denis hesitated, then said, "We'll talk about it. Come on. Follow me down." He needed to find out what, exactly, she remembered. If her memory loss was sufficiently complete, there might be no need for extreme resolutions.

She gripped his jacket with both hands. "Please, Denis, ride with me. Don't make me go by myself."

"Shh, it's okay, all right." He could pick up his car later. Right now, the important thing was to get Jane into the shower and scoured clean. He couldn't think with her looking like this, like an avatar for some mud-goddess.

He went to the passenger side of her car and opened the door, the mud from the handle smearing his fingers. He got inside and wiped the mud from his hands onto the upholstery. The smell struck him right away, though it wasn't strong—just a whiff of ripeness, a hint of urine and feces. "There's a nasty smell in here," he said.

Jane got into the car. The internal light came on when she opened the door, and Denis got his first clear look at her. No part of her body was uncovered; even her hair was caked, dreadlocked with mud. "I only smell the earth," she said. "It smells good."

Denis grunted. He rolled the window partway down to let fresh air in.

Jane drove, her hands leaving muddy prints on the steering

wheel and gearshift. She didn't talk much, though she answered readily enough when Denis asked questions. "It's all scrambled," Jane said. "I wanted to pick you up, and make amends. We drove into the hills, made love . . ." She shook her head. "What happened then?"

Denis improvised wildly. "You took me home, then realized you'd left some things there, your blanket, I'm not sure what else. You said you were going back to get them. I didn't hear from you after that, and when I called your house Nancy said she hadn't seen you, so I drove up here tonight to make sure nothing had happened to you." He hadn't picked up the knife or their trash, he realized, but he supposed it didn't matter now, since Jane was alive and reasonably well—it wasn't a crime scene anymore.

"I must have been caught in a mudslide, and thrown from my car . . ." She shook her head, and a little rain of dirt pattered down onto the seat. "It doesn't make any sense. There are all these gaps in my memory . . . I could have been killed, you know?"

"I know."

"But the goddess saved me." Jane's voice, content and sure, chilled Denis. "She spared my life, and consecrated me into her service. Baptized me in mud."

"Baptize" was an inherently Christian term, unsuited to such a pagan sentiment, but Denis refrained from pointing that out, though it did indicate the extent to which Jane's ordeal had affected her, replacing her typical precision with muddy inaccuracy.

"I'm still so confused, but some things are clear," she said.

"You'll feel better once you have a shower."

"*You'll* feel better once I have a shower," she said, with a touch of her old venom. "I like being muddy. It makes me feel *strong*. There was this bitch at the coffee shop—"

"You went to the coffee shop?" Denis said. "Looking like *this*?"

"This is the way I look. That's the way it is."

Marvelous. So now other people knew Jane was crazy. Maybe no one had recognized her; she wasn't exactly a regular at Genius Loci. Though, oddly, she seemed to be driving toward the coffee shop again, not slowing down for the turn to his house. Denis touched the steering wheel lightly. "Turn right here, Jane," he said.

She looked at him, blinking, then nodded and made the turn.

Jane pulled into a parking space in front of his apartment. "We'll get your car washed tomorrow, too," Denis said, getting out.

"I don't know. I like having a mud chariot. A vehicle created by the patriarchy, but consecrated to the goddess."

"Okay, Jane."

She got out of the car and went to his door. Denis followed. He couldn't decide if he wanted to jump into the shower first and clean off the traces of her touch, or let her clean up right away. They could always shower together, though that would mean watching the filth stream off her, turning the floor of the shower brown. . . . No, thank you. He could wait.

In the light of the living room, Jane looked terrible, hardly human at all. Her face, which he'd thought merely pale, was actually covered in white clay, as if she were made up for some primitive death-festival.

Jane went into the bathroom, then came out again. "I

don't want to use your towels," she said, half smiling. "I know how you are about stains. And I'll need clean clothes. I washed some things at the Laundromat, before I picked you up and we went into the hills. I remember that. The laundry bags are still in the car. I'll get them."

"No, I'll go," Denis said. He suppressed a shudder at the thought of Jane touching clean laundry with her filthy hands.

"We'll both go."

Denis sighed. She never let him do anything for her, as if the very offer of assistance were an act of male oppression. "Fine."

They went out to the car. Jane swung the hatchback open and reached inside for a bag of laundry.

Denis just stood, staring.

There was a body in the back of Jane's car. A woman's body, naked, mud-streaked, and curled up, long hair hiding her face. Jane seemed completely unaware of the corpse's presence as she grunted and tugged on the laundry bag. She couldn't get the bag loose because the dead body was lying on top of it. With a final yank, Jane pulled the bag free, and the body rolled over.

The corpse's hair fell away, revealing the face.

It was Jane, her features slack, her eyes blank and glazed.

Denis drew breath to scream, but before he could, the *other* Jane, Mud-Jane, said, "Well, are you going to help or not? Grab the other bag. I don't know which one has the towels."

Denis exhaled, counting to nine in his mind, calming down. This was Jane, too. He was sure of it—only Jane talked to him that way, looked at him that way. Her expression of half-amused annoyance was instantly recognizable, even through a mask of mud.

Maybe Jane hadn't gone crazy. Maybe Denis had. His guilt over leaving her trapped had conjured this corpse in the car to haunt him. It was just a hallucination, and would fade away. That was the only reasonable explanation.

"Sometime this year, lover," Mud-Jane said, shouldering the bag and walking to the apartment.

Denis hauled out the other bag of laundry, then stood looking at the body and the inside of the car. There were muddy handprints on the windows. While Jane was trapped, she must have crawled from the passenger seat into the back, beaten on the glass. But why? Because there was more room to move back there? Because it was more comfortable to lie curled on a bag of laundry? Because there was nothing else *to* do, there in the suffocating dark?

I have to get rid of the corpse, he thought. But he didn't have to, not really, because there *was* no corpse. This was just something his mind was doing to him, a torment, a hallucination. He would wake up tomorrow, or later tonight, and everything would be fine again. Denis had a resilient mind. It would bounce back from this. It *would*.

He closed the hatchback and hauled the laundry into his apartment. As he put down the laundry bag on the living room couch, he heard the water start running in the bathroom. She must have found the towels in the other bag. Denis sat down, legs shaking, and put his head in his hands. He had to think, calm down. He counted to nine, then to multiples of nine.

After she'd been in the shower for about two minutes, Jane began to scream.

Tarantula Juice

Marzi pushed her way through the throng standing around the bar at the Red Room, one of the most popular nightspots in Santa Cruz, until she reached the back corner, where Lindsay and Jonathan sat chatting. Jonathan nodded when he saw her, looking pleasantly buzzed and about as laid-back as it was possible to be while remaining somewhat vertical.

"I've just been showing Jonathan how to get free drinks," Lindsay said, almost shouting over the thumping music and crowd noise.

Marzi took an unattended chair from another table and sat down. "Oh, yeah?"

"Three different guys in one hour," Jonathan said. "She goes up to the bar, talks to a guy, touches his elbow, and bang: She gets a drink."

"He didn't even mention my smooth dismount," Lindsay said, speaking in an overprecise way that Marzi knew from long experience meant she was more than a little drunk. "I left those boys flattered and wanting more."

Marzi smiled at Jonathan.

"So she left you to entertain yourself while she worked her wiles?"

"I have a rich inner life," he said. "And I've been watching the crowd."

There were plenty of people to watch. The Red Room was one of the prime places to see and be seen in Santa Cruz, and it was thronged tonight by people wearing silk, velvet, black boots, short skirts, tight shirts, and shining smiles. The bartenders moved with the efficiency of Swiss clockwork figures behind the bar, dispensing drinks in an endless stream.

"I tried to get him to pick up girls with me, but he wouldn't." Lindsay pouted.

"Working with her would just highlight the inadequacy of my own meager skills," Jonathan said, without cracking a smile.

Marzi poked Lindsay in the side with her forefinger. "I ran into Alice tonight."

"*Alice* wouldn't mind if I picked up girls," Lindsay said. "So long as I shared."

Marzi opened her mouth to say more about Alice—to convey, at least in part, the gist of their peculiar conversation—but decided against it. This wasn't the time or the place; it wasn't a conversation that would work well when shouted to a drunk listener.

"I'm for another drink," Lindsay said, downing her gin and pushing back from the table. She went to the bar, squeezing in and leaning beside a man in a blue polyester shirt. She smiled at him with every watt of her considerable charm.

"And Lindsay says she isn't pretty," Marzi said, shaking her head.

Jonathan nodded. "She does. She told me she gets by on bluff. She dazzles them, so they don't look too closely. I thinks she actually believes it." He sipped his drink. "This is fun. I didn't expect to be out on the town. I figured on spending the night—hell, the whole summer—holed up in my room, working, but Lindsay wouldn't hear of it."

"Lindsay's good people," Marzi said. "Being friends with her is like being friends with the whole town—she knows everybody."

He shook his head. "I couldn't be that social. I get tired just watching her."

Marzi nodded. "She's got a gift. So. How're you liking the Pigeonhole?"

He looked blank for a moment, then grimaced. "Is that what you call it? My apartment?"

"Yeah. Well, Hendrix calls it 'the Pigeoncote,' but he's pretentious."

"When I talked to him about renting it, he called it 'cozy.' "

"That's one way of putting it."

"The shower's like a coffin stood on end, and if you sit up in bed you hit your head on the slope of the ceiling. But I have to admit, I've lived in worse places. Never *smaller* places, but worse ones. And it's cheap."

"Cheapest rent in downtown Santa Cruz," Marzi said. "I think it's the lack of a kitchen that keeps the price down."

"And the fact that the café is open until one in the morning."

"Also a factor."

"It doesn't bother me. I'm a night owl. The café's pretty quiet during the day, right?"

"When Hendrix refrains from blasting Megadeth, yeah. His taste in music is loud and antediluvian. Still, I couldn't live in the Pigeonhole. It would make for a shorter walk to work, but really. Too claustrophobic."

"I wouldn't want to make it a permanent residence. But for now, it suits me. And it's close to my work."

"You're studying Garamond Ray, right?"

Jonathan nodded. "The murals are some of his last works. They're fascinating."

"Good thing I convinced Hendrix not to paint over them, then."

Jonathan's eyes widened, the first sign of strong emotion Marzi had seen in him—he hadn't reacted that much even to Jane's attack. "He wanted to paint *over* them?"

Marzi leaned close, to speak near his ear. "Yeah, last year. Some little old ladies complained about Harlequin, said he was making them nervous, grinning there on the wall. And then some guy who called himself a color therapist told Hendrix that the Ocean Room was an unhealthy hue, and that Hendrix should paint everything pale green. Hendrix was really going to do it, too, but I got all the regulars to threaten to boycott the place if he did. Well, almost all the regulars—Denis told Hendrix he'd like to see the walls painted white and decorated with this 'Abstract Prismatic' series of paintings Denis did. A bunch of soulless paintings of crystal matrices. Hendrix actually gave that serious thought, too. I swear, the guy has a brain like Silly Putty, he's so impressionable. But Hendrix pays attention to business first, so when the regulars complained, he left the murals alone." Marzi thought the *real* kicker had probably been when she threatened to quit if he painted over the murals; Hendrix seemed to have an almost supernatural dread that Marzi would stop working there. Probably knew he'd never find another dependable assistant manager who'd work for such shit wages.

Jonathan shook his head. "I can't imagine. Those paintings are irreplaceable."

"I didn't realize Garamond Ray was such a big deal," Marzi said. No one would ever be so zealous about protecting *her* work.

Jonathan shrugged. "He's not well known, but he's a fascinating figure. He did murals in New York in the seventies, and also did a lot of poster work, album covers for punk rock bands, stuff like that. Had a few shows, picked up a small cult following. He was quite a character, apparently, used to hang out in bars and hold court, tell stories, get in fistfights. He specialized in these sort of mock-cutesy images with a sinister overlay—sort of Norman Rockwell viewed through a mescaline trip, nightmarish Currier and Ives. Then Ray moved to California, doing more underground illustration, murals here and there. Genius Loci used to be a shared-house artists' collective; lots of people moved in and out, but Ray lived there for years—he was the linchpin. In 1989, he disappeared. The murals in Genius Loci are his last works, as far as anyone knows."

Marzi hadn't known that, about the café's history. "Ray disappeared after the earthquake, right?"

Jonathan shook his head. "*During* the earthquake. He was seen that morning, but once the quake hit, that was it. No more Garamond Ray. He's not officially listed as one of the fatalities, because his body was never found. Nobody knows for sure what happened to him. He was a real hog for publicity and attention, though, and most people think that his being silent for so long means he's definitely dead."

"And now you're studying him."

Jonathan spread his hands. "I want to be the leading expert on the life and works of Garamond Ray, Beats ditch-digging. I had a little extra money, so I thought I'd come to Santa Cruz, live where Ray lived, surround myself with his work, and finish the writing here. The photos I've seen don't do the murals justice. That one, of the street café, with the gods—"

"The Teatime Room," Marzi said, nodding. The mural in the Teatime Room featured a host of Egyptian gods seated at a Parisian-style sidewalk café. Thoth dipped his beak into a fluted glass, Anubis sipped from a porcelain cup brimming with blood, and Sekhmet held a tea-press that contained a human heart. "I love that painting. It should be creepy, but it's somehow just . . . *peaceful*."

He looked interested again, and Marzi wondered if art was the only thing that cracked his cool. "All the rooms have names?" he asked.

"Unofficial ones, sure. As far as I know, Ray never titled them."

"Still, it's a useful shorthand I can use in my paper. What are the names?"

Marzi counted on her fingers. "The Circus Room, the Ocean Room, the Teatime Room, and the Cloud Room. Then there's the main room—if we called it anything, we'd call it the Space Room. And there are some mutant-looking sunflowers painted in the kitchen—they have stems segmented like crab legs—but we don't have a special name for the kitchen."

"So that's six rooms, counting the kitchen. But aren't there supposed to be seven rooms? That's what I always heard. There's supposed to be another—"

Just then Lindsay came over, holding a drink in one hand and leading a boy with the other. Marzi felt strangely relieved by the interruption. She didn't want to talk about the seventh room, the closed-up storage room behind the kitchen. She wasn't sure *why* she wanted to avoid the subject—there was no big mystery, it wasn't like Bluebeard's guestroom or anything—but the aversion was unmistakable. She'd been inside that room only once, just a couple of weeks before she dropped out of college. Maybe she simply associated the seventh room with that bad time in her life, the medical withdrawal, the hospital . . .

"This is Daniel," Lindsay said. The boy—who Marzi guessed was at least a year too young to be in the Red Room legally—smiled. "He's an art student."

"Aren't they all," Marzi said.

"Hey," Jonathan said, then turned back to Marzi. "Anyway, I heard there's a seventh room, with a desert motif. I guess you'd call it the Desert Room—"

The whole world lurched around Marzi. Her first thought was "Earthquake!" but this was a wholly internal shifting. She felt as if the bones in her skull were moving, as if doors she'd always kept closed had been jerked wide open—her head felt full, overfull, like a barrel spilling over in a heavy rain.

The room . . . changed. Not physically, not *fundamentally,* but there was a sort of visual superimposition, as if the barely visible ghost of another place were occupying the same space as the Red Room.

Marzi looked around, and mixed in among the hipsters and drunks she saw the dim forms of grizzled cowboys and worn-down women. The ghost of a honky-tonk piano stood in the far corner, played by a man with an absurd mustache and sleeve garters, and she could almost make out the strains of his jangly song. Marzi squeezed her eyes shut, hoping to banish the hallucination, but when she looked again, the ghostly forms were even more substantial, now sepia-toned like figures in old photographs.

The Red Room was being overtaken, or replaced, or *merged* with another saloon, a place with a name like the Bucket of Blood, the Trail Blossom, the Saddle Sore. The carpet occasionally gave way to patches of plank flooring, and the real bar seemed to float atop another bar, one made of a splintery board laid across stacked crates. The young, efficient bartenders were joined by a hulking, slow-moving man polishing a beer glass with a filthy rag, and as Marzi watched the real bartenders passed through the sepia-tone phantom without any of them taking notice.

This ghost saloon wasn't quite like the ones you saw in movies—the floor was too dirty for that, the whores were too fat, and the men had rotten teeth. This was a scene from *history*—or from Marzi's comic, *The Strange Adventures of Rangergirl,* somehow transformed from black ink on white paper into full-color reality.

Jonathan, Lindsay, and Daniel were all still with her, sitting around the table, which now shared space with a ghostly table of pitted wood. Their clothes seemed to shift and change before her eyes, changing to shadowy period garb and back to normal again. At the moment, Jonathan wore a black shirt, black jeans, and a black hat, along with an onyx-and-silver bolo tie. Lindsay wore a red, ruffled Miss Kitty saloon-girl dress. Daniel was dressed like an Eastern dandy, a banker, maybe, who'd walked into entirely the wrong bar, and now sat stupidly with his back to the room, drawing glares from the other customers.

If Marzi stared hard at any particular place in the Red Room, the ghostly saloon receded entirely, but still swarmed in her peripheral vision. She was . . . having an event. A stress reaction. Maybe even the beginnings of a seizure. But she held on to that oldest hope for health and happiness: *If I ignore what's wrong, maybe it will go away.*

"Daniel, tell them what you told me, about what happened in Dr. Maltin's class," Lindsay said, beaming in drunken benevolence. Her clothes shifted back to normal when Marzi looked at her.

"Oh," Daniel said, unaware of the grimy prospectors watching him, the cowboys spitting spectral tobacco juice toward his chair. "I came into class late, and—"

The crowd of cowboys and miners suddenly began moving, clearing away from the middle of the bar, rushing toward the far walls. Worse yet, the *real* people were moving, too, more slowly and apparently unconsciously, just drifting aside to clear a path from the front door to Marzi's table.

Marzi moaned softly. Jonathan leaned closer. "You okay?"

No. She wasn't okay. She was cracking up, seeing things— this was even worse than her experiences from two years before.

Someone approached from the front door, though Marzi hadn't seen it open, and strolled across the floor unhurriedly.

Where his boots touched, the carpet seemed to disappear, replaced by the rough planks of the ghost saloon. The figure
was coming right toward them.

It was the Outlaw.

The principal villain of Marzi's comic was an ancient sorcerer of indefinite origin, known by many names, most recently called the Outlaw. He embodied the spirit of savagery
and bloodshed in the West, and he masterminded most of
the nefarious activities that took place on the far side of the
Western Door. His appearance was as mutable as his
motives were cruel, and he appeared in a variety of guises.
When Rangergirl first saw the Outlaw, the day she opened
the strange door in the western wall of her tiny apartment,
the villain appeared as a tall cowboy in a duster and a beaten
hat, his face a mass of impenetrable shadow, his gnarled
hands resting on the worn wooden gun butts at his hips.
The Outlaw cast a long shadow even at high noon, even in
darkened rooms, and the sound of his boot heels reverber-
ated like a hammer on steel with each step he took, whether
he walked on sand, stone, or wood. In later issues of the
comic the Outlaw appeared as women, children, city slick-
ers, and monsters, but always that long shadow, the sound of
his heels, and the smell of gunsmoke gave his true identity
away.

Now the Outlaw was here, in a faded sepia form that
flickered and disappeared if she looked straight at it, but still,
here. Marzi wanted to move, to run, but she was paralyzed,
overwhelmed by the impossibility of the creature before
her. She looked away from him, to a far corner of the room,
and stared until every trace of the ghost piano and its music
disappeared.

When she looked back around, the Outlaw was gone, nowhere to be seen, and all traces of the sepia saloon had vanished, too. The moment had passed, and Marzi exhaled heavily. Just her imagination taking on a life of its own. But why was she having hallucinations now? There had been pressure the last time she cracked up—the stress of school, her mother's breast cancer. But Marzi's life was good now. A little lonely, but good. Did there even have to be a cause? Maybe her mind was just rotten all the way through, collapsing under its own weight.

"Marzi?" Jonathan said.

She blinked at him. She wasn't okay, but she could fake it. "Yeah. I just thought I saw someone I knew, across the bar—"

The Outlaw reappeared, right behind Daniel's chair, though the ghost saloon didn't. The villain was more substantial than ever now, face a clot of shadows, body almost real enough to smell of gunsmoke and ancient sweat. Marzi felt the temperature drop when his shadow fell upon her.

The Outlaw reached out and touched Daniel on the shoulder. Daniel turned his head to look behind him . . . at no one. He frowned, clearly confused, a little annoyed. Marzi started to rise from her seat, but the Outlaw's shadow made her cold and lethargic and slow.

The Outlaw put one of his long-barreled guns—Colt .45 Warmakers, Marzi called them in the comic—against Daniel's right eye. Without hesitation, without delivering a one-liner, without any ceremony at all, the Outlaw pulled the trigger. The gun went off without a sound, like something from a silent-era Western film, and Daniel's head snapped back. Marzi couldn't shout, couldn't even scream, as the shadow across her—or the shock within her—rendered her numb. The Outlaw started to turn, and disappeared before he even began walking away.

Daniel fell across the table, knocking glasses and bottles aside. Lindsay shouted, and a few people in the Red Room turned their heads, curious. Marzi leaned forward and touched Daniel's shoulder, then, when he didn't respond, she shook him. That was enough to send him tumbling off the chair to the floor. Lindsay, Marzi, and Jonathan knelt around him, saying his name, Marzi feeling at his throat for a pulse, finding nothing, no thump of life.

Daniel's eyes were open. His left eye was normal, but the pupil of his right eye was obscenely dilated, the white streaked with blood.

Cactus Country

DENIS CLOSED HIS EYES and waited for Jane to stop screaming. He counted to nine three times, but the screaming went on, so Denis acknowledged the inevitable. He would have to go in there, into the presence of whatever-she-was, and see what was wrong.

He knocked, and the screaming choked back to a sob. "Jane? Are you all right?"

Her voice was like rocks falling down a well. "No. I'm not all right."

Denis hesitated. "Should I come in?" Maybe she'd say no.

"Please." Her voice was low, troubled, like a storm front far off, but fast approaching.

Denis turned the knob and pushed.

Jane stood in the middle of the floor, in a puddle of brown ooze, her mud splashed all over the toilet, the floor tiles, and the sink. The floor of the tub was streaked with mud, and dirt swirled around and around the drain as water sprayed down from the showerhead.

Jane stared at the tub. "I

keep scrubbing, and the mud keeps washing away, but . . ." She
trailed off. Still looking at the tub, she put her hand against the
wall and wiped, as if wiping at a fogged window. Mud smeared
across the wall. "I can't get clean. I can't even find my skin,
Denis. I'm afraid. Look." She extended her right forefinger and
pressed it against the palm of her left hand. She pressed, apply-
ing a steady pressure, and her fingertip dimpled her palm, then
sunk in, then pressed *through*, her finger poking out the other
side, right through the back of her hand. "What's happening to
me?" she whispered.

Something deep inside Denis, some secret mechanism,
switched on. Denis often imagined his internal organs as
clockwork devices. The messy chemical factory of meat and
acid and bacteria disgusted him, and so he thought instead of
flywheels, levers, and gears, imagining himself as one of those
terrifically complex clockwork mechanisms from the eigh-
teenth century. He knew it wasn't true, but the idea comforted him, distracted him from the shitting shedding bleeding
truth of his own human nature. Somewhere in the red-glass
mechanism of his heart, a switch flipped, and the fear and disgust and horror he felt . . . went away.

She's a golem, he thought. *Something made of mud, to look
like a woman.* But golems were mute, they were blobby, they
had the word for "Life" written in Hebrew on their foreheads.

More importantly, golems weren't real. But reality suddenly seemed like a particularly negotiable currency.

He thought of the body in the back of Jane's car, *Jane's*
body. He wanted to believe it had been a hallucination, but
now he thought otherwise. Jane was dead, and this thing before him . . . this wasn't Jane. Not exactly. It was a revenant, a
returning spirit. A ghost in a body made of mud. Something

unnatural, something to be destroyed. He imagined plunging the knife into her, again and again, three by three times, and in that imagining he could see the blade come out stained with mud, not blood, and Jane only looking at him quizzically, her wounds closing, filth welling forth to seal the openings his knife made.

He couldn't tell her she was a ghost, couldn't tell her that he'd killed her, because then she could take her revenge, and how could he stop her? He had to tell her . . . something else. She was vulnerable now, afraid, weeping muddy tears. She would believe him, if he came up with the right sort of story.

"The goddess," he said suddenly. What had she been babbling about before, the power of the goddess, imprisoned somewhere?

"What?" she asked, bewildered, but no longer mewling and moaning, at least.

"The goddess. You said you had to rescue her, you said that she's the spirit of the earth . . ." He pointed to her, to the mud dripping from her extremities. "Now you're the spirit of the earth. You've been . . . empowered."

Jane looked at her hands. "Empowered," she said, as if tasting the word. *It must taste like minerals and worms,* Denis thought. *But it must also taste good.* Jane smiled; her teeth, he noticed, were small white stones. "When we made love in the mud, it made a real connection, didn't it? It woke the goddess, showed her my devotion."

"That must be it," Denis said.

Jane squeezed her hands into fists. "I'm a mud-girl now, a daughter of the earth."

"Looks that way."

Jane threw her arms wide and embraced Denis. He

gasped, his throat filling with the harsh mineral fragrance of her, the mud smearing against his clothes, his skin. Denis tried to flip the switch inside himself again, tried to detach and make this experience less than unbearably horrible. The best he could do was stifle the scream that wanted to emerge from his throat, turn his revulsion to stillness. He could not bring himself to hug her back, not knowing what she was, but she didn't seem to notice.

"And I couldn't have done it without you," she said, her earthy voice in his ear. "Our sex woke the goddess. You're in this with me, Denis. We made this together."

"Yes." Denis's voice was a croak. It was true. She couldn't have done this without him. If he hadn't let Jane die, she couldn't have come back as . . . whatever she was. And now she thought she was on a mission from a goddess, when the whole idea of gods—

—was just as absurd as the whole idea of ghosts.

There was madness now, either in Denis, or in the world.

"I'm unstoppable," she said.

Denis greatly feared that she was right.

"Let's get in the shower," she said. "I want to anoint your body with running mud. And then . . . we'll set the goddess free. I'll bring my new body, and you can bring a crowbar." She let go of him and stepped toward the shower, then looked over her shoulder at him, coquettishly.

Denis's stomach churned. That was a come-hither look. Jane had given it to him dozens of times before. She twitched her ass as she got into the shower. He was trapped. He mustn't reveal his revulsion.

"Come on," she said. "The water's fine. The mud is even better."

Wild Mare's Milk

"I'M NOT REALLY SUP-posed to let people in after hours," Marzi said. "But I think tonight calls for an exception." She put the ornate old key into the brass plate and unlocked Genius Loci's front door. Once it was open, she went to the security system keypad and deactivated the alarm. Lindsay and Jonathan followed, still shaken by their experience at the Red Room. They'd talked to the police there, but only briefly. The paramedics said Daniel had died of an embolism, just a faulty blood vessel popping in his brain. Marzi had seen . . . something else, but she kept that to herself.

Marzi felt strangely re-signed, as if pivotal events had transpired, unavoidable happenings set in motion. The consequences couldn't be stopped, only endured and—maybe—deflected. Marzi felt close to understanding, that she only needed a few crucial pieces of information to bring this confusion into some kind of clarity, a sort of grand unification theory of the madness in her life. A way to make sense of the sandstone-colored savage from her dream, the Outlaw in the Red Room, even her old phobia about closed doors.

Or maybe that sense of just-out-of-reach enlightenment was merely symptomatic of her growing insanity.

I need coffee before I think about things like this.

"It's nice of you to let us come here," Lindsay said. "Industrial quantities of beer and coffee are in order." Lindsay's voice was a ghost of its usual self, but Marzi was cheered to see her attempt lightness.

Jonathan sat down on the couch under the bay window, arms crossed over his chest, frowning. The walls in this room were painted flat black, with stars done in phosphorescent paint. Cracked and pitted planetoids adorned the walls, and Garamond Ray had also painted a strangely insectile satellite or space probe, with a cluster of solar cells that looked like faceted eyes, sensory arrays like dragonfly wings, and extended pincers. The satellite held a shred of thick white fabric in its pincers, blood staining the cloth, and the letters NA could just be made out on the shred of uniform, in the familiar style of the NASA logo. He looked at the walls for a long time, then said, "This painting is all about distance and alienation, isn't it? Or am I just projecting?"

"I always figured Garamond Ray just watched *2001* too many times," Marzi said, switching on a lamp and walking behind the counter.

"He might have been a friend," Lindsay said abruptly, dropping into an armchair beside the never-lit fireplace. "Daniel, I mean. He was an artist. I don't know if he was any good, but . . . well . . . now we'll never know what he might have made. It's funny. He died right in front of us, and I feel like I should feel *something* for him, but there's nothing.

Which is almost worse." She put her elbows on her knees and her chin in her cupped hands, looking at the floor glumly. Her glittering outfit, which had seemed so festive earlier in the evening, now struck Marzi as terribly sad, misplaced and tattered finery, a ball gown worn to a funeral.

Marzi drew a Guinness for Lindsay without even thinking, then set the glass aside. Lindsay didn't need more alcohol tonight. An Italian soda would be better. Marzi took a pitcher of iced coffee concentrate—"liquid crack"—from the fridge and poured herself a tall one, two parts water to one part coffee. Her synapses felt sluggish, her whole brain felt like a turtle left out in the snow, cold-blooded and bewildered. As if the Outlaw's shadow falling across her had lodged a little bit of desert night in her soul.

"I had an uncle who died of an embolism," Lindsay said, still staring at her boots. "He popped a blood vessel sitting on the toilet. The doctor said it happens like that sometimes, you're straining to take a shit, you push too hard, and 'pop.' My uncle died on his toilet with a porno magazine in his hands." She shook her head. "Daniel didn't go that badly, I guess. Though he didn't live as long, either."

Marzi, thinking of the Outlaw's long gun, wondered how easily Daniel *had* gone. At the last moment, had he seen what Marzi saw? Death in a long coat, Death like a Western cliché? Or had he seen something else, something appropriate to his own personal mythology, through his blood-soaked eye?

"Which porno magazine was it?" Jonathan asked.

Marzi and Lindsay both looked at him, and Lindsay laughed, a beautifully unfettered sound. "You know, I never thought to ask. My aunt was mortified enough as it was. She wouldn't have even mentioned the magazine, but my mom heard about it from a cop she knew. . . ." Lindsay shook her head. "And how could I not know that detail? It makes or breaks the story."

"It's a whole different kind of pathos if he was reading *Butt Pirates* than if he was reading *Big Bare Beavers*," Marzi said, which made Jonathan chuckle and sent Lindsay into paroxysms of laughter. *She's probably just hysterical,* Marzi thought. But a hysterical Lindsay was something she could deal with, something she could understand—not like a sad, existential Lindsay, which was too alien to bear.

Marzi brought Lindsay a cherry Italian soda, and then handed an ice-filled glass to Jonathan.

"What's this?" he asked, sniffing it.

"It's a vanilla train wreck. Go ahead, try it."

Jonathan sipped. "Mmm. It's good. And the name's appropriate. I feel like I've been in a train wreck tonight."

"Well, sure," Lindsay said. "Sure, the train wreck part. But please, dear Jonathan, don't tell me the *vanilla* part is appropriate, too. The *last* thing I need to hear tonight is that you're *vanilla*. And I had such high hopes." She grinned, superficially quite recovered from the trauma of seeing Daniel die in front of her. Marzi was sure Lindsay was overcompensating, trying to distract herself with laughter and innuendoes.

So what if she is? Marzi thought. *Whatever gets you through the night.*

"I only just met you," Jonathan said. "So I'll keep the secrets of my personal proclivities to myself, for now."

Lindsay looked at Marzi. "He must be shy." She turned back to Jonathan. "*I'm* not shy."

"She's really not," Marzi said. "I know, you thought she was shy, but it's actually a clever subterfuge."

"I was completely fooled," Jonathan said.

"Oh, shut up and drink your train wreck," Lindsay said, but fondly.

They were quiet for a time, sipping their drinks, looking at the ceiling. Not exactly avoiding one another's eyes, but not making an effort to connect, either. Marzi looked into her cup for a long time. Lindsay was her best friend, and Jonathan . . . well, he was still essentially a stranger, but he'd tried to pull Jane off of her, and she liked the way his eyes brightened when he talked about the murals, and sometimes you had to take a chance, didn't you? Marzi had talked to a lot of doctors during her three weeks in the mental hospital, and they'd spouted a lot of jabber and nonsense, but one thing rang true, and stuck with her: that Marzi *held things in,* that she didn't ask for help, ever. Hell, she'd only agreed to take a medical withdrawal when she could no longer physically make herself open doors and walk into classrooms, because the fear of what might be waiting beyond the doors became too great. She'd had a dozen anxiety attacks before she mentioned her troubles to anyone. And what had that gotten her? Only more fear and loneliness. One of the doctors had summed it up perfectly, saying, "Marzi, you don't *need* to be the Lone Ranger. And even he had Tonto."

Marzi smiled a little. Wouldn't Lindsay just *love* to be compared to Tonto?

She looked up and caught Lindsay's eye. Jonathan had wandered off to stand near the far wall, peering intently at a ringed planet painted in fuzzy hues of blue and green. Marzi went to sit on the couch near Lindsay's armchair, close enough for their knees to touch. "Can we talk for a sec, Lindsay?" she said softly. She didn't exactly *mind* if Jonathan overheard, but she wasn't going to pull him into it. Lindsay already knew all the backstory, so she'd understand if Marzi was feeling a little . . . fragile . . . about her sanity, and she wouldn't freak out about it. "Things've been sort of weird for me lately."

"The bad dreams you mentioned?" Lindsay said. "About the savage Indian guy?"

"Partly that," Marzi said. "But . . . well, for instance, tonight, in the Red Room, I thought I saw—"

"Huh," Jonathan said, his voice strange and flat. They looked up, and he pointed toward the front door. "Remember that crazy mud-girl? She's out on the deck." He squinted. "And she brought a friend."

"THERE ARE LIGHTS on in there," Denis said, standing on the corner with his hands shoved deep in his pockets. There was dirt under his fingernails, and as long as he kept his hands out of sight, he didn't have to think about that much. The worst thing was, he was almost getting *used* to the nastiness. When he'd been in the shower, with Jane, there were moments when he felt real pleasure. The sensation of making love to the mud-girl was bizarre but not unpleasant—cool, yielding, slick. If only he could do something about her mineral smell, he might even be able to bear the thought of fucking her again. At least they didn't have to worry about pregnancy. And the mud certainly washed off easily enough, when they were done. As long as they always made love in the shower . . .

But Jane the lover was gone now, replaced by Jane the zealot. She was naked, except for the mud, of course, but Denis had gradually accepted that the mud was more skin and substance than it was clothing or armor. Her hair was tentacle-thick, dreadlocks sculpted from mud. "What are they *doing* there?" she seethed. "It's three o'clock in the morning! The café should be empty!" She whirled and glared at Denis. "Are there usually people here so late?"

"I wouldn't know," he said, stifling a yawn. "I'm normally in bed by now." Though not normally sleeping, he admitted to himself. He slept no more than four hours a night, usually, and often sleeping that much was a struggle. More often he simply lay in bed, imagining crystal lattices filling the air. And when he slept, he dreamed of a great machine, a steam-powered contrivance of chrome and gears and treads. A grinding machine that tore up trees, houses, and streets, using everything in its path as fuel to feed its hungry engine of a heart. And to what purpose? Why did the machine go on? Simply so that it could obtain *more* fuel, he supposed, and continue grinding, leaving only a scoured plain in its wake.

"Do you suppose they're guards?" Jane said, as if thinking aloud rather than actually asking a question. "Do you think they're *guarding* the goddess? Or tormenting her, laughing at her bondage?"

"I hate to ask, lover, but . . . if this prison is so secure, if it can successfully contain the spirit of the earth, how are we supposed to get your goddess out?" Denis had come to regret his lie. Telling Jane she'd been transformed by the goddess had seemed a neat way to sidestep the issue of her death and to prevent further hysteria, but now it had led to this unpleasant little field trip . . . and he *still* had mud on his boots. And mud under his fingernails, as far as that went. How could he lure her away from this nonsensical quest?

Maybe it would be best to let her break into the café, he thought. *Let her see there's nothing imprisoned there, put her face-to-face with the absence of her goddess. Though I'm sure she'd incorporate that into her delusional system, too.*

"It's always easier to break into a prison than it is to break out," Jane said. "Besides which . . . I have *gifts*." She held up her hands, and the mud began to run down her forearms. Her hands were *melting*, disappearing. Then new digits began to grow from her wrists, longer than fingers, sharper, thicker. Fingers like spikes, or chisels. "I can break down doors, gouge my way through walls. Mud can be soft, Denis, or it can be dried and fired and made solid as bricks. It can ooze through the tiniest cracks, or it can fall down a hillside and destroy a village." She turned her face toward him, and the glow from a nearby streetlight gleamed on the wet white mud that was her face. "I will set her free. I won't be stopped." She walked toward the café then, straight for the main steps, up onto the deck.

Cursing under his breath, Denis followed her. That thing she'd done with her hands . . . Things shouldn't be that mutable. Things should have a form, and stick to it. And if things absolutely had to change, they should only grow *simpler*. Lately Denis's life had become increasingly, unpleasantly complex.

Why couldn't you have stayed dead? he thought venomously, looking at Jane's back. If he drove a knife between her shoulder blades now, it would effect no change whatsoever—it would just pass through her, as she'd pushed her forefinger through the palm of her hand earlier tonight.

Not for the first time, Denis felt a surge of real fear at what Jane had become.

Denis climbed the steps and stood beside her, looking into the main room of Genius Loci. Marzi was there, and her friend Lindsay, and a man that Denis didn't know. They were all looking out the window, and the man was pointing.

Jane knew them all, apparently. "Those three," she said, through clenched teeth. "They struck me before—they *mocked* me. They led *others* in mockery." She lifted her altered hand, as if to wave at them. "I will not be mocked."

Denis reached out, to touch her shoulder, to calm and restrain her, but then he thought of the feel of the mud, and the mixed feelings of lust and disgust that Jane's new texture awakened, and he lowered his hand. He was tired; he was resigned. Let her burst through the bay window into the café. Let her rip all their heads off, and tear up the floorboards, and look for her goddess. Denis couldn't bring himself to care anymore.

He heard footsteps behind them, and turned, expecting a police officer, or a homeless person, already deciding how to deal with either one.

But it was only Beej, holding a wadded-up black garbage bag. "Hi, Denis, mud-girl," he said, bobbing his weasellike head. "Have you come to be acolytes of the earthquake god, too?"

"Puppet of the patriarchy," Jane spat.

The front door of Genius Loci opened a crack, and Marzi

stuck her head out. "Sorry, folks," she said. "We're closed. Why don't you go to the Saturn Café? They're still open."

"Hi, Marzi," Beej said cheerfully. "I've come to liberate the earthquake god."

Curiouser and curiouser, Denis thought. But before he could say or do anything in response, Jane snarled, rather dramatically, and launched herself at Marzi, and Denis had little choice but to give the ensuing events his full attention.

Hole Up

"FUCK!" MARZI SHOUTED, and pulled the door shut just as Jane slammed against it. For a moment, Marzi's face was mere inches from Jane's, only the thin pane of glass in the door separating them. Marzi stumbled back from the fury in Jane's expression. "Get lost, or we're calling the cops!" she shouted, and Jane flinched, more at the volume than the threat, Marzi thought.

Beej ambled up the steps, smiling sheepishly. He held up a pair of red-handled wire cutters. "Sorry," he said. "I cut the phone lines, when I saw you guys in there. See, there's this earthquake god, and if you called for help—"

Jane shoved Beej aside, sending him stumbling into a table. Denis came hurrying up the stairs, saying "Jane" in a half-pleading, half-threatening tone. Jane whirled and began arguing with him, gesturing fiercely at the door as Marzi watched.

"The phone's out," Jonathan said, and Marzi turned to see him standing by the counter, holding the receiver in his hand. Marzi opened her mouth, then closed it again. What could she say? Things had gotten pathologically weird in the past two minutes. Beej had *cut the phone lines*? Marzi couldn't begin to assimilate that—it was too bizarre, too made-for-TV-movie.

Lindsay rolled her eyes. "What, do they think this is 1981?" She reached into her purse and withdrew her cell phone. She dialed, then said, "Yeah, we're at one sixty-one Ash Street, Genius Loci café, and there's three people outside threatening us, trying to break in." She paused, then brightened. "Yeah, hey, Joey! They got you on night dispatch, huh? So, could you send somebody over to—great. Sure, I'll stay on the line, let me pass on the good word." She put her hand over the mouthpiece. "It's Joey Montaigne, you remember him, he used to skateboard down by the boardwalk all the time? He's a cop now, isn't it wild? Anyway, he's sending some guys, and since the police station's only a couple of blocks away . . ." She held up her forefinger and cocked her head, listening.

Marzi listened, too, and heard sirens approaching.

"The sirens are a nice touch, Joey," Lindsay said into the phone. "Though I think they're scaring off the bad guys."

Denis grabbed Jane's arm and tugged her toward the street, looking around, panicked. Jane looked into the café, her face white and baleful. Marzi grinned at her and waved. "Bye now," she said.

Jane bared her teeth and hissed, like one of those exotic cockroaches, and then allowed Denis to lead her down the steps and along the sidewalk, away from the approaching sirens.

Jonathan came to stand beside Marzi, looking out the door. "This may be the strangest night of my life," he said.

"It's climbing the charts for me, too," Marzi said.

Beej appeared in the doorway like some lateral jack-in-the-box. He scratched his fuzzy scalp with the end of the wire cutters. "Hey, Marzi, let me in," he said. "Sorry I came on so strong, cut the phone lines and all; I got a little too James Bond, I know. But see, I'm supposed to free the earthquake god, and it'll only take a minute, really—"

"*Beej,*" Marzi said. "What the hell's wrong with you? Have you totally lost your mind?"

"My mind's been *found,* Marzi," he said, so earnest it made Marzi's heart break. "I've got a purpose now." He put the palm of his hand flat on the glass. "Let me in, please?"

A police car pulled up to the curb. The passenger door opened, and a young officer emerged, his hand on his holster. "You, on the steps!" he shouted. "Police! Turn around with your hands in the air!"

Beej's face fell. He looked at the wire cutters in his hands. "Didn't work, did it?" he said mournfully. "I screwed up."

Marzi, absurdly, felt the urge to say *You did your best.* But she only shook her head.

Beej turned around, holding his hands up. At the cop's instruction, he dropped the wire cutters and came down the stairs to the pavement, where the cop quickly cuffed him and shoved him in the back of the car. Moments later, three other police cars arrived, lights flashing. Marzi, Jonathan, and Lindsay stood in the doorway, watching. Lindsay kept chatting with Joey for a while, then Marzi heard her say, "Shouldn't we free up this line? I mean, for other emergencies?" She hit the disconnect button and grinned. "I let Joey cop a feel off me when we were fifteen, and he's been willing to do anything for me ever since."

"Lucky for us," Marzi said. What would have happened if the police hadn't come, if Denis hadn't been there to restrain Jane? Marzi didn't want to think about it. But Jane was still out there, in the night, and she definitely seemed to have something personal against Marzi. She'd be back, muddy and feral, and what would Marzi do then?

DENIS DROVE HOME slowly, scanning the streets and sidewalks for signs of the police. He imagined a SWAT team— men in black body armor, with webbed belts full of tear gas grenades, holding complex guns with the strange curvature of modern abstract sculpture. On one level, he knew such fears were absurd, but that didn't erase them.

Jane sat fuming and quietly furious in the passenger seat; *literally* fuming, faint trailers of white steam rising from cracks in her muddy body. Her smell was overpoweringly earthy, fragrant, mineral. He could feel the heat of her fury, and wondered if her skin would harden, dry, and—dare he hope?— crack into fragments.

"We were *this close*," Jane said.

"Didn't you hear the sirens? We would have gotten caught!"

"No cell can hold me. I'll never be a political prisoner."

That's all very well for you, Denis thought. *What about me?* "I'm not so formidable," he said, turning a corner, careful to obey the speed limit. "They could still be coming after

us! I'm sure Marzi recognized me. There might be cops waiting for us at home!"

"We didn't do anything," she spat. "What, trespassing?"
She flicked her hand in dismissal, sending a glob of mud flying, to stick on the dashboard. "And anyway, if we'd gotten
inside, freed the goddess, none of that would *matter*, the cops
would be stripped of their power, the patriarchy would topple, the—"

"Would you just shut the fuck up?" Denis said, surprised
at the calmness in his voice; he felt like his brain was boiling,
but his words came out tough-guy cool. Jane could disem-
bowel him with one hand, turn her fingers into chisels and
open him alive. He knew that, but he could take no more.
"I'm tired. Maybe you don't need to sleep anymore, but the
goodwill of the goddess doesn't sustain *me*." He pulled into
the parking lot of his apartment building, a knot of tension in
his belly dissolving when he saw there were no police cars
waiting. Yet.

"I'm going home," Jane said, through clenched teeth.

"Fine by—" he began, then stopped. How could he have
forgotten?

The body. Jane's body. If Mud-Jane was a ghost, then the
corpse was *real*, and it was still in the back of her car, rotting
in place. Jane might not notice it, but what if someone else
did? Especially if the cops investigated, went to Jane's apartment, became curious about her mud-covered car . . . He had
to get rid of the body, and that meant Jane *couldn't* leave and
take her mud chariot away.

Forcing himself not to hesitate, he put his hand on Jane's
knee. His fingers sank in slightly. She didn't react, but she

didn't get out of the car, either, just sat, still, like an unfinished statue.

"Janey, darling, I'm sorry. I'm a jerk. I am. I know how important this is to you."

"It's important to the world, Denis. The world is filthy, it's a wreck, and men made it that way." She didn't look at him, still gazed out the window, but Denis did his best to seem attentive. "I'm in a unique position to change things. You can't imagine the forces moving through me. The goddess who gave me these powers . . . she can change the world. Remake it. Shape it like . . ."

"Like clay?" he said.

She nodded slowly. "Yes. She can give the world a better shape."

Jane took a breath—something she did quite irregularly, Denis had noticed; breathing seemed to have become optional for her. "You've been good about this, Denis, helping me through my transition, keeping me from panicking, showing me the benefits of my situation. But this is more important than *anything,* than the possibility of jail, than our relationship, more important than *art.* Do you get that?"

"I'm beginning to understand," he said. "Will you come inside with me? Get some sleep, and then we'll figure out what to do next?"

"Yes," Jane said simply, and got out of the car.

Denis sighed in relief. Now he had time to think. The police would almost certainly come sooner or later, but he was pretty sure he could talk his way out of *that.* He and Jane hadn't really done anything, after all. Beej was the one who actually vandalized things. Denis could come up with a story for why he and Jane were out walking. . . .

Denis went into his apartment, after Jane. She was sitting on his white couch, looking blankly at the wall, perhaps deep in thought, perhaps not thinking at all. "Sweetheart," Denis said. "I'm, ah, going to move your car."

She turned her head and regarded him wordlessly.

"You don't have a visitor's pass, and they'll tow cars from this lot. There's barely enough parking for all the tenants, you know that."

"Fine," Jane said.

"If anyone comes to the door . . . don't answer it, okay?"

"I will speak to no one but the goddess this day, Denis. I have much to think about."

"Right. Good." He went out to Jane's car, opened the filthy door, and slid inside. He shuddered. The smell of urine from the back, the coating of mud all over the car—it repulsed him, but this was necessary. He tried to decide what to do.

It wasn't as if he'd killed her. Her body would show no signs of foul play. She'd died of suffocation, he assumed—would they be able to tell that? Denis didn't know much about forensic science, just that it could be incredibly revealing. Surely it would be obvious that she hadn't been murdered? Not *exactly* murdered, anyway. But they would be able to estimate time of death, and Denis had been seen with Jane since her death, and other people had seen her—or the mud-her, anyway. What would the police make of that?

Denis had to get rid of the body, and it wouldn't hurt to get rid of the car. Getting rid of Mud-Jane would be nice, too, but he wasn't sure how to do that, how something like her could be disposed of.

Denis started the car and drove, hunched over the steering

wheel, tense and wishing for invisibility. He took back streets, heading steadily up into the hills, until he reached the place where Jane's car had been buried, where all this mess began. It was four in the morning and there was no traffic, no one up on these dark roads. He drove the car close to the heap of drying mud and stopped, steeling himself for what was to come. Finally, he opened the hatchback and looked at Jane's still body. He breathed through his mouth—the stink was stronger back here—and concentrated on the clockwork of his glands, on calming himself down. He lifted her body out of the car, reminding himself the corpse wasn't a *person*, just meat, and he could stand to touch meat. It was difficult to lift her, far harder than he'd expected. She'd stiffened in death, and seemed heavier than she'd ever been in life. Strange bubbling sounds came from her stomach, gases expanding, he supposed. Denis dragged her toward the mountain of mud, where her car had been buried before she managed to drive it out. He dropped her body in the cavity where her car had been, a place surrounded on three sides by high walls of slowly drying mud. Then he went back to her car, started the engine, and drove it into the heap of mud, slowly nudging with the car's front end. Under the pressure from the car, the mud walls collapsed, burying Jane's body. Denis backed the car away and looked at the mound of mud in the uneven light from the dirt-caked headlights. It looked like a mudslide, that was all—a big mudslide, but certainly not *suspicious*. And back here, off the road, with nothing but mud and trees around anyway, who would bother to dig through it? Who would come looking? There were animals here, mountain lions, but it seemed unlikely they would smell her body and dig through hundreds of pounds of mud to get to it.

Satisfied, Denis got out of her car. He opened all the doors, and the hatchback, too; let the animals and the elements in, let them destroy any evidence there might be of Jane's death in the back seat. He noticed the remains of their picnic, still on the ground—some trash, the butcher knife, the half-eaten loaf of bread—and picked them up. He tossed them into the back of Jane's car, too. Standing with his arms crossed, Denis surveyed the scene. The car would be found eventually, but Denis was confident that its presence wouldn't be connected to him. This was the best he could do, for now. Mud-Jane was the more significant problem in his life at the moment. She had a tendency to draw attention to herself, after all. And what would he tell her about her car? She'd expected him to take it back to her apartment. He'd just tell her he'd left it there, and when she found it missing, let her assume it had been stolen, or hauled away as a presumed derelict, or something.

He went to his own car, still parked among the trees from his earlier trip here. He drove home, parked, and sat in the car for a while, going over the night's events in his mind, as if he were running his tongue over the gap left by a missing tooth. Facing Mud-Jane again was the last thing he wanted to do, but waiting wouldn't make it any easier. He got out of the car.

"Jane?" he called when he entered the apartment. "Are you here?"

She wasn't in the living room; there was just a smear of mud on the couch. He checked the bathroom and the bedroom, too, but she wasn't in the apartment. Where had she gone? And why? Would she try to break into the coffee shop again? Maybe she'd just stepped out to get some air, and would come back soon. How far could she go, without a car? He was too tired even to worry properly.

Denis kicked off his muddy boots. He *had* to get those cleaned soon. He went into the kitchen and washed his hands thoroughly, even scrubbing under the nails. Then he went into the living room and turned over the couch cushions that Jane had dirtied. That was only a temporary fix, of course—hiding dirt did not eliminate it, as Denis well knew—but it would do for the moment.

He was just about to wearily search the kitchen for a much-needed bagel when he was startled by a sharp knock at the door. Denis opened the door wide and made himself smile. "Hello, Officer," he said.

AT 5:30 IN THE MORNING. Marzi finally got home, exhausted from talking to the cops, and from talking to Hendrix, who'd been none too pleased to be rousted out of bed before dawn. He was annoyed that Marzi had been in the café after hours, but quieted down when she pointed out that if she hadn't been there Beej and the others would have been able to break in quite easily. Granted, there was the alarm, but Marzi had kept them from getting inside at all, and Lindsay's call to the police had brought faster results than the alarm would have.

Beej had been charged with vandalism for cutting the phone lines. If he didn't plead guilty, Marzi would probably be called to testify against him. Marzi found it more likely that Beej would try to tell the judge about his attempts to liberate the earthquake god, which would lead to a series of very necessary psychiatric appointments for Beej. He was clearly two screws short of a hinge these days, and could use professional help. The police were going to question Jane and Denis as well. All in all, talking to the cops had been a less painful experience than Marzi had expected, but she was still exhausted. It had been a night of death and madness, and Marzi was looking forward to sleeping the day away.

She stripped, splashed water on her face from the sink, and dumped double handfuls of it through her greasy, smoky hair. Not for the first time, she was thankful that she'd cut it so short; it was easier to keep clean, and that was one less thing she had to worry about. The doctors had told her to streamline her life as much as possible, to reduce sources of anxiety, and the first thing she'd done when she got out of the hospital was cut her hair down to a couple of inches, which now tended to stick up wildly from her head. Lindsay had helped her dye it pink that autumn, but the color had long since faded, leaving her hair the color of straw. She crawled onto her futon and pulled the sheet over her body. For the first time in what felt like forever she relaxed, tension bleeding from her body, muscles loosening. She was home, in bed, alone, safe.

She closed her eyes.

MARZI SOARED ABOVE Santa Cruz, looking down at the curve of the bay, boat sails the color of butterfly wings dotting the water, sea lions basking on a rock. Every roof was as familiar as the lines on her own palm. There was Genius Loci, there Logos, there Bookshop Santa Cruz, there the Saturn Café, and the sluggish, mud-colored river, which she and Lindsay

*always called "the raging San Lorenzo," bisecting the town,
the west side her home, the east side home to countless taque-
rias, the old Rio Theater, the Seabright Brewery. Marzi could
see it all, the hidden parks, the tangle of rusting shopping carts
by the river, the old Victorian houses—and she could sense the
people moving through the city like blood through the limbs
of a sleeping god.*

This is what it's like when a city has an out-of-body experience, *she thought*, no longer moving, now hanging there,
cloudlike.

*As if the thought were a cue, the city beneath her began to
die. The river dried up, revealing river-bottom mud the color
of shit. The roofs fell in, exposing rafters and support beams
that reminded her of broken ribs. The streets cracked, potholes appearing like open sores. Dust and sand rushed in to
choke the streets, burying the smaller houses entirely, and
blowing sand scoured the paint from remaining structures,
taking everything down to bare wood and metal. After a few
seconds, the scene below looked like something from the
Mojave, but even in that desert there was life, growing things,
and animals, however well hidden. What Santa Cruz had
become was . . . desolation. And not just Santa Cruz—the
neighboring communities, too. Capitola, Scotts Valley, Boul-
der Creek, Aptos. The redwoods in the hills were charred by
fire, blackened pillars sticking up at odd angles from still-
steaming heaps of mud. If Marzi could have flown higher—
she couldn't seem to control her own movements—she felt
she would have seen even more destruction. The coast road
collapsing into the ocean. The mountains leaping up and
falling down in the passing ripple of an earthquake. Wildfires*

destroying Oakland. San Francisco and Los Angeles falling into the sea, reclaimed by something older than life, reclaimed by the way of the world before there was life on Earth.

Marzi began to cry. She knew, somehow, that this was her fault. Not her fault because she rode in gas-powered vehicles or sometimes forgot to recycle her plastic containers, not the general culpability for the environment that rested on the shoulders of the developed world, but her fault directly. She could have stopped this. She could have done something.

A gust of wind spun Marzi in the sky, turning her toward the bay again. Without willing it, she began to drift lower and closer to the water, toward the tangle of hotels and liquor stores and one-way streets on the beachfront. Toward the boardwalk, with its two roller coasters, bumper cars, Tilt-A-Whirls . . . and the building closest to the water, Neptune's Kingdom, the arcade where Marzi and Lindsay sometimes went to play air hockey. Neptune's Kingdom had somehow survived the doom that came to Santa Cruz, its pennants tattered but still flapping, its sign broken and lying on the sidewalk, but the structure still intact.

Marzi knew the Kingdom wasn't empty. Something lived there. Something . . . denned there. Marzi drifted lower, until the Kingdom filled her entire field of view. Something moved inside with an enormous dry rustle, as if a nest of old bones and newspapers were shifting beneath a mammoth weight. Could this be it, then? The home of the Outlaw, the thing that had killed Daniel?

No. The voice was unmistakably feminine, husky, smoke-and-whiskey roughened. Marzi seemed to hear it inside her head. The rustling came again. No, I am not your enemy.

The Outlaw could come in many guises, she knew. He could make his voice feminine, of course. He could pretend—

The voice laughed, a deep, genuine chuckle with no guile in it. That convinced Marzi. The Outlaw could laugh, but it always rang false or cruel, because he didn't really understand *laughter, except the laughter of mockery, the laughter of joy at causing pain. This was a true laugh, but that didn't make Marzi feel much better, because now there was an unknown quantity, a new being, something she didn't understand and couldn't account for.*

I am not your enemy, *the voice said.* Nor am I, exactly, your friend. But I am an interested party. If you would prevent this desolation, Marzipan, you must be willing to make sacrifices. You must be willing to open some doors, and close others.

"Why me?" *Marzi shouted, not really expecting an answer.*

To her surprise, the voice responded immediately, with dry irony. Because you have a responsibility as an artist, Marzipan, *it said, and then chuckled again.*

Another wind picked up Marzi and spun her away from the Kingdom. Do not look for me here, *the voice said, its volume fading.* I live in a different palace in the West. Look for me there, in the West beyond the West.

If it said more, Marzi didn't hear. She spun higher into the sky, and it was no longer the peaceful drifting of a cloud but something faster and more terrifying, something like free fall with no parachute, in reverse.

Black dots appeared in the distant sky, over the water, and as they approached, Marzi recognized them. They were giant vultures. Diseased, scabby, starving, dropping feathers as they came, but still enormous, their yellow beaks opening hungrily, their eyes flat and black and desperate.

This land was so dead that even the scavengers and carrion-eaters were dying.

Then the vultures were upon her, beaks opening for her flesh, no longer caring if their prey was still alive and kicking, transformed into predators by their privation, and as they took their first bites, she woke.

MARZI SAT UP in bed, the sheet stuck to her sweaty body, her heart pounding as if she'd just run flat-out for a mile. She looked around the room, vaguely surprised that there weren't piles of sand in the corners, that the walls were intact, that the whole coast hadn't been bludgeoned by earthquake and razed by fire and buried in mud and choked in sand.

She got up, pulled on clothes, and stumbled to the kitchen. She couldn't remember the last time she'd been so thirsty. The inside of her mouth felt as rough as an iguana's back. She poured a glass of water, guzzled it down, poured another, and drank it more slowly. The clock on the microwave read 12:17. She'd slept enough, but she was exhausted, as if she'd been running in her sleep the entire time.

Her answering machine blinked at her insistently, a stuttering red light. She distantly recalled hearing it ring earlier, but she'd just buried her head in the pillow and slept on. Marzi pressed the button, the machine beeped, and Beej's voice spoke through a hiss of static: "Um, Marzi, hi, it's Beej. At the police station. This is my one phone call and you're it and I hate to bother you, but could you bail me out? I'm good for it, I'll pay you back, you know, or else the system will collapse and money won't matter anymore but . . . anyway. I'll be here." A long, long pause. "Guess you're sleeping. Sweet dreams."

Marzi listened to the rest of the tape, but it was just a couple of hang-ups. She imagined Beej, holding a greasy black phone to his ear, staring bug-eyed into the middle distance, knowing he didn't have any better friend than Marzi. It was so sad and crazy she almost wanted to call the police, just to have them tell Beej she couldn't bail him out. But he'd figure it out when she didn't come. He probably wouldn't even hold it against her; that wasn't his way. He'd just be a little hurt, a little bewildered. Maybe Beej would be able to get some psychiatric help now. Hell, it had done wonders for Marzi, hadn't it?

She brushed her teeth and took a shower, the hot water making her feel more human, less like something crumpled and thrown on the floor. She needed coffee, rather desperately, and then she'd be altogether okay again. She walked to the front door, took a deep breath, and seized the doorknob. Before, when she had trouble with doors, it had always been an unreasoning fear, born from the fact that she *didn't know* what was behind the door, that it could be *anything*. But this time, she knew what she feared. Streets full of sand, the smoke of wildfires, buildings cracked by earthquakes.

Marzi opened the door, and sunlight streamed in over her. Birds chirped. Some punks on skateboards glided by on the sidewalk, looking bored.

Marzi let out a ragged breath. "Good morning, world," she said, and went out.

Gun Wise

MARZI AMBLED UP to Genius Loci for coffee, and to look for Lindsay or Jonathan, but neither of them was around; just Hendrix, leaning on the bar and scowling. When she said hello, he just grunted. He was still pissed about that mess the night before, she figured. His glare had probably driven Jonathan away. "So," she said. "What'd the cops say?"

He shrugged tectonically, his dreadlocks swaying across his pale round face. "We're pressing charges against Beej, the little shit, since he pretty much confessed to the vandalism. We didn't bother with the other two, though."

Marzi frowned. "Denis and Jane? You just let them walk?"

"The cops talked to Denis this morning, and he said he and his girlfriend were taking a late stroll when they saw Beej fucking around with something on the side of Genius Loci. He said they saw you inside, and came up the steps to tell you about it, but that you wouldn't let them in."

"That is *not* how it happened!" Marzi said.

"You said they were beating on the glass and yelling. Denis says they were beating on the glass and yelling. The cops don't see a discrepancy there."

"It's bullshit. I don't know what they wanted, but they were *crazed*. Jane was, at least. And you heard about what Jane did yesterday, jumping on me, and—"

"I believe you. Look," Hendrix said, and beckoned her around the counter. Marzi came, curious, and Hendrix pointed to the wall just beneath the phone.

A blurry picture of Denis hung there, alongside a crisper one of Beej, both taken in Genius Loci. A hand-scrawled note above them read "Banned for Life."

Marzi whistled, impressed. This was unusually decisive action for Hendrix. He and Denis were even sort of *friends*. But Hendrix was loyal to the café; Marzi knew that. Denis and Beej shouldn't have fucked with Genius Loci.

"Wow, Hendrix. They're regulars, too."

He snorted. "Beej buys one tea bag and gets free refills on hot water all fucking day, and Denis never tips. I'm not sorry to see them go. You saw all the mud Denis tromped in here a few days ago, and Beej freaked out and started screaming in the Cloud Room . . . nah, good riddance. They're a fucking disturbance."

"There's no picture of Jane here," Marzi said.

"I don't even know if she's ever been in here, and I certainly don't have a photo of her, Marzi, but I'll tell everybody not to serve a mud-covered crazy woman, okay?" He stomped back to the counter to serve a customer.

Once he'd finished, Marzi said, "Hey, thanks for doing this, Hendrix. It's good of you not to give me shit."

"Jonathan lives upstairs, and you're a manager, and

Lindsay's here more than I am, so what do I care if you hang out after hours? You've got a key for a reason." He softened. "Besides, like you said last night, if you hadn't been here, who knows what Beej and company would have done?" He shook his head. "This fucking place. I used to love this job, but now people are trying to break in, and I'm hearing shit . . ."

"Hearing shit? Like what?"

He frowned. "I don't know. It's just weird echos or something, probably, but I keep hearing, like, *voices* when I'm in the kitchen lately. They sound close by but I can't make out what they're saying. I'm probably just getting old and going deaf and fixing to die."

"Nah, you'll live forever," Marzi said, and clapped him on the shoulder, feeling more friendly toward him than she had in a long time.

Marzi went out into the sun and walked along Ash Street. An aging hippie street vendor grinned at her, showing brown gapped teeth, and gestured to his stained blanket and the wares spread there: old engine parts, loose tarot cards, mason jars full of seashells and marbles, a leather rose, and a lone plastic scorpion, unevenly painted red.

"Cheap wonders," he said. "And I know *just* the thing for you." He rooted around in a leather satchel while Marzi stood, uncertain. She would've just walked on, but he seemed nice enough, maybe a little loopy in the head, but no harm there.

"There's probably better business on Pacific Avenue," she said, thinking of the kids who sold beaded necklaces and hemp bracelets there, the airbrush artists, the Famous Legendary Street Poet who sat on an upside-down bucket and intently read slim volumes of Beat poetry between recitations.

"One can throw oneself into the crowd," he said sagely, "or one can choose one's customers. I prefer the back ways of things. Ah, here it is." From deep in the bag, he drew forth—

—a gun. Marzi gasped and stepped back, thinking he *wasn't* harmless, he was a nutcase, and now she was a goner—

But he held the gun out to her, butt first. "This is a genuine antique," he said, nodding. "They don't even make caps for it anymore, though I have a full package, yes I do, two hundred shots."

"It's a cap gun," she said, relief flowing into her limbs like water, and she took it from his hands. The gun was lightweight, but the barrel was made of actual metal, even if the grip was made of some Bakelite-era protoplastic.

"Well, yes," he said. "If I wanted a real gun I wouldn't buy a Colt forty-five Peacemaker anyway. They were reliable enough for their time, but I'd probably go for a Desert Eagle or—"

"A Colt forty-five?" she said, intrigued. That was the gun Rangergirl used, and, in a way, the gun the Outlaw used, too, though his were called Warmakers.

"Wyatt Earp style," the man said. "With the extra-long barrel for increased accuracy."

"That's apocryphal," Marzi said. "He probably didn't really have guns like that."

"But it's a good *story,*" the man said. "Don't miss the point." His expression was deeply serious, face creased like an old leather satchel.

Marzi grinned. "I don't guess you have another one, do you? They're better in pairs."

"Alas, times are not what they once were, and I only have the one. Do you want it, or not?"

"How much?"

The man looked at the sky thoughtfully, his eyes a placid ocean blue. "Three dollars and eighty-eight cents," he said finally.

Marzi took a five from her pocket. "Here you go."

"We regret that we cannot provide change," he said.

"I figured as much. Call it a tip."

"No, no, you have to get your full value. I'll throw in the caps. The package isn't even opened." He dug around in his satchel some more until he retrieved a battered yellow cardboard box. A grinning cartoon cowboy beamed at Marzi from the package, holding up a pair of six-shooters. "200 Shots!" the lettering proclaimed.

Marzi took the package, pleased.

"Don't point that at anybody," the man said. "Unless you mean to use it."

"Thanks for this," Marzi said.

"You'd better put it out of sight," he said. "Toy guns these days are all bright yellow and fake-looking. If the cops see you with that, they might not know it's a toy. Cops in this town, bang-bang, talk to you later, you know?"

Marzi nodded. "You know, I always wondered—"

"Why criminals don't paint their Uzis fluorescent orange and carry them down the street right in the open? Yeah, I've wondered that, too. There's just not a lot of whimsy in the world when it comes to guns. Maybe that's for the best."

"Yeah," Marzi said, and put the gun and the caps into her bag. Hell, it probably was an antique—she'd probably just gotten it for a steal. "Take it easy."

"Happy trails," the vendor said.

Marzi continued on her way, humming. A little while ago

she was in her house, terrified to even go outside . . . but things hadn't been so bad since then, once she actually got out. Hendrix had acted like a human being, and now she had a cool new toy. Denis and his crazy girlfriend had rattled her, that was for sure, and seeing Daniel die had shaken her profoundly, but those things were *explicable*. Stress, not enough sleep, overwork; surely that accounted for the things she'd seen, the weird visions. Her mind didn't feel close to any breaking point at all, right now. She felt basically sound, even potentially happy.

Today she'd rest and follow her whims, she decided. No work, and no drawing unless she wanted to. She'd get lunch somewhere, then see where the afternoon took her—the park, the beach, the bookstores, wherever. She wouldn't think about Beej, or Denis, or dead guys, or anything. No vultures, no voices from Neptune's Kingdom, nothing bad. Just peace. Maybe she'd hook up with Lindsay or Jonathan at some point. Marzi whistled, and tapped her fingers against her bag in time, feeling the smooth contours of the gun beneath her touch.

She ambled toward the Saturn Café, the all-night vegetarian diner with the tattoo-themed décor, walls boldly painted with skulls, mermaids, dice, hearts, and devils. The place was barely inhabited at this hour, only a few of the booths along the curving walls occupied. Jonathan sat at one of the tables, a cup of coffee and a mostly demolished plate of huevos rancheros pushed off to the side. He was reading something intently—poring over it, actually. "Jonathan," she said.

He looked up, for a moment seeming not even to see her,

an oddly wonderful faraway look in his eyes. Then he focused, smiled, and said, "Hey, you. Have a seat."

She slid into the booth. The tables in Saturn were all uniquely decorated, and this one had old pulp paperback covers underneath a glass top: women in red dresses, menaced by shadows; men in spacesuits; elaborate UFOs; even a few gunfighters. Then she saw what Jonathan was reading, the pages before him, the stack beside him on his seat: what looked to be the entire run of *The Strange Adventures of Rangergirl*. "Aw, crap. You don't want to read those things, they'll rot your brain."

Jonathan closed the cover on the issue he was reading—number eight, the cover depicting a group of dusty townspeople running a monstrously muscled creature out of town on a rail. "Is that what they're doing to my brain? It felt nicer than that. Lindsay loaned me the whole run. They're wonderful."

Marzi ducked her head and looked around for a waitress. "Yeah, well. It's what I do. I'm just lucky they get published. Tropism Comics doesn't pay much, and the distribution could be better, but I've got creative control."

A waitress came over—she had a tattoo of a bass clef on her left cheek, and her hair was shockingly pink—and took Marzi's order, cheese fries and a cup of French onion soup, and coffee, of course. "Help yourself to the fries," she said, "they always give me a thousand more than I can eat."

"Thanks." They both reached for the fries, their hands brushing, and Marzi felt that half-strange, half-familiar tingle that comes from touching someone you might perhaps be attracted to for the first time. When she glanced up at him he was glancing at her, too. They looked away, each taking a cheese-dripping fry, neither one saying anything. Such a little romantic-comedy sort of moment, but there it was, and Marzi had to admit that the reason it worked in the movies was because you felt it in life sometimes too, though the consequences never worked out as neatly as they did on screen.

Jonathan picked up the stack of comics and put them on the table, thumbing through the issues. Once the waitress was gone he said, "I think my favorite is the first one. Not that the other issues aren't good—they are—but you do such a great job introducing Rangergirl, showing her punk sensibility, and her reaction to finding the door in the wall of her apartment. . . . It's all in the art, in the linework and the shading. It's remarkable. You do all this yourself?"

Marzi shrugged. "Lindsay usually helps with the lettering. She's got a steady hand. She won't let me credit her, though. Says it's my party, and she doesn't want people to think she deserves credit for anything, not even for putting the words in people's balloons. It was her idea to put those vicious little serifs on all the words the Outlaw speaks, that jagged sort of lightning-bolt quality."

"It's a nice touch," Jonathan said. "But what I love most is the cover for issue number one." He picked through the stack of comics until he found the first one, placing it in the middle of the table, as if to admire it better.

That cover was the image that *started* the comic, for Marzi, that made a bunch of free-floating ideas solidify into something tangible, something she could imagine transferring from her mind to paper. The cover depicted Rangergirl, short-haired, wearing a skirt, standing in her apartment, in front of an open door. On the left of the door stood a table, with a vase and a very Georgia O'Keeffe flower set upon it. Rangergirl stood facing the door, a little off to one side, and through the door a line of storefronts stretched, with hitching posts in front—a scene familiar to anyone who'd ever seen a Western, a look down the length of Main Street. Down at the far end of the street, the Outlaw stood, a black figure, really just a silhouette of a hat, a long duster, and boots. The classic position for a showdown, hero and villain facing off on a dusty street. Marzi had done her best to infuse the Outlaw with menace, to make him a blot that sucked up light. Some days, she thought she'd succeeded. Other days, she thought he was just a blot.

"I like the issues where Rangergirl goes back and forth from one world to the next," Jonathan said. "Where we see her trying to hold down her job on one page, and on the next page she's rescuing a wagon train from a spine-cat. The juxtaposition works well, and the strain on her is so clear. You can tell sometimes she'd ditch it all if she could, just have a normal life, but she can't—because she opened the door."

"It's her responsibility," Marzi said, and the words felt strange in her mouth, both true and unwelcome. "She can't stop. There's too much depending on her."

"Yes. And you're so good at piling on the details," Jonathan said. His voice had the same liveliness she'd noticed when he talked about Garamond Ray's work. "Like the town where the people have the heads of dogs, and then you work in all that stuff about Egyptian mythology, with the jackal-headed god of the underworld. I love your notion that all deserts are one desert, that Rangergirl might just as easily encounter Bedouins as Navajo Indians, that she could find a ghost town or a dead pharaoh's counting house beyond the

next gully or dune. And the rattlesnake sphinx is remarkable.
I can't wait to see how that turns out."

She frowned. "The rattlesnake sphinx is in the last issue,"
she said. "I thought you were only on number eight?"

"I'm on number eight the second time through. I read
them all once for the story, and the art. I'm reading it again to
see what I missed." Jonathan tapped the page in front of him.
"Like this, when the sea monster's fin surfaces from the rain
barrel, I missed that the first time, so it was a surprise when
the townspeople found out that was what had been killing all
the cattle."

"There was an actual sea monster," Marzi said. "It didn't
live in a rain barrel, and it didn't eat anyone, but a sea serpent
was caught, at Newport Beach. It was over thirty feet long.
They say another one, ten times as long, got away. There's a
photograph of the dead serpent, with people lined up along
its length to provide scale. It looks like a giant eel. The body
disappeared, though. A lot of the stuff in the comic is based
on history, actually. I twist it out of true, but the seed is often
historical. Charles Hatfield was a real rainmaker, and that
stuff about Pancho Villa's head is all true, and—"

"And Aaron Burr," Jonathan said. "I don't know much
about him, except that he shot Alexander Hamilton in a
duel."

"Burr was nearly convicted of treason. There's evidence
that he planned to found his own empire in the West, using a
cache of stolen gold to finance the economy. That didn't
work out for him, in the real world. But in my story, Burr
succeeded in founding that empire, and he rules the land be
yond the Western Door."

"But the Outlaw is really the one in charge."

"No," Marzi said. "Burr is a bad guy, but he's a builder. He builds towns, empires, alliances; all for his own gain, never for a good reason, but still. The Outlaw doesn't build. He tears things down. He's an earthquake wearing boots."

Jonathan nodded. "I get it." He closed the comic. "Anyway. I didn't mean to go on and on."

"Yes, please, by all means, stop praising me." The waitress came back with the rest of her food, and Marzi leaned in to smell the soup, closing her eyes as she inhaled. She was hungrier than she'd realized.

Jonathan looked as if he were about to say something, but then he just half-smiled and looked down at his coffee cup.

"What?" Marzi said.

"Nothing," Jonathan said. "Just . . . I just wanted to say thanks. You and Lindsay have made me feel really welcome here."

"Please. It's been all spilled beer, crazy people, and—well. Other things." She didn't want to mention Daniel, or even think about him, dead in the Red Room, victim of bad brains or something stranger. She pushed her plate over a little, to cover a Western book cover that depicted a masked man aiming his guns at a stagecoach.

"It's been an eventful couple of days, sure," Jonathan said. "But it hasn't been all bad."

"No. I guess not."

"I was wondering . . ."

"Yeah?" She dipped a cheese-covered french fry into a puddle of ketchup and popped it in her mouth.

"Ah. Is Marzipan really your name?"

Marzi rolled her eyes, chewed, swallowed. "Yeah. It's the curse of having unrepentant hippies for parents. It could've been worse. One of our neighbors had a little boy named Sunbeam. If I ever have a daughter, I'm going to name her Jennifer or Sue or something." She cocked her head. "Is that really what you wanted to ask me?"

"Well, no. I was going to ask if you had any plans today, but then I decided maybe you wouldn't want to spend time with me, since it hasn't turned out well the last couple of times."

"Maybe we should go someplace where we're unlikely to be assaulted, then," she said.

He spread his hands. "It's your town."

"I can think of a place, but it requires driving."

"I've got gas money if you've got wheels," Jonathan said. "Or do you lead a carless, monastic life?"

Marzi seesawed her hand. "I've got a beat-up little Honda that used to belong to my dad, but it mostly just sits in my parking space at home. I wouldn't trust it on a road trip, but it'll do for a few miles. Just let me finish eating."

"You SURE THIS IS the right place?" Jonathan asked, as Marzi eased her car over one of the calamitously deep potholes on the side of the road.

"Yep. Been here a million times." They'd driven down Highway 1, the scenic coast road, past fields and ocean views. A few miles outside of town, she'd pulled off onto a wide patch of scraped dirt on the shoulder that served as an ad-hoc parking lot. "Just be glad it's not the rainy season. Some of these potholes turn into little ponds. Lindsay got stuck up to her fenders once going through one." She stopped the car and pulled up the parking brake. "See the trail?"

Jonathan nodded, and they got out. Jonathan looked west, toward the sea, and whistled. "That's beautiful. I've never been to a beach where cliffs went right up to the water like this."

"Ha," Marzi said, walking around him. "You haven't seen anything yet." She led him over the railroad tracks, to the edge of the cliff, then toward a steep incline where the barest suggestion of a path switchbacked down to a cove below. "Be careful, some of the rocks are loose."

"Is this where you dump the bodies?"

"Ha. You try getting down there with a victim wrapped in burlap thrown over your shoulder." She led the way, picking her steps but moving quickly, with a smoothness born of familiarity. Jonathan came after, more tentative. Marzi waited for him at the bottom. He jumped the last few feet, landing on the sand in a squat, then stood up and looked around. "This is lovely," he said. The beach was a sandy semicircle, scattered with a few boulders, bordered by cliffs behind them and on both sides, with the gently rolling blue-gray Pacific beyond.

"We call it the hole in the wall," Marzi said.

Jonathan nodded, still looking around, then frowned. "Why?"

"You'll see." She took his hand and led him toward one of the largest rocks, then around it, revealing an arch in the cliff wall, nestled in the shadows and blocked from casual view by the rock. Like a doorway to Wonderland, a mouse-hole-in-the-baseboard-shaped hole in a rock wall, just big enough for two people to pass through, walking side by side. They walked through, to the long expanse of beach beyond the arch, that stretch of sand that was always a surprise and a revelation, inevitably bigger than Marzi remembered, with water on one side and nearly vertical cliffs on the other. It stretched on for hundreds of yards, a narrow band of clean sand that ended in a tumbling wall of rocks, the collapsed remains of a natural bridge stretching out into the sea.

"Oh, that's like magic," Jonathan said, and Marzi could only agree. She realized she was still holding his hand, and though he hadn't complained, she let go.

Marzi walked about halfway down the beach and then sat down, facing the water. The sky beyond was cloudless blue and infinite, the blurry horizon revealing the curvature of the earth.

"I've never seen the Pacific before," Jonathan said, sitting with her. "I've been to the Atlantic Ocean lots of times, but this is the first time I've looked at the Pacific. It's . . . different, somehow. Hard to say why. Maybe just the rocks, the sky, the cliffs . . . I don't know. There's some qualitative difference here. It looks more peaceful, deeper, somehow, than the Atlantic. Not as gray."

"Really? I've never been to the beach on the East Coast, really, just visited Washington, D.C., and New York a couple of times. You're from North Carolina, right?"

"Born and raised."

"You don't have much of a Southern accent."

"Yeah, well. I worked hard to avoid one." He picked up a handful of sand and let it sift through his fingers. "My mom's from the Midwest, and she taught me to talk, so I'm fortunate enough to have a bland accent."

"I don't know. Accents can be sexy." Marzi wondered at herself. She was flirting, wasn't she? Well. Why not? Hadn't she closed herself off long enough?

"The *Gone with the Wind* kind of Southern accent, maybe, but that's not the way they talk in eastern North Carolina, the land of pickup trucks and tobacco fields and turkey houses and swamps. Doesn't matter how smart the person talking is—to anyone from outside the area, hearing that accent, they think 'hick.' It's too bad. We've got the best barbecue in the world down there."

"So you like it there?" She settled back on her elbows in the warm sand.

"Never really lived anywhere else. I've visited a few places, New York and Boston and such, but never lived in them for any amount of time. Grew up in the country, then moved to Raleigh when my mom got a better job. The move . . . was pretty hard on me. I left all my friends behind, went to a new high school, and fell in with a different sort of crowd."

"Oh, yeah?" Marzi remembered Lindsay's talk of Jonathan's desperado vibe, which she'd never particularly noticed. "You've got a dark past?"

"Well, you know. Raleigh's not a big city by some standards, but it was the most urban place I'd ever been. I rode my skateboard, smoked weed, stuff like that. But one of my buddies was a drug dealer, and there were a few times when things got . . . unpleasantly heavy. Pissed-off customers once, and once another dealer. My mom talked about throwing me out of the house for a while, told me I was following in my father's footsteps, which was funny, since I'd never met the guy."

"Wow," Marzi said. "That's rough. How'd you go from juvenile delinquent to art student?"

He shrugged. "I realized I was being stupid, and decided to stop."

"That simple, huh? Just woke up one morning and decided to change your life?"

He sighed. "Not exactly." He lifted his T-shirt. "See that?" She did, right away: a white line of scar tissue, three or four inches long, running diagonally just to the left of his right nipple, standing out against his skin. She reached out, unthinking, and touched the leading edge of the scar, then drew her hand back. "It's okay," he said, and she pressed her fingertip there again for a moment, feeling the raised texture.

"What happened?"

He let his shirt drop. "My buddy Rob was making a drug deal in a park, and I was hanging out with him, when the customer pulled a knife and demanded Rob's whole stash. Rob, who was never the brightest bulb in the box, tried to knock the guy's knife away, and he *stabbed* Rob, right in the stomach. I'd never seen anything like it." Jonathan was staring out at the ocean, but his eyes were focused beyond the horizon. "All the color ran out of Rob's face, he went pale as milk, and without even thinking I rushed the guy, because he'd just stabbed my friend. But I was stoned, so I couldn't exactly bring overwhelming force or good reflexes to bear. The guy came at me with the knife, and I went down with this horrible pain in my chest."

"Did . . . did your friend die?" Marzi reached out and took his hand again.

"No. He was in the hospital for a while, but he lived. I got by with some stitches. The doctor told me how lucky I'd been. If the knife had come at a different angle, the blade might have punctured my heart, or a lung. As it was, it just hit my ribs and slid down, and left me this."

Marzi squeezed his hand, and he shook his head, losing the thousand-yard stare, and squeezed back. "So after *that* I made some changes in my life. My mom was married to this real asshole by then, and home was not a fun place to be, so I spent any time I wasn't in school at the library, and then in the art galleries and museums as I got more interested in art. Mom assumed I was still raising hell at all hours, but my grades were suddenly good, so she left me alone."

"Looks like you turned out pretty good, coming from a background like that."

He shook his head. "Sorry, I'm not trying to throw a pity party. Lots of people have it harder than me. I got a scholarship, got to go to college, got into a decent grad school, and now I'm out here, following my dreams—or at least, studying Garamond Ray's dreams, which is just as good for the moment. All that other stuff's just the past."

"I don't know. It's hard to outlive your own history." She considered telling him about her door-opening phobia, her stint in a mental hospital—wasn't it fair to swap a confession for a confession? But she hesitated, unwilling to open those doors, and the moment passed.

"Tell me about this place," he said. "How'd you find it?"

"Lindsay did, actually. She grew up in Santa Cruz, and she's been coming here since she was a teenager."

"Ah, Lindsay. She's something else."

Marzi laughed. "Yeah. We wound up as roommates when we were freshmen. I thought she was flaky and insincere—turns out I was right about the first one, but dead wrong on the second—and she thought I was a granola-eating self-righteous hippie because I spent a few years on a commune with my parents. Once I realized she really *was* interested in people, and not just faking it, and once she realized I wasn't a proselytizing vegetarian and that I owned a good stereo, we bonded. She brought me out here one afternoon, and we spent all day throwing a Frisbee." They'd done more than that, actually—they'd brought down a jug of vodka and orange juice, and gotten drunk, and Lindsay had kissed her. Marzi had gone along with the kiss—what else was college for, if not such experiments?—but hadn't felt any particular thrill or sparkle, and had gently discouraged Lindsay's other efforts to get intimate. Always one to pick up on hints, Lindsay had stopped, and their relationship hadn't noticeably changed after that. For Lindsay, it was just something to try, and Marzi saying no hadn't particularly bothered her. After a few weeks of feeling odd, Marzi got over it, and they'd been best friends ever since. At least, until Marzi dropped out of college. These days, it seemed they were best friends more in name than in fact. "That first time, Lindsay took me all the way down there." She pointed to the tumble of rocks at the far end of the beach. "There used to be a natural bridge there, centuries ago, I guess, and it collapsed, so now there's this weird plateau of rock you can climb up on. It's a lot of trouble to get up there, slippery and slick with algae, and she wouldn't tell me why she wanted to go. But once we made it, she took me out a ways, where the remains of the bridge stick out into the ocean pretty far, and she showed me the tide pools. Dozens of them, these tiny self-contained worlds, like miniature universes, you know? Just puddles in the rocks, but full of life. We spent hours there, looking at the sea anemones and starfish. There were fish and crabs, too, which I found so amazing, things that *move*, living in a cleft of rock, a sun-warmed pool, and maybe they had no idea about the whole ocean just beyond them. For all they knew, their tide pool was the whole world. Lindsay and I just stretched out on the rocks and looked into them, watching the fish swim, the crabs scuttle, the plants wave. The water was so clear . . . That was one of the best days of my life."

"It sounds beautiful," Jonathan said.

"We tried to go back a few times, but we could never make it. When the tide's too high, the rocks are totally inaccessible, pounded on by waves, and you can't climb up there. It seems like the tide's always too high, whenever I come here. I can't ever seem to get back to that place anymore." She felt the start of tears, and blinked them back.

"Maybe it's not too high now," Jonathan said. "Why don't we go see?"

Marzi nodded, slowly. "Sure. It's worth a try." She led the way to the end of the beach, and they climbed up the head-high wall of uneven rock, finding foot- and handholds. She pulled herself up over the edge, to the top, and offered her hand to Jonathan to help him up. "This way," she said, and set off over the uneven rock toward the ocean. The waves were breaking hard on the rocks, white foam spraying, but the way was passable. "We probably have an hour or so before the tide's too high," Marzi said, pleasantly surprised. The window of opportunity to pass by was limited here, and she'd never managed to get the timing right since that first night with Lindsay. "We might get splashed, but we can make it."

"I won't melt," Jonathan said. "Let's go."

They went carefully down the rocks, spray flecking them both as the waves broke, and then across a narrow ridge of rock to the largest part of the tumbled natural bridge. This place was tilted, pocked, and ridged, surrounded almost entirely by water, attached to the land only by the thin umbilicus of rock Marzi and Jonathan had crossed over. "I claim this land for us," Marzi said. "Look, there—tide pools." They went down on hands and knees to look into the clear water, at starfish and waving sea plants. They moved on, looking into others, exclaiming over mussels and crabs, and then Marzi saw a familiar pool. "Oh, this is the one," she said. "I remember this." This was the largest tide pool she'd found with Lindsay, a narrow cleft nearly ten feet long, an alleyway teeming with life. Marzi stretched out on her stomach, the better to see in, and Jonathan lay down beside her. They watched tiny silver fish dart through the water, past anemones like strange flowers. "There," she said. "Under that little shelf of rock? I saw a crab." A moment later the crab scuttled out sideways, claws upraised, followed by a pair of smaller crabs.

"Oh, that's awesome," Jonathan said, and Marzi caught something in his voice, some reverent echo of her own thoughts. She looked over at him, at his dark eyes and fair skin, and felt for the first time in ages that she was truly *with* someone, sharing something beyond the civil or superficial.

He turned his head and caught her looking at him, but she didn't turn away. He leaned his head toward her, a little, and she moved her head toward him in return, and in a moment they were kissing, and unlike the *last* time Marzi had kissed someone here, there was a thrill and sparkle now, and she thought she could go on kissing him for some time. He must have thought the same, because they did keep kissing, until their position on the rocks became too uncomfortable for Marzi, and she broke contact to sit up.

"That was nice," Jonathan said, still stretched out, looking up at her with his eyes half closed against the sun. "I'm glad we ran into each other this morning."

"Me, too." She'd let herself open up to someone, a little, and the sky hadn't fallen. She didn't feel endangered or scared. Trouble was easier to bear when there was a little joy in the midst of it. "We should get back, before the tide comes in."

"Right. I need to get some work done this afternoon, but maybe, if you're not busy, if you wanted to do something later . . . I told you about my sordid past, but I want to hear about yours. This commune stuff intrigues me."

"I'd like that. But the commune stuff, really—not as interesting as it sounds, unless the theory and practice of milking goats excites you. I'll drop you off by the café. I've got some errands to run downtown. Meet you at Genius Loci around six, we can get some dinner?"

"Consider it a date."

Three-up Outfit

Marzi came up the steps to Genius Loci late in the day, after an afternoon spent reading Terri Windling's *The Wood Wife*, sitting in a park, watching ducks in a pond, and thinking about Jonathan. She'd put caps in her toy pistol, too, and fired it a couple of times—it was satisfyingly loud, with none of the kick of a real gun.

The lamps outside the café were already on, though dark was another hour away, and moths were clustered hungrily around the pale white globes, seeking some ethereal nourishment. Jonathan sat at the table just outside the double doors, at the top of the steps, the neon "Genius Loci" sign bathing him in red light. "Jonathan," she said, and he looked up from the oversized art book he was leafing through.

"Hey, Marzi. Lindsay was here earlier, looking for you."

"Everything okay with her?"

"Yeah, she just wanted to see how you were doing after everything last night. We hung out for a little while here. She, ah, asked me about the afternoon, and I told her how it ended. I hope that's okay."

Marzi laughed. "Lindsay's like the Spanish Inquisition with glittery nail polish. What'd she say?"

"Just that if I broke your heart, she'd break my fingers."

"Only your fingers? She's going soft. Is she going to be around later?"

"She said she was going out."

"Hot date?" Marzi asked.

"So I assume. She's meeting Alice—" He frowned. "Well, she *said* she was meeting Alice, but there she is now."

Marzi turned around in her chair to look. Lindsay came bouncing up the steps, smacking gum in her mouth. "Damn, girl," Marzi said. "You're looking good."

Lindsay flounced the skirt of her sundress and batted her lashes. "I know. I'm hot as hell tonight." She dragged a chair across the deck with an awful scraping sound and flopped into it, then crossed one sandaled foot over the other. "But, alas, Alice stood me up."

"She wouldn't have done that if she'd gotten a look at you," Marzi said.

"I daresay," Lindsay agreed. "She left a message on my answering machine, said something came up, she was really sorry, yadda yadda. All very vague." Lindsay put her elbows on the table, crowding an empty glass out of the way, and put her chin in her hands. She exhaled huffily, dramatically, but with an undercurrent of genuine sadness, Marzi thought; Lindsay was always one to cover actual distress with melodramatic lamentations. "Methinks she's had her fill of me. That, or she doesn't like the idea of being seen out on the town with me. She hangs out with a pretty hard-core crowd—those women don't believe in bisexuals, and they sneer at anything in a skirt, though they'd also like to get up *under* those skirts, as often as not."

Marzi thought of her conversation with Alice. "I don't think that's it, Linds. I ran into Alice last night when I was out walking, and she seemed very much into you. She *did* seem like she had something on her mind, though, so maybe something really did come up."

"You're too trusting," Lindsay said, poking Marzi in the arm. "You've got to learn to expect the worst. That way, you can only be pleasantly surprised." Lindsay took Marzi's hand, then Jonathan's. "Speaking of pleasant surprises . . . "

"Are we having a séance, Lindsay?" Marzi asked.

"Yes. We're going to call up the spirit of my dearly departed fun night out. Do *you* know what I think we should do, Marzipan?"

"I shudder to think."

"Young Jonathan has never been to the boardwalk. Young Jonathan has never eaten a deep-fried Twinkie a mere hundred yards from the ocean. Young Jonathan has never ridden the oldest wooden roller coaster in the tricounty area. Do you see where I'm going with this?"

"I think so, yes." She glanced at Jonathan.

He shrugged. "I'm up for a night on the town."

"I bet you're up for all sorts of things," Lindsay said, "but we'll have to settle for the boardwalk, for now. We'll eat hot dogs and ice cream for dinner. When I was a kid, I thought I'd eat meals like that every night when I grew up. Let's be true to our younger selves!"

"My parents would be proud," Jonathan said. "Is it far?"

"No, it's just down by the wharf," Marzi said. "We can walk there in fifteen minutes or so."

After a brief detour for Jonathan to put his book away in the Pigeonhole, they set off toward the setting sun, passing neatly painted little houses on Washington Street. They chatted amiably for a while about inconsequential things, then Marzi said, "Oh, guys, you won't believe this. When I got up today, there was a message on my answering machine from *Beej*, asking if I'd come bail him out of jail."

"Jeez," Lindsay said, shaking her head. "I hope he gets some help. He's always been weird, but I think he went over the rainbow recently."

"It's strange," Marzi said. "Beej talked about a god, the earthquake god, the other day, and he mentioned something about it at the café, too. And Jane, in between totally *attacking* us, talked about setting her goddess free. Remember, she asked me why I hadn't embraced the goddess yesterday, when she jumped me on the deck?"

"I can't say I was paying that much attention to what she said," Lindsay said. "I was shocked, mostly."

"I remember," Jonathan said, looking off at the horizon, a worry line marking his forehead. "That *is* odd, that they'd both be talking about some god—"

"And both assaulting the coffee shop," Lindsay interjected.

"Yeah. Converging delusions," Marzi said, but not with any great conviction. There had been so *many* odd things in the past two days. The vision of death-from-a-Western in the Red Room, the recurrence of her problem with doors, that dream of Santa Cruz destroyed—all of it was taking a toll on her. There was something else, too, something she could *almost* remember, and for a moment she had a brief vision of a door opening in a yellow wall, and sunlight pouring in from the space beyond, light as harsh as ground glass, and then a man, or something at least mostly man-*shaped,* rising up before her—

"This is bumming me out," Lindsay said, and that broke Marzi's connection to whatever she was remembering—for that, Marzi was simultaneously annoyed and grateful. She'd had a good day, and possibly a good night ahead, and she didn't want to spoil it with shit like this. But on the other hand, Jane, at least, was still out there, perhaps still mud-spattered, probably still crazed. "You guys are supposed to be soothing my injured ego since I got stood up," Lindsay said. "So let's refrain from dwelling on the habits of your garden-variety crazy guy."

"Agreed," Jonathan said. "Is that the roller coaster?" He pointed to an arch of red-and-white showing just above the trees.

"That's the Big Dipper," Lindsay said. "It was built in nineteen-early-something. It's made of wood, and when you ride on it, it sounds like it's going to fall into the ocean any minute. This whole boardwalk is famous, actually. It was in *Lost Boys,* you know."

"That vampire movie with Pee-wee Herman?" Jonathan said.

"No, no, that was the original crappy version of *Buffy the Vampire Slayer. Lost Boys* is the one with Kiefer Sutherland, playing his career-defining role as a wicked vampire lieutenant," Lindsay said.

"I'd forgotten that," Marzi said, distracted. Thinking about vampires and the boardwalk made her think of *other* monstrous things, like the rustling creature in her vision, the one denned inside Neptune's Kingdom.

"Ah, and here's the skate park," Lindsay said, nodding toward the fence-enclosed patch of asphalt, with ramp and rails chained down inside, and a few teenagers standing around holding their skateboards and smoking. A ten-year-old wearing a helmet and knee pads rolled slowly back and forth on his Rollerblades in the half-pipe. "Skater boys always did it for me when I was just a wee teenybopper," Lindsay went on. "Something about the way they slouched."

"I used to skate," Jonathan said. "I haven't done it in years, though. Guess I'm getting old."

"You're still a champion sloucher, though," Marzi said.

"Good posture is crucial," Jonathan said.

Pedestrian traffic thickened as they approached the wharf. They passed thin teenage girls with their sweaters tied around their waists, an Asian boy in a long black trench coat trying to look remote and cool, a few surfers, dripping wet and walking intently away from the sea, all walking across the street, ignoring the traffic lights with the blithe assurance that such a critical mass of jaywalkers was a match for any car. Marzi, Lindsay, and Jonathan jostled together, clustering up close out of necessity. "Are these all tourists?" Jonathan asked.

"Mostly," Lindsay said. "They start to come as soon as it stops raining every year, pretty much. More on the weekends, of course. Everybody streams in from over the hill in Silicon Valley for fun and sun and so on." Lindsay put her arm around Jonathan's waist. "But you're no tourist! You're a Santa Cruz native by association."

"Lindsay bestowed the same honor on me years ago," Marzi said.

"Oh, you're from Humboldt County," Lindsay said. "Your people are my people. Come. The boardwalk beckons."

They passed the arcade, Neptune's Kingdom, and Marzi couldn't resist glancing inside as they passed. The decorating motif was faux-nautical, with life preservers and fishing nets hanging on the walls—like a bad seafood restaurant, only without the grease stains. Just inside the door a fake bathysphere with pincer arms moved slowly up and down on wires, claws opening and closing, and a surprisingly lifelike animatronic pirate climbed a long rope to a crow's nest suspended from the ceiling. Steps led up to the second floor, where you could buy overpriced food with kitschy names like Barnacle Burgers and Foot-Long Sea Dogs. The rattle of pinball machines and the hum of arcade games drifted out. No rustling, no monsters, no oracles, nothing unusual at all— Neptune's Kingdom was as prosaic as ever. That should have reassured Marzi, but it didn't. Instead she felt the resurgence of her old feeling that there was a world just beyond the visible, that behind any door she might find monstrous wonders and wondrous monsters. Lindsay and Jonathan didn't slow down as they passed the arcade, Lindsay chattering away and Jonathan nodding, so Marzi didn't break stride, either, but the hairs on the back of her neck rose as she passed the building. Having Neptune's Kingdom at her back gave her the distinct, ridiculous feeling that she was being watched.

Lindsay led the way, turning right to cut between two bright yellow buildings, onto the boardwalk proper. "And here we are. The world-famous beach boardwalk."

Jonathan scuffed his boot heel against the concrete. "If it's a boardwalk, shouldn't there be actual boards?"

"I thought you were an artist," Lindsay said. "It's an impressionistic boardwalk!"

"Yeah," Marzi said. "Why be so literal? It's a boardwalk in *spirit*."

"There's even Skee-Ball!" Lindsay said. She arched an eyebrow. "You don't look impressed, Jon-jon."

"I'm reserving judgment," he said.

"Perhaps a deep-fried Twinkie will do the trick," Marzi said, pointing toward the Extreme Fried Foods! booth.

"Those were invented in the South," Jonathan said. "We've had them at state fairs for years."

Lindsay poked him in the shoulder. "Fine, be unimpressed. Go get us some tickets. Lots. I like to ride the rides and play the games." She pointed toward the ticket booth, and Jonathan walked amiably in that direction.

Marzi leaned toward Lindsay. "He's a hard sell," she said. "He thinks our boardwalk is lame."

"Oh, we'll get him," Lindsay said. "You'll note I'm wearing a white top, and no bra, and I have every intention of going on the log flume ride, which, as you know, has copious splishy-splash tendencies. We'll see if me all dripping wet and clingy cheers him up."

Marzi knew Lindsay's lasciviousness was as natural for her as breathing, and quietly quashed the little upsurge of jealousy she felt.

"Maybe you should save something for the second date," Marzi said dryly.

"Speaking of which, I hear this is *your* second date with

him, Marzipan," Lindsay said. "Something about true romance amid the tide pools?"

"We had a moment, but who knows what'll happen? He's
only here for the summer anyway." She was reluctant to express hope for something deeper, to even *allow* herself such
hope.

"A summer can be like a *lifetime,* if you do it right,"
Lindsay said. "I'm glad you're giving him a chance."

Jonathan returned, holding a roll of blue tickets and looking amused. "Bumper cars," Lindsay said, and grabbed their
hands.

As Lindsay demanded, they rode the rides and played the
games. Jonathan admitted to being impressed by the unusual
amount of maneuverability on the Space Race bumper cars,
but was less than wowed by the house of horrors. As they
creaked slowly along the tracks beneath red lights and artificial cobwebs, Marzi found herself wishing that her fears were
as simple as this—big spiders, mummies, screams in the dark.
Her fears were entirely too baroque. Lindsay was squished in
close next to her, with Jonathan sitting in the seat behind
them, distinctly not screaming in fear at every new scare.
Lindsay whispered, "I want. To suck. Your—"

"Blood," Marzi said firmly.

"Well, if you insist on being so *traditional* about it," she
said.

Jonathan leaned forward, resting his head between theirs.
"Can we do something that goes fast next?"

So they went to the Big Dipper, the centerpiece of the
boardwalk, and ratcheted up the track, zoomed down the
incline, and whipped through the curves. There were no

loop-the-loops or spirals, not on a roller coaster that old, but the structure rattled and shuddered and seemed to tremble as they rode, which was terrifying enough. As they got off, Jonathan said, "That was sort of the Model-T Ford of roller coasters, but it was fun."

"Time to get wet," Lindsay said, and they got in line for the log flume waterslide. It was a short line. The night was turning cool, and most people weren't eager to get wet, but Lindsay, of course, could not be discouraged. "If we get cold, we'll just huddle up," she said. "This is my date, so no arguments!"

The log-shaped boat was divided into two compartments, with each big enough to fit two people sitting single file, straddling the long, narrow central seat, so that the one in front was necessarily tucked up against the one in back. Lindsay climbed into the front, and when Marzi tried to get in behind her, Lindsay slid back and said, "Nope. I need the space." She grinned, and Marzi scowled, but she climbed into the back, where Jonathan had already situated himself. There was no choice but to slide back snugly between his open thighs, and he had nowhere to put his hands but the sides of the boat or around her waist. He held on to the edges of the boat.

"I didn't expect us to get so cozy tonight," Marzi said. The closeness was oddly more uncomfortable since they'd kissed earlier in the day. Being snugged up between his thighs seemed like too much too fast.

"I can wait for the next log, if you want to ride alone," he said, and just the fact that he'd offered made her more comfortable riding with him.

"I'll be okay," Marzi said. "At least with two of us back here, we're less likely to fall out and die." And it did feel good, leaning back against him, feeling his warmth.

"And all this weight in the back will lift the nose of the log, so Lindsay will get splashed all to hell and back," he said.

"I'm counting on it!" Lindsay said, and the log started forward with a jerk, sliding out along the flimsy-looking chute, which wound its way sedately through riverlike S curves, sloshing gently. Jonathan kept his hands on the side of the boat, and Marzi held on to the divider between her compartment and Lindsay's. She looked out at the ocean, the sailboats bobbing, the moonlight on the water, and for a moment it struck her as terribly romantic, being nestled up against a cute boy on a spring night.

The log approached the final, precipitous slope, the nose edging out briefly into empty air until the weight made it topple forward into the near-ninety-degree drop. Lindsay gleefully chanted, "Oh shit oh shit oh shit," Marzi felt her stomach lurch and have its own out-of-body experience, and Jonathan wrapped his hands around her waist in what could only be pure terror. Having his arms around her made Marzi feel both safer and more stomach-tinglingly nervous as they hurtled down. When they hit the straightaway, a great gout of water leapt up and soaked Lindsay, but only splashed Marzi and Jonathan.

The log coasted to a halt, and they climbed out, Lindsay happily dripping. Her top was not particularly transparent, though it did cling. Marzi wiped water out of her eyes, but Jonathan was mostly dry. "I didn't get wet at all, sitting behind Marzi," he commented.

"Mmm," Lindsay said. "I wonder if Marzi can say the same thing about sitting in front of you?"

Marzi smacked her on the arm. "We don't all get damp as easily as you do, Linds."

"I'm glad I'm too young and innocent to know what you're talking about," Jonathan said. "And on an unrelated note, we're almost out of tickets. One more ride?"

"Something that doesn't leave my stomach a hundred feet up in the air would be appreciated," Marzi said.

"I suppose we should ride the sky glider," Lindsay said, looking up. "Your stomach will still be way up in the air, but so will the rest of you." Jonathan and Marzi tilted their heads back, too, and looked at the slowly moving basket-shaped seats that hung suspended from a continually spooling loop of cable above them, like a chair lift at a ski slope. The sky gliders ran the length of the boardwalk, affording good views of the town and the ocean. Most of the seats were empty—it was hardly a thrill ride—but it looked like a pleasant end to their boardwalk experience. They went up the concrete steps and waited their turn, and when an empty car arrived, Lindsay told the attendant, "I'm riding by myself," leaving Marzi and Jonathan behind before they could protest. The attendant showed Lindsay where to stand, and when the seat slid up behind her, Lindsay did a little hop and sat down. The attendant put the bar down across her lap, and Lindsay was off, looking back at them, grinning.

Marzi and Jonathan got into the next car—they were built for two—and sat, their knees touching, Marzi holding her bag in her lap. It was noticeably cooler up here, above the board-walk, and as they rose higher, above the roof of the haunted house, nearly on level with the highest peak of the Big

Dipper, a breeze began to blow, and the basket swayed. "Are we being matchmade?" Jonathan said. "Lindsay seems to be going out of her way to put us together."

"As far as she's concerned, the match is already made, and it's all her doing anyway."

"I'm sure she just wants you to be happy," Jonathan said. He hesitated. "She told me so. She worries about you being lonely, I think."

Marzi started to say "I am happy," but that wasn't really true, and the air up here was so cool and clear, she couldn't bear lying. "I'm not unhappy," she said, which was perhaps a bit of misdirection, but at least not a lie. Her life, at best, was a sort of pleasant neutrality, characterized more by a lack of fear than by joy. A day without an anxiety attack—lately, a day without a *hallucination*—was a successful day. And she did have her comic. That filled a lot of the dark corners of her life with light. "Things aren't so bad."

"A ringing endorsement." They rode for a while in silence, swaying, and Marzi looked out at the lights of Santa Cruz in the distance, then looked the other way, over the dark beach and the ocean. Tiny lights, right up against the void. It was enough to make a person get all symbolic and metaphorical. She waited for the vision to shimmer and decay, for rotting vultures to come flying in over the ocean and perch on the big seahorse sculptures that topped the arcade, for sand to cover the lights. But nothing changed. No vision this time, at least. The world was whole and safe for another moment.

"You're a good artist," Jonathan said, and such a sentiment was so far from Marzi's thoughts that for a moment she didn't even understand what he was saying, any more than if he'd cried out in the voice of a gull. When sense caught up with sound, she blushed and shook her head, a motion of modesty so instantaneous as to be almost reflexive.

Jonathan went on. "I mean it. Your comics are very good. I have a lot of respect for people who can do what you do, turn their thoughts into pictures. A lot of respect, and maybe even more jealousy."

"You want to be an artist?"

"Oh, I can draw. I've got a steady hand, a decent eye. But whatever it is that drives you, that makes you stay up late working, whatever lights you up inside and guides your hand . . . I don't have that. I wish I did. I wish I could get that passionate about anything."

"Don't confuse drawing and religion," Marzi said. "It's not so much a sacred fire as it is a lot of sweat and effort. Ten percent inspiration and ninety percent perspiration, remember."

"I know," he said. "It's become unfashionable to say that artists are touched by the gods. But that ten percent inspiration is pretty crucial. Anyway, I've come to terms with my limitations. I'm an appreciator, more than a creator. What I'm trying to say is—I don't really know you, or Lindsay, beyond the fact that you're both nice, and brave, and funny. But I've read your comic, and I've listened to you talk, and, all matchmaking aside, I want to get to know you better."

"I'm not going anywhere," Marzi said lightly, but the breeze that made the basket sway seemed to blow through her whole body, now, as if her nerves were exposed to the air. "And I don't think you're without passion. You got pretty excited about Garamond Ray."

Another ghost of a smile. "I get passionate about passion in others."

"No wonder you like Lindsay so much."

He laughed. "She's fun, yeah. But I was talking about you."

Unsettled, Marzi looked out toward the lights of Santa Cruz. The aerial view reminded her uncomfortably of her vision of the city destroyed. Santa Cruz was thriving now, though, a town bisected by a slow river, a town of hills and redwood cathedrals, of duck-filled ponds and long, graceful footbridges, of fanciful outdoor sculpture and houses full of sleepless, brilliant graduate students. Maybe a town haunted by something monstrous. Or maybe just a town inhabited by one Fine Art school dropout comic-book artist who was going rapidly insane. Though that hypothesis didn't explain Beej's behavior, or Jane's.

The car approached the platform at the far end of the boardwalk. Lindsay's arrived first, and she hopped off and waited for them on the stairs. Jonathan and Marzi arrived, and followed suit, and they all went down the stairs together. "Well?" Lindsay said. "Did you get even *better* acquainted?"

"You're not even a little bit subtle, are you?" Marzi said.

Lindsay shrugged. "What can I say? Even in the depths of my horrible solitude, I want to make other people happy. Come. Now we walk on the beach." She set off, and they followed.

"I used to go running on this stretch of beach," Marzi said, walking close to Jonathan, heading toward the place where the San Lorenzo River touched the bay, next to a crumbling sea cliff. "I'd come out here early and run from the rocks at the far end, past the pier, all the way to the river, and back again, two or three times. It was a good workout, and there was something wonderful about being here just after sunrise, with just a couple of boats on the water, and almost nobody else on the beach."

"Why did you stop?" Jonathan said.

"Oh, this was when I was in college, before I dropped out. Now that I work evening shifts, it's a lot harder to get up at dawn."

"Did you drop out to concentrate on the comic?" Jonathan asked.

Marzi hesitated. Her dropping out—and the real causes behind it, the phobia, the anxiety attacks—wasn't something she felt ready to talk about after all. And, in a way, it *was* tied up with her comic. *Rangergirl* had been born after she left school. "Pretty much," she said, but she could taste the half-truth in her own mouth, and thought she sensed a subtle shift in Jonathan's body language, as if he understood that a wall had just been erected, a door closed between them.

Lindsay came back to them, pointing. "Hey, look at that," she said. "There's someone building a monstrous big sand castle by the river."

Marzi squinted, and now that she was looking for it, she was able to resolve shapes from the shadow of the sea cliff. Someone was piling handfuls of sand onto an already waist-high mound of sand.

"Who builds sand castles in the dark?" Marzi said.

Lindsay shrugged. "Dunno. Let's go take a look. I'm a sucker for sand castles, but the ones I make always look like anthills."

They drew closer to the sand castle, which didn't look like much but a pile of mud at this point; the turrets and gates and moat, Marzi supposed, would come later.

"Hi, there!" Lindsay called. "Wow! You must've been

working on this for a while. It's gonna be a hell of a castle when you're done."

"It's not a castle," the builder said, voice low. Marzi couldn't tell if it was a man or a woman, not from the voice, or from the body, as the builder was mostly hidden behind the mound of sand.

"Oh?" Lindsay said. "What, then? A giant turtle? A whale?"

"It's a practice burial mound," the builder said, and jumped to the top of the hill of sand, which shifted under the weight but didn't collapse. The builder crouched on all fours, moving her head forward to peer at them, dreadlocks swinging.

"You," Jonathan said, disgusted. "You again. Shit."

"Shit and mud and ashes," Jane said agreeably, and leapt, driving herself off the mound of sand, straight at Marzi.

Jonathan shouted wordlessly and shoved Marzi aside, putting himself in Jane's path instead. Marzi fell into the sand, landing hard on her elbows and her ass, wind whuffing out of her, leaving her stunned and still for a moment. Jane slammed into Jonathan, and the two went down in a tangle, Jonathan gasping, Jane laughing, almost a witch's cackle. Lindsay helped Marzi to her feet, and they rushed to where Jane was thrashing Jonathan. She'd somehow half-buried Jonathan, his legs and one arm covered by wet sand, trapping him. Contemptuously, Jane kicked a shower of sand toward Jonathan's face, and he turned his head away, coughing. As Marzi approached, Jane stood up, smiling dangerously, her teeth like polished white shells.

"Jane, take it easy," Lindsay said. "We'll go our way, and you go yours, okay? We didn't mean to bother you."

"Shut up," Jane said. "I don't want to talk to you. I want to talk to *her*. To the prison guard, the traitor to her sex, to *Marzi*." She spat the word.

Marzi should have been terrified, and in some distant compartment of her mind she was, but mostly she felt a sort of cold rage, a steel core of determination whose origin was mysterious to her. She shook Lindsay's hand off her arm and stepped forward. "What's this all about, Jane? You've got a problem with me? What is it?"

"I changed my mind," Jane said. "I *don't* want to talk to you. There's no use talking to a door, to a *lock*, and that's all you are, the lock on a prison for a goddess. You're just the bars in the window. An obstruction to be broken down." Jane lifted her hands, her fingers long and impossibly sharp. Marzi thought of swinging her bag at Jane, but there wasn't much weight in it, just a sketch pad, a paperback book, and the toy pistol inside—

The pistol. Suddenly that seemed like the perfect solution, exactly what Marzi needed in her hand, exactly what she needed for this showdown. But before she reached into her bag, she realized that didn't make any sense. The gun was a toy, just metal and plastic; it wouldn't even *scare* Jane, it certainly wouldn't *hurt* her.

Then Jane's hands closed around Marzi's throat, squeezing, choking her at arm's length. Marzi and Lindsay clawed at her arms, but they might as well have been scratching stone.

Suddenly Jonathan was there, covered in sand but standing, coming up quickly behind Jane, and once he got into striking distance, he planted one foot and brought the other leg around in a hard, sweeping roundhouse kick, right into Jane's side. *Should have gone for the knee,* Marzi thought, the voice in her mind cold but recognizably her own. Hitting her in the side would piss her off, maybe knock her down, but wouldn't disable her.

But Jane didn't fall down; at least, not right away. Jonathan's foot, clad in a heavy hiking boot, passed *through* Jane's body, mud spraying where blood might have been expected, and he spun almost completely around, stumbling before regaining his footing.

Jane howled, releasing her grip on Marzi's throat. She stared around, eyes wide and white, and then her torso fell away from her waist, thumping on the sand, leaving her bodiless legs standing for a moment, separated. Jane had been kicked messily in half.

"Great holy fuck," Jonathan said, and for the first time Marzi heard real fear in his voice. She recognized the tone—it was the sound of someone who has realized his part in an irrevocable action.

Jane's legs fell over, next to the rest of her body.

Jonathan stared down at her, his mouth opening and closing, soundlessly. "I—I didn't—" He didn't complete the thought.

"That's impossible," Lindsay said, and she took hold of Marzi's arm again, squeezing too tightly, her voice high, touching the lower registers of hysteria. "Marzi, that's not—"

"She's moving," Marzi said, calmly, and she found that this development was not entirely unexpected, that somewhere inside she'd thought something like this might happen.

Jane rose up on her arms, looking at them all, still grinning. "You see?" she said. "The goddess has made me immortal. I am one with the earth. Will you try to lock up the earth itself, Marzi?"

Marzi took two steps toward Jane and kicked out, driving her foot straight into Jane's face, mud spraying on impact. Lindsay and Jonathan gasped. The small white stones that made up Jane's smile scattered. Her torso fell over—though not, Marzi knew, for the last time. She wouldn't die that easily. Maybe if they threw her into the sea, she would dissolve . . . but even that might fail, and Jane might emerge later, dripping, composed of mud from the ocean floor.

Marzi knelt and picked up a pebble from the sand. One of Jane's teeth. She clenched it in her fist.

"Let's go to my house," Marzi said. "I think I've had enough of the beach."

Shadow Riders

DENIS SLEPT FOR most of the day, and when he got out of bed he decided to clean his boots at last. There was no point in pretending things were normal anymore. Better to acknowledge the mess his life had temporarily become, and turn his attention to moving on. He knelt and scrubbed his boots in the tub, which had quite a ring around it now, thanks to Jane. He wondered where Jane was, what havoc she was wreaking, whether he'd see her again, but as he washed the mud from his boots, he tried to rinse her from his mind, to cleanse himself of her stain. He wanted his mind to be smoothly oiled antique machinery again, all brass flywheels and golden screws, not clogged with the grit of her. He shook the water off his shoes and put them in the sink to dry.

It was time to get on with his life, and put this lunacy behind him. Jane had gone wherever spirits go; her body was buried where it wouldn't be discovered for a long time, if he was lucky. People would realize she was missing, yes . . . but there were plenty of people who could confirm that she'd been acting strangely lately. Denis had already dealt with the police, and if necessary, he could do so again. As long as he kept his wits about him.

The phone rang. Denis gripped the basin of the sink with his hands, the mud remaining on his fingers marring the white porcelain. He listened to the phone ring. After nine rings, the answering machine picked up.

"Denis?" said a cheerful, faintly bewildered voice, instantly recognizable.

Denis sighed, relieved, then wondered what he was relieved about, what he'd been expecting—cops? Jane? But it was only Beej.

"You're my other one phone call," Beej said. "They're not so strict around here, really, it's not like it is on TV. Anyway, somebody could come bail me out, and I wondered if it could be you? I'd pay you back, you know, if you want money, I can find money, but I can put in a word for you with the earthquake god, maybe you can stand with me in the calm places, and not die, how'd that be? That'd be worth some bail money, I think." Beej's voice dipped, conspiratorial. "See, I have to get out, because I have to set the earthquake god free, because then everything can *begin*. My whole life's been nothing but a waiting room, and I can't believe there are these silly bars between me and my destiny, it seems like such a small thing, metal that could be torqued into spaghetti by the right ripple of the earth. . . ."

And on and on. *Why the hell did I get a digital answering machine?* Denis thought. If he had an old-fashioned answering machine, with a tape, Beej would've been cut off by now, but he could keep rambling for *hours* if he wanted, and the machine would turn it all into numbers, little bits of data that could be played back, binary lunacy.

Denis went into the living room and picked up the phone. "Don't call here again," he said.

"Hey, Denis! You're there!"

"Not for long. I can't help you, Beej. I'm sorry."

"Oh," Beej said. "You don't have any money?"

Denis started to respond with something cutting, vicious—if anyone deserved to have some sense lashed into them, it was Beej—but he was too tired for that. There had been too much venom and tension in his life since Jane's accident in the mud. "Yeah, Beej. I'm sorry, buddy, but I'm broke. Good luck, though."

"It's not so bad here," Beej said. "Except for being imprisoned. The food's okay."

"Glad to hear it. I have to go."

"Could you do me a favor? Could you go to Genius Loci and free the earthquake god? If something happens, and I can't do it myself . . ."

Denis frowned. There was the shared delusion again, the gender-flip of what Jane had raved about. "What's all this about an earthquake god?"

"It's the spirit of desolation, what happens when the earth grinds its teeth, and it's trapped. I don't know where—in the building, under the building, *through* the building. But I'm pretty sure anyone can set it free, that all it will take is a crowbar, maybe not even that; maybe just a hand in the right place."

"Right. If I see the door to the prison, I'll open it, okay?"

"You're the best, Denis!" Beej said. "Uh. Gotta go." And

then a click. Presumably Beej was being taken back to his cell.

"Crazy little fuck." He'd found Beej interesting, for a while—for all his repulsive mannerisms and basic lack of sophistication, he had some fascinating ideas about art, and there was no doubt of his talent; his photo montages were eerily resonant and emotionally affecting, even for Denis, who prided himself on an intellectual approach to art. But lately Beej had grown steadily stranger, and his usual poor hygiene had become something nastier, bordering on the pathological.

Maybe the cops will give him a good delousing, he thought, and then dismissed Beej from his mind.

It was time to get back to his own work, to his paper about the French surrealists. The same subject that had precipitated his falling out with Jane, which had led to their making up, and the aftermath . . . but that didn't bear thinking about. If his mind was a mechanism, surely there was a way to route its operations *around* the areas pertaining to Jane, to slice every bit of her existence out of the operant loop?

Denis put on his jogging shoes and went out into the fading afternoon, walking to Genius Loci. He went to the café at the same time every day, if possible; his days were easier when they had a focal point to orbit around. The usual scattering of people sat on the deck, neo-hippies and goths and punks, bikers and clean-cut students and desperately uncool freshmen with dyed hair and fresh body piercings, reveling in their illusory freedom. Denis went up the steps, feeling subtly *wrong*, and in a moment he realized why: He was used to the solid reassuring thump of his boots on the nine wooden steps. The jogging shoes were too soft and silent, and it felt strangely like he was going into a different place, a changed place, though of course it was he who had changed. He would get strong coffee, sit at a table in the peaceful blue corner of the Ocean Room, and think about the surrealists. Their dreams were far more baroque than Denis's own. He dreamed almost solely of the machine that grinds, all threshing arms and chrome, too neat by half for those artists with their bird-headed matrons, their talking cats, their fantastic landscapes superimposed over cheap furniture. Denis couldn't imagine having dreams like that, like the aftermath of a mental tornado.

He'd only gotten three steps into Genius Loci when Hendrix began shouting at him, his pale face rising from behind the counter like the proverbial bad moon, his dreadlocks flying as he shook his head. "No, Denis, beat it, get out of here, you're banned for life."

Everyone in the café within earshot looked at him. A few people even stood up from tables in the other rooms to see what the fuss was about. Denis froze, feeling like a bug pinned under a magnifying glass. "What?"

"You. Are. Banned. For life." Hendrix flapped his hand—like he was waving away a gnat—and said, "Beat it. Don't ever come back. Go to Javha House or the Marigold or something."

"But . . . you don't understand . . . this is where I *go*, every day." Denis was appalled to realize he was whining, when all he wanted to do was bring logic into this improbable argument. "I'm a *regular*." In truth, the coffee shop was integral to his life. Denis took comfort in his habits and routines—routines that had been brutally upset in recent days. Losing Genius Loci on top of all that was just too much, and he felt the leading edge of hysteria rising, and forced it down. He wasn't sure how much longer he'd be able to control his uglier emotions, though, if the stresses assaulting him didn't ease up.

"Look, I don't care where you go, but you can't come here. We won't serve you, understand? And you can't hang out in here if you aren't buying something."

"That's a catch-twenty-two," Denis said.

"Good literary reference. Two points," someone said, and laughter followed. Denis whipped his head around, but there were several people looking at him openly and chuckling, so he couldn't single out any one for his glare.

What would you do, anyway? a small voice in his mind wondered. *Stab him? Suffocate him?*

"In about ten more seconds, I'll decide you're trespassing, Denis, and I'll have to call the cops. Then you can join your buddy Beej in jail."

Light dawned. This wasn't as Kafkaesque a persecution as it had seemed at first; it was just a misunderstanding. "No, Hendrix, you don't understand. I wasn't trying to break in here last night. I just saw Beej and came to see what the fuss was about. I explained it to the cops, you can ask them—"

"You think I haven't talked to the cops enough already? Since five in the morning I've been talking to cops! I don't care what you told them; I know what Marzi told *me*. You and your crazy girlfriend are *both* banned for life." He looked at his watch. "I believe your ten seconds are up. Banned for life. This is your final official notification. Piss off."

Denis turned away. Marzi! He'd never thought about her

much before. She was either a service drone—and thus a total nonentity—or she was that comic-book girl; she didn't interest him greatly in either aspect. But now she'd arranged to have him kicked out of his favorite place, a place where he spent more of his waking hours than he did at home. And for what? He'd tried to *restrain* Jane, he'd held her back from smashing in the door and doing whatever it was she felt she had to do in Genius Loci! He'd done Marzi a favor, and this was his reward?

Only a few days before, Denis would have found the concept of "getting back at her," of any sort of revenge, ridiculously simplistic, something from the movies, something far too messy to attempt in real life. But recently, he'd discovered a higher tolerance for messiness than he'd previously believed himself capable of. Perhaps revenge wasn't outside the scope of possibility. Perhaps there were ways to sting her as he'd just been stung. Or worse.

He went down the steps in his soft shoes. It didn't sound like he was leaving the same place. It didn't sound like he was the same person leaving it.

BEEJ HUMMED in his cell, shifting his weight on the hard bunk. It was more comfy than the beach, where he'd been sleeping lately, or the temple of the earthquake god, where he'd tried to sleep one night, until the religious experience of his dreams had proved too powerful to allow him rest, but he still didn't like it. The cell was too clean and antiseptic, all concrete and steel. One good quake would shear the bars, twist the walls out of true, render all right angles meaningless.

Beej listened for earthquakes, but didn't hear any coming. He had the feeling that the earthquake god had expended a lot of energy reaching through the door of his prison to touch Beej. Surely *someone* would throw open the door to the god's prison. Beej knew it would be easy; the prison was designed to keep the god *in*, not to keep anyone *out*. The god said there were guardians—one guardian outside the prison, and one on the *inside*—but that they could be easily side-stepped, that all it would take was a little plain human muscle to open the door. And then . . . Beej had dreamed of the after-math, the world a jumbled mess, like a photo collage in three dimensions, like the world's biggest found-object sculpture, strange juxtapositions of cars and steel girders, humped-up concrete, water running where it wasn't meant to, fires illuminating everything.

When the earthquake god burst out, the whole *town* would become a work of wrecked art.

Beej went to the bars of his cell and held on. He closed his eyes and turned himself into a seismograph, the newly shaped plates in his head poised to vibrate in sympathy with any tremors in the crust of the earth, but nothing came.

"That's okay," Beej said quietly, cheerfully, to no one, opening his eyes. "I can wait."

Dream Sack

THE THREE OF THEM walked back to Marzi's place quietly, all wrapped in their own thoughts. Marzi let them into her apartment, and Lindsay went straight to the kitchen. "We're drinking your wine, Marzipan," she called.

Marzi flopped onto her couch and tried to relax, tried to pretend the world hadn't gone insane by degrees over the past days. "Make mine a double, barkeep."

Jonathan stood outside the doorway for a moment, brushing the last bits of sand from his body and taking off his shoes before coming inside. He stood in the middle of the room, scowling at the carpet, and finally said, too loudly, "Why is no one talking about the fact that I just *kicked* a woman in *half*?"

Lindsay came back with three wineglasses in her hands, held by the stems, and the way the glasses rattled delicately together revealed her trembling. She put them down, carefully arranging them on the table, and said, "I'm not sure that's what I saw. It was dark. Really dark. Maybe you just grazed her, and she fell."

Marzi didn't speak. She *knew* what she'd seen, and she couldn't unsee it now, but Lindsay and Jonathan hadn't used up their reserves of rationalization and repression yet.

Jonathan shook his head. "This isn't the first fight I've been in. I connected, but it was like kicking . . . I don't know. I've never kicked anything my foot went right through before. I saw the dirt go flying—"

"She was covered in mud," Lindsay said, annoyed, as if this discussion should already be behind them. "You kicked her, and some mud flew off her, so what? I'm not saying you didn't do good, you *did*, but . . . there's no way you kicked her in half." Lindsay knelt by Marzi's stereo, sorting through her CDs with occasional sniffs of disdain, tossing aside Uncle Tupelo, the Two Dollar Pistols, Whiskeytown, Wilco, all her cowpunk and insurgent country discs, until she finally found a Portishead disc and put it on.

Jonathan sat down on the couch, poured a glass of wine for himself, and then one for Marzi, and leaned back. "But at the end, when Marzi kicked her . . ." He looked at Marzi, pointedly.

Marzi shrugged, gazing into her wineglass. She decided to lie, to spare their minds. There was no need to put them through the torturous self-doubt she'd experienced herself so recently. "I just kicked a bunch of sand in her face, let her know we weren't going to back down. After you knocked her down, I think the fight pretty much went out of her."

"It sorta looked like you kicked her head right off," Jonathan said.

"It's hard to see anything in the dark," Lindsay said,

testily. "And as far as I know, Marzi isn't some secret kung-fu master with the power to decapitate people with her feet. Look, can we talk about something else? I don't want to waste any more mental processing cycles on psycho Jane."

"Motion seconded," Marzi said.

Jonathan sighed. "I could've sworn . . . but it was dark, and there was plenty of adrenaline to go around. I guess I don't know what I saw." He shook his head. "This summer isn't turning out the way I expected so far."

Lindsay leapt on the chance to change the subject. "So what do you plan to do this summer, exactly? You're studying Garamond Ray, right?"

Jonathan shifted on the couch, but nodded, apparently willing to leave Jane behind. "I want to talk to some of the people who knew him—lots of the artists from back then are still living in the area. Ray taught a few classes at the university, so some of the faculty may have stories to tell. I've been corresponding with some of them. And of course I need to take pictures of the murals in Genius Loci. Which reminds me. I meant to ask you about it earlier, but isn't there another room, one with a desert motif?"

"A desert?" Marzi said. At the mention of the Desert Room, her blood temperature seemed to instantly drop ten degrees—this was thin ice, tightrope territory, creeping past a cave with a monster inside.

"Sure," Lindsay said. "You told me about it, ages ago. The old storage room, right? All rotten and crammed full of junk, and big water stains on the walls?"

"I think," Marzi said, her voice hollow in her own head, distant, like the echo of gunshots or a cattle stampede in a far-off box canyon. "Sure, yeah, I remember."

"Water stains?" Jonathan said. "That's terrible. I'd love to get a look at the mural, though. Whatever's left of it."

"No," Marzi said. Her voice slashed down, hard, harsher than she'd intended. "It's dangerous in there," she said, trying to push back the hot ache that filled her skull, trying to speak normally. "The floorboards are all rotten; you have to know just where to step. Hendrix won't let anybody in there—he's scared of the liability, you know? Besides, you can't see anything, there's crap leaning against all the walls, you'd have to move everything out of the way, and Hendrix would never let you do that." All those things were true, she *knew* they were true—but had Hendrix ever actually told her that? Or had *she* told *him* it was too dangerous, knowing his native paranoia would cause him to agree with her, and declare the room off-limits?

"Huh," Jonathan said. "Too bad. Are you all right, Marzi?"

"Yeah, babe, you don't sound so good." Lindsay touched her leg. "But then, after the night we've had—"

"I have to go," Marzi said, standing suddenly, feeling like she might vomit at any second. "Bathroom." She stumbled across the room, toward the bathroom. The door was closed, and when she reached out to touch the knob, her vision filled with light, harsh and white, and she tumbled out of normal space and consciousness, into something else, a different time, another, half-familiar, space.

SOMEONE PULLED OPEN a door once, but Marzi isn't sure who—was it Rangergirl, curious as always, opening the nailed-shut door in her tiny apartment way back in issue number one? Or is it Marzi herself turning the brass knob on a painted-over door in the Desert Room, the crammed-full storage room in the back of Genius Loci, where Hendrix sent her on her second day at work to shift the junk around?

Either way, the door swings open as if pushed by fierce winds, and a bright high sun blinds the girl for an instant. When her eyes adjust (Rangergirl's eyes? or Marzi's?), she sees a long, dusty street lined with weathered storefronts and hitching posts. In the distance, jagged mountains make angular cutout shapes against the sky. She is more fascinated and awestruck than afraid, this girl, and she takes a hesitant step toward the doorway and the strange new world beyond, but she does not pass over the threshold. Somewhere an out-of-tune piano mangles a rollicking tune. The air over there smells of sage and sand, of heat and gunsmoke.

Then someone steps into the far end of the street, a black figure in a duster and a cowboy hat, at least nine feet tall and casting an impossible shadow that stretches nearly to the girl's feet. The girl recognizes him, and is comforted: This is the Outlaw, and so the girl herself must be Rangergirl and not Marzi. That means this is a thing of the imagination, not something real, not something that ever truly happened.

Then the man moves and suddenly he is *there,* right up close, his face inches from the girl's own, each one standing on their own side of the doorway, only the thickness of the doorframe dividing their worlds.

The man's face is not human. His eyes are smoking gun barrels, his teeth ribbons of barbed wire, his face cut deeply by wrinkles that are really gullies and arroyos, desert formations. This face is not from the comic book—Marzi has never drawn anything so horrible, has never even imagined it. The Outlaw's face is just shadow under the brim of his hat, and he is an evil, ancient man, but *this*—this thing embodies the wasteland, and promises to give the whole world over to dust.

The girl who opened the door knows she isn't truly here, that this isn't really happening now, but still she is terrified, in part because the scene seems familiar, and not because it's something she drew in a comic book once.

The thing with the wasteland face says, in a voice of smoke and rattlesnake and mummification, "If you can get in, then I can get *out*."

The girl (who is Marzi; she knows herself now; there can be no doubting, no hiding behind a character) steps back. She slams the door in the creature's awful face.

That creature was never in Marzi's comic. Rangergirl goes through the Western Door again and again, she has adventures, fights the Outlaw in all his guises, but Marzi would never be so brave, never risk her life, because her life is *real,* she is flesh and blood, not ink and paper, and she does not have the safety of turning to the last page and being done. Faced with a door to another place, Marzi would not become a brave adventurer— she would slam the door and never touch the brass knob again, never enter the room that *held* the door again. She would try to hide the door from others, try to forget about the thing with the wasteland face, try to *make it not be real*.

Marzi knows herself, and she also knows this dream, this vision, is not from her comic, not something she made up.

It is not fiction.

She knows, then, that it must be memory.

*   *   *

MARZI OPENED HER EYES to find Lindsay and Jonathan kneeling over her, looking down in fear and concern. "Aw, hell," Marzi said, doing her best to sound calm, wondering if they could hear the thud of her heartbeat, like horse hooves pounding on a coach road. "Shouldn't have had that wine on an empty stomach." In truth, she had never felt more sober. For the first time in two years, her memories were complete and unbroken—an absence she'd never consciously noticed had been filled. So what if the things she found in her newly restored memories were impossible? Hadn't she seen other impossible things since then? "How long was I out?"

"Just a few seconds," Jonathan said, touching her forehead as if checking for a fever. "You reached for the bathroom door and fell down, and we rushed over, and you opened your eyes."

"Felt like I was down for a lot longer," she said. "Just . . . stress, I guess. The adrenaline crash, after what happened with Jane." She thought about telling them, describing her vision, but feared they wouldn't believe her—they were well on their way to convincing themselves that Jane hadn't been kicked in half, after all. Marzi knew the power of repression, understood the vast human capacity for forgetting the impossible, even if her own capacity for self-delusion had been burned out tonight, overwhelmed by one too many impossible things. Besides, if her vision was true, this was *her* problem to resolve. Jane had said as much: Her fight was with Marzi. There was no reason to drag her friends into it. Jonathan had saved her life tonight, kicking Jane that way, and she would do her best to protect his life, now.

"Do you want to go to bed?" Lindsay said. "We can take off."

The thought of lying in her bed, looking at the ceiling, alone, was unbearable; she would only brood. She had things to think about—serious things, dangerous things, deeply confusing things—but she couldn't face them now, in the dark, in the night. "I don't think so. I want to drink lots of water and sit on the couch. And . . . could you stay?"

"I'm not planning to walk to my car," Lindsay said. "Not after the night we had. I'll stay overnight, if you want."

"Yes," Marzi said, making her way to the couch. "Please, both of you. I don't feel safe by myself." Though, in truth, she was more worried about them going out, alone. Jane might have put herself back together by now.

"I'll get you some water," Jonathan said.

Marzi nodded. The memory of the Desert Room had parched her to the bone, and her mouth felt as dry as sun-baked rocks. Jonathan brought her water, and she held a swallow in her mouth, her eyes closed, tasting the coolness, probing her memories. It was all there, unmistakable. She'd just started working at Genius Loci, and she went into the storage room—the Desert Room—to put away some old broken tables and

and

and she saw a door. A painted-over door with a tarnished brass knob. And she opened that door, because she was curious, as anyone would be.

Marzi swallowed, then looked at Jonathan and Lindsay, their faces hovering before her like anxious moons. She forced a smile. "Hey, guys, I'm okay. It's been a long night, you know?"

"God, yes," Lindsay said. "Do you think we should call the cops, about Jane? If she was really hurt . . ."

"I think she's still in one piece," Marzi said, phrasing it that way deliberately, looking for some reaction in their faces, but seeing none. So. They'd managed to forget the impossible parts of what had happened on the beach. She touched the white stone in her pocket, and knew that she would not be able to forget. Maybe she'd never be able to forget anything else ever again. "I doubt they'd be able to find her anyway."

"I don't want to talk to the cops, particularly," Jonathan said.

Lindsay nodded, and flopped back down on the carpet. "This was supposed to be a *fun* night," she said. "Like me and Marzi used to have. I wanted us to go out dancing after the boardwalk. I remember when you could drink frat boys under the table, Marzipan."

"I got over *that* little affectation years ago," Marzi said. It was true; she'd almost forgotten what the *old* Marzi was like, how she'd been when she first came to college. Free from her parental constraints, Marzi had overindulged in all the usual ways, going to raves, dropping ecstasy a couple of times, getting drunk, and neglecting her classes. At that point they didn't have grades at Santa Cruz, so it wasn't totally obvious she was fucking up; being out of high school meant having to be her own moral compass, and that was *hard*. She'd met Lindsay when they were both party girls, though Lindsay had always been serious about her art, too. Lindsay managed to keep everything under control by only sleeping four or five hours a night, apparently running on raw enthusiasm and talent the rest of the time.

Then, in her junior year, Marzi got her summer job at Genius Loci, and went into the Desert Room and—and all that shit went down, and she had to go to the hospital for a while. She'd never really been the same after that, she realized. Something had sobered her to the bone. She took a medical withdrawal, stopped going to parties, managed to get back her job at Genius Loci, and finally decided not to go back to college at all. She settled down to work on one of the half a dozen ideas she had for a comic book. One of her ideas was for a sort of cowpunk contemporary retelling of old Western yarns set in a city, maybe a vaguely dystopian frontier-town kind of vibe, and that had become *Rangergirl*. It wasn't supposed to be overtly supernatural at first—all that shit about the door, and the Outlaw, and being a guardian, all that came later, *after* Marzi opened the door in the Desert Room, after she got out of the hospital.

It was like it hadn't been her idea at all, but something planted in her mind. The conceit of the Western Door had almost certainly made *Rangergirl* a better comic, a better piece of art, than her original idea would have been. She'd undergone something deeply traumatic, which may have had repercussions of which she was still largely unaware, and that had affected her work positively. But how had it affected her otherwise? She suspected she was going to find out soon.

Marzi looked at Lindsay with new appreciation. Lindsay was the only one of her friends who'd stayed by her, the only one who'd written to her while she was in the hospital, who'd brought her flowers afterward, who'd never pried into things Marzi didn't want to reveal. She'd simply accepted her, been the same old wisecracking Lindsay, even though Marzi was scarcely recognizable as the person she'd been before.

Marzi realized, with an almost physical rush, that Lindsay *loved* her—perhaps, even, was *in love* with her. She started crying, and her friends just held her hands. She'd seen horrible things these past few days, but there were good things, too, good *people,* to balance that. These were her guards, her protection, her deputies, her posse, her friends. They could face any showdown together. They could win any shootout. They could pick up the pieces after any disaster, and build something new. Marzi closed her eyes, and felt the emptiness inside her recede; felt the deserts in the greater chambers of her heart shift, and begin to blossom.

Outside Man

MARZI WOKE, STRETCHED, and heard Jonathan and Lindsay talking in the other room. Their presence, even at this remove, soothed her, and kept darker thoughts at bay. But eventually they would leave, and Marzi would be alone, and she would have no choice but to face the things she'd remembered, and the consequences she feared. Everything decayed. Everything turned to dust.

Marzi sat up in bed, shaking her head sharply, as if to dispel cobwebs from her face. Why did she have this dark tide in her, this terrible undertow of loss and dismay?

But she knew why. Because, two years ago, she'd glimpsed the face of total desolation. She didn't know what it was, that thing with the wasteland face, not in any absolute, objective sense, but she knew it intended to grind the world down to nothing, to make the earth a molten waste, a heaving place in which no blade of grass could take root, on which no bird could land, in which no trust could be found. She'd opened a door, and almost let that force, that tornado with intentions, loose on the world. But she'd stood in its way. Somehow, her presence had been enough to keep it from passing through, and Marzi had shut the door in its face, and then locked the memory away in the deepest vaults of her mind. So why had she remembered now? Sometimes repression was a *good* thing, right? It let you get on with your life.

Except it hadn't, not really. Marzi had been in stasis, avoiding relationships, even keeping sweet Lindsay at arm's length. The only thing that had involved her heart at all was her comic, and even that had been shot through with dark threads of alienation, influenced by her glimpse of the thing that lived behind the walls in the Desert Room. What was it? Where did it live, really, what meta-space did it inhabit? Marzi had heard of the medicine lands, the world-behind-the-world, that some Native Americans believed in, where the forces that secretly shaped the world lived. Had she glimpsed that place?

Possibly. If so, she'd seen the thing that *lived* there, maybe the thing that was imprisoned there. Maybe—as much as she hated to think of it—the thing she was supposed to guard.

Some guard I am, she thought. *One look at the prisoner, and I have to check myself into a loony bin.*

She got out of bed, pulled on her thin summer robe, and went into the living room. "Morning, troops," she said. Jonathan and Lindsay sat together on the couch, looking bleary and rumpled. "The shower's free, if you want it."

"Mind if I go first?" Jonathan said. "I've still got sand in all sorts of unmentionable places."

"Don't feel like you can't mention them to *me*," Lindsay

said. "But, sure, go ahead." She leaned her head back on the couch and closed her eyes, losing herself in her own thoughts, or else still in the waking-up process.

"I'm going to make coffee," Marzi said.

"Coffee," Lindsay said, without opening her eyes. "Coffee good."

Marzi went into the kitchen and started a pot of coffee, thinking. How much of what had happened in the past few days had to do with the thing she'd seen behind the door? The vision of the Outlaw in the Red Room, that bizarre dream of Santa Cruz in ruins, Jane and Beej both babbling about imprisoned gods, the tattooed Indian she'd seen disappear into the Teatime Room just before the earthquake . . . The god's prison was weakening, and Marzi could no longer live in ignorance. She was needed to actively guard against the wasteland thing's escape. The thing—Beej's earthquake god, Jane's goddess—was pressing against the door, whispering at the cracks, peering through the keyhole, influencing the world. It was trying to get someone to let it out, to fling the door wide. If it could do this much from behind the door—make Jane into mud-girl, hitch Beej's inherent craziness to its own agenda—what could it do if set free?

Shit, that's easy, she thought. *It can turn this whole coast into a desert.*

Marzi had to consider the *other* possibility, of course, the alternative explanation to the things she'd seen, and the things she'd remembered: She might be crazy. It had all been very believable last night, with the memory of Jane breaking apart still fresh in her mind, but now the doubts were creeping in. She still *remembered* it all, but she doubted the truth of those memories. They were unbelievable, after all, though she found herself believing them anyway, and wasn't that a sign of madness? She had to find a way to prove this to herself one way or another. The first step, she decided, would be to go back into the storage room—the *Desert Room*—and look at the door to the wasteland. Not open it, she wasn't ready to risk *that,* but just look at it, touch it, confirm its empirical existence. But more than that, she needed to face her fear. She'd subconsciously avoided the room totally for two years, and she'd suffered a recurring phobia of opening any doors at *all,* because of what she'd glimpsed there. Fuck that. Marzi didn't want to be a victim of her own inability to cope. She'd go in there, and have a look around. That's what Rangergirl would do. And Marzi might not *be* Rangergirl, but she'd invented her, and that meant her better qualities had to exist in Marzi somewhere, if she dug deep enough, right?

Marzi poured herself a cup of coffee, and another for Lindsay. This was going to be a long day.

"BAGELS ARE. LIKE. *God,*" Lindsay said. They sat in the courtyard behind the Bagelry, where the fruit trees were blossoming, white flowers scenting the air and falling down like perfumed snow.

"Interesting theological position," Jonathan said, sipping what must have been his fourth or fifth cup of coffee for the day. He wasn't even slightly jittery, and he wasn't asking for decaf. Marzi was in awe. He propped his feet up on an empty chair, wiggling his toes.

Lindsay held up the uneaten half of her bagel, smeared

with raspberry cream cheese. "The major religions agree: God is round. Raspberry is divine. Ergo."

Marzi laughed. "So what've you kids got planned for the day?"

"Work!" they chorused, then looked at each other and laughed. "I haven't been to the studio in a couple of days," Lindsay said. "My work in progress is probably, like, dormant. I need to talk to my adviser, too. I'm supposed to TA for this summer class." She shrugged. "It's beer money."

"I've really got to knuckle down on my thesis," Jonathan said. "I'm only here for the summer, and while that seems like a long time now, it's going to go *fast*." He glanced at them—Lindsay in particular was suddenly looking blue—and said, "Hey, I'll have time to hang out, don't worry, it's not like I have to work twenty-four-seven. I just want to get into the habit of working every day."

"What I love about him is his professionalism," Lindsay said.

"And here I thought you liked his ass," Marzi said.

"It's a very professional ass, isn't it?" Lindsay said, leaning back in her chair and eyeing Jonathan's bottom.

Jonathan waited patiently for them to finish, then said, "Could I ask you a favor, Marzi?"

A cold coil of fear grew in Marzi's stomach. She knew what he wanted, if not in particular, then in general. "Shoot."

"I understand I can't go into the Desert Room, but I was wondering, could you take a few snapshots of the walls for me? If the floor's unsafe, you could just stand in the doorway. I know I won't see much, but anything would help, really. It'll probably just be a footnote in the thesis, about how even the few remaining major works by Garamond Ray are being lost, but I'd like to have as much documentation as possible—otherwise, it's just apocrypha."

Marzi was pleasantly surprised that she didn't vomit, black out, or have an apocalyptic vision when he said the words "Desert Room," but otherwise, there was nothing to be happy about. How could she refuse without calling attention to herself, without making Jonathan and Lindsay suspicious? It wasn't like Jonathan was asking for much; it was a reasonable request.

Why shouldn't *I do it?* she thought. She'd planned to go to the Desert Room again anyway, to see how reality matched her memories. Granted, she'd planned to do it at some as yet unspecified future date, while doing it as a favor for Jonathan would likely be more immediate . . . but that was a good thing. Otherwise, she might put it off indefinitely. This way, she had some outside motivation. It was good to do the hard stuff right away, wasn't it? Do the hardest thing first, and then everything else was easier.

That was good advice . . . unless going into the Desert Room *wasn't* the hardest thing she'd have to do, just the *first* thing.

She smiled, wishing she were a better actor, hoping they would ascribe any strangeness in her expression to residual hangover. "Sure, I'll do it. I don't know how well the pictures will come out. The room's moldy and full of junk, but I'll do what I can."

Lindsay finished her bagel in a few quick bites. "What're you doing today, Marzi?"

"I want to finish a couple of strips for the paper," she said.

"You do a strip for a newspaper?" Jonathan asked.

"Yeah. It's called 'Glass Eyes'—your basic alternative-newspaper-broody-shadows-no-punch-line type of thing."

"Only it's *good*," Lindsay said.

"Dunno about that. But it keeps me in beer money. At the rate of about one beer per week, anyway. I'm working at the coffeehouse from five 'til close. I'll see you guys around?"

"I'll come down and give you my camera around five," Jonathan said. "Is that all right?"

"Actually, I'll get there a little early, around four, and take a few pictures then. Might as well get it over with, right?" She was in no great hurry to go into the Desert Room, but she wanted to do so during daylight, with lots of people in the café; otherwise, she might not have time to do it until after closing, when she was alone in the building, and there was no *way* she was going to do that.

"Sure. I might even be able to get the photos developed tonight."

"I'll try to stop by later, if I can," Lindsay said. "No promises, though. I'll get in touch tomorrow, if nothing else."

"All right. Back to the ink mines," Marzi said.

"To the pigment mines!" Lindsay said.

"To the, ah, theory mines?" Jonathan said.

"Academics," Lindsay said, and rolled her eyes.

Painted for War

MARZI LOST HER- self in her work that morning, happily for- getting every danger real and imagined, emo- tional and visceral, in favor of scratching out sketches with her pen. "Glass Eyes" was in many ways her bread- and-butter work, at least in terms of visibility—it ap- peared weekly in several free California papers, the indie press, and was archived on- line. Most people who knew her name knew her more for the quirky comic strip with its ever-shifting ensemble cast than for *Rangergirl*. It wasn't a punch-line kind of comic; Marzi put the characters in odd situations, quite a few of them drawn from Lindsay's picaresque and picturesque life, follow- ing one viewpoint character for a while, then switching to someone the character had interacted with, a process she called relay racing. The title came from the first strip, when a blind man with two glass eyes was accused of ogling a woman in a short skirt. The blind man ap- peared occasionally, usually lurking in the background, making cryptic pronouncements, or more often behaving in a completely prosaic fashion. After almost eighteen months of writing the strip, Marzi was gearing up for a series about the blind man, most of which would actually center on his pet peacock, Argus.

It was totally, utterly unlike *Rangergirl*, which was admittedly her consuming passion, and working on "Glass Eyes" was a nice respite from the emotional effort writing her comic book entailed.

Now, though, she found herself doing a series of strips about a Stranger coming to town, a sort of *Waiting for Godot* meets *The Iliad*, her usual cast of artists, busboys, bus drivers, beachcombers, and surfers milling around in a city park at some vast picnic, making cryptic comments about "that guy" and "that bastard," complaining about all the things that happened the *last* time the mysterious Stranger showed up. All the while, the clouds overhead gradually darkened, going from happy cottony fluffballs to menacing sacks of rain and lightning. By the time Marzi looked up from her sketch paper, her fingers twisted in a cramp, she'd filled half a dozen pages with rough sketches, every comic filled with uncomfortably hobnobbing characters relating dark anecdotes about the Stranger—the time he got a dance club shut down, how they changed the rules at the skating rink because of him, how he'd ruined a chartered fishing boat company in some complicated scheme involving nude scuba diving.

Marzi blinked and groped for her glass of water. The comics were good, though a bit more brooding than her "Glass Eyes" work usually was. The strip tended to focus on misunderstandings, comedies of errors, mistakes in perception, so this was a different tone from the usual. They weren't bad, and most of these sketches could be transformed into finished strips, but what was her subconscious getting at? Who was this stranger? Jonathan? No, that didn't make sense, he wasn't ominous. . . .

She sighed. It was the Outlaw. The thing with the wasteland face, the lurker beyond the threshold, her nightmare come true. Now even "Glass Eyes" was infected by it. Oh, well. It wasn't like she could keep something so monumental from appearing in her work. But what could she do about it? This thing was trapped, and it was somehow reaching through the door, affecting people, trying to make someone set it free. Marzi had, however inelegantly and accidentally, prevented that for now: Beej was in jail, and Denis and Jane were banned from the café. Had the thing reached out to anyone else? How could she be on the lookout all the time?

Maybe she was ignoring the obvious. Why not just nail a few boards across the door, or take off the doorknob, or put a bunch of big padlocks on the thing? Hendrix would think she'd gone crazy if he caught her, but she could probably get away with it. He never went into the Desert Room, which was probably a good idea, as his weight might strain the creaky floorboards to the breaking point. The idea was something to consider. Even if she *was* crazy, and there was nothing behind the door but the back of some aluminum siding, locking the door would give her some peace of mind. Theoretically.

It was 3:40 now, so she had to hurry to meet Jonathan. She went out, locked her apartment, and looked around for wild mud-people, faceless giants in gray dusters, or other assorted monsters. Seeing none, she set out for Genius Loci. The day was cooling off already. The café looked lovely, its sprawling decks inviting, its big windows lending it a feel of airy openness. How could this be the prison for an ancient evil? The café didn't feel dangerous to her. It felt like home.

Maybe that was part of its . . . what? Magic? *That* wasn't a word Marzi was prepared to say out loud any time soon, not in connection with her own life, and it felt funny to even be thinking it. So say "power." Maybe the café attracted Marzi because she *was* a guardian, for whatever random or preordained reason, and it made sense to make a guard want to spend time in the place that needed to be guarded.

Or maybe she just liked big funky coffeehouses with murals and scrounged secondhand furniture. She liked to think it was an inner rather than an imposed affection for the place. That was the problem with accepting the supernatural: It brought up all kinds of unpleasant questions about fate and destiny and free will, things she'd rather not question too closely. Maybe she had to think about them, though. The monsters were coming up out of the basement. The doors were coming off their hinges. She had to deal.

Jonathan sat on the deck, a half-full pint of beer in front of him, another pint sitting untouched across the table. "Bought you a beer. Payment in advance. Got time to sit down?"

"Thanks, yeah."

"No problem. Drinking alone depresses me."

"Did you get much work done today?"

"Eh. Some. I went back to the beach today, just to make sure . . . I don't know. That Jane wasn't still there, unconscious or something. We knocked her down pretty hard. Self-defense, I know, but it worried me. There was nothing there. Even the pile of sand had mostly blown away."

Marzi nodded. "I thought she would be up and around

again soon. I just hope she'll leave us alone, now." She knew Jane *wouldn't,* but she didn't want to get into that at the moment. Or, preferably, ever.

"That would be nice."

She glanced at her watch. "Do you have a camera for me?"

"I do." He reached into his bag and drew out a bulky silver-and-black contraption.

"I figured you for the slim digital type."

"Wish I could afford one. This was a hand-me-down from my grandmother. She was kind of an amateur photographer." He handed the camera over to her.

Marzi took it, surprised at the weight—this was no little plastic-and-cardboard disposable number, which was more or less the only kind of camera Marzi had ever used. There were knobs, dials with numbers written around them, switches, silver doodads . . . "I think this is beyond me, Jonathan."

"I'll set it up for you. Don't worry; all you have to do is point, focus, shoot, advance the film . . ." He trailed off, smiling.

"Consider me reassured." She handed it back to him. "Show me how it works, and I'll go take your snapshots."

"You're sure I can't come in with you . . . ?"

"Hendrix would have kittens. I'm going to have to sneak past him as it is."

He sighed. "I had to ask. But I appreciate your help. I just wish I could see the room for myself."

Jonathan showed her how to work the camera, and though she had the feeling it *could* be a lot more complicated, she thought she'd be able to get the job done. She'd take a few pictures of moldy, cluttered walls, and that would be it . . .

except it wouldn't. She wasn't going into the Desert Room to take pictures, not really—that was just the pretext, and the goad. This was . . . what? A scouting expedition. A bit of reconnaissance. She was getting the lay of the wasteland, or at least its anteroom.

Or, maybe, she was going to prove herself seriously delusional. Which would, in many ways, be better than the alternative.

"Okay," she said, and finished her beer. "I'm going in. If I don't come out by nightfall, send in a search party."

Jonathan nodded, unaware of how black that bit of lame humor really was.

"I'm going to try to move some of the crap around and get clear photographs of the walls," Marzi said. "So it might take me a while." She wanted to see the murals in their entirety, if she could. It didn't seem like simple coincidence that the doorway was in the Desert Room, after all, and there might be something for her to learn from the paintings. She remembered them pretty well—now that her memory had opened up again—but she hadn't seen the parts of the walls obscured by stacked boxes and other junk.

"You're going above and beyond the call of friendship," Jonathan said. "I owe you."

"Hey, you bought me a beer. That's at least partial payment, and up front, too." She stood up. "I start work at five o'clock. Give me a few minutes after that to get settled, then you can come bug me for your photos, okay?"

"Sounds good. There's a one-hour photo place over on Mission. I can probably get the pictures developed tonight."

"Great." She waved and went inside.

Hendrix was busing tables in the Teatime Room, his

broad back turned to her, so Marzi just scooted around the counter, nodded to Tina, who sported a fresh piercing in her eyebrow, and went through the kitchen.

Marzi took a deep breath and looked at the door to the Desert Room, painted an innocuous blue, the same as the kitchen walls. Garamond Ray had painted sunflowers in the kitchen, big jaunty blooms with strangely segmented stems, like crab legs, but there were no flowers painted on the door. Maybe he'd tried to paint flowers, and they'd withered, wilted, and died from the heat baking through the door from the other side, all the searing nastiness radiating out from the Desert Room . . .

Marzi shook her head. Damn. She was getting schizo-melodramatic, here. This was no big deal. This was just open-ing a door, and stepping inside. Anyone could do it. People did it every day.

She knew that was a lie, that this was more than the ordi-nary crossing of a threshold, but she took comfort from the thought, from the everyday nature of the act. *See, you turn the knob, there, it twists cool and easy in your hand. You push the door, and it swings open without even a squeak, though it hasn't been opened in months at least, though no one's ever oiled it, and this isn't even the* important *door, this is just the door to the room that holds the door.* Marzi thought of airlocks: This room was a buffer zone, the place where the wasteland and the world were kept apart, the demilitarized zone. No-man's-land. The metaphors were obvious, and they were more than metaphors, actually—they were analogues. She groped for the light switch, there on the right side of the door, just where she remembered, her fingers touching the cool plastic before she could begin to really worry about strange hands closing over hers, or about scorpions and black widow spiders scuttling over her fingers. She flicked the switch, and it clicked on with a dry snap like a bone breaking cleanly. Dirty flyspecked light filled the room from a single unshaded bulb, but Marzi cast her eyes down instinctively, not ready yet to look at the walls, or at the door which she knew was straight ahead on the far wall. Instead she looked at the dusty floorboards, stepped inside, and closed the door behind her.

When she looked up, the first thing she noticed was how *small* the room was. In her memory it was vast, but in reality it was just a small back room, nothing special. It smelled of mildew and dust, not of alkali or desert wind. The room was filled with junk: the remains of a tarnished brass espresso machine atop a battered gray metal cart, scrap boards leaning against the walls and littering the floor, like the remains of a barn scattered after a tornado. The walls on either side were mostly uncluttered, but she didn't dare look at the murals yet.

She tried not to think of all the scorpions and rattlesnakes and sleek poisonous spiders that could be living among the junk, unseen, but she wasn't very successful. The Desert Room, though surely no better insulated than the rest of the café, seemed to shut out all ambient sound. She couldn't hear the Metallica disc Hendrix was playing, or the babble of customers.

Now that she looked up, Marzi couldn't even see the door in the rear wall. Broken shelving leaned against the back wall, covering the door and the rest of the wall almost entirely.

That was a relief. She could face the door whenever she wanted, and didn't have to be confronted immediately with the locus of her fear.

She finally turned her attention to the two mostly visible walls; the murals were impressive, despite the blossoms of mold that marred them here and there. Huge rocks seemed to project from the walls, an illusion helped by the fact that the walls really *did* bulge in places from water damage, lending an indisputable sense of three-dimensionality. Bald vultures perched on top of cartoon cactuses. Oversized scorpions swarmed over the rocks, stingers and claws upraised. Rattlesnakes coiled on sand dunes. Vile yellow light saturated the whole scene, and a poison-yellow sun filled one upper corner of the room, painted on two walls and the ceiling, though water spots obscured the spiky flares on its upper reaches. It was a mural like any of the others, just done in a desert motif, sort of like the Road Runner and Coyote cartoons, but more menacing—this was a desert alive with things that would kill you. But even that was somewhat reassuring, because the monster Marzi remembered didn't want any life at *all*; it wanted everything scoured down to the bare rock. Marzi lifted Jonathan's camera, pleased to see that the room looked even more harmless from behind the viewfinder. She snapped shots of the two side walls, then lowered the camera, chewing her lip.

The floor wasn't really that rotten. There were a couple of bad places, enough to fuel Hendrix's paranoia, but mostly the structure was solid, and there were boards laid across the most dangerous bits. Chunks of the plaster ceiling might fall on her, but that was the extent of her danger. The room felt like a *room*, not a wasteland confined within four walls, despite its soundproof qualities. Her thumping heart had slowed, and the adrenaline no longer sang in her veins.

She went to the center of the room and turned around to get a picture of the interior wall. She felt a bit nervous turning her back to the rear wall, the one with the door that led nowhere . . . but it was just a door, covered up with boards besides, and altogether harmless.

The mural was painted across the wall and the door that led to the kitchen, and depicted a distant dune with a coyote howling in silhouette, and sharp rock outcroppings in the distance. Marzi took a photo.

She put the camera down on top of a pile of boxes and turned her attention to the rear wall. This was the sticking point, wasn't it? The real test. Now that her memory had been restored, Marzi remembered placing the boards there to block the door, leaning them against the wall with zombie-like efficiency, already repressing the memory of what she'd seen behind the door. She should have nailed the boards up instead, but she'd been working in shock, after all. It was amazing she'd done even this much. She started moving the boards out of the way.

When the wall was one-third uncovered, Marzi noticed the difference.

The door was still blocked, but she'd cleared away enough of the shelving on one side to see the painting. It was not as she remembered. There should have been more boulders, more scorpions and dunes, more of the same desert-scape that adorned the other walls. Instead, the painting depicted buildings, weathered wooden storefronts with hitching posts out front, the classic view-down-Main-Street scene from a thousand Westerns. This was the street where the comical sidekick would die in the second act, where the hero and the villain would shoot one another in the third.

I'm just remembering it wrong, Marzi thought. After all, the buildings *did* look familiar—she'd drawn them in the first issue of *Rangergirl,* as part of the ghost town that lay beyond the Western Door. She'd assumed she was drawing on a lifetime of experience with Western movies, but apparently the scene was an outright theft from Garamond Ray. Was impaired memory a suitable excuse for plagiarism? Unless the wall hadn't *always* been like this . . .

No. The wall hadn't changed—that was absurd. *As absurd as a mud-girl,* she thought. *As absurd as ghost cowboys in the Red Room.*

Marzi went to the other side of the still-blocked door and cleared those shelves away. More buildings, marching off to the vanishing point, painted in perspective. She moved on to the middle, took a breath, and moved the boards away.

She stood back and looked at the whole wall. The door was still there, tarnished brass knob and all—she'd been careful not to touch that knob when clearing the shelves away, careful without acknowledging the reason for her care. The middle of the mural depicted the street itself, a dusty stretch lined by buildings. She'd expected to see a shadowy figure painted at the end of the street, a man in a hat and a long duster, but the street was empty. Otherwise, it was perfectly familiar, the land just beyond the Western Door, which she'd drawn so many times. Marzi was profoundly shaken—she didn't remember the mural looking like this at *all.* She'd take her last picture, and get out of here, and then seriously consider getting professional help. Again.

Marzi stepped back and lifted the camera, peering through

the viewfinder. Her finger depressed the button, and the shutter clicked, obscuring Marzi's view for a fraction of a second.

When the shutter opened, the painting had changed.

Now a shadowy man stood at the far end of the street, visible through the viewfinder. A blob of mold obscured his face.

Marzi gasped and dropped the camera to the floorboards.

When she looked at the wall with her own eyes, the man was gone. She picked up the camera, which seemed undamaged by the fall, and almost put it to her face again. But no. She didn't want to see if the figure came back. Nor would she look at the developed photographs, if she could avoid doing so. She didn't want to know if the figure appeared in them.

Without putting the boards back, unwilling to stay in the room a moment longer, she reached behind her and opened the door to the kitchen. She backed out of the room, never taking her eyes off the rear wall. Once outside, she flipped the light off quickly, and then slammed the door.

Marzi leaned her forehead against the cool wood and breathed deeply. She would have to go back in eventually, she knew—it was imperative that she nail boards over the door— but she couldn't face it again, not so soon.

She headed outside to get some fresh air before her shift started.

LINDSAY WAS DEEP in her canvas, slashing color across the upper third of the painting, when Alice came in. This painting was a cadmium-and-cobalt scream of primal defiance, a repudiation of the dark that seemed sometimes to be pressing in from all sides, an act of violence committed against her own growing melancholy.

Then the source of her melancholy appeared. Alice walked in, her chunky motorcycle boots clomping against the floor. She looked shy and out of her element among the covered canvases, the neat workbenches, the jars of turpentine and soaking brushes. But beautiful, too, her strong features, cropped hair, slim body in a leather jacket, plain white shirt, black leather pants, a little silver charm of a gorgon's head hanging on a green thread around her neck. She'd ridden with a lesbian biker gang called The Gorgons for a while. Lindsay loved those stories, loved hearing Alice recount her vivid history. Lindsay put her brush and palette down and smiled. She wanted it to be a dazzling melt-her smile, but couldn't manage it; the look on Alice's face was so odd, confused and determined all at once.

"Hi, tall, dark, and handsome," Lindsay said, wishing she'd held on to her brush so she'd have something to do with her hands. Her voice was too loud in the quiet studio.

Alice stopped, a little too far away even for a conversation between strangers, much too far to stand from a lover, and the distance made Lindsay ache.

"Lindsay," Alice said, her voice wavering. "I'm really sorry about last night." Alice Belle, uncertain—it was as wrong as a fish flopping on the salt flats, incongruous as a cursing monk.

"It's okay. Stuff comes up." A beat, a twisting moment. "What came up?"

Alice looked around, found a stool, pulled it over, and sat. She slumped, seemingly exhausted, and Lindsay noticed the bags under her eyes, like faint smears of ash, like war paint for a dispirited brave. "I wanted to talk to you about that. I'm . . . did Marzi tell you she saw me, that we talked?"

"She mentioned it, but she didn't say much, just that you had a lot on your mind." *Like I'm too young,* Lindsay thought. *Too femme, too perky, I try too hard, I'm bad in bed. . . .* Which of those? Something else? Would Alice lie, try to spare her feelings; would Lindsay know it for a lie?

"I told Marzi I'm afraid of becoming a pyromaniac," Alice said, and *that* was unexpected. Lindsay was flummoxed, then abashed at her own self-absorption, and, finally, confused and alarmed.

"What?" Lindsay said.

Alice shrugged. "I think I'm going crazy, is all. I've always liked fire, but lately it's been more than that. These past couple of days I've thought about *starting* fires. That's why I didn't go out with you last night. I went riding, tried to clear my head, and . . . it doesn't make sense . . . but once I got a few miles away from town, I felt better. I felt like myself again, not some crazy firebug. So I came back, and it started to happen again, that *urge,* like there's a huge speaker downtown blaring the word 'Burn' over and over, a thousand decibels, and as I get closer it gets louder and louder until I can't hear anything else, it fills up my head . . ." Alice, amazingly, was crying, tears spilling from the corners of her eyes, and Lindsay went to her without thinking and held her, wrapped her arms around Alice's body. She was so much smaller than she seemed.

Alice was so stiff, it was like hugging a light pole, but then she relaxed suddenly, stood up from the stool, and embraced Lindsay fiercely. "I'm so *scared,*" Alice said. "I'm so scared of *me,*" and Lindsay couldn't think of anything to say to that, could only think of Marzi's brief breakdown, when the sight of a closed door was enough to make her weep uncontrollably. Both Marzi and Alice were *strong*—Lindsay would have bet her eyes they were stronger than she—and yet they'd both broken in such peculiar ways.

"Alice, it'll be okay, we'll work it out," but Alice pulled away, shook her head.

"No," Alice said. "What, I'll go to therapy, they'll say my mom and dad hurt me, which they did, and that's why I want to start fires? But it's *not*, not now. This is coming from *outside*, and I know that's crazy, that thinking it makes me even crazier, but I believe it's true."

It did sound crazy—paranoid, specifically. But how could she say that, especially when Alice acknowledged it herself? How could Lindsay help?

Alice said, "Something wants me to burn down Genius Loci, the coffeehouse. I dream about it, I daydream about it, I almost *plan*—oily rags, gas cans, smoke and flames belching out the windows, the roof lifting off like a rocket, Lindsay." Alice's eyes were bright, glassy; Lindsay realized that talking about this *excited* Alice, even as it disturbed her. "And I see something beautiful, rising from the flames—a phoenix, a dark angel made of fire, with a beautiful face and snakes made of smoke for hair, a goddess of fire, cleansing, taking everything down to ash and the end, a goddess with supernova eyes—" and then Alice grimaced and shook her head. "Shit," she said. "You see? I'm almost talking myself into it. You see?"

"I see," Lindsay said, willing herself not to step away. She touched Alice's hand. "Don't hurt yourself, baby."

"What I don't get is how specific it is," Alice said, scowling. "It began as a vague thing, you know? I wanted to fire-dance more, then I wanted to play with open flames, but then for the past couple of days it's been so strong, and it's this one particular place I want to burn. What's so special about a coffee shop?"

Lindsay shrugged helplessly, strange connections knitting together in her mind. Jane had tried to break into Genius Loci, howling about an imprisoned goddess, and Beej had calmly pledged fealty to an earthquake god while *he* tried to break in, and now Alice had visions of a phoenix-gorgon-goddess—Why? Why were all these people drawn to this ordinary place? Lindsay had an open-door policy when it came to strange ideas, and she'd dabbled in tarot, Eastern healing practices, numerology, astrology, and various forms of divination, but nothing really *stuck*, and she had no strong attachment to any particular mystical system—but surely this mass obsession with Genius Loci meant *something*.

"So I'm going away," Alice said, almost but not quite too softly to hear, and Lindsay blinked at her, then shook her head and said, "Oh, no," unable to summon any laughter or offhandedness, none of her many protections coming easily to hand. She had no illusions about forever or eternal love with Alice, but they'd just *begun;* there was so far yet to go before the end, and now it was over?

"I feel better when I'm farther away," Alice said. "Please understand, it's even hard to be here, this close. I don't trust myself, and that's terrible. I hate this feeling, but I had to say good-bye to you. I had to see you before I left."

"Alice," Lindsay said, and nothing else; there seemed to

be no words. Protests were futile, and what could she say? So "Alice" again, and Lindsay kissed her lover's eyelids, her forehead, her lips. They shared a hungry kiss and an embrace, and there was heat; so much heat.

Alice broke away, and smiled shyly, that unlikely smile she had. "Maybe—" she began, then stopped and shrugged.

Lindsay nodded, understanding, her lips still warm from Alice's. "I know. Maybe."

Short-trigger Man

WHEN MARZI GAVE him the camera, Jonathan said, "Thanks again." He looked down at the camera and said, "Oh, there's only one picture left. Smile." Before Marzi could protest, he snapped a picture of her.

"I bet my eyes are half closed and I look like a pug dog," she said.

"I'm sure you're very photogenic."

She snorted.

"I'm going to get these developed," Jonathan said. "I'll see you later." He went down the steps quickly, al-most skipping. It was nice to see him excited. She suspected it wasn't a side of him that most people saw, and she felt privileged to glimpse it.

Hendrix was gone for the night, and the only other person working was Pouty Peter, who had long bleached-blond bangs and almost never talked—he was nice enough, she supposed, but uncommunicative to the point of pathology. The café was dead empty, only two or three customers who were in for the long haul with their laptops, books, and magazines; most of the student clientele had fled for the summer, and everyone else apparently had better things to do with the evening than hang around here. Pouty Peter sat on a chair near the refrigerated drink case, reading a book written in German, sipping intermittently on a Red Bull. Marzi tried to think of some manager-type stuff to tell him to do, but really there was nothing. It had been a slow day, too, apparently, and everything was as neat as it ever got, except for the stuff they would clean up after closing.

The first hour was uneventful. Marzi served exactly one beer, and spent the rest of the time reading, until she finished *The Wood Wife*—there were desert spirits in that book, but they were different from the one she had to contend with. Then she doodled in a notebook, sitting on a stool behind the counter, keeping an eye on things, though there wasn't much to keep an eye on—Beej behind bars, Jane scared away or no longer interested or maybe busy being crazy someplace else, Denis no doubt humiliated down to the soles of his boots. A boring night like a thousand others, but not since last summer had it been *this* quiet, and Marzi had forgotten what it was like. It took some effort to get her mind down to the proper cruising speed.

Around seven, Pouty Peter said, "Shit, do you hear that?"

Marzi cocked her head, but didn't hear anything except someone faintly tapping on a laptop in the Teatime Room. There wasn't even music playing; the last CD had stopped, and she hadn't even noticed. "No, what?"

"It's like . . . I dunno . . . a black buzz. Bees or flies or a fan that's almost broken . . ." This was more than Marzi had ever heard Peter say at one time, and it wasn't proving him a lucid or interesting conversationalist. "Almost like it's words, but I can't quite make it out . . ." He looked bothered; more than that, *spooked*. "Maybe it's just somebody listening to head-phones, or something playing down the street."

"Maybe," Marzi said. "You've got better ears than me, I guess." She listened—after all the strange things she'd been through lately, she couldn't dismiss *anything* out of hand—but still didn't hear anything.

Peter stood up. "Look, I don't feel so well, do you think I can take off? I know you'd be here all alone, but—"

Marzi waved her hand. "I'm going to close early anyway. Go on." She'd been thinking about sending him home for a while anyway. It was that kind of night. She couldn't imagine there being a rush here that she couldn't handle by herself.

Peter gathered his things. "If you get super busy, call me on my cell, I'll just be at home." He lived in a shared house not far from the café.

"Sure, don't worry about it."

Then Marzi was alone, bored, listening to the nothing-at-all noises, certainly no black buzzing. She wished Jonathan would come back, even though he would want to show her the pictures; she wished Lindsay would come in, smelling of bubble gum and vanilla, bringing some radiance with her.

All at once, the handful of people in the café stood up, rat-tling their chairs, stuffing books into bags, closing laptops with snaps. Marzi frowned, wondering at the synchronicity, coming around the counter to glance into the other rooms. Everyone was leaving, looking suddenly worried or furtive or curiously Buddha-blank-faced. They all left without a word, even though a couple of them were regulars with whom

Marzi ordinarily exchanged greetings. "Hey, guys, where's the fire?" she said as they left, but no one spoke, or even glanced back; they didn't hurry, just left as if they'd remembered someplace else they urgently needed to be.

Marzi thought of animals spooking before an earthquake. People said the animals always knew first, felt the vibrations before they even happened, that the animals *knew*, without even knowing what it was they knew. So why didn't she feel anything?

"Shit," Marzi said aloud, mostly just to hear herself speak. It didn't help, and in fact seemed inappropriate, like cursing in the ruins of a possibly haunted church. Marzi considered putting on some music, really blasting something up-tempo, but couldn't quite bring herself to do so. What if there were something she needed to hear? Something like Pouty Peter's black buzz, or whatever made the customers leave?

The Fiesta-plate clock ticked loudly. Marzi shivered, hugging herself. Had the temperature in the room suddenly dropped, or was that her imagination? She thought of shutting the front doors to block the breeze, if there was a breeze, but it would also make it harder to run away, if . . .

If what? She was being ridiculous. She was—

Something flickered in the front window, the big one that looked over Ash Street. It was a flash of light, an incomplete reflection. Marzi frowned, coming around the counter, squinting. It looked like someone was trying to project film on the window, which wouldn't work, of course, not really, since the window was transparent. But the darkness beyond the window and the dirt on the glass allowed hints of dancing light and shadow to briefly resolve. Marzi turned and looked behind her, and of course there was nothing, no dancing beam of light, no projector. It was just something outside, the reflection of a reflection of headlights, maybe, or—

We should talk, a voice said, emanating from nothing, from the walls, from the blackness of the spaces between Garamond Ray's painted stars. *Chew the fat.* The voice was gravelly, and underlaid by a faint hiss, as if it were a severely degraded soundtrack.

Marzi spun around, looking behind her, toward the Desert Room beyond the kitchen, but no one was there. She looked back toward the window, where the flickering on the glass was more obvious now, more substantial, as if something were gathering substance from the air.

"Who am I talking to?" she said, amazed at how calmly the question emerged. She thought, *What would Rangergirl do?* It didn't seem at all like a foolish question. *She would be brave,* Marzi thought. She wondered if she could manage that.

I don't have a name. I come from a time before names, a place without them. You're the one who names things. The voice was more substantial now, too, and seemed to emanate from that thickening patch of air, a space above the couch where the light seemed to stick together and swell. *You could never decide what to name me. You call me lots of things.*

"The Outlaw," Marzi said. "You're telling me you're a character from my comic book?"

"A character from your comic book is *me,* more like," it said, and now the voice was no vague emanation; it came from right in front of her, a rough, human voice. The curling whiteness—the glare of light reflected off a window, but with edges—was taking on a roughly human shape, two tendrils spinning down into legs, a widening torso, arms, something like a misshapen head.

Marzi retreated behind the counter. "You can't get out," she said, her jaw tight. "You're *behind* me."

"I'm *not* out. Not that I can't *get* out—you can't fence me in—but I'm not out yet. This is nothin' but pretty lights on a screen. I've been hammerin' on that old door, darlin', and I've managed to open it a crack, to reach out a little, and touch the world. But this?" It stepped forward, having feet to step with, now, looking like a white man-shaped balloon, featureless, but the head was all wrong, lumpy, strange. "This is nothin'. I just thought we should have a powwow, is all, sit down and talk man-to-man. Or what have you. I'm not a man, and neither are you, but I don't care overmuch about the particulars."

"Why are you talking like that? Like some B-movie cowboy?" Marzi wasn't afraid, exactly—it was almost too surreal to be terrifying. Or else, on some level, she'd been prepared for this, expecting it.

"It's not up to me, how I talk. I don't talk at all, given my druthers, but you make me want to ramble on. I'm callin' you out, but you're the one who chooses the time and place and weapons."

"I don't understand you."

Improbably, the thing spat, turning its lumpy head and spewing a neat stream of whiteness that disappeared before it hit the floor. "No. I reckon not. Listen, I'll make you a deal. You've got until sunup to get out of town, free and clear, and no one will follow you. There's no shame in walking away from a fight you can't win."

What would Rangergirl do? Well. That was easy, now. "I'm not walking away from anything. Besides, last time I checked, you were still locked up. What are you going to do to me? I guess you're the one who's been pushing Beej, and Jane, huh, making them do things?"

"Nobody makes anybody do anything. I just help them do what they want to do anyway. They're just getting in good with the winning side. But yeah, they're my gang, even if they don't know that, exactly."

"Well, Beej is *locked up,* just like you, and Jane is gone. Not to mention crazy. And I'm here, and I'm going to keep you in. Tomorrow I'm coming back with boards, and I'm nailing your door shut, and that's going to be the end of it."

The thing laughed, cruel and mocking. It reached up, lifted the top of its head away, and rubbed its arm across its forehead.

Marzi burst out laughing, and the thing's own laughter suddenly stopped. "What's funny, missy?"

"Is that thing supposed to be a *hat*? That big lumpy thing on your head, that's supposed to be a *cowboy hat*?"

"There's no call to insult my hat," it said in a wounded tone, and suddenly Marzi wasn't in the middle of a dramatic movie anymore, she was in a comedy, something like *Blazing Saddles,* maybe, and the thing before her didn't seem dangerous at all, just foolish, a nothing dressed up in a cowboy's clothes, nothing to be afraid of at all.

"Oh, go to hell," Marzi said. "Screw you and the nag you rode in on."

The thing diminished, slumping on one side like a punctured beach ball, and began to dissolve, the light that made up its body dispersing, giving way to everyday shadows. "You have until sunup, missy. If you're still here tomorrow it won't go easy on you. I'll see to that. I've killed your kind before. You're not the first one to guard my door." It sank to its knees, which came apart underneath it, and its ludicrous lump-hat lost what feeble definition it had.

"We'll see about that," Marzi said, feeling boisterous, watching the light-puppet come apart. "You've never had to fight me before. There's a new sheriff in town." She leaned on the counter, and added, as an afterthought, "Bitch."

The thing came apart completely, and then there was nothing.

Maybe that wasn't exactly how Rangergirl would've handled it, but Marzi thought she'd done pretty well, all things considered.

She turned away and saw someone coming up the steps, slowly, and it took her a moment to realize it was Lindsay, because Lindsay didn't shuffle, she didn't plod; even when she was exhausted from being up for a night and a day working or partying, she didn't walk like this. She came into the café, and there were tears on her face. "Oh, Marzi," she said. "Alice left. She left town. She's gone."

Conversation Fluid

DENIS HAD SPENT the past day trying to find a replacement coffeehouse, to fill the hole in his routine left when he'd been banned from Genius Loci. He'd tried Javha House, but there were actual *pigeons* roosting in the rafters there, which was too disgusting to contemplate, and he'd tried the Marigold Café, but the noise of a nearby jack-hammer had made concentration impossible. Now Whooping Coffee, the café of last resort, was also proving untenable. There was a primitive dance stu-dio in the back of the building, full of mostly unattractive people con-torting and leaping about ridiculously, pre-sumably at least in part for the enjoyment of the café patrons, who seemed, by and large, fascinated by the goings-on. Denis could not, of course, work in such an environment, and being re-minded of the primitive movement in *any* art form was enough to annoy him. He hated primitives; prac-titioners of such art were determined to recapture a nonexistent state of innocence, and in the pursuit of that spurious goal, they threw away everything a thousand generations of artists had learned about perspective, straight lines, linearity, self-referentiality, irony, postmodernism, all the artistic virtues that Denis held dear. Had he lived in the dimness of prehistory, he would not have been content with scratching pictures of elk and bison onto cave walls through some misplaced trust in sympathetic magic. Indeed, he would have been moved to do something not yet recognizable as art under those circumstances, like the formulation of mathematics and geometry, perhaps. He would not be at home among primitive, mud-streaked . . .

Denis put down his coffee cup with a gently shaking hand. He looked around the café, which was, naturally, decorated with primitive art, from ugly wooden masks to reproductions of cave paintings to "modern primitives," the refuge of the artless would-be artist. There were pictures of women, those huge-breasted, wide-hipped, ant-headed über-mothers, and while none of them looked a bit like Jane, the association was there nevertheless. Jane had become something different, fundamentally—he'd known that, but now the nature of that change was more obvious to him. She was no longer capable of artifice. She had become a basic—a *direct*—creature. A modern primitive, violent, straightforward, mud-smeared.

Denis found it terrifying. Jane was now his very antithesis, and he had no idea where she was. Perhaps she was trying to break into Genius Loci now; perhaps she had gone to make love to a landslide; perhaps she was waiting in his apartment, having puzzled out the truth about what had happened to her, about what Denis had done, or failed to do. The old Jane, the Jane he'd dated, would have reacted in a certain way to improper actions on his part: She would have left, not talked to him for a while, stewed in her own juices, and become increasingly frustrated, all actions that didn't interfere with Denis's life in the slightest. But this new Jane . . . who knew what she might do? She wasn't the woman he'd known. She was a monster, and there was no telling what action she might take next.

Denis found such unpredictability profoundly unsettling.

He rose from his chair and gathered his things, leaving the noise of thrumming drumbeats and bare feet slapping against the studio floor, walking out the door toward his car. What if he went home, and Jane was there? What then?

He had to get rid of her. It was as simple as that. Her very existence would weigh on his mind, make him paranoid, diminish his enjoyment of life. But how could he hurt her, when she was made of mud, when he'd killed her once already? Exorcisms and the like seemed absurd to Denis, but perhaps he should look into them. After all, ghost-animated mud-dolls seemed absurd, too. Getting rid of Jane, *really* rid of her, was the only way he could think to restore normalcy. And he would do whatever proved necessary to achieve that end. Without his routines, he would lose his mind, and in madness, his dreams of the machine that grinds would cease to be terrible, and would instead become a portent of some final solution.

"So what I want to do is get drunk," Lindsay said, once she stopped crying—just sat up, wiped her eyes with her sleeves, and looked at Marzi earnestly, her eyes mascara-streaked. "Will you kindly be my enabler, barkeep?"

"Lindsay, sweets, are you sure you want to get wasted? How about we . . ." What? "Eat ice cream or something," she said finally. "I guess we're not culturally programmed with a lot of options, are we? We could talk about it, though."

"Sweet lady liquor will loosen my tongue, Marzipan." She sat back on the couch under the window, disappearing a little into its voluminous cushions, looking very small. "I just don't want to think about it right now. I had this idea, this mental picture, of what the summer would be like, and Alice was a big part of that, bigger than I realized. I keep thinking about the way she's gone, the hole that leaves in my under-standing of things, it's like hamster wheels spinning away in my brain . . . so I want to get drunk, and not think about it. Sometimes, if you repress enough, if you distract yourself enough, you can get so far ahead of the curve of grief that you never have to deal with it at all."

"That's a healthy attitude," Marzi said.

"Fuck healthy," Lindsay said softly. "Just be my friend, okay?"

Marzi nodded. "All right. But I'm going to make sure you drink lots of water, too."

Lindsay took a twenty-dollar bill from her purse and handed it over. "Then beer me, dearie, and keep 'em coming until the money runs out. I have to go to the powder room." Lindsay rose from the couch with none of her usual pixielike grace and walked through the Ocean Room to the tiny bath-room.

Marzi got up and drew a beer, wondering what had hap-pened between Lindsay and Alice. There hadn't been a lot of narrative sequence in Lindsay's initial outpouring, just that Alice was leaving town on seriously short notice. It wasn't as if they'd been involved for long—as far as Marzi knew, they'd only started flirting about three weeks ago—but with Lindsay, in this case, it was clearly more about missed chances and sudden disruptions than anything else. And maybe Lindsay had been prepared to give more of her heart than she usually did. Most people only got to enjoy the surface glitter of Lindsay's personality, but Alice had touched something deeper in her, Alice with her quiet kindness, her true attention. Sure, it was hard for Lindsay. Sure, getting drunk wouldn't ultimately help much. Sure, she would do it anyway.

"Hi, Marzi," Jonathan said, appearing in the doorway, dressed all in black as usual. He looked as mournful, in his way, as Lindsay. "The pictures you took didn't turn out. They're overexposed." He sat down in the ragged armchair beside the couch and put his feet up on the battered coffee table, right where the cowboy made of light had stood earlier. Marzi sat on one end of the couch, close enough for their knees to touch, almost.

Shit. All that effort for nothing. Well, not for *nothing*—she'd needed to go back into the Desert Room anyway, but . . . "Did I do something wrong? I knew that camera was too much for me."

"No, it wasn't you. The guy at the photo lab said it looked like the film had been exposed to the sun, but that doesn't make sense. Even if it had been exposed, that would have ruined the whole roll. I'd taken a few pictures before I gave you the camera, and they all turned out fine." He reached into his pocket and took out an envelope, fanning several photographs onto the table—pictures of beaches, pelicans, seals, surfers, sunsets. "And there's the picture I took of you, the last one on the roll." Jonathan pulled that picture from beneath the others. Marzi thought she looked like a startled rabbit in the picture, but at least she didn't have visible pimples or closed eyes. "It's just the pictures you took for me in the Desert Room that didn't come out. You can see it on the negative, they're just *wiped*."

"So it *is* my fault. I have the black thumb of photography." That had to be it, right?

"No, I don't think so. It's some kind of equipment malfunction. You didn't leave the lens cap on or anything—the *film* was ruined. I'm beginning to think the universe doesn't want me to see this room."

An equipment malfunction. Film that had never been shown to the sun, nevertheless exposed. Did it qualify as objective proof of the supernatural? The light-cowboy was flamboyant, sure, and pretty dramatic, but it was also wholly uncorroborated, and could have been nothing but an apparition from the depths of her diseased mind. That exposed film, though . . . that wasn't just inside her head. That must mean something, right? What if the Outlaw, the thing behind the door—what if it was real? Then the Outlaw was the cause of her mental breakdown, not a symptom of it, and taking refuge in the notion of her own madness was just ducking her responsibility. Not at *all* what Rangergirl would do.

Jonathan sighed. "You know, meeting you aside, the past few days have royally sucked. Mud, fistfights, and frustration." He rubbed his eyes. "I'm not sleeping well, either. I get insomnia a lot anyway, but it's been especially bad lately. I don't think I'm used to the Pigeonhole yet. The acoustics in there are really strange. I hear distant voices all night long, coming up from the street, I guess. But I've been so excited about the work, and the murals, that I didn't mind. But now this happens, and I *still* can't see all the murals." He shook his head.

"It's just one room, right?" Marzi said. "You've got the other murals; they're good examples of Garamond Ray's work. Isn't that enough?"

"Yeah," he said. "Sure. They have to be enough. I just hate that I'm so *close* to this other major work, and I can't even *see* it. It gets to me." He looked up at her. "I don't suppose . . . Hendrix isn't here, nobody's here, nobody'd know if I went into the Desert Room and looked around, right? Could I?"

Marzi exhaled heavily. "Jonathan, please don't put me in this position." There was no way she'd let him go into that room, harmless as it had seemed while she was there. It was so *close* to bad things, it was thin ice, and who knew what might happen? She was the guardian, for whatever reason, like it or not, and she couldn't let Jonathan in. She hadn't even covered up the door again when she left, so it would be right there in plain sight. . . . "I stepped through a rotten board when I went in there this afternoon. I covered it up with an old piece of wood so Hendrix wouldn't notice and flip out, but it's just too dangerous. If you got hurt, and we had to call an ambulance . . . Hendrix already had to get out of bed to come here the other night because of Jane and Beej and Denis. I don't want to wake him up again."

Jonathan raised his hands. "Fine, sorry, I shouldn't have asked."

"Sure," she said, a little stiffly, feeling bad about the lie, but what else could she do? "It's okay. It must be driving you crazy."

"You'll have to give me a good description of the room, at least, so I have something, an eyewitness account. Maybe it'll give the story a little drama—the lost room of Garamond Ray."

I wish it were a "lost room," Marzi thought, and said, "Absolutely."

Lindsay came out of the bathroom, makeup washed away from her eyes, lending her an oddly vulnerable look. She nodded to Jonathan. "Did you tell him?" she asked.

"No, babe. I figured you'd want to."

Lindsay came over, dropped onto the couch, and addressed Jonathan. "I've been jilted by my lover. Well, maybe not jilted, maybe it's worse because it's not even really about me, I'm not that important, but anyway, she left. She had good reasons, and I'm being childish and unfair, but I don't care, she *left*, and I'm sad, and I'm going to drink, drink, and keep on drinking. Will you comfort me?"

"Of course," Jonathan said.

Lindsay smiled at Marzi. "You're a comfort. You're both comforts."

"I'll get a couple more beers," Marzi said, because what else could she do? They would get each other through the night, in whatever way possible. If she told them she was the only thing standing between Santa Cruz and an otherworldly force of destruction, they'd call up the hospital and get her some help, with the best of intentions. She had to carry this herself. The Lone Ranger.

Marzi poured herself a beer.

THREE HOURS AND many pints of beer later, Marzi finally shut the front doors of the café and turned off the neon sign in the window. There had been no other customers, as if whatever effect had driven them out earlier still lingered, like the smoke from citronella candles keeping mosquitoes away. Lindsay and Jonathan were apparently immune, but they both had other things on their minds, after all. Marzi was the soberest of the three, if only because she'd felt some sense of duty to her job, and had limited herself to two beers. It wouldn't be right to get sloshed when she was the only employee here. The three of them had talked about many things, distracting themselves from their troubles, and now they sat together on the floor, feet spread out before them, half-empty pints sitting between their legs.

"What it is, is women," Lindsay said.

Jonathan raised his glass.

"I love women." She looked at Jonathan, blinking. "I like boys, too. I do. I'm flexible. But women." She gestured vaguely, perhaps making an hourglass shape in the air, perhaps intending something less obvious. "I love them. But they're rough. I'm one, I don't understand it. Confusing. How do you do it, huh? You, Jonathan, how?"

"You muddle through," Jonathan said.

"Mmm," Lindsay said meditatively, as if considering what he meant. "Alice, did I tell you why she left?"

"No, you didn't say," Marzi said.

"This place." Lindsay gestured at the walls and the ceiling. "She said she wanted to burn it down."

Marzi sat up straighter, and cleared her throat, and said, "Ah. Why did she want to do that?"

Lindsay corkscrewed her finger around her temple. "She said it was an *urge*. That she was turning into a pyromaniac. She didn't want to be a pyro, so she left. Said it was easier to resist, when she was far away."

"Huh," Jonathan said. "That's bad. But better than if she'd stayed, and done it, right?"

"I told her, I said, get professional help. Right? That's what you do, when you get crazy thoughts, you can't keep them down. Right, Marzi? Right?"

"Yes," Marzi said. "I guess so." She hoped Lindsay wouldn't bring up the fact that Marzi had been the recipient of professional help once; she didn't want to deal with that, with Jonathan's questions or even his speculative glance. She was busy thinking about Alice. Alice had told Marzi she was becoming more obsessed with fire, but she hadn't said anything about arson fantasies centering around Genius Loci. "So Alice just wanted to burn stuff, anything, or was it this place in particular?"

"Oh, this place." Lindsay held up her beer, sniffed at the glass, made a sour face, and put it back down again. "She dreamed about it. Daydreams, night dreams, that if she burned this place down, an angel or a phoenix or something would rise from the ashes. To cleanse the world. Which I thought was funny, on account of Beej and Jane and what they were talking about."

"The earthquake god, and the goddess," Jonathan said. "Mass delusions. Is three a mass?"

"Maybe it's ley lines," Lindsay said. She gestured again, making her hands vaguely perpendicular to one another. "Lines of converging force. Or because we're close to a fault line."

"Maybe it's the paintings," Jonathan said. He stretched out on his back, hands on his chest, and stared up at the ceiling.

Marzi swallowed and looked around, at the deep blacks of the Space Room, the dim blues in the darkened Ocean

Room, the peacefully monstrous faces of the gods in the Teatime Room. The paintings. Was it the paintings? Did the thing behind the door have something to do with Garamond Ray? He had worked here, in this building, for a long time, and he had disappeared right after—maybe even during—the big quake in '89. But how did he fit in? How did *anything* fit in? The thing behind the door had tried to recruit Alice to its cause, it seemed, and Marzi hadn't even realized it.

Marzi was so far out of her depth, she couldn't even see land.

"Hey. Whatsit," Jonathan said.

"Hmm?" Marzi said.

Jonathan stretched out his arm and pointed at the ceiling. "That. Square bit in the ceiling. What's it?"

"That's the door to the attic," Marzi said. "Your apartment, the Pigeonhole, used to be part of the attic."

"Huh," he said. "I never noticed it."

"Well, there's a *carpet* up there," Lindsay said, rolling her eyes. "The trapdoor is under the carpet."

"It's nailed shut, anyway," Marzi said. "Hasn't been used for years and years."

"Huh," Jonathan said.

Marzi roused herself. "Okay, kids. This has been fun, but I want to clean up, close up, and go to bed." She hesitated before the lie. "I'd invite you guys over, but I've got a headache, and I want to get some sleep."

"You've been hospitable," Lindsay said. "More than that. No problem. I want to sleep in my own lonely bed and mope anyway."

"You okay, Linds?" Marzi said. "Want me to walk you home?"

"Nah," she said. "I'm made of iron. I'm unstoppable." She stood up, and Jonathan rose to his feet as well. They said their farewells and left, Lindsay walking steadily, carefully down the street, Jonathan tromping up the stairs outside to the Pigeonhole, head hung low. He looked flat-out exhausted.

Tomorrow Marzi would find some boards to nail over the door in the Desert Room. That was a priority. That would give her some peace of mind. Maybe she should just do it now . . . But it could wait. Going in there this afternoon had been traumatic enough—she didn't think she could stand another foray into the Desert Room tonight. She'd get up early in the morning, come over before Hendrix opened up the café, and do it then.

Marzi went about her cleaning-up chores, wondering if the cowboy made of light would reappear, what she'd do if he did. He was simultaneously absurd and threatening, a manitou with a taste for singing cowboy movies. That taste had, apparently, affected her, made her write a Western comic, given her a small obsession . . . she paused in the act of cleaning the espresso machine. But she'd *always* liked Westerns. She'd read about Calamity Jane and Wild Bill Hickok when she was a little girl, read Louis L'Amour and Zane Grey novels by the crateful, watched spaghetti Westerns and John Wayne movies. She'd eventually read a lot about the real history and found even the bloody, dusty truth fascinated her. What had interested her the most, though, was the divide between the *actual* "Wild West" and the public perception of that time, the mythologization of the West, which began way back in the mid-1800s, with dime novels and self-consciously quirky outlaws like "Black Bart" Boles, who left nasty little poems at the scenes of his crimes. Marzi loved the imagined

West, found it fascinating, and always had. That fascination couldn't be laid at the feet of the thing beyond the door. Why would her enemy choose to appear in such a guise, anyway? The dust-and-hardpan associations were obvious, but the West *wasn't* about desolation, not really; quite the opposite. It was about dragging a living out of an unforgiving land. The resemblance between the landscape of the imagined Old West and the world the thing beyond the door wanted to create was only superficial, so why did it appear in such forms? It didn't make sense. But she wasn't capable of figuring it out, not tonight. She had to seal up the door, so she wouldn't have to think about this anymore.

She finished her work and thought, briefly, of going to see if Jonathan was awake. Maybe now was the time for them to talk. But if they did, their conversation would surely turn to darker matters, and Marzi might not be able to resist telling him the truth about the Desert Room, and what lived beyond it. Their relationship was new, and she didn't want to spoil that by making him think she was insane. She would deal with the door tomorrow, and *then* they could talk, when her mind and her conscience were clear.

Marzi walked home, thinking about nails and plywood, trying to believe her problems could be solved with something as simple as a hammer and a few hard swings.

Deadfall

JONATHAN LAY AWAKE in the Pigeonhole, where the day's old heat went to die, listening to the whispering in the corners of the room. Something about this room, the way it was shaped, made it an echo chamber or something—distant, scratchy, indistinct voices, rising and falling in volume, but constant. He might have thought he was going crazy, if not for the fact that he only heard the voices here, in this room.

He'd dozed in and out of consciousness for a few hours, but had woken before dawn from a suffocating, claustrophobic nightmare, and couldn't get back to sleep. Reality wasn't much better than the dream of suffocation; the dimensions of the Pigeonhole had never seemed so stifling. This attic room was tiny, tucked in under the sloping roof, the walls painted eggshell white. The single small window looked out over Ash Street, but there wasn't even a sill, and no place to put a fan. The bed was pushed up under the lowest part of the ceiling, leaving a little space at the end to walk around. The bathroom was slightly more spacious than an airplane lavatory, and the shower was approximately the size of a telephone booth. No kitchen, no storage except the space under the bed—at least it was cheap, and the location couldn't be beat.

Jonathan lay, naked, considering the dimensions of his new home, his exhaustion a constant thing now but bearable, the better part of his drunkenness seemingly gone—he'd forced himself to drink several glasses of water from the sink before falling into bed. He was afraid to look at the clock and see how many hours were left before first light.

Jonathan thought about getting up and doing some work. If he was going to be awake and sober, he might as well be productive. He hadn't worked in the Pigeonhole yet—it was nicer to go downstairs to the café, though he could easily lose track of time staring at Garamond Ray's paintings. The depth and texture of the murals were extraordinary, far superior to the rest of Ray's work. All the articles about Ray talked about the house in Santa Cruz where he'd painted his last murals, where he'd disappeared during the Loma Prieta quake. His last works were his greatest, everyone agreed, and there had been a few small, bad photographs, enough to pique Jonathan's interest. So he'd come to Santa Cruz, and looked for the cheapest apartment he could find—which was, miraculously, in the same house as Ray's paintings. It was almost enough to make him believe in Fate.

But work seemed like too much trouble now. His thoughts drifted, and focus seemed impossible. He closed his eyes and tried to sleep again, but the darkness pressed in against him, oppressive, and the voices in the corners murmured. He gave up and looked at the digital alarm clock sitting on the chest of drawers: 4:17 A.M.

Groaning, he rolled over in bed, thinking about the past few days, trying—his eternal struggle—to focus on the positive, and not the frightening, the frustrating, or the irritating. He'd gotten into a lot of fights when he was younger, in high school, but he'd never come up against anything like Jane before, someone so off-the-charts crazy. Jonathan had straightened himself out and gone to college, and he didn't like these recent, brief bouts of violence in his life; they brought back bad memories. But there were good things here, too: Lindsay had made him feel welcome, Marzi made him feel all *sorts* of things, he had a lot of new ideas about the thesis, and the murals were better than he'd imagined, from the blood-stained dignity of the gods in the Teatime Room to the leering Harlequin in the Circus Room to the saturated air of the Ocean Room.

Which made him wonder, as he'd been wondering all night, about the Desert Room. Marzi had described it, but only vaguely: a poison yellow sun, swarming scorpions, cartoon cacti. He couldn't *imagine* it, not really, which was why he was an art theorist rather than an artist himself, he supposed. If Marzi had come back with photographs, that would have been good enough to appease his curiosity, but the camera had screwed up somehow, and he had nothing. If only he could *see*! So what if the floorboards were rotting in the Desert Room? He could be careful. It was maddening to have his life's work thwarted by something so trivial.

He sat up, thinking he might go down the street to the

open-all-night Saturn Café and have a steamed milk to make him drowsy, so he could sleep into the later morning, maybe.

"Trapdoor." The word came from the ceiling somewhere, in a dry, spidery voice, more distinct than the usual acoustic ghost voices, and Jonathan jerked his head up in surprise, but there was only darkness there, of course, no one clinging to the place where the wall met the sloping ceiling. Jonathan stepped to the desk and turned on the lamp anyway, peering into the corners. Was it someone shouting down the street, their voice bouncing to him from an odd direction? He looked out the window, but there was no one in sight.

"Trapdoor," Jonathan said, and then looked at the ragged green carpet under his feet. Jonathan didn't have a great sense of spatial relationships, but he knew his room was directly above the main room—the Space Room—downstairs. And the old access to the attic was a trapdoor. He'd noticed that earlier tonight.

Jonathan knelt and peeled the carpet away from the wall. It wasn't even tacked down—it was just a remnant cut to fit, more or less, the strange dimensions of the Pigeonhole. The carpet came up easily in his hands, and he tugged it back from the corner, revealing the scarred wood underneath.

There. A plywood panel set flush into the floor, with a couple of nails driven in, more to hold it in place than to truly secure it. Jonathan went to his bag and rummaged until he found his Swiss army knife. He opened the short blade, slid it under the edge of the plywood, and pushed. The edge of the board popped up, nails barely resisting. The plywood had been cut to size and nailed over the trapdoor, which was now revealed, just a thin board held up by a rusty old spring-and-hinge assembly. Jonathan set the plywood covering aside.

Still kneeling, he pressed experimentally against the trapdoor.

The hinge squealed horribly, making Jonathan wince, but the door moved. It swung down.

Jonathan chewed his lip. He could get down there, now, he knew, take his flashlight and slip into the Desert Room and finally get a look. No one would ever have to know. He could write about the room with authority, but claim his sources were all secondhand. It wasn't so much for the paper, anyway; it was for *him*, for his need to know. The only problem was getting back up to the Pigeonhole afterward. He could wedge something in to keep the trapdoor open, but it was about ten feet from the floor, at least. He could lower himself and drop a few feet without ill effects, but how would he get back up again? There were alarms on the doors and windows, and Jonathan wasn't James Bond enough to confidently disconnect them, so he couldn't just walk outside and go back up the stairs to his room. Maybe he could make a rope of his clothes . . . He shook his head. Yeah. That would work, because this was a bad movie, right? Jesus. Better to just forget it.

"The side door," the spider voice on the ceiling whispered, and this time Jonathan stood up and said, "What the *fuck*?" The voice was too distinct, too *close*. But he remembered, now: There was a door in the Teatime Room, blocked off by tables, and it opened onto the space underneath the stairs that led to the Pigeonhole. Maybe that door wasn't connected to the alarm. He couldn't remember if there were wires on it or not. Maybe not—it clearly wasn't in regular use, there was a table in front of it, so maybe no one had thought to attach it to the alarms. It was probably locked, but it could be unlocked from the inside, and he could slip out that way, couldn't he? And if that didn't work, he could always just *leave*, alarm be damned. He wasn't planning to steal anything, and he could be back in his room long before the cops arrived.

He got dressed slowly. He was really going to do this. Drop *Mission: Impossible*–style through the ceiling, take a look around, and get out. The flashlight would help at first, but he'd be able to turn on the light in the Desert Room, since there were no windows there to reveal his activities to potential witnesses outside. Jonathan slipped his little flashlight into his pocket, then sat on the floor, on the edge of the trapdoor. He pushed open the trap with his feet and began to lower himself down.

The spring-loaded trapdoor pushed against his back, trying to close. Jonathan felt as if he were in the jaws of a particularly weak mousetrap. He held on to the edge of the trapdoor and eased himself down, like lowering himself from a pull-up. The trapdoor, still trying to close, scraped up his shoulders, his neck, and along the back of his head, all rather painfully. Then Jonathan was past it, his head clear—and the trapdoor, no longer held open by his body, whipped closed, its edge slamming brutally against his knuckles. "Fuck!" he cried, and let go. He fell, his fingers dragging against the edge of the trapdoor with sharp wet stings of pain. Jonathan dropped a few feet to the floor, which hurt his ankles more than he'd expected, a pair of stabbing agonies shooting through his joints. He crouched and cradled his fingers against his chest, then put each knuckle to his lips, one by one, tasting blood on all of them, feeling the little curled bits of flesh where the skin had been scraped.

So much for *Mission: Impossible*. He stood, shaking his hands against the cool air. There was more light here than he'd expected. The streetlights out front shone through the bay window and glass front doors. He could see well, but people outside might be able to see him, too. Fortunately, there weren't many people out at four-thirty in the morning . . . but early risers would be getting up soon. He should hurry.

Jonathan went into the dark kitchen and turned on the flashlight, a weak beam of light illuminating the mutant sunflowers on the walls. He washed his hands in the sink, hissing as the water hit his scraped knuckles.

Then he turned. There it was. The door to the Desert Room. All he had to do was open it, and step inside.

Jonathan touched the doorknob, almost reverently, and turned it. The door opened smoothly and silently. He didn't shine the flashlight in, because he didn't want to see the room piecemeal. He wanted to see the murals all at once, in full light. He aimed the flashlight at the floor and groped along the wall on either side of the door until he found the light switch. Then, with his hand resting there, he stepped inside and shut the door behind him. He switched off the flashlight and stood for a moment in the total dark, listening to the silence, smelling the mildew.

He flipped on the light, the bare bulb overhead briefly dazzling him, though it was dusty and low-watt. Blinking and squinting, he peered around as his eyes adjusted. The paintings were not the first thing he noticed. The room really *was* filthy and cluttered, and he took in the broken shelves, the monolithic old espresso machine, the jagged pieces of Styrofoam packing material, the sagging floor. He'd have to watch his step. He'd had enough falls for one evening.

Then he looked at the paintings. They were remarkable, despite the blooms of mold. But they weren't at all like Marzi— or the art books, for that matter—had described them. The mural was always described as desert-themed, and while there was desert aplenty here, that wasn't the prevailing motif. Jonathan would have called it the Old West Room, or the Cowboy Room, though there were neither cows nor their keepers in evidence, or any other living things. What of the cacti, the scorpions, the vultures he'd read about? There were none of those.

The murals depicted a ghost town. The storefronts were weathered, signs faded or hanging by one corner, bat-wing doors splashed with blood, windows dusty and broken. A pair of photorealistic snakeskin boots lay in the street near a pile of desiccated horseshit. There were hitching posts with ragged tethers tied to them, the animals they'd secured long since escaped or stolen. Jonathan turned around slowly, noticing more small details. A skull rested on a windowsill, and a wind chime made of fingerbones hung over the general store's porch. The skeleton of a cat lay, paws outstretched, just inches from the skeleton of a rat; that should have been black humor, Tom and Jerry go to Boot Hill, but the bones were so finely detailed, down to the bits of gristle still clinging to the joints, that it was chilling instead. The ground was dust, glittering with flecks of mica. The windows of the sheriff's office were shattered, and through them Jonathan glimpsed the shadowy hulks of medieval torturing equipment: a rack, a wheel, and the smooth curve of an iron maiden. The murals were astonishing, a monstrous reconsideration of the popular conception of the "Wild West," and Jonathan was already composing paragraphs in his mind about Ray's intentions. The room was a masterpiece.

Then he noticed the door on the far wall. Noticed the doorknob, actually, since the door itself looked like part of the painting, a door leading into an unmarked storefront. But the brass knob jutted out into the room, proving its reality. Was it a bit of three-dimensional sculpture, a knob Ray had nailed to the wall in order to make the door look more real? Or *was* it a real door?

"Open it," the spider voice said, and this time Jonathan didn't flinch. He simply stepped forward, enchanted by the notion of opening a door *into* the painting—because that was what seemed likely to happen, what *must* happen. Ray had done his work well, and created the illusion of entrance, suggested that it would be possible for Jonathan—for anyone—to go from observer to participant, to step into the painting itself. It was a masterly stroke, one which Jonathan could explore at length in his paper, and already he was thinking of comparing it to various famous trompe l'oeils—though really, this was the *opposite* of a trompe l'oeil; it wasn't a painting designed to look real, but instead something real designed to look like part of a painting—of talking about Ray's desire to truly engage viewers, to bring them into his work.

Jonathan reached for the polished knob. He expected the brass to be cool, but it was warm, almost pulsing in his hand. He turned the knob easily and tugged open the door, which, once started, seemed to open by itself, as if something on the other side were pushing. Light poured in from the doorway, blinding and searing compared to the dusty bulb overhead, and Jonathan couldn't see anything, couldn't understand what was happening. Then something grabbed him, seized him by one arm and the back of the neck, and dragged him through the door, into the light. Jonathan struggled against the thing that held him, the thing that stank of gunsmoke and dry snakeskin and whiskey and blood. The thing thrust its hand against Jonathan's chest, somehow *into* his chest, dry fingers squeezing his heart, and then it threw him down into the dirt.

A door slammed, and then there was silence, and light, and dry heat.

Jonathan lay still, unable to summon the will to move, or even to close his eyes against the sun. A numbness spread from the places the thing had touched him, radiating out from his heart, robbing him of hope, of strength, of intention; mummifying his will to live. He knew he would never stand up again. He would become a skeleton in the street, part of the painting, rotting in color on the wall. He knew, and he couldn't care.

Then someone picked him up, a man who smelled of tobacco and licorice and whiskey. The man carried Jonathan toward the saloon, with its bloodstained bat-wing doors, and Jonathan didn't even wonder what was happening. The light was already starting to fade.

Grave Patch

THE EARTHQUAKE woke Marzi from a restless sleep. Her dreams were a sinister nonsense montage: cowboys made of fire, drawing plastic cap guns that melted in their hands; wagon trains in which the wagons were somehow alive, but dying, struggling along like starving oxen, ragged bloody holes opening in the canvas; flash floods tearing through the streets of Santa Cruz, clocks and park benches and potted plants bobbling and tumbling in the white rush of water; Marzi painting on the ribs of the sky with a bloodied brush, her one-pigment palette a sucking wound in her own chest. The last dream, the one she woke from, was of a machine like a chrome bulldozer, chewing up the terrain before it, leaving nothing but antiseptic whiteness in its wake.

Marzi leapt out of bed, not even half awake, as the quake hit. The pictures on her walls swayed, creaking. Her lamp fell over, the bulb breaking with a tinkle. The wind chimes in her bedroom window jingled wildly, and her bookshelf gave a little bounce, disgorging its contents onto the floor. Marzi stumbled through the shaking room to the doorway, standing in the threshold, holding on to the doorjamb, blinking her eyes and coming into consciousness. By the time she'd awakened enough to realize what was happening, the quake was over. It wasn't even a very bad one; she'd felt bigger in her time, though any quake you noticed was disconcerting, bringing a brief but profound sense of dislocation.

After setting her upset possessions right again, Marzi sat on her bed and looked at the clock. Almost five A.M. She could sleep, but not for long, not if she wanted to get to the café before Hendrix did, and nail shut the door. Better to get up now; she could sleep more later in the day. She was sort of hungry anyway. Wrapping a robe around herself against the morning chill, she headed for the kitchen.

Her back door was open, showing a slice of sky and the path to the sidewalk. Dawn was creeping into the sky, lending everything an in-between, twilight feel. Marzi stood still, her heart thumping suddenly hard, and listened. Had someone come into her house, or had the door been jounced open by the quake? Normally she locked the door, but she'd been so distracted last night it was possible she'd forgotten. It was also possible someone was in her house, or had been, a burglar she hadn't even noticed.

Marzi didn't hear anything. Her place wasn't that big: her bedroom, the kitchen, the living room, bathroom. There weren't many places for a person to hide. The couch was against the wall, the armchair too spindly to make a good hiding place, and if someone had been crouched under her drawing table, she'd have been able to see them from here.

Marzi swiftly pulled open a drawer, grabbing her butcher knife, and turned with her back to the cabinets. "All right, bastard, come on out," she said. No one answered. Her stomach grumbled loudly.

She sighed. The door must have popped open during the quake, that was all. She closed the door and twisted the deadbolt, then turned back toward the fridge.

Someone was standing in her living room.

Marzi gasped, and then, ridiculously, her stomach growled again. She still had the knife, and she raised it before her, wondering if she could dash for the door, turn the bolt, and get out before this whoever-it-was could reach her. It didn't seem likely.

"Guess who busted out of jail?" the stranger said, voice gravelly. "None of my own boys could break me out, but it turns out they didn't need to. It was an inside job." The stranger stood in shadow, beyond the range of the kitchen light, but its body seemed to shift and ripple, unable to settle on a given shape.

"No," Marzi said, not understanding the particulars, but grasping the essential: The thing behind the door was no longer behind the door. "This is a trick, like in the café."

"Nope. No fool's gold here, sweetness. I'm the real thing, cut loose and walking up and down in the world. Somebody popped my hinges for me." It stepped a little closer to the light. "I'm just here to talk, for now. I don't mind telling you, I'm not strong enough to do much else. Yet."

Marzi held up the knife. "I can take you, then." The words seemed false and hollow, but she had to say something.

The thing laughed, softly. "Oh, darlin'. You're too green

to hurt me. I'm a grizzled old hand, and you're so wet behind the ears your shoulders are damp from the dripping. No, if I thought you could hurt me, I wouldn't be here. I'd be holed up in the hills somewhere. I've been watching you, though, peering out of the keyhole, through the walls. You thought you were so tough. Like it's hard to keep a door closed and locked. You're not the one who *caught* me, and you never will catch me, now that I'm loose again."

"If I'm so green, why are you wasting time with me at all?"

The thing shrugged. The light was touching it a little, now, enough to show cracked leather boots, dark jeans, a leather vest, but its features were still in shadow. "Because you're the law around here. I don't much like the law, not the kind people make. The laws of nature are good enough for me. Things fall apart. Water seeks the lowest level. Everything becomes dust. Those are all the laws the world needs, the only ones I want to obey, but you're here, mucking things up with the way you look at the world, the way you look at *me*. This can go one of three ways. I can kill you, or I can run you out of town on a rail, or you can leave on your own."

Marzi thought about leaving. It was a tantalizing idea, to just throw some things into a bag and buy a bus ticket, get away from doors that opened onto impossible places, away from spectral cowboys and mud-women, away from the madness that had so swiftly overtaken her life. If there were nothing at stake but her own happiness, she wouldn't have hesitated, but yielded, and given this creature his free rein. She'd never asked for such responsibility, after all. But there was more at stake than that. Lindsay lived here—how could Marzi leave her behind, to be terrorized? And if she took

Lindsay with her, did she also have to take Alice Belle? And
what about Jonathan? And even Hendrix, Denis, and Beej—
did they deserve to be swallowed by sands, pecked to pieces
by vultures? And, moreover—this was her *town*. Santa Cruz
had survived disaster in the past, but if she left this time,
pretty soon there'd be nothing left to come back to.

Staying was bad, but leaving would be worse.

"You caused that earthquake," she said.

"Just a little whoop of exultation," it said. "I was happy
when I got out, and I told the world I was back, and rattled a
few windows. It wore me out, too. I'm not strong yet. Been
locked away too long, in the lands beyond the lands, where
the living is easy and everything flows like water. This world
is harder to change, but when you do things here, they're
more permanent." It cocked its head. "Don't you want to
know how I got *out*?"

The thought had crossed her mind. What did he mean, an
inside job? Had Hendrix opened the door? But it had been
closed tonight when she left, she knew it, so—

Shit.

"Jonathan," she said.

"That's the one," the thing said. "He just had to get an
eyeful of the Desert Room, the one Ray painted to lure me in.
Oh, how we wrestled there! We shook the whole damn coast
that day."

Marzi wanted to ask about that. What did this thing have
to do with Garamond Ray? But she was more concerned
about Jonathan. "He broke in?"

"Dropped through the ceiling like an angel from heaven.
Though I had to whisper him down. He sauntered in, had a
look around the Desert Room—which looks a mite different

now, since *you* were there earlier, sweating out changes, exhaling transformations—and when I whispered 'Open the door,' he did it, the idjit. And I flew free. Your own boyfriend set me loose." The thing cocked its head—which seemed to be topped by a vaguely misshapen cowboy hat again—and said, "I never used to gloat. That's just one of the changes you rang in me. I like gloating, but I can see how it might get in the way of more important things."

Marzi was scarcely listening to him. Had Jonathan been hurt? She was more worried about him than pissed off, but if he was okay, she'd get pissed off very quickly. Then again, she didn't know how persuasive the whispering of the thing behind the door—now the thing in her living room—could be. It had, presumably, driven away all her customers last night, perhaps driven Beej mad, or at least helped speed along the process, pushed Jane into a mud-smeared frenzy, maybe even gotten into Alice's head and sent her running for the hills. And Jonathan lived right above the door; he was subject to the thing's whispering constantly. He'd even said something last night about hearing voices, and she hadn't realized what that meant! She was the worst guardian ever.

"But back to my *point*," the thing said. "I'm not really strong enough to kill you yet, and my gang's in bad shape, mostly thanks to you, so the first option's out. Running you out of town on a rail is difficult for the same reasons. So I'm asking you to leave, before I get strong enough to stomp you, which won't take long. I said last night that I'd give you until dawn to get out of town, and that still holds—though dawn's coming up fast, so you'd best saddle up, don't you think?"

"Go fuck a rattlesnake," Marzi said.

"I figured that's what you'd say. Well, the gist of it, anyway.

So." It stepped out of the shadow, into the light. Its face was much as Marzi remembered, though mercifully farther away, not exhaling on her. Its skin was ravaged and lined, more like landforms seen from above than flesh, nose a black mineshaft hole, eyes black circles, smoking slightly. It smiled, and its teeth were wound with barbed wire, its lips shredded and bloody. Marzi steeled herself and showed no reaction. She'd seen worse in horror movies, seen worse in photos of wartime. It was just special effects, meant to scare her, and she wouldn't give it the satisfaction. The thing didn't seem to care, just smiled its bloody-lipped grin. "Turns out there's a fourth option. It's a doozy, too. Your boy, Jonathan—I left him on the other side of the door."

Marzi blinked. "What?"

"It ain't complicated. He opened the door. I drug him in and threw him on the ground. I walked out, and slammed the door behind me. I wasn't the only thing living back there, you know. The lands beyond the lands are *teeming,* and I didn't want nothin' following me out. Besides, I figgered it might come to this, you being pigheaded, me being too tuckered out to take the direct approach, and I thought having your boy on the other side of the door could be useful. There's stuff there that can hurt him, darlin'. Stuff that can eat him alive. You can leave him there, I reckon, while you try to deal with me. Or you can go in and get him. I imagine he could use a cavalry right about now. I touched his heart, and I doubt he's coping at his best."

"What do you mean, you touched his heart?"

"A fella's gotta have his secrets, now. You'll find out, unless you leave him to die. And he will die. Or worse, he might not. Not for a good long time. Think on that."

Marzi sneered, trying to feel brave. "Sure, I go in after him, and the door shuts again, and we're *both* trapped. You'd like that."

"You dumb green sage hen," the thing said mildly. "You can't be locked in there. Just about anybody else can, but not you. You're the *guardian*. You own the door. Oh, if I was still on the other side, and you came in, you'd never get out again, I'd see to that—I'd beat your ass every time you went near the door, just like I did to Garamond Ray. I probably couldn't kill you, not over there, but I could keep you from getting away. Hell, if you had any sense, you wouldn't even try to get out, because then there'd be a chance I'd escape with you, and you'd have to find a way to put a whirlwind in a box again, to bottle a mudslide, and that's a tough job. But without me standing in the way, you can come and go through the door as you please."

"You're lying," she said.

It shrugged. "Maybe. But your boy is over there fixin' to die, and that's the truth. Hell, everything I said's the truth. I'm not a liar by nature, and you haven't made me be one, especially."

"You lied to Beej, to Jane, told them you were a god, imprisoned—"

The thing took a long step forward and it was *in her face*, teeth bared, eyes penetrating twin abysses.

Marzi shrieked and slashed upward with her knife. She felt resistance, but not much, and heard a sound like paper tearing, and a buzzing, like she'd disturbed a wasp's nest. The thing's expression didn't change. Marzi might not have moved at all.

"I never lied, not to any of them," it said, voice soft and

reasonable, and this time its breath didn't smell of gunsmoke. It smelled of salt flats and alkali. "I *am* a god. I lived here in the West before there was anything touched by man or beast, before life knew what it was to be alive. And I *was* imprisoned. Maybe I let my followers use their imaginations as far as what that *means,* what I might *do* for them if they let me out . . . but Beej, at least, he knows what I am, and he pledged allegiance anyway. And Jane . . . let's just say that Jane knew working for me was better than the alternative. But I did *not* lie." It stepped back, sliding off the knife, frowning, shaking its head. There was a tear in its chest from the knife, but it wasn't bleeding. The thing laughed, abruptly, a sound like rocks rubbing together. "I never used to get offended, either. Just another one of your gifts. Not as much fun as gloating, I must say."

Marzi didn't know what the thing was talking about—though she suspected it was important—but the foremost thing in her mind was a concern for Jonathan. What if the thing was telling the truth? Then Jonathan was in trouble, and only Marzi could help him.

"I'll be back for you," Marzi said.

The thing nodded. "Sure. I'm not trying to get out of the showdown. I'm looking forward to it. I just want to get up to my fighting weight first, and keep you busy in the meantime."

"Get out of my house."

The thing looked around, as if seeing its surroundings for the first time. "I will. And then I'll flatten your house. All the houses. Return everything to dirt and dust and nothing." It strode past her to the back door, turned the bolt, and threw the door wide.

"I *love* opening doors," it said, and walked into the slowly rising dawn.

Marzi looked at the clock over the kitchen sink. It was almost five-thirty. Genius Loci opened at seven, and Hendrix would be there at six-thirty or so, probably. She didn't have much time.

She had to find Jonathan. There was no question about that. What had happened to him was her fault, for not being honest with him, for not telling him and Lindsay about the dangers they faced. Besides, she *owed* him; he'd kicked Jane in half, probably saving Marzi's life. Marzi had been running from her responsibilities for too long. She wouldn't run from this one.

But she couldn't go after Jonathan alone. What if the thing *was* lying? She'd need someone on this side, who could open the door for her if she got stuck. There was only one person in the world she could call: the *other* person she should have been honest with, the other one she should have warned. Marzi picked up the phone and dialed Lindsay's number.

THE EARTHQUAKE WOKE Beej about an hour before it happened. He felt the vibrations thrumming through the bones in his skull, an exquisitely blinding sensation somewhere between pain and orgasm. He lay awake on his hard bunk, looking into the dark above him, whispering softly to himself, begging forgiveness for his trespasses, pledging fealty, occasionally giggling. The world would break like an egg, and Beej would be there at the place where the crack began, standing at the epicenter, at the right hand of a god.

When the quake came, Beej bounced out of his bunk and

landed hard on the concrete floor, but he didn't care—it didn't even hurt. He sat cross-legged on the floor of his cell while the cops cursed and poked their heads in to make sure everyone was okay. Beej waved at them jauntily, and they scowled, like always. Beej hummed a little and watched the windows as light crept into the sky, everything in his head going *la la la* in anticipation. Because something had *happened*. That hadn't been a natural earthquake, and the epicenter was close-close-close; just down the street, in the prison where the god lived, or used to live. Beej had half-expected the walls of the jail to crack open when the tremors began, but they hadn't. The building was probably on a floating foundation, or at least earthquake-safety retrofitted. After Loma Prieta rearranged the face of the town, the people of Santa Cruz had become a bit more careful about such things. Not that their care would protect them. Oh, no. Everything would be shaken down to bits around them, and they would be broken up, too. That was too bad. Beej didn't have anything against people, not really. He would have just as happily pledged himself to a god of love and light, but those gods had not revealed themselves to him. Beej's only revelation had come from the god of the earthquake, and so that was the god that earned his loyalty.

When he heard bootheels clicking on the floor, Beej rose to his feet. None of the cops sounded like that when they walked, every click of heel on floor clear and distinct, each a miniature crack of doom.

The earthquake god walked into the holding area, and Beej stood still on the other side of the bars, unable to believe his good luck, to be looking on the god-in-the-flesh, not a smoke ghost or a brief apparition, but the real thing walking around. It was man-shaped, the color of sandstone, naked from the waist up, clothed below in a leather cloth. It wore deerskin moccasins, but each step sounded like bootheels, a small and strange thing that struck Beej as very godlike—a walking sense of dislocation, a living, sentient example of cognitive dissonance. The god stood just on the other side of the bars; its face was impassive, its eyes polished black stones, its teeth the color of flint. "Beej," it said, voice toneless and uninflected. Its breath smelled like rocks baking in the sun.

"My god," he breathed.

"I need you to do something for me."

"Anything." Beej imagined himself driving a bulldozer, or manning a wrecking ball, or just walking through town, opening fissures in the ground with every step.

"Much as it pains me to say this . . . I need you to build me something."

Beej frowned. He hadn't expected that. Unless he was supposed to build something that would later wreak greater destruction. . . . "Of course. Whatever you want."

The thing reached through the bars and touched Beej's cheek, which made Beej shudder with pleasure, though the god's flesh was hard and rough. "You are my pet artist, you know. I chose you because you are mad, and you can make things. You're a shaper. Under other circumstances, you might have been the one holding me prisoner."

Beej winced. "Never, I would never—"

"Oh, I don't know. All you want is duty, a set of devotions, a *reason*. Keeping me prisoner might have given you that. But you've got too many snake pits in your head to make you a good candidate for that sort of responsibility, I suppose. Marzi was a better choice."

Beej smiled a little, hearing her name.

"You like her, don't you?" the god said.

Blushing, Beej looked at the floor. "It's not important," he mumbled. "Flesh is grass."

"And we know what happens to grass, don't we? It gets dry, and it burns, and it floats away. Your flesh too, eventually. But even full of snake pits, you have power, enough to shape things, enough to make you valuable to me. You can build what I need."

"What should I make?"

"Sort of a sculpture, Beej, and sort of a tide pool. Something like a door, and something like a shadow box."

"A sculpture?" Beej said uncertainly. "I'll try, but . . . I'm not so good with making things in three dimensions. I can paint, I can do photo collage, I can draw, but when it comes to building things, my eyes don't meet my hands."

The god did not look pleased. It blinked, once, like a lizard. "Ah. I see. You're not that kind of artist."

"Now, if you want a good *sculptor*," Beej said, "that'd be my friend Denis. He used to make the most amazing things. He worked with metal, mostly, because he liked the clean lines, but he did other stuff, too, with wire and found objects . . ." Beej trailed off, belatedly realizing that pointing out his uselessness to the god's plans might be a bad idea. But he couldn't very well lie to his deity, could he? Better the god know now than find out later.

"Denis." The god sounded unhappy, the first inflection that had touched its voice. "I see. And do you think you

could work with Denis? The door will need to be embellished. Imbued. And you're the one with the power to do
that, Beej, to make it more than just a sculpture. I shudder to
think where a door Denis made by himself might lead to, but
I can guide *you*. Could you . . . collaborate with him, do you
think?"

"Oh, sure," Beej said. "That'd be great. I've always wanted
to work with Denis, but he never wanted to."

"I suspect we can convince him," the god said.

Beej looked around, then said, confidentially, "Of course,
the problem is, I'm in *jail*." He shook the bars by way of
demonstration.

"Oh, not to worry," the god said. He slipped his pinky
finger into the lock and wiggled it a bit, meditatively. The
lock clicked. "I'm good at opening doors. I like it. It's my
new thing." The god stepped back, and the door swung open.

Beej stepped into the corridor. "But there's getting *out* of
here, and that's tricky, too, there are police . . ."

The god shook his head. "Don't worry. They're all . . .
asleep." The god smiled, and Beej suspected that the police
weren't asleep at all, that something worse had happened to
them. He felt bad, thinking about that, because those cops
had been nice to him, mostly, and even the ones who hadn't
been nice didn't deserve . . . Well. It wasn't about what people
deserved. It was about the god's will. Beej served the god's
will. Anything else was a distraction.

"Let's find your clothes, shall we?" the god said. "We
can't have you running around in that ugly jumpsuit."

Throw In

MARZI COULDN'T BRING herself to go into the café yet. She sat on the steps, wishing for a cigarette, looking dully at the trash in the street beside the sidewalk: a condom wrapper, a ragged bit of newspaper with the word "Run" in screaming thirty-six-point type. There was no heat in the air, and she wore a sweater, but she was still cold. She had her toy gun, loaded with caps, and she turned it over in her hands, taking comfort from it like it was a lucky charm, which maybe it was. She'd gone up to Jonathan's room, hammered on his door, but he wasn't home.

The door under the stairs to the Pigeonhole was standing open. It was the only door into the building that wasn't alarmed; Hendrix had probably forgotten about it when he had the system put in. It was locked anyway, and the key was long lost, but the Outlaw had gotten through it with no difficulty. At least it hadn't just walked through the wall; that was reassuring, to know it had to use doors, even if it could open them without difficulty. Apparently prowling around bars and appearing as a spectral cowboy were the supernatural equivalent of remote telepresence. Now it was out for real, walking around in the world in something like a body, and it had to use doors. So maybe, if it was physical enough to need doors, it was physical enough to kill. But why was it physical at *all*? Why did a sentient earthquake need a body? In a sense, it wasn't even a *thing*—it was a potentiality, an event, a process, a conscious disaster.

And why did it keep appearing to her in the form of things she'd written about in her comic books? Sure, there was a degree of accuracy in the comparison, a certain satisfying symmetry, but its fundamental form couldn't possibly be that of a villain from a Western. So what the hell *was* it?

Lindsay arrived, parked at the curb in front of Marzi, and popped out of her car. She didn't look at all puffy or half-asleep. She'd been awake when Marzi called—"The quake bounced me out of dreamland," she'd said—and agreed to meet right away, almost no questions asked. Just one: "Is it bad?" And Marzi said, "Well, yeah," and Lindsay said, "Give me ten."

Lindsay sat down beside Marzi on the curb. "Hey, babe," she said.

"Hey." Marzi leaned her head on Lindsay's shoulder, then abruptly, and to her own great surprise, began to cry.

Lindsay put an arm around her and made soothing noises.

"Ah, Lindsay, I fucked up," Marzi said. "I didn't want the job, but I got it, and I screwed it up bad."

"Nothing we can't fix," Lindsay said. "No such thing as a problem we can't handle."

Marzi shivered. What could she and Lindsay do to stop the thing with the wasteland face? It seemed afraid of Marzi, which suggested there was *something* they could do, but if Marzi could hurt it, she didn't know how. How did you fight a willful mudslide, a living wildfire? You *couldn't*—you could only pick up the pieces afterward. But if the Outlaw had its way, there would *be* no afterward. Just desolation spreading in all directions.

"I should have told you about this before, but I didn't entirely believe it myself. Even now, even though I *am* sure, I'm also sure you're going to think I'm crazy," Marzi said.

"Wouldn't be the first time."

"I'm serious." Marzi looked at the asphalt, the trash in the gutter. Not at her best friend.

"Tell me," Lindsay said.

Marzi almost smiled. Lindsay was good people. "Well, in a nutshell . . . Two years ago, when I first started working here, I was storing some stuff in the junk room . . . the *Desert Room.*" She had to force herself to call it that, but she didn't stutter, this time. "And I found a door in the back wall. A door to nowhere."

"Okay."

"Well, I opened the door, because, shit, that's what you *do,* if you're stupid, if you're me." *Or if you're Jonathan,* she thought, but she'd save that revelation for later. "And I saw this . . . thing. It had . . . it sounds too stupid, if I describe it, but it was alive; it had a face."

"I don't guess you mean you found a rat in the crawl space." Lindsay sounded serious, at least, but not in a humor-the-lunatic way.

"No. I didn't even find a crawl space, unless it's the crawl space for the whole world. The door opened on a place, Lindsay. A whole other place."

A moment of silence, then, "Sounds like your comic."

"Yeah. Art imitating life. Anyway, I slammed the door, and then I slammed a bunch of doors in my own head, repressed the shit out of the whole experience, buried it all so deep I've only just started remembering it this week. But it was coming out in bits and pieces all along—I had a breakdown, I had anxiety attacks when I tried to open doors. You remember. That was right after I saw the thing beyond the door."

"So what made you start remembering?"

Marzi wanted to ask Lindsay if she believed her, but that was too dangerous, and not really necessary. Because Marzi intended to show her the door, and Lindsay would either see what was behind it—the lands beyond the lands, as the Outlaw called it—or not. If the former, she'd believe, and if the latter, well, no problem. Marzi would call her old therapist, tell her she'd had a . . . what would she call it? A relapse with escalations.

"I started seeing shit. Hallucinations, I figured, stuff from my comic, pretty much, but walking around in full color, big as life. And I had this dream, or vision, where I saw Santa Cruz destroyed, and I heard this raspy old-lady voice saying a bunch of crap I didn't really understand. Remember Beej talking about the god of the earthquake? And Jane going on about the goddess? And . . ." She trailed off.

"Alice," Lindsay said. "She talked about a phoenix, a god of fire, rising from the ashes of Genius Loci. Shit, Marzi. This thing you're talking about, it's what made Alice go?"

Marzi nodded. "I think so. Yeah. So if I'm crazy, I guess it's contagious."

"I guess," Lindsay said, clearly troubled. "I'm not one to

laugh at stuff I don't understand—I was the only one who believed Seth when he said he'd been abducted by aliens, remember, back when we were freshmen? But this . . . I hate to say that line about how I believe *you* believe, but that's the best I can do for now. Beej, and Jane, and Alice . . . It doesn't seem like it could just be coincidence, but this is way beyond tarot or prophetic dreams, you know? This is the far side of far out."

Marzi had scarcely dared to hope for even that much belief. "It's worse now, because the thing behind the door got *out*, earlier this morning. I fucked up, and I didn't watch the door, and now it's loose. That's what caused the earthquake, when it escaped."

"Heavy," Lindsay said, and shifted a little on the sidewalk. "I mean. Shit."

"The thing came to my house. Stood in my living room. I saw it. It was a monster, like a cowboy made of wrecked earth. . . . I'm not making any sense. It was horrible, and it pretty much talked trash to me, tried to scare me into leaving town." Marzi glanced at Lindsay, who was looking meditatively off into the middle distance. "I guess this qualifies as full-blown psychosis, huh?"

"Mmm," Lindsay said. "The thing to do is to get independent verification, right? I don't guess it told you anything we can check out?"

"It told me Jonathan was the one who set it free."

Now Lindsay looked at her. "Say what? Your Jonathan?"

"Yeah. He wanted to see the Desert Room, so he pulled up his carpet and came through the trapdoor. He went into the Desert Room, he opened the door, and he let it out. But not before it locked Jonathan in, left him on the other side."

"Um. So, have you tried knocking on Jonathan's door? If he's home, then everything's okay. Apart from your possible mental health issues, that is."

"Yeah, I knocked. Nobody's home. So I figure the thing was telling the truth." Marzi sighed. "Or else, you know, I went into a fugue and chopped Jonathan up, and I just don't remember it."

"You'd be all bloody if you'd done that," Lindsay said.

"So maybe I smothered him."

"Hardly seems like your style."

"So," Marzi said. "Hendrix will be here in half an hour. Before that happens, I want to go through the door, find Jonathan, and bring him back. But I need your help."

"What do you want me to do?"

"I want you to be my doorman. You make sure I don't get trapped on the other side, like Jonathan was. I'd just leave the door standing open, but I think there's other not-so-nice stuff living there, things we don't want wandering around town. The thing told me I could open the door from the inside, because I'm the prison guard, so it's my door. But I don't quite trust that, you know? So I'd like you to watch my back. Will you come?"

"Of course I'll come. But just for the sake of argument, let's say the door opens up on bricks or something. What then?"

"Then I call Dr. Mitchell, and you give me a ride to wherever she tells me to go."

Lindsay nodded. "So long as we've got a contingency plan. And that's better than chopping me up to hide your shame."

"I'll always share my shame with you. You're taking this awfully well, you know."

Lindsay shrugged. "I feel like I've been called up from re-serve best-friend status to active duty. Helping you dye your hair or something is easy. *This* is what friends are for."

Marzi stood up. "Thanks, Lindsay. I mean it." She shook her head. "Most people . . ."

"Most people suck. Come on." She stood, too, and they went up the steps. "I can't decide if I want you to be crazy or not. I don't know which would be better."

"That's easy. If I'm crazy, it's just me who's in trouble. If I'm not . . . we're all seriously fucked."

"Yes, but if you're not crazy, that means it's *real,* that there's magic in the world. It would be worth a lot to know that for sure, even if no one else believed it, even if bad things came along with the magic. It can't *all* be bad magic, can it?"

"I don't know," Marzi said. "The good stuff isn't making itself obvious."

Marzi unlocked the door, stepping inside to quickly punch in the alarm code. Once Lindsay was safely inside with her, she shut and locked the door, and carefully rearmed the alarm.

"Looks like this place got quaked," Lindsay said.

Marzi turned and surveyed the damage. All the bottles of Torani syrup had tumbled from the shelf to the floor, a bunch of chairs had fallen over, and there was a crack in the glass on the dessert case.

"It could be worse, I guess," Marzi said. "This being the epicenter and all."

"Hmm," Lindsay said.

Marzi went around the counter, stepping carefully over the drying puddles of hazelnut, raspberry, and Irish Cream syrup. "Hendrix can clean it up. I'm not even supposed to be out of bed yet."

Lindsay followed her into the kitchen. The door to the Desert Room was standing ajar, but not enough to allow a view into the room.

Marzi took a deep breath and pushed the door open. It swung inward, silently as ever, letting a little ambient light spill onto the trash and dust on the floor. "Moment of truth."

"I'll go first," Lindsay said, and bustled past her, into the room, glancing around and flicking on the light switch. She whistled, low and appreciative.

Marzi stepped into the room, and gasped.

The mural had changed drastically. It was no longer a desert scene, but something from a ghost town, with faded store-fronts, tumbleweeds, hitching posts, rain barrels, and water troughs.

"Did you paint this, Marzi?" Lindsay asked. "Paint over whatever used to be here before, or . . ."

"No," Marzi said. "I . . . it's not even my style. I don't paint like this. It's like something by Garamond Ray."

"Somebody could copy that style." She glanced at Marzi, then quickly looked away. "Somebody must have. This isn't what you described, what Jonathan said the books described. No scorpions or cacti or rocks or anything."

"It's weird, but honestly, Lindsay, it doesn't register all that strongly on my weird-shit scale. I've seen stranger today. See the door? With the brass knob?"

"What door?"

Marzi pointed. Lindsay stepped forward, put her hand on the wall, on the door, and whistled again. "It looks like part of the painting. I didn't even know it was real."

"I've had that feeling a lot, lately."

Lindsay took a deep breath. "So what's behind Door Number Only?"

"Either a place that doesn't quite touch the world, or nothing at all, or . . ." She shrugged.

Lindsay touched the knob. "Shall I?"

"I don't—Maybe I should—Shit. Sure. Open it."

Lindsay turned the knob and pulled the door open. Marzi stood behind her, and when the harsh light from the lands beyond the lands poured in, it turned Lindsay into a shadow, just a black silhouette standing in a door frame. This *was* the door from her comic, then, essentially, opening onto the West beyond the West. Lindsay looked exactly like page three of the first issue of *The Strange Adventures of Rangergirl*, and Marzi realized with a pang of wonder that she'd put a lot of Lindsay into that character, that in a way the character was a love story about her best friend. Perhaps not the kind of love Lindsay would want from Marzi, if the world were a place of perfect congruency, but something deep and true all the same.

Lindsay stepped back, and stumbled into Marzi, but didn't fall. Marzi blinked against the light until her eyes adjusted, and she could see what lay beyond.

Lindsay reached behind her, fumbled for Marzi's hand, and gripped it hard. "I see . . . a dusty street, and wooden buildings." Her voice was tight and too high. "Is that what you see?"

"Yes," Marzi said, and it was like an ice floe had broken loose from her heart and drifted away. She wasn't crazy. Lindsay could see it, too. "The first time I saw this, Lindsay, my mind just shut down. I dreamed about it, I *drew* about it, but I didn't remember it. And I didn't even see this, not really. The buildings . . . they're bigger now, more substantial. It was mostly just a desert before. Then the thing came at me, and its face filled my vision."

"Why haven't I fainted?" Lindsay said, still squeezing. "In the movies, people are always fainting. It seems like a great way to get out of a difficult situation, you know? To skip the awkward intermediate moments. But it never happens to me."

"It's because you're so stout of heart."

Lindsay turned around and looked Marzi in the face. "Are we going in there?"

"I have to go in. Jonathan's in there, I think. But I need you here, to make sure I can get out again."

"Look," Lindsay said. "You go through, and I'll shut the door, and you see if you can open it again from the inside, okay?"

Marzi searched her face for some sign of incipient hysteria, any indication that Lindsay was near her breaking point, but she looked fine, just a little pale.

"Okay," Marzi said. "I guess that's the first thing to do." She stepped toward the door. She couldn't see much of the lands beyond the lands—mostly weathered two-story buildings and a dusty street, blocking the view to the horizon. It smelled like sand and sage and heat there, but not horseshit, or piss, or gunsmoke, or whiskey. It didn't smell like anything alive or human lived there, despite the buildings. She glanced at Lindsay, who stood with her hands clasped before her, as if about to recite a poem for a class. "If I'm not out in ten seconds, open the door, okay?"

"I'll open it in five."

Marzi nodded, looked back at the lands beyond the lands, and stepped through.

There was no *frisson*, no sense of dislocation, just a dramatic increase in the heat; this was a dry, baking place, quite unlike Santa Cruz. The sky overhead was a faded barely-blue, as if the sun had bleached the color from the atmosphere. She pulled the door shut behind her, before she could think too much about what she was doing.

The door was set in a free-standing fragment of wooden wall, as if it were the only remaining part of a house that had otherwise been demolished. She didn't move from the shadow of the standing wall, didn't make a sound, just counted slowly to three and then turned the knob. It opened easily, out into the Desert Room, and Marzi stepped through again, back to the world she knew, and shut the door behind her.

"Looks like I can come and go as I please," she said, shaking a little.

"Good," Lindsay said. "Then you don't need me to play doorman, and I can go with you."

Marzi stared at her for a moment, then shook her head. "No. No way."

Lindsay touched her arm. "Marzipan. I'm going with you. You think I'd let you go over there by yourself? No way. I'll be honest, I thought you were losing it when you told me about this outside. I thought you needed help. But I was wrong, except it turns out you *do* need help, and the help you need is *me*."

"This isn't a comic book," Marzi said. "This is its own

thing, and it's not a good thing. What if something happened to you?"

"What if something happens to *you*, huh? And I'm out here, all by myself, no you, no Jonathan, Alice is gone, who do I have? Where would I be then? You say this bad thing is loose in the world, you want to leave me alone to deal with that? I have to go with you. I have to make sure you come *back*. I need to do this. I don't want to be a sidekick or a lovely assistant, Marzi. I want to be there beside you. You think I'd let you go by yourself, let you get eaten by basilisks or giant rattlesnakes or some shit?"

"Okay," Marzi said, relieved, pleased, and apprehensive all at once. It would be better, with Lindsay there. But if anything happened to her, Marzi would never forgive herself. Or the Outlaw. "Okay, we'll go together."

Lindsay looked at the closed door and sighed. "I wish it wasn't a Western, though. You know I never really liked Westerns."

"Aw, c'mon. We're a team. Frank and Jesse. Hart and Boot."

"Rangergirl and her fearless native guide." Lindsay frowned. "But this . . . the way it is . . . it *must* have something to do with you. It used to be a desert before, but now it's like something out of your comic, a door that leads to a weird Old West, that's so *you*. I don't understand it, but this isn't some . . . some static situation. It's dynamic. You're affecting the world over there. Somehow."

"Yeah. Somehow. But I don't know how, and there's no time to figure it out." She took Lindsay's hand. "Come on. Time to follow the no-brick road. Time to find Jonathan."

With her other hand, she reached for the brass knob, and opened the door.

THE EARTHQUAKE WOKE Denis, too, but once the tremors subsided he got back into bed, pulled the blanket over himself, and went back to sleep. Unpleasant dreams had broken his rest all night—not his usual dream, but new ones, messier ones. Dreams of mud-women pursuing him through ditches and gullies, all eager to wrench his arms and legs from his body, to stuff his mouth and rectum with slick mud. He hoped for a few more restful hours in bed before trying to work on his paper. He had an office on campus he could use, but he seldom went there, because he also had an office*mate*, a greasy cupcake-devouring manatee named, appropriately enough, Whalen. Whalen worked at his desk often, and after a few attempts to share space with the man, who farted without shame and had a distressing tendency to sing top-40 pop songs to himself, Denis had requested another office. He'd been laughed at. Space was at a premium, and none of the other grad students wanted to trade places with Denis. Whalen's odor and idiosyncrasies were well known in the department. So Denis had started doing his work at Genius Loci, and that had worked fine until . . . the recent unpleasantness. Now he would have to try working in his office again, and hope Whalen was away for the summer, which seemed unlikely.

After the earthquake, Denis dreamed of being repeatedly swallowed and disgorged by an enormous whale with phosphorescent, leprous patches on its skin.

He woke again to the sound of something falling over in the next room, and a muttered curse. Denis lay still in bed, listening, and heard footsteps and the creaking of his couch cushions. Someone was in the living room.

It had to be Jane. Who else but his dead ghost lover would enter this way? Had she come back to make up, to kill him, to fuck in sullen silence? Denis got out of bed, already dressed enough, since he slept in shorts and a T-shirt. He opened his door and went into the living room.

It wasn't Jane. It was Beej, sitting in the middle of the couch, hands on his knees, smiling tentatively. "Hey, Denis. Sorry to barge in, but—"

"Barge in?" Denis's weariness was replaced by outrage. "I think you mean *break* in, Beej. Get out of my house, before I call the police. Speaking of which, why aren't you still in jail? Who would bail you out?"

Beej looked uncomfortable, insofar as Denis could see his features in the half-light from the curtained windows. "Sorry to come in unannounced, but see, something's happened—"

"How fascinating. Leave now."

"Denis, I can't go yet. I brought someone to meet you." He leaned forward, and pitched his voice low. "I brought the earthquake god. He escaped from his prison this morning, and then set me free."

Denis sighed. "As much as I'd enjoy meeting your imaginary deities, Beej—"

"I believe I can make my own introductions." The voice came from the kitchen, dry and full of malicious good humor. Denis looked, and saw a tall man—absurdly tall; his head seemed almost to brush the ten-foot ceiling, but that couldn't be—standing by the stove, mostly in shadows.

"Okay, Beej, you coming here is one thing, but you bring your weirdo friends—"

"Could you give us a few moments, Beej?" the man in the kitchen said, and Beej sprang to his feet.

"Sure thing," he said, and hurried to the front door without a backward glance, letting himself out, shutting the door behind him.

Denis knew he should be shouting, demanding that this man leave, threatening to call the police, but all that seemed so banal, predictable, exhausting; after all he'd been through these past few days, he couldn't work up the energy. "What is it? What do you want?"

"First, let's establish my credentials. I *am* a god. Beej may be misguided about a lot of things, but he's got that much right." The man didn't move from the shadows in the kitchen, and Denis didn't approach him; he could still dodge back into his bedroom and lock the door, if necessary.

"Okay," Denis said. "Nice to meet you. I'm an atheist."

"I don't know how you can doubt what I say. After all, I raised a woman from the dead. I gave her a new body made of mud. Aren't those the sort of things a god is expected to do?"

Denis swallowed, suddenly thirsty. "Ah. I don't think . . ."

"Yes, Denis," the man said, patiently, pedantically. "I'm talking about Jane, whom you killed—"

"No," Denis said, holding up his finger, trying to stay in control, counting rapidly in his head, up to nine and back down again, up and down. "I never killed anyone."

"Oh, really?" the man said, and stepped forward, his shoes—they seemed to be pointed cowboy boots—clicking on the floor. "I suppose you'd say that at worst you're guilty of negligence, that the only crime you committed was the crime of inaction. You didn't kill Jane, a mudslide did." Another step, and now enough light touched him to reveal a brown duster, jeans, and a ragged cowboy hat, which threw shadows on the man's face. "Which means I killed her, because I am the god of the mudslide, god of the swift and slow endings of life. Maybe so." The man came into the light completely, and when Denis saw his face, he screamed, something he never would have imagined himself doing—screaming in shock was so pulp-fiction, so hackneyed and inauthentic.

But he screamed, because this man had no face. This man wasn't a *he* at all, but an *it*. It had a chrome skull, with barbed wire for teeth, and threshing hooks turning slowly around and around deep in its eye sockets. The thing took no notice of Denis's brief shriek. "But do you think Jane would buy that excuse, son? That she'd say, 'Oh, well, you didn't *kill* me, you just *caused* me to be killed by your own inaction, well, that's a different story, no harm done.' Or do you think she'd be, maybe, a little angrier than that? See, I'm going up into the hills to pick her up. She had a little run-in with the good guys, got kicked in half, and she made her way back to the place where she was born, to bury herself in mud and recuperate. When I dig her out, I can tell her what you did. That you left her to die. I can show her the corpse you left behind—"

"Ha!" Denis said, and shook his finger at the chrome cowboy. "She can't even see her body! It's invisible to her!"

"You dumb shitheel," it said. "Why do you reckon it's invisible? Because I *made* it invisible. Jane's close to my heart, she's important to me, and I wanted to spare her that pain. She thinks she's merely been transformed—it might upset her to find out she died in the process. But if you don't go along with what I want, boy, I can cure her blindness. I can

let her see what you did, see the body you left. I believe she'll
be cross with you, if I do that. Who knows what she might
do to you then?"

"Ah," Denis said, thinking furiously, and getting nowhere. If this thing really was responsible for making Jane a
mud-revenant—and look at it, who knew what a being like
this was capable of?—it had all the power here. Desperately,
Denis said, "How do I know you aren't just some . . . some
robot, some art project Beej made, with a speaker in your
face?"

The thing stared at him, necessarily expressionless. "Oh.
Right. You see me as metal, mostly, right? Within certain . . .
annoyingly immutable limits, most people see me as they
like, as they interpret me. Beej thinks of me as the earthquake
god, and he sees me with skin made of cracking sandstone.
But you . . . oh, I know your dreams, Denis. The machine
that grinds, wearing down all the ugly imperfections, that
killing engine of chrome and spikes. My goals and your dreams
aren't so different—I want to dip the world in a killing jar,
too. I want to scour the earth. I *am* the machine that grinds,
Denis."

Denis swallowed. "You know my dreams."

"Ayup. When people dream about me, I *know*."

"Then . . . I guess you are what you say."

"Good boy. I take it you'll be joining my band of merry
outlaws, then? I didn't want you, particularly—you're too
fucking contrary by half, like a mean horse that'll throw you
for no good reason—but my wildfire girl ran off down the
owl-hoot trail, so I've got an opening at the disciple level.
You do what I say, and I won't tell Jane what you did to her."

"Fine," Denis said, because what else could you say to a

chrome-faced god? "But can't you kill me yourself? Why be so roundabout, why threaten me with *Jane*?"

"Because you're more scared of Jane than you'll ever be of me, Denis. Because Jane is something *you* did, and there's nothing you're so scared of as your own well-earned consequences." There was silence for a moment, broken only by the steady whir of the threshing machines in the god's head. "Damn. I never used to be insightful. The things that girl's done to me."

Denis ignored that—he had a well-honed ability to discard trivial or confusing information—and nodded. This thing had him over a barrel. "So what do you want? To scour the earth, big killing jar, blah blah blah, I know—but what do you want to *do*? Practically speaking?"

"You and Beej are going to do a little art project for me. I'll tell you all about it. But first, we're going to go pick up Jane. Won't that be fun?" It couldn't grin, but there was definitely mirth in its voice.

"Delightful," Denis said, thinking that he was going to get his just-cleaned boots all muddy. Again.

Sage Rat

When Marzi and Lindsay stepped through the door, hand in hand, their clothes changed.

"What the hell!" Lindsay said. Marzi gaped at her. Lindsay had been transformed into the image of a saloon girl, in a red corseted dress, her hair ringleted and red-ribboned. She lifted her skirts and looked at her feet. She was wearing red heels. "This is not funny. Why do you get to be Billy the Kid, and I'm a hospitality girl?"

Marzi looked down at her own clothes. She wore unassuming gunslinger garb: jeans, boots, and an undyed cotton shirt. The most interesting thing was the gun belt, soft old leather with a plain metal buckle. A heavy Colt .45 hung backward on her left hip, so she could reach across and draw right-handed. Marzi drew the pistol, careful not to point it anywhere near Lindsay. "I think this used to be my cap gun," she said. "I tucked it in my pocket before we came through, and now it's gone . . . but I've got this."

"Is it loaded?" Lindsay

asked, holding up her skirts like a woman frozen in mid-curtsy.

Marzi opened the gun, and found a bullet in every chamber. She snapped it shut. "Looks that way."

"Do you know how to use it?"

Marzi shrugged. "My grandfather used to collect guns. Mom and Dad never approved of him showing me the collection—they're hippies to the bone—but he taught me how to shoot a little when I was a teenager. I'm not good, but I could hit a barn at twenty paces, I guess. It's been a long time since I've tried." Marzi wasn't quite being truthful; she had a natural gift for shooting, that rare synthesis of hand and eye that made sharpshooters. The skill was useful in table tennis, too, and that was mostly where she employed it. Her grandfather had been stunned when, after a few lessons, Marzi could shoot almost as accurately as he could. He'd offered to buy her a piece of her own when she graduated from high school, but Marzi had declined. She was comfortable enough with guns, but she didn't feel any particular passion or affection for them, and she'd read too many stories about people being killed accidentally or deliberately by their own handguns.

She hadn't held a firearm in years, but this was a good one, well balanced, and it seemed authentically period, from the late 1800s. The Colt Peacemaker was a good weapon, for its time, less prone to exploding in the shooter's hand than some of its contemporaries.

"As long as you can kill otherworldly monsters, I'm happy," Lindsay said. "And scare off any horny cowboys who come after me." She flounced her skirts in irritation. "Really, this sucks." She glared around at the worn-down buildings.

"As long as I don't have to shoot more than six horny cowboys," Marzi said. "I don't have any more ammo."

Lindsay ran her hands down the front of her dress. "I think this thing has whalebone in it. We've got to find something else for me to wear, Marzi, if we're going to be here for long. Whose bright idea was it to dress me like this, anyway?"

Marzi walked to a building and put her palm against the rough wood. "I don't think any of this is exactly real. It *is*, but I think the way we're perceiving it is sort of . . . optional. Arbitrary. The clothes are like that, too. You're just dressed to fit the theme."

"That's lame," Lindsay said.

"When in Tombstone," Marzi said, shrugging. "We should find Jonathan and get out of here."

"This place doesn't look that big. There's only one street. Where do we start? Should we yell for him?"

"I don't know. The thing . . . the Outlaw . . . said there are other creatures living here. Maybe we shouldn't call too much attention to ourselves."

"Too late for *that*," drawled a man's voice, from the porch of a building on the right.

Marzi spun, drawing and cocking her gun with an unthinking ease that went beyond her meager training, into something like instinct.

A man sat in a rocking chair beneath a wooden awning. He was sun-darkened and barrel-chested, wearing a striped Mexican serape spattered with unidentifiable stains. His face was round—though not precisely fat—and his gray-and-black beard needed a trim. His faded blue eyes watched Marzi's face, not her gun.

He took a long drink from an unlabeled glass bottle, then set it down on the boards beside him with a clink. He raised his arms slowly to show his empty hands. After matching Marzi's stare for a moment, he said, "Well, I guess you're the new sheriff in town. I'd be happy to hand over my badge, if I had one."

"Is he one of those other creatures," Lindsay said, "just disguised to look like the town drunk or something?"

The man frowned for a moment, then smiled mirthlessly, showing all his teeth, which were surprisingly white. "No, my posy, I'm not a creature. I'm Garamond Ray."

Marzi lowered her gun. "The painter? You?"

He beamed, lowering his hands. "My fame precedes me! I knew I'd become famous after I died. Not that I actually died—just the next best thing. Tell me, am I part of the canon, now? How long have I been gone?"

"Marzi," Lindsay said, "if we're going to chat, can we get in under the shade? Whalebone is hot, and I don't mean sexy."

Marzi nodded, still looking at the man on the porch. Sunburned. Middle-aged. Half drunk. This was *Ray*? How could that be? He should be in his sixties at least by now . . . unless he hadn't aged since his disappearance in 1989.

The building behind him was a saloon with bat-wing doors. The faded sign hanging above the doors depicted a pool of blue water and a couple of palm trees in flaking primary-color paint, and a name, "The Oasis," in sinuous faux-Arabic script.

"Sure, come in out of the sun," Ray said. "I never could do a damn thing about the heat. It's built-in." He pushed himself up, the arms of the rocker creaking under his weight.

Marzi and Lindsay walked into the shade, instantly cooler by several degrees. "Oh, that's way better," Lindsay said.

Ray looked her up and down with obvious appreciation, and Marzi thought about how long he must have been here, if he'd been trapped since the day of the Loma Prieta quake in 1989, when he'd disappeared. So many years, with no other people—or were there other people?—living in a ghost town. Marzi suspected that, under those circumstances, her own sex drive would have simply withered and dried and disappeared, but from the way Ray looked at Lindsay, his was definitely still functional.

Or maybe this place was full of nymphs or succubi or something, and Ray had sex daily with jackal-headed women. What did she know? She didn't even understand precisely where they were: the backstage area for the material world? Under the floorboards of rational space? In Faerie, or the medicine lands, or the Dreamtime? Or was that all the same place?

"I admit," Ray said, voice broad and ironic, "that I haven't experienced a social occasion in a long time, but isn't it customary for strangers thrown together by circumstance to introduce themselves?"

"Sorry," Lindsay said. "I think we're still shaken up, just being here."

"Oh, that's understandable." Ray held out his hand. Lindsay shook politely. "I am, as I said, Garamond Ray, once a painter, lately a stationary nomad."

"I'm Lindsay," she said. "And you should know, I am so totally gay. Sorry."

Ray stared at her, blinked, then laughed, a sound too big for this dry place. "My apologies. Once upon a time I had a bit more tact, but I haven't been in the company of others for a long time. Your sexual unavailability is duly and regretfully noted."

Lindsay dropped an ironic little curtsy.

"And you must be my esteemed replacement," Ray said. "The Wild West theme is certainly a switch. There's whiskey, now, which is nice. I'd ask how the apocalyptic doorman job is treating you, but since your prisoner escaped a little while ago, I think I can hazard a guess."

"I'm Marzi," she said, not offering to shake hands. "You seem to know a lot more about this than I do."

He shrugged. "It's all on-the-job training, but you get the hang of it after a while. I've been doing it longer than you have. I am a bit confused as to why you're here, though—shouldn't you be out capturing the man in the black hat, or whatever you've imagined our adversary into? Or else buggering off to some tropical paradise with a low incidence of geological upheaval?"

"We're looking for our friend," Lindsay said, crossing her arms, clearly annoyed.

"Ah," Ray said, and stared up at the awning above them meditatively. "Then I suppose you'd better come inside."

He pushed through the bat-wing doors, Marzi and Lindsay following. The interior of The Oasis was familiar from countless Westerns: sawdust on the floor, scarred wooden tables scattered with dog-eared playing cards, a long rough bar, a honky-tonk piano with yellowing ivory keys, stairs to a second floor with a few closed doors. It might have been the same bar Marzi saw in her vision of Daniel's death, but made even more unnerving by its emptiness.

Jonathan was stretched out on the long, wide bar, like a corpse laid out at an old-fashioned wake.

Marzi pulled her gun and trained it on Ray, who sighed and raised his arms again. Lindsay ran to Jonathan, touched his cheek, then leaned over to press her ear to his chest. She listened for a moment, then raised her head. "His heart's beating, but it sounds all rattly, like if you shake a half-full salt shaker. Like he's full of sand."

"What did you do to him?" Marzi demanded, stepping closer to Ray.

"Apart from picking him up out of the dirt and bringing him out of the sun and making him as comfortable as possible?" Ray said. "Not a thing. Now put that gun down, before I take it away from you."

Marzi stiffened. "I'd like to see you try."

Ray snorted. "You couldn't even keep our adversary locked away, when I did all the hard work of getting him here in the first place, and you think you could *stop* me?"

"Can you guys compare dicks later on?" Lindsay said. "I'm worried about Jonathan."

Marzi lowered the hammer on her gun and went to Jonathan. His every breath rattled. Marzi took note of his clothing: He was dressed in dandified Western clothes, a black shirt with silver embroidery around the cuffs and collar, little pearl buttons, and a string tie with a silver clasp in the shape of a bull's head; the eyes were turquoise. Jonathan's boots were hand-tooled, shiny leather, worked with complex lasso designs. He looked like what the old-timers called a "mail-order cowboy," someone from back East with a head full of dime novels and no real sense. Someone who didn't belong in a place like this. "The Outlaw told me he'd touched Jonathan's heart," Marzi said.

"The Outlaw? That's what you call it?" Ray grunted. "I always called it 'the djinn.' And while I realize these things are largely subconscious and beyond our control, I have to say, things were better when it was a djinn. It's easy to trap a djinn—you lure it into a bottle, then seal the bottle. It was just my bad luck to get sealed inside with it. But now that it's a cowboy . . . well. There are all sorts of new complications."

"Marzi, do you have any idea what this guy's talking about?"

Marzi shook her head. "Not really. I'm out of my depth."

Ray sighed. "Let's sit, then, and have a little powwow." He gestured to a table, like all the others except it held a shot glass and a bottle of whiskey. Marzi hesitated, looking at Jonathan. "Don't mind him," Ray said. "I think he'll keep. The desert is a wonderful preservative. I haven't aged a day in all the time I've been here, and my beard hasn't grown. I haven't even taken a shit. I don't even know how long I've been in here, either. The sun never sets, you know, so it's hard to keep track. I tried piling up stones for a while, but I ran out of stones, and marks in the sand don't last."

"You've been here for more than fifteen years," Lindsay said. "Your beard is no longer in style."

"Shit," Ray said. "I thought, maybe five years, but . . . shit."

Lindsay and Marzi sat down with him, Lindsay angling her chair so she could keep an eye on Jonathan. Ray sat back in his chair, hands crossed over his belly. "You've been the guardian for a while now, Marzi. I don't know how long exactly, but I'd guess it's been a couple of years since we developed a Western motif around here, since the seals started cracking and the door began to give. For a while, I hoped I'd be rescued." He shook his head. "I gave up on that, though. Tell me what happened."

Marzi shrugged. "Two years ago, I found the door. I saw the thing, the Outlaw. I slammed the door. That was it."

"Oh, I remember. There were sandstorms around here for weeks after that, and then the buildings started to appear, the spring dried up, and I got a well and whiskey instead . . . but go on."

"I had sort of a breakdown. I repressed everything. I only realized there was a real monster, behind a real door, a couple of days ago."

Ray whistled. "I'd assumed you were making plans, taking precautions, all this time. No wonder the djinn—sorry, the Outlaw—managed to make a crack in the door." He ran a hand through his short, going-to-gray hair, and for a moment he looked lost and vulnerable. "We're in the shit here, now. Sorry I was nasty to you before, but I thought you'd just screwed up out of incompetence. Ignorance is a bit more excusable."

"You're so gracious," Lindsay said, but she didn't take her eyes off Jonathan.

Ray ignored her. "I'd begin at the beginning, but what's that? I don't know if the djinn—no, the Outlaw, I have to get used to that—I don't know if it's been around forever, or just since people were around to recognize it, to believe in it. You know the idea of the genius loci?"

"It's the name of the coffeehouse where I work," Marzi said. "The house where the door is."

Ray stared at her, then laughed. "Ah, Christ, it leaks. It

gets to people, influences things, no matter what. Whoever named the place must have felt its presence, way down deep in the cellars of their brain. I did my best work in that place—it's a coffee shop now? Damn. It was a shared house, a studio. A bunch of us lived there in the eighties and painted and got high. Santa Cruz was a haven for old hippies and aging punks back then."

"Still is," Lindsay said.

"That's good to hear," Ray said. "I had some of the best times of my life in that house, and did my best work there. Did my murals survive?"

"Yeah," Marzi said.

"It's wonderful work," Lindsay said, still not looking at Ray, but in a softer tone.

"Yes, it is," Ray said. "It wasn't until I finished all the murals that I realized I had painted gods."

Marzi blinked. Lindsay said, "Come again? Sure, in the Teatime Room, there's Thoth and Ra and all, but there aren't any other gods . . ."

"It makes more sense when you're on 'shrooms," Ray said. "Anyway, when you've been saturated by the place, and the images are pushing against your eyeballs from the inside . . ."

"I think I get it," Marzi said. "He's right. There are big and little gods. The serpent, in the Ocean Room—"

"I love the names," Ray murmured appreciatively, not really interrupting.

"It's what, the Midgard serpent?" Marzi asked.

"Maybe. Or more like Leviathan. 'That which gathers itself together in folds,' that's what 'Leviathan' means, literally.

I think I was painting a metaphor for this place." His gesture encompassed the whole of the lands beyond the lands. "A place where space and time are folded in on themselves. Möbius territory."

"And I guess Harlequin is a kind of god," Lindsay said.

Ray nodded. "Chaos personified." He frowned and see-sawed his hand in a gesture of equivocation. "Well, that's oversimplifying, but you get the idea. Harlequin was my first attempt to paint our adversary, and I didn't even realize it. But Harlequin is a joker, and the Outlaw doesn't have a sense of humor. Not inherently, anyway," he said, glancing at Marzi. "And neither djinns nor gunmen are known for their sense of whimsy. I'm glad I didn't go on thinking of our adversary as Harlequin." He shuddered. "God, can you imagine? Harlequin, striding around on stilts made of bone, burning down the world, dragging around entrails like strings of sausage—"

Marzi gasped as the room around them changed, the walls turning from wood to brightly colored, tattered canvas, Ray briefly made up in the dead-white greasepaint of Pierrot, Lindsay in a red dress with lipstick to match, transformed into Columbine. Then Ray slapped Marzi across the face, hard, and everything snapped back to normal. Marzi stared at him, her mouth open. Lindsay whimpered.

"Sorry," Ray said. "I shouldn't have been so . . . vivid . . . in my description. I have a lot of practice at keeping my imagination under control—that's important, in this place—but you're in charge of things now, you're the one who de-fines the point of view, and really, as bad as it may be to think of our enemy as a gunslinger, it would be infinitely worse if he were Harlequin. You can't start thinking of him that way.

Harlequins are . . . unpredictable." He shook his head. "Keep your imagination under control."

"I understand," Marzi said, almost whispering. "It was me. I made him into the Outlaw. He didn't influence me; I influenced *him*."

"You define his shape," Ray said. "And this place is fluid—it's the medicine lands, it's all potential, it's all clay. You can shape things here so easily. You saw the face of total desolation, of a local spirit that was probably born when Santa Cruz was just water and rock and nothing, and it wants the world to be that way again. But you couldn't *understand* that, not really—I'm not sure anyone can look into the face of a wasteland and see its true features. You know that quote, about how if you stare too long into the abyss, the abyss stares back into you? I think what stares back is your *reflection*. Faced with all that emptiness, you try to fill it up with yourself. So when you saw that thing, you did what people always do: You made up a story, you personified. People see faces in the patterns of linoleum, they see rocking chairs and hunters in the patterns of the stars, they see the Virgin Mary in a knot on a tree trunk. People make patterns. They see gods in natural processes. I don't know if seeing makes it so, or if the potentialities would express themselves somehow anyway. . . ." He shrugged.

"Wow," Lindsay said after a moment.

"You painted," Marzi said. "You . . . sensed the presence of our enemy. Was it here all along?"

"Someone else trapped it, a long time ago," Ray said. "Maybe they imagined it as a creature of the night, and daylight banished it. Maybe they imagined it as a mountain lion, and painted its picture on a rock, and buried the rock. I don't know, but someone trapped it here. Then I came along, and accidentally stirred it up. I sensed it. I painted. The Teatime Room, the Ocean Room, the Space Room, I painted those things because I understood there were depths beneath the world, utter freezing vacuums, but *inhabited*. I painted the room with the castles in the clouds because I had a sense of shifting, inconstant places—maybe of this place—of strange territories inhabited by giants. Then . . . I found the door. I think I thought there had to be a door. Too much Narnia, maybe. The door appeared in the last room, the one I was painting to look like a desert. One day I opened the door. Shit, wouldn't you?"

"I did," Marzi said.

Ray nodded. "Yeah." He poured himself a drink, looked at it for a moment, but didn't drink it. "So I opened the door, and the thing came out. A beast of smoke and fire. A devil in the desert. A djinn. Because that's how I really imagined it, deep down, like a monster from the Arabian nights."

"It got loose . . . and it caused Loma Prieta," Marzi said.

Ray looked blank.

"The big quake," she said.

Ray nodded. "Yeah, it did that, after a couple of weeks and a lot of mischief. Everybody else moved out of the house, weeks before I opened the door—they just weren't comfortable there, said they heard a horrible buzzing all the time. So nobody knew about it but me. The djinn had to work up to causing that earthquake. Being locked up had weakened it. Life's too easy here, strangely enough—it can cause storms and quakes here with a thought. The real world is a lot more solid. It resists. But, yeah, it worked out, it got strong, and it made a big quake."

"But the epicenter wasn't even in Santa Cruz! It was, like, ninety miles away!" Lindsay protested.

Ray shrugged. "So it expanded its borders. This is just the place where it was trapped, a long time ago. I expect it could tear down the whole coast, given time."

"But you trapped it," Marzi said. "So there's hope. We can capture it again."

Ray shook his head. "It used to be a djinn, Marzi. It's not all that hard to trap djinn. Solomon did it; he sealed them in clay pots. There are countless stories of genies in bottles. Once I understood what it was—or what I believed it to be—I was able to trap it. I read about djinn. I researched. I *imagined*. I finished painting the Desert Room. I painted a pot over the door, a picture of a huge clay pot, inscribed with seals of tempting and trapping, and I lured the djinn inside. It wanted to get rid of me, to be free of my perceptions, of the form I imposed on it, and once it got strong, it came to kill me. I lured it into the room, and opened the door, and it was sucked into the pot. The pot I'd *imagined*, you see? But before it was sucked in . . . it grabbed me, and dragged me with it. So here I am."

"I didn't see a pot in the painting," Marzi said.

"I expect not. Things started changing as soon as you became the guardian. And no, I don't know why you, or why me, except I'm an artist, and I assume you are, too. We're imaginers. We *can* do it, and someone has to, so we get the job. You didn't think of it as a djinn, didn't perceive it that way. You saw it as an outlaw, a gunslinger, poisoning wells, kicking up dust."

"Aw, fuck," Lindsay said. "I get it. You can trap a djinn in a bottle, but you can't do that to an outlaw."

Marzi nodded, staring at the tabletop. "Jails don't hold outlaws. Not in Westerns. The bad guys always escape, or get busted out by their henchmen. There always has to be a showdown. So we can't trap it the way you did again."

"You begin to see the nature of the problem," Ray said, and took the shot of whiskey, grimacing as it went down.

Range Boss

"YOU KNOW." DENIS said, "it hardly seems appropriate for you to be riding in a car. Where's your . . . your godlike conveyance?"

"He can ride in a car if he wants to," Beej said from the passenger seat, glancing behind him into the backseat, which was improbably shadowy. "That's what being a god is all about, really. Being able to make choices."

"You think I should be riding, what, a stagecoach with wheel spokes made of thighbones?" the godlet said from the backseat, voice a distinctly John Wayne–style drawl. "Or maybe a pale horse?" He laughed. "No, *you* want me riding in something all shiny metal and curving blades, right? Shit. I'd be happy to travel in greater style. But I can't just snap my fingers and make that stuff appear. Maybe that'll be your *second* project, making me a proper mount. But I doubt it. There won't be anything recognizable as a street around here, soon. Once I get Janey woke up."

"I thought being able to create things was part of the

basic god skill set," Denis said, turning onto Bay Street and beginning the long, gradual ascent out of town and into the hills. He had the sense that he could push the godlet fairly far before being struck down. The monster needed him. And, more to the point, Denis *amused* him. He could tell, and it pissed him off, and made him even more likely to snipe.

Besides, they were going to get Jane, and that was scarier than the godlet's ominous presence.

"Nah," the godlet said. "That's a common misconception. Some gods are creators. Some are preservers. Some are destroyers. Me, I'm the last kind." The god spat, which made Denis's shoulder muscles bunch up—spitting! In his car! And what was he spitting? What did a thing of iron and homespun cloth spit *with*? "Which you'd best remember, next time you want to mouth off."

Denis sniffed. "I'm a creator, and you're not. You need me."

"I hate creators," the godlet said, and shifted in the strangely shadowed recesses of the backseat. "You'd better do everything you can to stay on my good side. Maybe then I'll let you take off among the willows before I finish scouring this place down to bare rock."

Denis fell silent, and Beej breathed a sigh of relief. Denis glanced at him. Beej had definitely gone all the way strange. They'd been . . . friends, sort of, insofar as Denis could be friends with someone who had only a passing familiarity with personal grooming. At least Beej knew his art, and Denis had to respect that. But he'd turned into the doomsday equivalent of a Jehovah's Witness, all smiles and crude attempts at conversion. He couldn't imagine why anyone would choose *not* to worship the god of earthquakes, mudslides, and wildfires! It was all part of his native inferiority complex, Denis

thought. Beej couldn't find any real value within himself—
there wasn't much to find, after all—so he had to look to
outside sources for validation. The godlet certainly had a *presence,* and his very existence unpleasantly jostled many of
Denis's most fundamental beliefs, but when you came right
down to it, he was a thuggish prick with a cowboy fetish.
What sort of god wore *spurs?* It simply wasn't right.

"Stop slowing down," the godlet growled. "I realize this
car's a piece of shit, but you can go faster than this, even uphill."

"Sorry," Denis muttered, pressing the accelerator. He'd
dropped to about ten miles per hour without even realizing
it. "My mind was wandering."

"Thinking about your sins, huh?" the godlet said.

"I don't believe in sin," Denis snapped. "We don't live in
a moral universe. There's no such thing as an objective 'right'
or 'wrong.' There's no final judgment."

"I find that temporary judgment is pretty effective,
though," the godlet said. "Especially since 'temporary' can
still last a damn long time."

"I hate it when you two fight," Beej said miserably.

Denis saw the turnoff coming up, but he didn't slow
down. He would drive right past. He would claim he didn't
remember where he'd left Jane. He would—

A freezing hand touched his shoulder—it was like metal
kept in a freezer, burning cold right through his shirt. "Turn
left, hoss," the godlet said, right in his ear.

Denis spun the wheel, and bounced over the edge of the
pavement. He slowed the car and stopped in sight of the half-
collapsed mound of mud and Jane's abandoned car.

"Yee-haw," the godlet said, without apparent irony, and
the back door clicked open. The shadows in the backseat

departed suddenly, and the interior of the car brightened enough to make Denis squint.

"This is amazing," Beej said. He looked at Denis and smiled, tentatively—Beej always looked like a dog that was hoping for a pat on the head but expecting a kick. "To be in the company of something so powerful, to be of *service* . . . we're extraordinarily lucky."

Denis just stared at him, not blinking, not letting any expression at all touch his face, and Beej blushed, looked at his lap, mumbled something wholly unintelligible, and got out of the car.

Denis stayed in his seat, his hands clutched on the wheel. It dawned on him, suddenly, that he could *get away*. The godlet couldn't fly, couldn't reach him; clearly he required mundane transportation. Denis could just put the car in reverse, back out onto the road, and drive *away*. He could escape. Hadn't the godlet said something about another member of his posse, one who'd gotten away—gone down the owlhoot trail? Escape was possible.

But he would have to go far away, he knew. He'd have to give up everything: his studies, his life. He was not yet convinced that those things were irretrievably lost. Denis had great faith in the power of the status quo. The godlet could talk about scouring life from the West Coast, but Denis thought life, *normality*, was more resilient than that. The world was inertial; it resisted change. Look at all the stupid hippies who still lived in the hills around Santa Cruz, waiting for a revolution that had never come, that *would* never come. Things would probably work out in the end, wouldn't they?

Then there was the matter of Jane. She didn't need to sleep, or eat, or piss, or anything. If Denis took off, the godlet would surely make good on his threat, and tell Jane what Denis had done. She would pursue him, and she would, inevitably, find him.

Even if she didn't pursue him, he would always wonder. He'd be looking over his shoulder for the rest of his life. Could he live with that much tension?

No. He would snap.

He didn't drive away.

When the godlet had its back turned, it was somehow easier to look upon. It didn't overwhelm the senses quite so much. Wasn't there something, in the Bible or somewhere, about how God had shown His backside to one of His prophets, because the sight of His full-frontal divinity would have proven too overwhelming? At any rate, now the godlet looked almost human, though extraordinarily tall, wearing jeans and a leather vest and a large, rather misshapen cowboy hat. The bit of uncovered—well, not *flesh*—substance between the hat and the collar shone dully, like tarnished chrome. The godlet might've been a special effect from a peculiarly genre-bending B-movie, a sci-fi Western, except for his incontrovertible reality. The godlet was as solid as the earth, more *there* than almost anything else Denis could see. He was as real as rocks and the sea, as inevitable as entropy and tooth decay. Denis shivered. Odd, that he should get a sense of the thing's power now, while watching him from a distance. Perhaps, closer up, Denis was too overwhelmed, too engaged in the complex business of maintaining his sanity, to appreciate it.

The godlet was walking around, looking at the mud from different angles, while Beej fluttered around. It was like that old cartoon, with the tiny yipping dog that bounced around the stately bulldog, trying for bigness by association. The godlet stopped walking, turned its head to look at Denis, the reflected flash of sunlight off its metal face briefly dazzling him, and then raised its arms like a conductor signaling a crescendo.

The mud rose up. That, too, could have been a good effect in a bad movie—damp soil shifting, rising, taking on vaguely human proportions, first a sort of lumplike golem shape, gradually acquiring definition; fingers, eyes, something like dreadlocked hair. And then it was Jane, absolutely and recognizably Jane, a figure sculpted in mud. She looked around suspiciously, squinting, and then her eyes fell on the godlet.

She collapsed to her knees and shouted "Goddess!" while raising her arms in what Denis considered a rather melodramatic gesture. He frowned. God*dess*? Well, hadn't the godlet said different people saw him differently?

"But why are you dressed like a cowgirl?" Jane said cautiously.

Within certain annoyingly immutable limits, Denis thought, and smiled, because really, it was *funny,* wasn't it—a god of destruction, a Kali for the Western world, dressed up like a *cowboy*?

For just a moment, the godlet flickered in Denis's sight; he suddenly had shiny black skin, and four arms, each tipped with hands dripping blood, and he—she—it wore a necklace of skulls. Just like an Indian goddess of destruction.

Except he still had on that misshapen hat, and though there were heads hanging from his belt, it was a *gunbelt,* complete with holsters. And Kali had never, in any depiction Denis had ever seen, worn leather boots and spurs.

Then the godlet was just himself again, metal and cowboy

clothes. That had been . . . strange. Denis hoped such a perceptive shift didn't happen again. He liked his supernatural intrusions into reality to be as consistent as possible.

The godlet gestured for Jane to rise, and she did, and then they all came back to the car, and there it was, that fundamental absurdity again: the mud-revenant and the god of earthquakes riding around in a decade-old Honda Civic. Beej took the passenger seat again, and Jane and the godlet took the back. Jane was lost in the godlet's shadows, but she reached out and caressed Denis's cheek, leaving a faint streak of mud there. "Hey, baby," she said. "I'm sorry I ran out on you, but I was so tired, and confused . . . I had to take a walk, to touch soil with my hands, and then I got hurt, and had to rest. But I'm not tired anymore. I feel strong."

"Good," Denis said, and concentrated on driving back down the hill.

"We're going to change the world," Jane said.

"Yep," Beej said, sounding happier than the proverbial pig in shit.

The godlet giggled, and for a moment Denis heard a burst of jaunty calliope music and smelled, of all things, sausages cooking, but then it was gone, and there was just the sound of tires on pavement, and the smell of Jane's mud and the godlet's sage-and-gunsmoke.

"Did anybody else hear—" Beej said.

"Sorry," the godlet said. "I just went all Harlequin there for a second. Nothing to worry about."

And though Denis had no idea *what* that meant, he didn't ask.

Snake Blood

"WE'VE GOT TO GET back to Santa Cruz," Marzi said. "We need…" She trailed off, looking at Jonathan's prone body. "We need to get him to a hospital."

Ray snorted. "Unless modern medicine has come a long way since my unfortunate incarceration, I don't think a hospital would do him much good."

"It's just shock," Marzi snapped, because she didn't want to believe it might be something worse. "When I first saw the Outlaw, I repressed it for *years*. And I'm the destined guardian!"

"Don't get too self-important," Ray said. "I don't know about being destined. You were able to do the job, and you were in the right place, so you got tapped. If I believed in Fate, I wouldn't worry so much; I'd just figure, oh, well, Fate will take care of it. Besides, I don't think your friend is suffering from shock. He probably didn't even get a good look at the Outlaw—I imagine it jumped out of here like a cricket from a brushfire."

"People in shock don't…

rattle," Lindsay said. She stood by the bar, holding Jonathan's hand.

"The Outlaw said something about touching Jonathan's heart," Marzi said. "I don't know what he meant."

"Hard to be sure," Ray said, leaning back in his chair, looking at the ceiling contemplatively. "But the thing to remember is, it's a wasteland walking. So . . . maybe it left a little piece of the wasteland lodged in Jonathan's heart. Maybe it salted the earth in his soul."

They didn't speak. Marzi finally exhaled. "Can I fix him? You said I could change the world, I could imagine things, right?"

Ray sighed. "How should I know? Sure, maybe there's a way. This is the medicine lands, everything's-possible territory. But I couldn't tell you how to do it."

The bat-wing doors creaked, and a shrouded figure stepped into the saloon, dressed in scraps of ragged fabric; the overall effect was that of a dishrag with legs. Its face was completely hidden, veiled by brown cloth.

"Nobody move," Ray said in a tight voice. "Sometimes, if you're very still, they just go away."

"What is it?" Marzi asked, barely moving her lips as she spoke.

"Something that lives here, in the medicine lands," Ray said. "That's honestly all I know. But they can be . . . unpredictable."

It swung its shrouded head to the left, and to the right, and then focused on Marzi. It lifted its arm and beckoned her. "Marzipan," it said, and its voice was rough, feminine, and familiar. "You are here, and your enemy is gone. This is not good."

"Holy fuck," Ray said, awestruck. "I've never heard a manitou speak before."

"Um," Marzi said. "I know you, don't I? You seem—"

Suddenly the bar was gone, as were Ray and Lindsay, and Marzi found herself floating in the air above Santa Cruz. But this was a Santa Cruz transformed, streets filled with sand, half-starved vultures roosting on top of buildings.

"I told you to look for me," the voice said, "in the West beyond the West. But you . . . forgot."

"I had a lot on my mind," Marzi said, squeezing her eyes shut. "I'd like to go back now, please."

"I can answer a question," the voice said, and Marzi opened her eyes. She was back in The Oasis. "I can be . . . something like an oracle."

"Who are you?" Marzi asked. "Why do you want to help me?"

"I am an interested party," it said flatly.

"That's not good enough," Marzi said, and crossed her arms. "Why should I believe you? For all I know, you're another *wasteland* thing, trying to trick me."

It laughed, and Marzi remembered the laugh, remembered that it had convinced her of the creature's truthfulness during her vision. "You waste time, but I have always been curious, too. I understand. I am a creature of the desert, a *spirit* of the desert, like your enemy. But we have . . . different points of view. Your enemy is the spirit of utter desolation, of alkali flats and ashes. When you think of deserts, you think of . . . dead space, don't you? All emptiness, sand, and dunes."

"More or less," Marzi said.

"But that's not true, is it?" Ray interrupted. "Deserts are full of life, teeming with it—but very specialized life, good at hiding, good at surviving. Deserts aren't just symbols of waste and desolation. The desert means other things, too—secret resources, beauty in unexpected places, hidden life. Right?"

"Yes," the rag-thing said. "I am a creature of that desert. The living desert."

"Why didn't you ever come to *me*?" Ray said. "I could have used a little help!"

"You were doing fine." The rag-thing might have looked at him. With the cloth over its head, it was hard to tell. "You had our enemy contained."

"Sure, but it was a pretty rough go! I could've used . . . shit, even some company! Some support! I've been here for years, alone, going crazy, fighting the djinn endlessly. And you show up now?" Ray was red in the face, shouting by the time he finished.

The rag-thing stepped up to Ray without seeming to cross the intervening space, a trick that was disconcertingly like something the Outlaw would do. "I am not your friend," it hissed. "I am the living desert. I am poison, and spines, and dehydration. I am the thirst that drinks whole rains in seconds. Not someone to chat with. I do not care if you're happy, or if you live or die. I only want my enemy kept in check."

Ray, leaning far back in his chair, nodded almost imperceptibly. His face was no longer red; it was pale and sweating.

The rag-thing stepped back, turned on its heel, and faced Marzi. "If you want me to help you, come to me. I live deeper in the West."

"What do you mean?" Marzi said. "You're here, now, and—"

"You'll need time to think about the proper question. You must be careful. And it will do you good, to walk in the desert. Besides, I am not really here. I am too . . . big . . . for this place. I would flatten your buildings with my bigness. This body you see is a messenger. An outstretched hand."

"If you're so big, why don't you smack the Outlaw down, then?" Ray muttered.

"Down to what?" the rag-thing said, amused. "We are of the same substance, he and I. I cannot hurt him. But I can help *you* hurt him. If you come to me, and ask your question, I will answer." It turned toward the door.

"Wait," Marzi said, panicked. What was she supposed to do, exactly? "Where do I—"

But the rags collapsed into a heap, and then seemed to *boil,* scorpions and little brown spiders and sand-colored lizards scurrying from the folds of cloth, racing for the door and cracks in the walls, gone before Marzi could think to step away, before Lindsay could finish drawing air to shriek.

"AT LEAST no one's here," Denis said, parking in the nearly empty lot just down the hill from the art building. "Fortunately."

"There are too many trees here," the godlet said. "I don't like being surrounded by so much cover. It's too easy to use it against me." His voice was gravelly, more human with every word.

"I suppose," Denis said. Santa Cruz University was not arranged in the traditional fashion, with buildings surrounding an open quad, and outlying facilities scattered as necessary on the outskirts. It was more decentralized than that, essentially a redwood forest with buildings scattered throughout, connected by a few roads and a number of footpaths. Denis had always felt the place had a nicely autonomous feeling—he didn't constantly encounter throngs of pot-smoking, beer-swilling students as he had at his undergraduate alma mater. You could walk across campus some mornings and see no one else at all.

"On the other hand," the godlet said, "a nice big fire on a dry day could cut this whole place down like a scythe through grain, couldn't it?"

"The hills are alive with the sound of ashes," Beej said, and giggled.

"To the studio," the godlet said, and unfolded himself from the car. Jane, Beej, and Denis all emerged as well, Denis looking around nervously. What if someone saw him consorting with a moron, a mud-girl, and—and—a primal earth-monster in a cowboy hat? But there was no one else around. He led the way—thus choosing to have Jane and the godlet behind him, which was nerve-abrading, but at least he didn't have to look at them—up the hill, through a stand of red-woods, around the back of a building, to an art studio's side entrance. He reached into his pocket for his keys, but the godlet said, "No, let me. I like opening doors." He stepped past Denis, brushing against his arm, and Denis staggered back against the walls as a wave—no, not a wave, more like a sandstorm, or a tornado full of ground glass—seemed to pass through his body invisibly. The world went gray, then beyond gray, to a colorlessness he'd never imagined. He gasped, coughed, and spat a little shower of sand. The grains sparkled as they fell. Jane was at his side instantly, stroking his back, cooing at him with concern, her mineral smell filling his nostrils.

The godlet glanced at him. "Sorry, pard. Didn't think about that. Beej has been, ah, altered to the point where he can suffer my touch, and Janey is beyond such concerns, but you're all ordinary glands and meat and weakness, and your kind and mine don't mix. I took down six lawmen today, just by touching them. I didn't make a point of leaving a piece of myself stuck in your craw, though. Count yourself lucky. Just be sure to stay clear out of my way in the future."

Denis clutched at his throat, which had been lacerated dozens of times on the inside by the tiny bits of sand he'd coughed up. Color gradually leaked back into the world, and after coughing a few more times, Denis felt cleared of sand. "Water," he said hoarsely.

"Soon, sweetie," Jane said. "We're busy now."

The godlet touched the door, and it swung open, though he didn't use a key or turn the knob. "If only all doors were so easy to open," he said, then stood aside. "After y'all."

Beej went first, then Jane, leaving damp brown footprints in her wake. "You, too," the godlet said.

"You hurt me," Denis said, looking into the godlet's eye-holes, at the lazily turning blades there.

"Won't be the last time, neither," he drawled.

Denis narrowed his eyes, thinking of *rust*, the unstoppable process of oxidation, creeping over the godlet's metal body—because it was a machine, a grinding machine, that would seize up, go dry, get vapor lock, lose ball bearings, break down into *nothing*.

A reddish speckle appeared on the godlet's face and spread from there, pitting, corroding, etching the metal.

The godlet laughed. "Oh, Denis," he said, almost affectionately. He held up an articulated-metal hand and looked at the flecks of rust now sprinkled there. "That's nice, a good cosmetic touch. But you can't hurt me. Your worldview isn't that powerful—you're outgunned. If you were in charge, you'd probably see me as a big ol' thing on tank treads with pincers and such, and everybody else would see me as some sort of machine. But I'm a gunslinger, Denis, that's the fundamental fact of my nature—and you don't kill an outlaw with rust." He chuckled, but with no real humor, as if he realized the nature of the conversation demanded gently mocking laughter, but didn't really understand why. "Do you think I'd keep a viper like you around if you could hurt me?"

"Outlaws aren't generally renowned for their intelligence," Denis said. "I'd hoped you'd be stupid enough to let me hurt you, yes."

"Outlaws aren't known for book-learning, it's true, but we do have a certain amount of cunning, and we're not good at forgiving betrayals. You *obey* me, Denis, and maybe you won't get crushed under my boot, understand?"

"I hear and obey," Denis said, rubbing his throat, counting to nine in his mind.

"Master," Beej said, poking his head out of the door. "I think you should come see this."

"You first," the godlet said, and Denis went inside, careful not to brush against him. He hadn't been able to hurt the godlet, not this time, but that didn't mean he couldn't be hurt at all. There might be other opportunities.

The studio was bright and spacious, with track lighting providing an even, uncritical light. Canvases in various stages of completion stood covered here and there, and workbenches broke the large space into individual artistic demesnes.

A rather attractive young woman that Denis knew slightly—her name was Caroline, he thought— was standing by a bench in the middle of the room, talking animatedly to Jane.

"—such a statement," she was saying, her face full of wonder. "To make your body into your art! I'm so impressed! Are you performing anywhere?"

Denis shook his head in distressed wonder.

Jane shifted uncomfortably, moving her weight from foot to muddy foot, though once upon a time she'd have thrived on a conversation like this. "Not performing as such. It's more a sort of open-ended thing, just . . . walking up and down in town."

"Well, sure," Caroline enthused, pushing her glasses up on her nose. "That's what art should be, direct communication with the people, free from artificial barriers like the stage—"

"What is this?" the godlet asked.

"This is the grease that keeps the art world turning," Denis said.

"Jane!" the godlet called.

Both Jane and the woman looked over. Caroline stepped back in alarm. Denis wondered what she saw when she looked at the godlet. Apparently not a god to be worshipped.

"Kill her," the godlet said.

"Huh?" said Beej.

"What?" said Denis.

"But, goddess," Jane said, glancing at Caroline, who was still staring openmouthed at the godlet.

"We're not playing cowboys and Indians with cap guns here," the godlet said. "This is serious. This is about planned extinction, human eradication. Kill that woman, Jane. She's part of the problem, believe me, she's a stinking sweating rutting spreading sack of scum, she's mold with a mind, *kill* her."

Jane took a hesitant step toward Caroline, who was beginning to realize the general outlines of her situation. "Jane, what are you doing?" she said. "That man, he looks so convincing, how much makeup did it take to make him look like that?"

"She's not a *man*," Jane said. "Why do you all keep calling the goddess 'he'?" She took another step. Caroline's lips tightened, and she picked up a utility knife and thumbed the catch to slide out the blade. She backed into a table and hesitated—she couldn't get away now without turning her back on Jane and threading her way through the tables, and she was clearly reluctant to do so. Her hesitation was the end of her.

"Jane, no!" Denis said, not because he cared about Caroline especially—they were barely acquaintances—but because he didn't want to see Jane puppeted around by the godlet.

To his surprise, it was Beej who stopped him, putting a greasy hand over his mouth, hissing into his ear. "The god will kill you, Denis, be quiet." Seeing the wisdom in this, Denis nodded, and didn't fight, but Beej didn't take his hand away.

"I'm sorry, sister," Jane said. "It's for . . . the greater good." She walked toward Caroline, slowly at first, but then seemed to steel herself, and rushed the woman. Caroline shouted and struck out with her knife, but the blade passed harmlessly through Jane's stomach, coming out muddy. Jane reached out, her hand now twice its normal size, and seized Caroline's face as if palming a basketball. Beej pulled his hand away from Denis's face, perhaps uncomfortable with the parallel. Jane put her other hand around the struggling Caroline's body, pulling her close, as if in an embrace. Caroline fought, punching, stamping down on Jane's insteps, all with no effect. Gradually, her struggles slowed, and ceased—Jane was filling her airways with mud, Denis supposed.

Jane kissed Caroline's forehead, leaving a smear of clay—like the word wiped off a golem's forehead, Denis thought, extinguishing life—and then let her body fall to the concrete, mud-spattered, unmoving.

"Show me the shop," the godlet said.

Denis stared at Jane. Jane stared at the dead girl.

Beej cleared his throat. "This way." He walked to the door that separated the sculpture shop from the rest of the studio, opened it, and looked inside. "No one's here," he called, relief plain in his voice.

"Pity," the godlet said, and went in after him.

Denis went to Jane and touched her shoulder, trying to ignore the body at her feet. "Are you all right?"

"I am only a vessel," she said, still staring at Caroline. "I . . . contain the goddess's grace. This was not my will. I am an instrument of Her will. That's all." She shook off his hand.

Denis glanced at the open door to the shop. "We can run," he said quietly. "We can get away." It had occurred to him that a way to keep Jane from chasing him was to run away with her. That would bring its own set of problems, but it was better than living in fear of her. His hopes of riding this out, of waiting for the world to make sense again and his life to return to normal, had died with the woman at Jane's feet. This corpse was a signpost: Denis was heading for country from which he might never return, a place where all routines were ruined.

Jane looked at him, her face a mask of white clay, and after a moment she shook her head. "I am in a great power's employ," Jane said. "I have proven myself loyal, and I will be exalted. The harder the path, the greater the glory."

"I'm not sure how you reconcile your feminist ideals with murder, Jane," Denis said.

"I'm not a woman anymore," she said, touching her mud-hips, her mud-chest. "I've changed. Feminism is irrelevant to my concerns, now. And this"—she gestured to Caroline's corpse—"is not murder. When an earthquake brings down an overpass, and crushes the people in their cars underneath, that's not murder. When a tornado blows apart a trailer park, and flings people into trees at hundreds of miles per hour, that's not murder, either. It's an act of god." She pressed her hands to her belly, as if assuring herself of her own reality. "I have become an act of god. I am a natural disaster."

Denis opened his mouth, but there was no answer to that. He wanted to say that natural disasters didn't *choose* to kill people, but in a way, the conditional refutation of that assertion was in the next room, wearing boots and a cowboy hat.

"Come, Denis," Jane said, and stepped over Caroline's body as if it were no more important than an old shoe. "I won't tell the goddess you wanted to run. Your fear is understandable. But I'm sure you can contribute to the cause."

"The cause of death," he said.

She patted his cheek with her slick hand. "Aren't you clever. The cause of the *earth*, Denis. Be happy." She went into the other room, and Denis followed, miserable, resigned. No amount of counting could soothe him now. He was screwed, right down to his boots.

Denis had spent a lot of time in the shop sculpting, last year, before he became more interested in crystal matrices. He'd briefly enjoyed making smooth metal analogues of biological things—frogs, flowers, crabs—and later had moved into a phase of building large metal models of small things— chrome amoebas that never changed shape, copper fleas. Some of those he'd sold, others were in storage, and those he'd deemed failures had simply been cannibalized for other projects. He was comfortable here in the shop, with the stained concrete floor, the high ceiling, the standing half-shaped stones, the unfinished metal and wood fabrications, the big steel lockers, and the utility room, a *Wunderkammer* of torches, hammers, masks, and saws.

"Tell him what I need, Beej," the godlet said, standing beneath an assemblage of polished wood that resembled a gallows, some student's work-in-progress. Jane stood beside him, looking like a work-in-progress herself.

"We have to build a door," Beej said. "I have the specs written down. Metal is best, something strong—nothing organic, if we can help it, not for the main structure at least. Once the basic framework is done, I'll do embellishments with wire, spikes, silk flowers, and so forth, but the actual door is your job. We need a freestanding frame, and a hinged door that swings one hundred and eighty degrees, so that it can open completely from either direction."

"And a lock," the godlet said. "A bolt you can close."

"Fine," Denis said. "May I ask why I'm supposed to build this?"

"It's a trap," the godlet said. "You're building the door to a trap."

"I just love these enigmatic half-explanations," Denis said.

"You wouldn't believe me if I told you," the godlet said. "You'll see soon enough."

"When do you want this done?"

"As near to now as possible. It doesn't have to be pretty—a little roughness around the edges would fit right in—just sturdy. And . . . potent." The godlet took off his hat and scratched his shiny head. "Make it *good*. That's your job. I don't know much about that part. A door's a door, as far as I can tell. The only thing that matters to me is which side I'm on, but you can make it into art. Now get your torch and start burning. Beej says there's enough metal here to do the job."

"And if someone should interrupt us?" Denis said, going to the closet to look for an apron and gloves.

"Oh, Beej will kill them," the godlet said.

Denis turned to look at Beej, who winced, but nodded.

"Me and Jane are off to wreak some havoc. We'll be back in a few hours, and you'd best be finished by then, understand?"

"I will be, or I won't be," Denis said. "You'll just have to come and see."

The godlet grunted and sauntered out. Jane followed, her gaze fixed worshipfully on the godlet's back.

"All right," Denis said wearily. "Let's move one of these workbenches in front of the door."

"Um. What?"

Denis sighed. "To keep people out, Beej. Unless you're really so keen on killing someone?"

"Oh. No, I guess not. Good idea."

"You should probably bring that dead woman in here first, so no one stumbles across her."

"I knew her name," Beej said. "It was Caroline."

"I know," Denis said. He went to the closet, thinking about torches, a face mask, right angles. Anything but Caroline's messy death. "Bring her. If there's one thing I've learned this week, it's that you have to be careful about where you leave your corpses."

Outriding

"SAY, MARZI," LINDSAY said, "what with your godlike powers and all, do you think you could give me a new outfit?"

Ray snorted. "She's the one who gave you that one, whether she meant to or not."

Lindsay ran her hands down the front of her bodice. "Hey, it's not like I don't love whalebone and red satin; it's just impractical for a desert trek."

"I'm still not sure you should go," Marzi said. "It could be dangerous."

"Oh, it'll be dangerous," Ray said, sitting on the piano bench, plinking the yellowed keys. "Quite dangerous. You don't see me volunteering to accompany you. I don't mess with big spirits, if I can help it— once was enough. This place is safe. It's an oasis. It used to have palm trees and a clear spring, but lately it's been a saloon, thanks to Marzi's psychic radiation." He hit middle C; it was flat. "I'm not complaining. Whiskey beats date wine every time. I might be piss drunk when you get back. I've held off until now, be- cause I thought I might have to deal with the Outlaw, but now that my shiny sheriff's star has been metaphorically pinned to your succulent breast, I'm ready to adopt the role of lovable town drunk."

Marzi didn't answer him. Her feelings toward Ray were a jumble: respect, annoyance, pity, gratitude. Mostly annoyance, at the moment. She knew she should cut him some slack—he'd been trapped here for a long time—but she had a feeling he'd been like this on the other side of the door, too: arrogant, with a streak of self-pity.

"Hello, fashion victim here," Lindsay said. "I'm going to have weird creases in my skin forever if you don't get this thing off me."

"Oh, I'll help you take it off," Ray said.

Lindsay scowled at him. "Modesty forbids."

"I was a great lover in my day," Ray said morosely.

"So *anyway*," Lindsay said, and looked at Marzi brightly. "Let's go, fairy godmother. Cinderella in reverse. Turn my party gown into tatters, or at least something that doesn't have stays."

Marzi stood from the bar stool, frowning. She looked at her hands, then raised them, like a conductor about to lead an orchestra. She had no idea what to do next.

"Oh, Christ," Ray said. "You don't do it with your hands, you do it with your *head*. Just imagine it, *see* it, the way you see a picture before your pen touches the paper. Just *see* it—"

Marzi looked at Lindsay. She thought. She saw.

Lindsay's Miss Kitty dress disappeared without so much as a puff of smoke. It happened with the speed of a camera trick—in one frame, Lindsay wore a terribly red dress, and in the next, she wore soft breeches, low-heeled black boots, a gray vest over a white shirt, a bowler hat, and two gun belts, crisscrossed low on her hips.

"Oof!" she said, patting the holsters at her hips. "These things are heavy! No wonder cowboys walk so funny."

"I think that has more to do with the endless horseback riding," Marzi said, pleased with herself.

"Not that those guns will do you much good," Ray said. "They're just made up, no more real than this piano. They won't hurt any of the things that live out there, if 'live' is the right word for mysterious forces of vast power."

"Yeah, but will they make a loud bang?" Lindsay asked.

Marzi laughed. She thought of telling Ray that her gun *did* have some substance in the real world, but why not keep a few secrets?

"I s'pose so," Ray conceded.

"Then I'm happy," Lindsay said, and tipped her hat back in a wholly unself-conscious gesture; not for the first time, Marzi marveled at her friend's ability to adjust to any situation. "So, we're off to see the wizard."

"More of an oracle," Marzi said.

"Shit," Ray said quietly. "I was wondering about that, how you'd see it, what it would be in your worldview. So it's an oracle, huh? Why do you say that?"

"I just . . ." Marzi trailed off, then shrugged uncomfortably. "It seems right, you know? That it will help, but only a little, and only if I ask the right question. There's a thing in my comic, a rattlesnake sphinx, and it—she, I think it's a she—reminds me of that: inscrutable, wise, and venomous." Marzi gnawed on one ragged fingernail, thinking ferociously, trying to pin down her thoughts; she'd always approached her art with faith in her subconscious, in her ability to conjure potent images from her own unexplored depths, but it was a process that needed to be examined, now, because her imaginings were taking on flesh and weight. "Only I think of this new spirit as more of a scorpion. A scorpion oracle."

"Okay," Ray said, nodding. "You're probably seeing through to the truth at the being's heart. Scorpions are dangerous, but there's probably no way you could think of this thing that would make it *safe,* any more than you could make the Outlaw into an environmentalist, but just . . . be careful." He pondered the ceiling for a moment. "At least scorpions are small."

Marzi decided not to mention that she imagined the scorpion oracle as vast, an enormous creature scuttling in cavernous shadows, an entity big enough to fill Neptune's Kingdom by the boardwalk. Why worry him?

"We should get going," Lindsay said. "Time's wasting, right? I doubt we're going to get back to Genius Loci in half an hour, like you'd hoped."

"It's hard to say," Ray said. "Time is funny here, I think. It doesn't move like time in the real world. Sometimes faster, sometimes slower . . . I don't know. It's just a feeling. Like I said, I haven't aged since I've been here, I don't have to eat, I don't sleep regularly. . . ." He shook his head. "These are the changing lands, but they're also the changeless lands. Just be careful. Don't get lost. Come back. I want you to trap the Outlaw again, so I can go back home. I miss the world. But I've got no desire to go there with the Outlaw running loose. I just want to retire in peace."

"Okay," Marzi said, hitching up her gun belt. "We're on our way, then."

"Can I ask one last thing?" Ray said.

"Shoot," Marzi said.

"You only get to ask the oracle one question, right?"

"Right," Marzi said, nodding.

Ray sighed. "Three would have been better, or a hundred, but you've got to go with your gut, I guess. What question will you ask?"

Marzi looked at Jonathan. She wanted to know what to do, how to save him. But she also wanted to know how to stop the Outlaw. She knew, intellectually, that saving Jonathan wasn't important, not compared to besting the Outlaw, but . . . She thought back to their time on the beach, looking into the tide pool; their ride in the sky glider over the board-walk; how brave he'd been later, on the beach, fighting Jane. There was something wonderful in him, and right now, it was full of dust. She couldn't bear that. The oracle would know how to save him. It would know how to stop the Outlaw, too. But maybe she could figure that out on her own; in a way, the Outlaw was her creature, subject to rules of her de-vising. Surely there was a way to exploit that? She was the guardian—didn't that mean she must have the resources to deal with the Outlaw?

But then, maybe the resource to deal with the Outlaw *was* the scorpion oracle, and asking about Jonathan would waste that opportunity.

Shit. What would Rangergirl do? Was that even the right question to ask herself anymore?

"I don't know," Marzi said. "I'll figure it out on the way."

"Just don't ask it if you'll ever find true love," Ray said. "Or anything like that."

Lindsay gave him a withering stare on Marzi's behalf.

"Just take care of Jonathan," she said, "and try not to get too drunk. We might need your help when you get back."

Ray grunted. "I passed my badge on to Marzi. As far as I'm concerned, I'm out of the law-and-order business."

"You're inspirational," Lindsay said. "C'mon, Marzi. Let's go. Into the Wild West."

They linked arms, and walked through the bat-wing doors, into the dust and the sun.

ONCE OUTSIDE, Lindsay looked at Marzi and said, "So, Sundance, which way do we go?"

"Well, call it a hunch, Butch, but I'm thinking we should go west."

"I'm hardly Butch," Lindsay demurred. "Maybe we should be Femme and Sundance."

Marzi laughed. If she had to be in this place at all, it was good to be here with Lindsay.

"West is a tricky proposition, though, since it's always high noon," Lindsay said. "There's no moss growing any-where around here, and I doubt we'll have a chance to sight on any stars, if I even knew how to do that, which I don't."

Marzi hitched up her gun belt, which was chafing her hips. "I think one of the particular truths of this place," she said, "is that *every* direction is west."

Lindsay nodded. "We're into something deep here, aren't we?"

"I'm sorry I got you into it," Marzi said automatically.

Lindsay shook her head. "That's not what I meant. This is something worth doing. I'm glad I'm here. There are times when I feel so separated from the world, Marzi, and that's what I see stretching in front of me for my whole future—that ivory tower of academia they talk about, up above everything. That's where I'm going to be for the rest of my life, too, unless I end up working in a museum or, God forbid, a gallery somewhere, and even those places are tiny little subcultures. This actually matters. What I do here really means something."

"I don't know," Marzi said. "Academia can mean something. The teaching part, anyway—I had some teachers who changed my life. And if *you* teach, the kids will love you."

Lindsay waved her hand dismissively. "Possibly. But teaching seems like small potatoes compared to stopping an ancient primal force of destruction from leveling the West Coast."

"Sure," Marzi said. "But after that, what do you do for an encore? You need something to fall back on." Marzi looked around at the yellow dust, the fading-almost-to-white blue sky, and said, "For me, I don't think I'll be drawing *Rangergirl* anymore."

"I guess I can see why," Lindsay said. "Though it's a shame." She hitched up her belts. "Shall we?"

"Off we go," Marzi said, and started walking purposefully forward. It didn't take long to get outside of town, where they settled into an easy walking pace. Once the town was behind them, there was just desert.

But that term, "just desert," was misleading, Marzi realized. Right now they were walking on hardpan, but off to the left she could see rolling Saharan dunes, and on the right, far in the distance, there were sharp high outcroppings of rock. There were patches of scrub, stands of saguaro cactus, prickly pears, arroyos, canyons, and what looked—somewhat disturbingly—like Pueblo-style cliff dwellings far

ahead. It was a collision of geographies. There *was* no archetypal desert, Marzi realized; all deserts were different, wildly
so in some ways. But wastelands . . . all wastelands were essentially similar. Only the color of the rocks varied.

"It's like a desert sampler platter out here," Lindsay said.
"I thought it would be a boring slog through a metaphysical
dust bowl, but it's not, is it?"

"Part of it is the nature of this place," Marzi said. "It's inclusive. And part of it's me, I think. We're walking through
my comic book now, for better or worse. I have some idea
what to expect, and maybe I have some control, but there's
nasty stuff in my comic, too."

"I know. I've read them." Lindsay pointed at the sky.
"What's that? Never mind, stupid question. I know *what*.
What I'm really wondering is what they're circling over."

Marzi looked. There were four vultures circling up on the
high thermals, and though at this distance they were little
more than black shapes with wings, Marzi knew they would
be shedding feathers, scaly-headed, and starving. Lindsay
was right—what *were* they circling? What was out there, far
in the desert, about to die?

Or maybe it wasn't about to die. Maybe the vultures were
desperate enough to watch anything that moved. "I don't
know," Marzi said. "But how about we don't go that way?"

"Agreed. How far do you think we have to go? How long
will it take?"

Marzi shook her head. "Couldn't say. Maybe distance is
variable here. This isn't the territory, it's the map, and you
can fold and crumple a map pretty much any way you want,
you know? And time doesn't work the way we're used to either, like Ray said."

"In the old stories about the land of Faerie, time moves differently. Rip Van Winkle and all that."

"True. But I thought Faerie was supposed to be *green*."

"The fields beyond the fields, sure," Lindsay said. "But maybe there are different kinds of fairyland."

"Medicine lands. The Outlaw called this place the 'lands beyond the lands.' It's spirit country."

"And we're going to meet a spirit." Lindsay shook her head. "So Jane was right about all that goddess of the earth stuff?"

Marzi shrugged. "I don't know. There are forces, beings, obviously, but I don't think they usually take a direct interest in humanity. They've got lives of their own, right? I doubt they're looking out for us."

"I can't decide whether or not that's comforting."

"I think it is. So far, direct supernatural intervention has done nothing but bad things for me."

"Oh, I don't know," Lindsay said. "You used to worry that you were crazy, right? At least that's cleared up."

"I'm past the point of thinking that this is all one big hallucination, sure." Marzi hadn't thought about that, but Lindsay had a point. "I'd been thinking of myself as this fragile thing, trying to keep from getting stressed out, because that's what the doctors said I should do. But you're right, it *wasn't* me that was nuts; it was the world."

"See? What this is, is a crucial part of the healing process."

"Let's hope it's not also the start of the grievous wounding process."

"Marzi, here in the desert, all we've got is hope."

They walked in silence for a while, exchanging glances when the hardpan became a rutted coach road, but neither of them saying anything about it. The heat was steady and strong, the air dry as a pumice stone and hungry for moisture, but Marzi wasn't thirsty, nor was she sweating overmuch. There were some advantages to wandering in a largely metaphorical desert, it seemed.

"Um, Marzi? What are those?" Lindsay pointed toward an expanse of reddish sand. It might have been the surface of Mars over there. Marzi squinted and saw tiny shapes, just blobs at this distance, approaching over the sand. They moved quickly, fluidly, growing larger.

Marzi knew what they were. It wasn't surprising that she could identify them, even from so far away. After all, she'd created them.

"Comanche," she said.

"Fuck," Lindsay said. "Should we run?"

"We can't outrun them. Besides, they like it when you run."

The Comanche in Marzi's comic weren't much like the real tribe, though they had a common origin. In reality, they'd been a fierce, warlike people—the name "Comanche" was taken from the language of a neighboring tribe, and literally meant "always against us." The real Comanche had been famed for their horseback-riding prowess and their skill with spears and arrows. While other tribes used horses primarily for transportation, the Comanche seldom left horseback, not even dismounting during raids, preferring to fight from the saddle. They were excellent trick-riders, too, capable of hanging upside-down beneath a galloping horse, firing arrows, or even throwing fourteen-foot lances. They were a proud, ferocious people, one of the great terrors faced by the settlers. Bad treaties and overwhelming enemies had finally broken the Comanche—but not in Marzi's comic. In the land beyond the Western Door, the Comanche had realized the futility of their battle against the white men, and made recourse to dark powers—such powers were always lurking in the pages of *Rangergirl*. The Comanche made a deal with demons in the desert, and received an army of chimerical monsters to use for mounts, mix-up beasts with wings, claws, scales, and fangs, each lethal, each different from the next. The chief rode a huge manticore, and was reputed to play chess with it. The battle leader rode a sphinx, and people whispered that the man and the monster were lovers. With the help of their vicious mounts, the Comanche retained control of a large part of the plains. They were not the Outlaw's allies—he wasn't the being they'd dealt with—but they were no friends of the beleaguered settlers, either. The tribe as a whole was slowly becoming monstrous, and some of the children were born with tails or the jaws of serpents or talons instead of fingers. The abominations were killed at birth, but that took its toll, too; the tribe's numbers were dwindling. Their territory was changing as well, the sand becoming red, the air taking on a bitter smell, fumaroles opening in the ground. The demons the Comanche had turned to for salvation were transforming them, making the Comanche like themselves, making their homeland a hell. Marzi hadn't decided yet what would ultimately become of the Comanche, whether they'd become irredeemably evil, or if some small part of the tribe might find redemption by destroying the rest. As the Comanche of her imagination approached her over the sands, Marzi wished she'd given that subject more thought.

Rangergirl had been in this situation once, faced by the

chief of the Comanche. What had she done? She'd parlayed, let the chief know she was tracking important prey, a monster from the depths of a silver mine that was rampaging across the plains, killing settlers and Indians alike. The chief had given her free passage across his territory, though his smiling, urbane manticore had wanted to devour her "womanly parts" as a toll.

But that was in her comic, and it wouldn't work out that way here. She had to remember that, appearances aside, these *weren't* her comic-book Comanche. They were denizens of the medicine lands who were, in some fundamental way, similar to Marzi's imagined tribe. And what were the basic qualities of that tribe?

Fierce. Proud. Violent. Not fond of intruders.

"Draw your guns, Lindsay. Shoot the guy in the lead, riding the sphinx."

"What, if he goes down, they all go down? Or they make you their new leader because you killed the old one?"

"No. He's just the most dangerous."

"But Ray said my guns won't work! They're just special effects!"

"I think he's mistaken. I think your guns won't *kill* the things that live here, but that doesn't mean they're useless. They'll be noisy, the bullets will hurt, but the spirits won't actually die."

The Comanche came, dust flying up around them, reddening the air, and they were totally quiet, without war cries or shouts; the silence was more unnerving than screams would have been.

"Marzi, they're throwing spears or something!"

"Yes," Marzi said. There was no time to tell her not to worry about the spears and arrows she could see. If you saw arrows coming at you, they were approaching at an angle, and would likely miss. The ones that hit you came point-first, and you couldn't see those at all. "Fire!" Marzi said, knowing Lindsay had never fired a gun before, and her accuracy would be for shit. The tide of monster-mounted Comanche presented a broad target, but still. She wished Lindsay had a tommy gun, something wildly inaccurate anyway, but that sprayed such a torrent it wouldn't matter; when it rains bullets, everyone gets wet.

Then she heard the deafening sound of automatic weapon fire, and Lindsay's thin high scream of surprise. Lindsay *did* have a tommy gun now, and against the laws of physics, she wasn't being spun around by the recoil, but stood her ground, firing. It was astonishing.

But then, Marzi had made sketches of a woman stagecoach robber armed with a sentient submachine gun, hadn't she? She'd just now imagined Lindsay into the role.

The chimera mounts began to fall as Lindsay swept her gun across them, blood spraying. Up close, Marzi saw that the monsters were horribly diverse—beetle mandibles, tentacles dragging on the sand, jointed crab legs, overlapping scales. The first rank of monsters fell, howling and thrashing, to Lindsay's gun, and they formed a barrier to the creatures rushing behind them, and even the uninjured mounts stumbled and tripped over their fallen fellows, throwing their riders. The unhorsed Comanche mewled and crawled weakly, helpless without their symbiotic mounts. The injured chimera were more than a wall, now; they were a trap, their spikes and flailing claws and grinding mouths inadvertently injuring their allies. They were making plenty of noise now, not war cries but howls of pain.

Lindsay's gun stopped chattering, and she and Marzi stared at the heap of groaning monsters a dozen yards away. The Comanche looked at Marzi and Lindsay with flat murder in their eyes, but none of them could do more than writhe or crawl among their fallen lances. The battle leader was pinned beneath his mount, the broken-legged sphinx licking at his bloodied face tenderly. None of them was dead, though.

Marzi's ears still rang from the gunfire. She'd never even pulled the trigger on her own gun. "Lindsay, let's get out—" she said, but then Lindsay screamed and pointed to the sky.

Marzi looked up and saw a black dot in the blue, growing rapidly larger, screaming down toward them through the air—was it a meteor? Whatever it was, she couldn't run, couldn't *move*, and then it was blotting out most of her vision.

The thing hit the ground with a heavy thump, but not an explosion, and Marzi looked at its dinner-plate-sized, mindless black eyes, its overlapping segments of armor, its six nastily barbed legs. It was a flea the size of a small car. It must have been at the rear of the initial charge, and *jumped*—a normal flea could jump four hundred times its own height—and landed here.

The Comanche on its back swung down. He wore an elaborate leather harness, tethered by springy cords to dozens of points on the flea's body, so he could have a full range of movement without leaving his mount. He swooped in close, snatched Lindsay's gun, and whooped, aiming at them and pulling the trigger.

The gun didn't fire. Marzi concentrated fiercely on that thought, that it *wouldn't* fire; it was a gun with a mind, and it wouldn't shoot its allies. Disgusted, the Comanche tossed the gun down, and the flea snapped it up with a flicker of its frightful jaws, and swallowed. The Comanche swung back up to his mount's back and took the reins.

Marzi drew and fired her Peacemaker into the Comanche's chest, then swung the pistol down to put a bullet in the flea's eye.

The flea fell, and its rider dangled upside-down in his web of straps, blood running down his chest, his neck, and onto his face. A few drops fell to the sand.

The other Comanche and their wounded mounts stopped howling. They all stared at the dead flea, its dead rider.

Dead.

"We'd better go," Marzi said.

"I don't think they're going to do anything else," Lindsay said. Her eyes were glassy. This was too much, too fast; it had all happened in moments.

"I know," Marzi said. "But I can't look at them anymore." She holstered her gun. She wanted to vomit. Rangergirl gunned down monsters all the time. Why had Marzi never written about the guilt, the shame, the outrage at one's own capacity for violence? It didn't even matter that it was self-defense—imminent danger made such action necessary, made it *possible*, but it didn't make it easy, or even right. They were the ones trespassing here, after all, not the Comanche.

For the first time, Marzi wondered if she'd be able to perform whatever acts of violence might be necessary to stop the Outlaw.

But she had to. It was that, or let countless people die, and she had to choose the lesser death. "Could" or "couldn't" didn't even come into it.

"Let's go," Marzi said, and they set off into the deeper desert, a tribe of silent wounded monsters at their backs.

As they left, they heard flapping wings, and saw enormous, almost humanoid vultures spiraling down to eat the dead.

Another Jump to Hell

THE LAND BECAME more hilly as they traveled, until the horizon went from a distant, hazy line to something sharp and up close, just the top of the next hill. They crested a hill and looked down at a black shape snaking across the valley, roughly perpendicular to their path. They stood watching for a while. "It's a steam engine," Lindsay said at last. "See the smoke puffing up?"

Marzi nodded. A black locomotive moved slowly across the plain in the far distance, black metal gleaming in the sun, cloud-white billows rising from the smokestack. There were passenger cars, a seemingly endless line of them, stretching away behind the engine.

"Who's driving it?" Lindsay said. "And who's riding on it? It looks like a *lot* of people."

"In my comic," she said, but Lindsay interrupted her.

"Oh, God, the bone train? You're telling me that's a locomotive to the *underworld*?"

Marzi shrugged uncomfortably. "It's something we're

perceiving as the train to the underworld, something similar in function, maybe, or . . . I don't know, maybe not similar at all, but just close enough. I don't really understand the rules."

"This is creepy stuff, Marzi. It's starting to get to me. And this sky, Jesus, it's so fucking *big,* it stretches from edge to edge, you know? It makes me feel tiny. . . ." Lindsay shook her head. "I never understood agoraphobia, but I think I'm starting to."

"I don't think people like us are meant to be in a place like this. Our minds are working overtime trying to translate all the data, trying to make the stuff we're seeing make sense to our eyes, projecting it all through the weird Western filter of my *Rangergirl* comics. It's bound to be a strain." And yet, it wasn't really a strain, not for Marzi—presumably because she was the guardian. Lindsay didn't have whatever special resources Marzi did, and she was starting to look a little wide-eyed and dazed. Marzi put her arm around her. "We can take it slow, stop whenever you want, you can close your eyes, lean on me . . ."

Lindsay nodded gratefully, squeezing her eyes shut. "I always thought I'd love to do the whole *Wizard of Oz, Alice in Wonderland* thing, going to a strange new world, but it's *hard.* I can feel things aren't right, or I'm not right, or something, and I see movement from the corners of my eyes, like the landscape is filling itself in, so it'll be whole by the time I look at it straight on." She inhaled sharply, then released a long, shaky breath. "I am not a proper astral adventurer."

"We'll get through it, Lindsay," Marzi said.

Lindsay opened her eyes and then, gently, kissed Marzi

on the lips. Marzi was surprised, but she didn't freeze or pull away. "Thank you," Lindsay said. She scowled. "Can't you do something about the sun, though? It's weird, being this hot and not being sweaty or anything."

"I don't think the sun's going to set anytime soon."

Lindsay rolled her eyes. "Oh, yeah. In *Rangergirl* there's that whole prophecy, right?"

Marzi nodded. "In the land beyond the Western Door it's always high noon, but once the land is free of evil, the sun will set, and the girl who won the West will walk away, into the sunset, never to return; giving her kingdom to the people." Marzi grimaced. "It didn't seem so silly when I wrote it."

"It's got a certain pulp majesty, I always felt," Lindsay said. "Bet you would've written your comics differently if you'd known you were going to have to walk through them, huh?"

"There would've been more restaurants, trees, and swimming pools, yeah."

"I don't believe I'd get into a swimming pool in this place. You'd probably find the Midgard serpent living at the deep end or something." She shaded her eyes and looked down. "There's the caboose, finally. I guess we should keep going."

They went down the hill, losing their whole-landscape view, and then Marzi stopped, listening to what sounded like distant thunder. "Aw, fuck," she said softly.

Lindsay raised her eyebrow. "What's that?"

"I think it's . . . buffalo."

Lindsay nodded. "Of course it's buffalo. What else would it be?"

"I just did *sketches* for this. It didn't make it into the comic because I couldn't see where it was going . . . shit. I think it's *white* buffalo. Bone white."

"You're going to have to be a little more explicit, Marzi," Lindsay said.

"In my original idea, the bone train was followed by a herd of stampeding, skeletal buffalo—they were like psycho-pomps, Western Valkyries, there to pick up stray souls, or people who jumped from the train, or . . . I never worked out exactly *what* they were, because I decided not to use them. But it sounds like they're coming."

"Or something like them," Lindsay said. "Something that likes to pick up stray souls?"

They looked at one another.

"I'd say 'run,' " Marzi said, "but I don't know where we'd run to. It sounds like they're pretty far away, running through another valley. . . . If they *are* following the train, we should be fine, right?"

"Right. I am officially reassured."

They hunkered down, protected from the thunderous noise by the hillside. The sound swelled, like the crescendo of an all-percussion symphony; there was the sound of bony hooves hammering hard-packed earth, and along with that the sound of bones clacking together, and in her mind Marzi could see the creatures, rushing in a herd shaped like a wedge. She could imagine every joint, every bone wholly scoured of flesh, if these creatures had ever *had* flesh. Then Marzi realized what they were: the ghosts of all the buffalo slaughtered during westward expansion. Those stampeding, skeletal creatures weren't shepherds or guardians; they were the vengeful dead, and the humans on the train to the underworld were finally in their territory again. If any poor souls missed the train they would be ground beneath those hooves forever, smashed and ground into the finest particles, into constituent—but still *conscious*—atoms.

Marzi moaned. Because if the noise over the hill *hadn't* been a herd of skeletal white buffalo before, it certainly was now. She had to get her imagination under control. She shaped this place, after all, she defined—

Marzi stood up, slowly. Lindsay tugged at her trouser leg. "Are you crazy?" She had to shout to be heard over the clattering thunder of hooves.

"No," Marzi said. "It's all right. We're safe. They can't hurt us."

"And you're *sure* about that?"

"Yes," she said simply, and that was enough for Lindsay, who stood up, too. "We're not dead," Marzi explained. "They hate the living, too, but they can't hurt us." That was true. She'd *decided* it was true. She went to the top of the hill, and Lindsay followed.

They looked at the bone white cloud of dust, which filled the sky in that direction, and then at the tiny-by-comparison herd of white buffalo running after the black train. They were broad-shouldered, thin-legged things, each one as white as fine china, making a sound like castanets, like maracas, but like nothing so much as thousands of bones grinding and banging together. After a few moments the sound began to fade, and the herd disappeared from view. The cloud of bone dust still hung in the air.

"We've gone far enough," Marzi said, and knew it to be true, *made* it be true. "The scorpion oracle is here, now."

"What—" Lindsay began, but Marzi held up her hand,

and Lindsay fell silent. Marzi pointed at the cloud of dust, which was beginning to dissipate.

In the depths of the cloud, revealed as the dust settled, a structure stood, part mountain, part walled fortress, a lumpish, squat thing of granite, imposing and vast.

"What's that?" Lindsay said.

"It's where the scorpion oracle lives," Marzi said. "Where the rattlesnake sphinx lives, in my comic, but they're not that different—wise and dangerous creatures. I think it's worth noting that the scorpion oracle appeared to me, not as something I'd *already* created, but as something I *might* have created. You see? The scorpion oracle is the other side of the coin from the Outlaw: It's life, it's creative, it's not totally dependent on me. But I *can* control it. A little, at least." She gestured. "That building is my version of the Arizona Territorial Penitentiary, the Devil's Island of the desert. In real life the prison was bordered by desert, a river, and a town full of people who liked nothing better than shooting escaped prisoners." As she spoke, the sound of running water filled the air, and a fast-moving river . . . *insinuated* itself into the landscape, curving around the prison. A town—clearly a ghost town, abandoned—grew on the other side of the prison, some buildings popping up like mushrooms after rain, others seemingly precipitating out of the still-settling cloud of dust. Lindsay gaped, but for Marzi it was just like drawing a picture, only on a bigger page. The hills faded away, flattening out into a brutal plain of hardpacked earth. "There was a Gatling gun on a turret over the courtyard, and once when a group of prisoners tried to escape, the warden's wife fired it into the crowd, mowing the prisoners down. This was the place where the worst criminals were sent. It's all granite, and iron bars, and as near to escape-proof as they could make a prison in those days. There's even a snake pit. An honest-to-god snake pit. And in my version, it's even *worse*, it's bigger and meaner, it grows like a tumor. It's a haunted prison full of hate and poison and snakes, and the rattlesnake sphinx, of course, lives in the snake pit." Marzi looked at Lindsay, who took a step backward, apparently startled by something she saw in Marzi's eyes. "But here it's a scorpion pit, and a scorpion oracle lives there. We have to go talk to it. We have to ask it a question."

"We have to ask it how to defeat the Outlaw," Lindsay said.

"No," Marzi said, looking back at the dark rock walls of the prison, the palace. "We have to ask it how to save Jonathan. To bring him all the way back to life. That's what this creature is, after all—the spirit of the living desert, of dangerous life lived in the moments of grace between dying of thirst and dying of the heat." She caressed the gun at her hip. "I'll take care of the Outlaw myself. I know how to do that now. I just figured it out."

Marzi set off down the hill toward the prison's monolithic front gates, and Lindsay followed.

"IT'S GOOD." Denis said.

"It is, isn't it?" Beej said. He extended his hand to Denis, and Denis shook it, solemnly. Normally Denis was reluctant to touch Beej, who probably had several unusual skin diseases, but it was the right thing to do. They'd partnered, and worked together, and made something good.

They'd made a door.

It stood seven feet high and three feet wide. The corners of the frame were joined with fat ugly welds, which was inevitable given the speed with which Denis had been forced to work, but it didn't detract from the piece; in fact, it added to the door's sense of menace. The hinges were mismatched, one black iron, one tarnished bronze. The door itself was barred, made of crisscrossed lengths of metal welded hastily together. There was no knob—you opened the door by pulling on the bars; there were plenty of handholds—but there *was* a lock, a tube of metal that slid into a bolt and locked with a twist. Of course, anyone on the inside could reach through the bars and undo the bolt, but Beej said that wouldn't be a problem. That was the basic form, what Denis had made, a freestanding dungeon door.

Beej had embellished it.

He had a locker in the studio, and it was full of his magpie acquisitions. Beej made collage out of trash and photographs, and he had a lot of trash. He'd glued rhinestones around the door frame, then painted them glossy black; they sparkled like the eyes of spiders. He'd wrapped barbed wire around the bars in the door, and smeared glue randomly on the door and tossed handfuls of sand at it, giving the sculpture a scabrous, mangy aspect. He had a bag full of shark's teeth, and he painted them all black and glued them to the door frame and the door itself, so the teeth interlaced when the door closed, making it resemble a ravenous mouth. The door was a gateway to desolation, and it seemed just on the verge of becoming animate, of lurching across the concrete floor, snapping its hinged jaws like something out of an early Stephen King story.

"And yet . . ." Denis said.

"It needs something," Beej agreed.

"Something . . . over the door. Like a horseshoe."

"But not."

"No," Denis said. "Of course not actually a horseshoe."

They gazed together at the door for a while. "I know just the thing," Denis said. "I'll go and get it."

"I can't let you leave," Beej said. "If you try to run, to get away . . ."

Denis stared at him. "I'm not going to leave before it's *finished*," he said.

Beej ducked his head, then nodded. "Okay. But hurry. If the earthquake god comes back, and you're gone—"

"What? He'll kill us? I suspect he'll do that anyway eventually, but for the moment, he needs us. Don't worry, I'll be back soon."

Denis returned fifteen minutes later, carrying a buffalo skull carefully, in both arms. "From the anthropology department," he said, ignoring Beej's look of stupid relief that he'd returned at all. "Part of some Native American collection. I tore off the leather thongs and feathers they had dangling from its horns." Denis *had* considered running away, of course, but the problem with that was the old familiar one: Jane. She could be an ardent pursuer, he suspected, and he preferred standing in the long shadow of imminent danger to a likely short lifetime of running and fear. Besides, there might still be a chance to strike against the godlet for the pain and humiliation he'd suffered.

Most importantly, though, he needed to finish the sculpture.

Denis bound the skull on top of the door frame, using epoxy to hold it in place. Beej wound wire through its eye sockets and nostrils, binding it to the door. They stepped back, and Denis nodded in satisfaction. The skull added a whole new dimension, a further hint of sentience, to the object. "It's like the door is the skull's mouth, a giant metal prosthetic jaw," Denis said.

"It's perfect," Beej said simply, and though Denis had a number of objections to that word on principle, he nodded.

"I don't think our patron is an art lover, though," Denis said. "So why did he have us make this? What is it *for*?"

"It's going to swallow Marzi," Beej said, and took a rolled-up, tattered comic book from his pocket. He tossed it to Denis, who flipped through it, first disdainfully, then incredulously.

"Oh, please. That's ridiculous. It will never work."

Beej looked at the door, as if he were looking into a mirror. "It will work," he said, "because I believe it will work."

Denis shivered, and felt briefly as if he were in the presence of something greater and more awful than himself. Then he remembered it was only Beej. "I see," he said. "Good for you. I never liked Marzi much anyway. She got me banned from Genius Loci for life. I *love* that place."

"I wouldn't worry about that," Beej said. "Genius Loci is the next place we're going."

Big Augur

MARZI AND LINDSAY passed through the wide-open gates, Lindsay craning her head to look at the tops of the brutally thick walls, the gun turrets, the crenellations. Marzi walked on, seemingly oblivious to the grandeur—but then, it had come from her imagination, hadn't it? "Aren't prison doors normally shut?" Lindsay asked.

"This isn't a prison anymore," Marzi said. "It's a den." She walked across the courtyard toward the immense main building, a block of solid stone with high thin windows.

"I don't understand why a spirit of life would want to live in a place that's all granite and sand and iron bars." Lindsay was whispering, the immensity of the courtyard too much like being in a church, in the presence of something divine and disapproving.

"You misunderstand her nature," Marzi said, not whispering, clearly preoccupied. "She's more the spirit of *perseverance,* of life in extreme circumstances. She doesn't have anything to do with jungles or forests. Maybe individual lives are difficult in those places, but life as a whole thrives in them easily. She's only interested in lives struggling to survive in the desert, or the deepest part of the ocean, or the frozen wastes." Briefly, the landscape flickered, the prison becoming a humped turtle shape, covered in white snow, and the land around them a freezing Siberian plain. Lindsay barely had time to gasp and shiver at the numbing cold that washed over her before the landscape changed again, became the desert and the prison. Marzi didn't seem to notice the change, any more than she would notice a brief digression in the course of her thoughts, Lindsay supposed. Maybe *Marzi* was the dangerous and divine spirit Lindsay sensed here. That was a sobering idea. "So in a way," Marzi went on, "a prison is the perfect den for her. People live in prisons, but it's hard living. Especially in this prison."

They went into the building, into darkness crisscrossed by shafts of light coming in through the arrow-slit windows. It smelled of dust and something Lindsay couldn't identify, something acrid. There were no interior walls here, just piles of rubble with bits of iron sticking out, fragments of chains and bars and gates. All the walls had been knocked down to make a vast cavern. Lindsay's eyes adjusted, but she couldn't see the ceiling, or even the far walls, and she was reminded of those stories about places that were bigger on the inside than they were on the outside—those stories had always seemed, to her, to be metaphors for the imagination, the heart, the mind, all the spaces inside people that were larger than the walls of bone and skin that circumscribed them.

In the floor ahead of them, across an expanse of rock-strewn stone floor, there was something like a crater, or the caldera of a volcano. A hole, with rubble heaped around the edges.

"The snake pit," Marzi said. "The scorpion pit. That's where she lives. That's where we have to go."

Lindsay cleared her throat, the sound echoing tremendously in the space. "Oh," she said. "Down there?"

"To the edge, at least," Marzi said, and calmly unholstered her gun. For a moment Lindsay thought she meant to charge the hole, shooting into the darkness, but she just set the gun carefully on a rock. She looked at Lindsay and gave her a smile, though it was distant, almost perfunctory—Marzi's mind was operating on some other plane entirely, most of her attention given to things Lindsay could not sense or see. "I don't want her to think I'm coming as an emissary of death."

"Should I put down my guns, too?" Lindsay said.

"Already did," Marzi said, and Lindsay looked down, seeing that she was right—her guns were gone. Marzi must have spirited them away.

"My gun's the only real one, anyway," Marzi said. "The only one with enough substance to kill anything here. But still, no reason to appear threatening. We're here as penitents."

"I don't get it," Lindsay said. "She *invited* us, so why all the hoodoo? Why the walk across the desert? Why couldn't she just answer our questions at The Oasis?"

"I needed to learn," Marzi said. "Learn how I could shape this place, and I couldn't do that sitting in Garamond Ray's Oasis. He never struck out into the deep places; he never tried to learn the extent of his abilities. He was content with trapping the djinn and using his own life for the cork in the bottle." She shook her head. "That's not good enough for me. Sometimes you have to wander in the desert to learn, Lindsay. And anyway, things mean more if you have to work for them."

"That's what my mother told me when I was sixteen and she wouldn't buy me a car," Lindsay muttered.

Marzi didn't laugh, didn't even seem to hear. She went to the edge of the pit and knelt among the rough stones, her head bowed. Lindsay stood back, unsure what to do—kneel, or just stay out of the way? *Sisterhood and solidarity,* she thought, and went to kneel beside her friend. It was uncomfortable, and the only sound was Marzi's regular, measured breath, and Lindsay began to wonder why they were sitting beside a hole in the ground.

"Enter," said a voice like the crackling of dry leaves, and then the rocks inside the pit changed—or else, Lindsay's *vision* changed—and there was a rough-hewn stairway, leading down into the impenetrable dark.

Marzi stood without hesitation and started down the steps. Lindsay followed, wishing absurdly that she still had the guns at her waist. At first, they walked down a gentle slope into the vast hole, but later they passed through a smaller opening, and the walls closed in around them. Lindsay expected total darkness, but instead the walls began to glow, lines of pale green fire twisting sinuously on the walls. Some of the glowing lines were moving, very slowly. Lindsay paused to examine the wall—Marzi kept walking—and saw that the light came from bioluminescent fungi, and thumbnail-sized glowing beetles. The beetles constantly shifted their configurations, but the patterns they made didn't seem random, more like letters in a language somewhere between Arabic and Sanskrit.

Was Marzi making them do this? Or did these creatures belong to the scorpion oracle?

Lindsay hurried down the steps, following the gentle curve of the stairway. It no longer looked like artlessly tumbled rocks, more like a secret passage in an old horror film.

When Lindsay reached the bottom of the stairs, she found Marzi waiting, looking down a short hallway that ended in an arch-shaped wooden door with iron hinges. The walls here were alive with fungi and bugs, all glowing, and Lindsay could see the fixed look of concentration on Marzi's face, her expression made eerie by witchlight. "When we pass through that door, we'll find the oracle," she said. "The physical manifestation of . . . for want of a better word . . . a god. We will ask a question, and it will answer." Marzi glanced at Lindsay. "You were always smarter than me. So listen closely when the oracle answers. I might need your help figuring out what it means."

"Glad to be of service," Lindsay said, and it was true; she'd felt essentially useless so far.

Marzi gave her a brief, summer-lightning smile, and went to the door. There was no knob, just a big iron ring, and Marzi closed her fingers around it. "Fucking doors," she said, without rancor, and pulled on the ring. The door opened, scraping loudly against the stone floor. *I hope we weren't counting on the element of surprise,* Lindsay thought. Firelight flickered beyond the door, and Marzi strode in, Lindsay following. The room was big—Lindsay could sense that— but poorly lit by a pair of torches in sconces nearby.

Something crunched under Lindsay's boots.

"Gross!" Lindsay cried. The floor was alive with crawling things—scorpions, their tails little upraised question marks, and sleek black spiders, and long centipedes. They scurried away from Marzi and Lindsay, creating a little semicircle of bare stone around them, except for the ones Lindsay had crushed. "It was an accident," Lindsay said nervously. "I didn't mean—"

"Shh," Marzi said. "No harm done. The scorpion oracle can be hard on her creatures. She doesn't mind if a few of them get crushed."

Hardly reassured, Lindsay tried to scrape her boot off on the rough stone floor. Maybe the scorpion oracle wouldn't care if she and Marzi got crushed a little, too—had Marzi considered that?

Suddenly the room filled with light, flames bursting into life all around them. Once Lindsay's eyes adjusted to the dazzle, she saw more of that twisting, sinuous language on the walls, carved into the rock, but still shifting, defying the stone. The light came from pedestals set at irregular intervals throughout the room, each topped with an ornate iron cage. Inside each cage, fierce white-hot flames burned. The room was suddenly as bright as an operating room, though infinitely more filthy. The flames in the cages moved strangely, seeming almost alive—and Lindsay gasped when she made out a head, and feathered wings, and claws in one of the cages. "Marzi," she said. "Are those . . . phoenixes?"

Marzi nodded, seemingly unsurprised. And why should she be surprised? She'd created this place, right? Or, at least, her perceptions had shaped it; she was clothing the god of perseverance in a costume she could comprehend. Lindsay looked around the room, and realized it *was* like something Marzi would draw—maybe it even existed already, in sketches for the next comic, the one where Rangergirl would finally meet the rattlesnake sphinx. There were stone statues of scorpions here, much bigger than life-sized, including one on a platform in the center of the room that was bigger than a car, its pincers monumental, its eyes dully glowing rubies. This place had a certain lost-temple grandeur, a slightly ironic pulp-adventure sensibility; it was, in other words, pure Marzi.

"All this is just . . . anteroom," Marzi said. "All this stuff, the statues, it's the sort of thing penitents and worshippers bring. This isn't what oracles are *about*—this is just the sort of thing that gets built up around oracles. Let's go to the heart of the place." She set off across the room, not even looking down, and the carpet of insects made way for her, scurrying aside as Marzi wove her way among the phoenix-filled cages toward the back of the cave.

There was a hole in the wall, like a cartoon mousehole in a baseboard, but rougher around the edges, and big as a garage door. It was simple, and dark, and no light came from inside. Lindsay knew there was no going into that place, not if you ever wanted to come out again. This other room was a temple, but *that* place—that was a den, where something frightening lived.

"I come as a penitent," Marzi said, speaking loudly. "I come to ask your aid."

There was a rustling in the cavern.

"Ask," a voice said, the same voice that had said "Enter" above.

"I want to know how to heal my friend Jonathan," Marzi said.

Lindsay suppressed a groan. Sure, Marzi had said she wasn't going to ask about the Outlaw, but Lindsay had held out hope that good sense would triumph. Yes, she wanted Jonathan to get better, too, very much, but wasn't it more important for there to be a place for him to get better *in*? If the Outlaw had his way, the whole West Coast would be a smoking ruin.

There was a moment of silence. "That . . . is . . . the wrong question," the oracle said, every word seemingly a struggle.

Marzi snorted. It was an astonishing sound, Lindsay thought—snorting at the scorpion oracle was like laughing at a hurricane. "You don't get to decide that. You just have to answer."

"You should ask about the Outlaw!" the oracle said, more confidently, but it sounded a little peevish, too, less elemental, more human.

"Oh, I've got that under control," Marzi said, and Lindsay wondered if that were true, or if Marzi was just playing it by ear. She wanted to believe Marzi had a plan, had figured out all the angles . . . but she knew how Marzi wrote. She never knew how her stories were going to end when she started a comic. She just found a beginning, had a few ideas and images in mind, and started working, trusting that everything would work out in the end. That worked for her, for comic books—but this wasn't a comic book, despite certain superficial similarities. "I need you to tell me something *useful*."

"Very well," the oracle said. "I am . . . constrained . . . by this shape. I have little choice in this matter."

"Damn straight," Marzi said.

"Very well," the oracle said. "The heart, once a temple of

blood, has become a tomb of dust; journey inward, and bring the sleeper in darkness back to the light."

There was a moment of silence.

"That's it?" Lindsay said. "That's the answer to how we help Jonathan?"

"I did not wish to speak cryptically," the oracle said, but Lindsay thought she heard a note of malicious satisfaction in her voice. "I wished to explain, very clearly, but when I tried to speak . . . well. You heard."

"Oracles are cryptic," Marzi said, shaking her head. "That's not something I can reimagine, something I can change—I believe it too deeply."

"So this was for nothing?" Lindsay said, despair threatening to crash in again.

"I wouldn't say that," Marzi said. "I think I understand, actually. I'm not sure what will happen when we try, but I think I know what to do."

"You understood?" Lindsay said, trying to keep the disbelief from her voice. "Really?"

"Sure," Marzi said. "In a way, I wrote the dialogue, right? I understand how this place works, now. Come on. I'll show you. But first . . ."

Marzi knelt by the opening to the cave. "Thank you, spirit," she said. "You have done me a great service."

"Return the favor," the oracle hissed. "Defeat our enemy."

"I'll do my best," Marzi said, and stood up. "Come on, Linds. Up we go." Marzi sounded cheerful, and engaged, and all there again, Lindsay noted. Dealing with the oracle had put some sort of bizarre strain on her—maybe it was the effort of creating this setting, of keeping the oracle more or less under control.

They passed through the anteroom, and went back up the stairs—only to emerge from a trapdoor in the wooden floor of The Oasis. Lindsay looked around, stunned, as she climbed into the bar. Garamond Ray, sitting by the piano, looked no less surprised. "But, what?" Lindsay said. "How did we get here?"

"We've done our time in the desert," Marzi said, climbing out, and then closing the trapdoor, which blended seamlessly into the floorboards—and maybe disappeared entirely, as far as Lindsay knew. "For now, anyway. There was no reason to walk back. Space and distance are flexible around here, if you know how to exert the right pressure." She walked to Jonathan, and laid her hand against his forehead. "We're about to get a demonstration of just *how* flexible." She smiled at Lindsay and Ray. "Are you guys ready?"

"For what?" Ray said, eyes narrowed. Marzi had proved more capable than he'd expected, Lindsay realized, and he was beginning to wonder if he was outclassed and outgunned, if the greenhorn had already surpassed the old gunfighter.

Marzi stroked Jonathan's cheek. "We're going to save him."

"How?" Lindsay said.

"By going into the temple of his sand-choked heart, and bringing him out again," Marzi said.

She sounded so sure that Lindsay allowed herself to believe, for a moment, that Marzi really did know how this story was going to end.

THE GODLET RETURNED, chrome gleaming, boots clocking on the concrete. He walked around the door, examining it from all angles, thumping his metal fist against the frame, making it clang.

I should be worried, Denis thought. *I should be afraid our esteemed master won't like it, but I'm not.* Even Beej, who turned into a lapdog around the godlet, seemed confident.

"Well?" the godlet said. "Is it good? It looks like a door, so that's all right, but I'm whatever the artistic equivalent of tone-deaf is, so I can't tell if it's good or not. I don't *like* it, but that doesn't mean much—I don't like anything that's made, anything where fragments get together into something whole. So is it good?"

"It's the best work I've ever done," Denis said.

"Ditto," Beej said.

"So it'll work, then?"

"I believe it will, my god," Beej said.

"That's all it takes, for a fella like you, Beej. Belief. And proximity to me, of course. The properly charged atmosphere."

"Listen," Denis said. "I read the comic, the thing about the box canyon—that's really what you plan to do?"

"Yep," the godlet said. "Trap Marzi in a tide pool, a solipsistic loop . . ." He paused. "Solipsistic. Damn. I'm spending too much time around you, Denis. Marzi's a big damn radio tower, and Beej is nearly as strong, but you're getting to me, too, and you're barely a shortwave. Solipsistic, hell." The godlet turned back to the door. "Let's heave to, boys. We've got to carry this thing to the café."

Denis snorted. "I somehow doubt it will fit in my trunk."

"No. That's why Jane's out stealing a truck. There's some construction on campus and she's off to rustle us up some transport. She should be here soon. You're a lucky man,

Denis. She's quite a woman, and you're what she loves best, after me, of course. She could hardly stop talking about you while we were out. She even asked if I could make you into a walking mudslide, too, so y'all could be together forever."

Denis shook his head and took a step back.

"But I told her no," the godlet said. "Told her your rampant masculinity would taint the earth, some shit like that. The truth is, I don't want you to have that kind of power. I like you weak. I imagine you'd go insane if I turned you into something like her, anyway."

"I suppose you're right," Denis murmured.

"Can I be mud?" Beej asked hopefully.

"Oh, no, son," the godlet said, laying his steel hand on Beej's shoulder. "You'll be more than that. You'll be the spirit of your own special place, just like me. C'mon, boys. Let's get moving." He considered the door for a moment, then grasped it firmly in both hands and lifted it over his head. Denis gaped—that door was all metal, it had to weigh hundreds of pounds. But why was he surprised? This was a god. Vicious, squalid, and mean, yes, but still a god.

The godlet trotted out, holding the door over his head, and Denis and Beej followed, each for his own reasons, each into his own uncertain future.

Riding into His Dust

"WE SHOULD LINK hands," Marzi said, and Lindsay took her left hand, Garamond Ray her right. They'd moved Jonathan to the floor, and now they stood around him. Marzi took slow, deep breaths, trying not to overthink things; if she thought about this too much, she was afraid she wouldn't be able to do it.

"Close your eyes," she said. "I think it'll be easier." She watched them obediently shut their eyes, then she did the same. Against the blackness of her eyelids, she imagined *going in*. There was no distance to travel, she knew, not here; distance was an illusion. Everyone had worlds inside them, deep strange places of their own, and perhaps it was a form of trespassing to go into Jonathan's inner realm—but what choice did she have? She was sure this was what the scorpion oracle meant. They had to go inside Jonathan, and bring out his soul, his consciousness, whatever it was the Outlaw had made desolate. The journey was difficult; she could feel the shape of the place she was trying to go, but it slid out of her mental grasp, proved elusive. Marzi gritted her teeth and tried harder; she *imagined* it better. She knew what it would be like, there, inside him, and after another moment she felt the quality of the air around them change, become musty and stale. She opened her eyes.

They were in a necropolis. There were a few pyramids and dozens of crypts, blunt straightforward stonework without embellishment. Standing high in the middle distance was a high cylindrical tower—a Zoroastrian burial tower, Marzi realized, a tower of silence. The dead were placed on shelves inside the tower, their remains given over to the air and the vultures. "Open your eyes," she said.

Ray and Lindsay did so. Ray looked around, frowning. "Where are we?"

"It looks like the Luxor in Vegas," Lindsay said. "Only realer."

"The what in Vegas?" Ray said.

"After your time," Lindsay said.

"We're . . . inside Jonathan," Marzi said, before they could start bickering. "Sort of. Metaphorically. But you know what metaphors are like around here. This should be a garden, with fountains, but the Outlaw touched Jonathan, and a bit of desolation got lodged inside him, and turned the garden into a cemetery."

"Today's only getting weirder, Marzipan," Lindsay said. "So what do we have to do?"

"Find Jonathan and bring him out," Marzi said with a shrug.

"Bring him out of what? Out of himself?" Lindsay asked.

"Yes," Ray said. "He's here somewhere, sleeping, almost

dead. We have to bring him back to life." He shook his head. "I can't believe this is what you asked the oracle about. I sure hope your boyfriend is worth it."

"Don't worry about the Outlaw," Marzi said. "I've got him figured out. We could use Jonathan's help once we get to the other side of the door."

"I hope you know what you're doing," Ray said. He sighed. "I should have had more to drink."

"Where do we start looking?" Lindsay asked.

"One of the pyramids, I think," Marzi said. "And watch out for vultures, jackals, ghouls, giant worms, and other stuff. I . . . have a hard time imagining a place like this without those things. Sorry."

Ray shrugged. "Monsters are in the nature of this place, I think. We've all got dark things inside us. I just hope we don't meet too many of Jonathan's."

"Well, Marzi's got a gun that works. She can protect us," Lindsay said. "Except, shit, didn't you leave your pistol in the prison?"

Marzi frowned, then patted her hip, where the familiar weight of her gun now rested again. "No, it's here. I just got it back. Like I said, distance is irrelevant in this place. But there's a problem with using my gun. Anything we see here, it's a manifestation of something inside *Jonathan*. It might look like a vulture or a mummy, but that's just the way we're interpreting it, the way it fits into my overriding worldview of this place."

"Think of it like a themed costume ball," Ray said. "Jonathan's fears, his neuroses, his streak of capricious cruelty, whatever, they're all running around dressed up like jackals or whatnot. And if we kill them . . ."

"We kill that part of Jonathan," Lindsay said. "Crap. Talk about radical personality modification. I guess we don't want to do that. Though you could probably make a good living bringing people through the door, and going inside them, and shooting their phobias and addictions and stuff."

"There are easier ways to make a buck," Marzi said. "We should start looking. Let's saddle up. Metaphorically, that is."

"I've noticed that," Ray said. "There aren't any horses here. Why not?"

"Horses are too girly for Marzi," Lindsay said promptly.

"In the comics, before Rangergirl even found the Western Door, the Outlaw killed all the horses. People who need to ride in my comic end up riding other things," Marzi said.

"Like big lizards, or giant dung beetles, or steam-powered horse-shaped automata. When Rangergirl needs to ride, she rides on the ghost of a famous horse that could do arithmetic, named Abacus, who's mostly invisible, like Wonder Woman's plane. You know, just sort of outlined." Lindsay grinned.

"How strange," Ray said. "A Western without horses."

"Well, the real reason is, Marzi's crap at drawing horses," Lindsay said. "They always end up looking like long-legged cows."

"Thanks for betraying my trade secrets, Linds. Let's go."

They walked slowly through the crypts. The paving stones on the path were just rough slabs at first, but then they became headstones, the carved names and dates weathered to illegibility, only visible as irregular indentations.

"I don't remember a place like this in your comics," Lindsay said, whispering. The hush of the place was getting to all of them.

"I never drew it, but I did have an idea for a kind of pan-desert afterlife, with pyramids and towers of silence and stuff like that, and various gods of the underworld vying for power." She pointed to a low rise between two pyramids, where wooden crosses rose from the ground. "There's Boot Hill," she said. "There's a saloon underneath the hill, like a Western hall of Valhalla, where all the dead gunfighters play poker and drink whiskey and shoot each other. I was going to write about that place a few issues down the line . . . but I don't know, now."

"You have quite an imagination," Ray said. "For narrative, anyway. I'm good at paintings, at scenes, but you're better with story, I think."

"We just have different perspectives, I guess. I always see an implicit story in good paintings."

"I wonder if the Outlaw is more or less dangerous, now that he's bound up in your narrative logic?"

Marzi grinned. In a way, that was the key to her idea for defeating the Outlaw. The Outlaw was locked into the narrative, trapped by its role, and it couldn't deviate from what the story required of it. But Marzi was still a free agent. She could act in ways the story didn't dictate—in ways a Western couldn't even *encompass*—and that was how she'd beat the Outlaw. She was sure of it. She didn't want to tell Lindsay and Ray about her plan yet, because in a way, they were locked into the story as well—not as much as the Outlaw, who'd possessed no more personality than a tornado before Ray and Marzi imagined ones for it, but still, they were playing parts, wearing costumes. They might not understand that Marzi's plan was the best way. They might, in fact, be horrified. They were thinking of Marzi as Rangergirl, but Marzi was going to win by doing something Rangergirl would *never* do.

"I think this is it," Marzi said, pointing to a small pyramid directly in the path in front of them. It was like the others, but instead of being made of rough stone blocks, it was made of blood-red bricks. "The temple of his heart."

"Not a single ghoul or zombie," Ray said, looking around warily. "Your boy must be quite well adjusted. I think if you went into *my* heart, there'd be jackals trying to eat your face right away."

"That pyramid is his innermost core," Marzi said—and wondered if, by saying it, by *believing* it, she made it true. "I think Jonathan probably has a well-guarded heart. We should be careful in there."

They reached the pyramid, and walked around it, looking for an entryway. The pyramid was no bigger at the base than a small house, though Marzi suspected that, like so many other places in this land beyond the door, it would be bigger inside than out. They didn't find a single break or point of entrance.

"It's sealed up," Lindsay said. She tapped the bricks. "Is this something the Outlaw did, or . . . ?"

Marzi shrugged. "I think Jonathan keeps things locked up pretty tightly inside, that it's hard to get in." She thought about the scar on his chest. Here, she could see the scars inside him. Would he have shown *those* so willingly?

"Then why doesn't he let us in now?"

"He's not himself," Marzi said. "But I wonder . . ." She began tugging and pushing at bricks, methodically working her way around the pyramid. Lindsay and Ray caught on, and they, too, started prodding at bricks.

They worked silently for several minutes—during which Marzi began to think she was deluding herself, that this would never work—when Ray said, "Ah-ha!" He pulled a brick out of the wall and peered into the rectangular hole it made. "Looks like a lever," he said, and reached inside. He grunted, narrowed his eyes, and pulled. There was a low click, and then the sound of vast amounts of sand pouring down on the other side of the bricks.

"It must be done with counterweights," Marzi said.

"Thinking makes it so," Ray muttered, but before Marzi could decide if he meant that resentfully or admiringly, a section of the wall lowered like the hatch in a movie UFO, creating a ramp they could walk up. "So you tug his lever, and you get close to his heart, huh?" Ray said, grinning. "Jonathan and I, it seems, are not so different."

"And yet, you seemed to enjoy tugging his lever," Lindsay said. "I didn't realize you swung that way."

"My dear, all innuendoes aside, after so many years on this side of the door, I would happily fuck *anything* that wasn't a figment of my imagination, Jonathan included. Though I would, of course, prefer to do it with you."

"You sure know how to make a girl feel special," Lindsay said.

"Okay, let's go," Marzi said, and walked up the brick ramp. She paused at the top, looking inside. There was a small anteroom, with an inner door marked with what looked like hieroglyphics. Marzi went inside and examined the markings more closely, and saw they were simple line drawings of everyday objects: coffee cups, cars, books, televisions, telephones, and so on. She touched the door, running her finger around the edges, but couldn't find a way to open it. She sighed. There was no other way. She concentrated, briefly, then said, "Lindsay, hand me that crowbar."

"I don't have a—oh." A pause. "Here you go." Lindsay passed over a short pry bar, and Marzi worked it into the crack beside the door. "Ray, you should get a torch," she said.

"Why not a flashlight?" Lindsay asked.

"Torches are better to burn up the evil nasty pyramid gases, right?" Ray said.

"Right," Marzi said. "The torch is on the wall right behind you, Ray."

"You could be a boon to interior decorators everywhere," Lindsay said.

"Got it," Ray said.

"Matches in your front pocket," Marzi said.

Ray sniffed. "I can take care of that much *myself*," he said. "I've got some control over this environment, too, you know. It may be your sandbox now, but I still have a shovel and a pail."

"Sorry," Marzi said absently. The torch flared to life behind her. "Everybody hold your breath," Marzi said, and leaned on the pry bar.

The stone squealed, and then the door popped open. A cloud of thick air swirled out, and the torch flamed bright blue for a moment in the new atmosphere. Ray waved the torch around, burning up whatever gas had come from the tomb, and when the air was clear again, they all exhaled and took tentative breaths. The air stank a little of rotting meat, but it was breathable. "Ray, do you want to lead the way?" Marzi said. "Or else hand me the torch."

"I'll go," he said, and stepped through the door. Marzi and Lindsay followed, into a narrow corridor with a distinct downward slope. The roof almost brushed Marzi's head.

"Like an iceberg. Nine tenths of the place is below the surface."

"That sounds like a fair description of Jonathan," Lindsay said. "Do you ever get the sense that he used to, like, steal cars or something? He's cleaned up his act, but he's still got this desperado vibe about him."

"I think it'd be safe to say he had a misspent youth, yes," Marzi said.

"Sorry to interrupt the fan club," Ray said. "But what should I be looking out for? Trip wires, flaming boulders, giant knives, pits full of spikes?"

"Yeah," Marzi said. "That kind of thing."

"Ah. Good. Inclusive." He coughed. "How about living crocodile statues?"

"Seems unlikely," Marzi said.

"Well, there's one fast approaching," Ray said.

Marzi looked past him, and there *was* something slinking up the corridor toward them. It was a walking statue, rough-hewn from red rock, and its proportions weren't quite right, but it was clearly a crocodile, struggling gamely along on slightly misaligned legs. Its jaws, however, seemed in good working order, with teeth shining like crystal. "Fuck," Marzi said. She concentrated, trying to create a pit in the floor before the crocodile, something for it to fall into harmlessly—and nothing happened. This was too deep, too securely inside Jonathan's heart, for her to make casual changes like that. "Um, guys, I think a retreat is in order—"

"No way," Lindsay said. She strode past Marzi, headed straight for the crocodile. Marzi reached for her, but Lindsay batted her hand away and kept going. Marzi drew her gun. She didn't want to kill this thing—whatever part of Jonathan it represented—but she wouldn't let Lindsay die.

The crocodile seemed baffled by this direct approach, however, and stopped walking as Lindsay approached. "Hey, you stupid boy!" she shouted, and the crocodile actually flinched. "It's *us*. I know you're in a coma or whatever, but it's *Lindsay* and *Marzi*. We're here to help you."

The crocodile opened its jaws and started forward again. Marzi wondered how many times people had told Jonathan they were trying to help him, right before they beat him up, or stole his money, or arrested him. She trained the gun on the crocodile, trying to justify it to herself—surely it was okay to kill this vicious, defensive part of Jonathan. It couldn't be doing him any good, it was an artifact of his old hard life, right? But she knew it was *his,* and that by killing it, she would diminish him. But if that was the only way to *save* him . . .

"Damn it," Lindsay shouted. "We've got your hero here, too, Garamond fucking Ray!"

"Hero?" Ray said, bewildered.

"He's a big fan," Marzi said.

The crocodile hesitated.

"Tell him you're here!" Lindsay hissed.

"Um," Ray said. "Yes, this is Garamond Ray. Care to, ah, let us pass?"

The crocodile tilted its head, sidled sideways, and began to climb up the wall, like a gecko. It reached the ceiling and hung above them, upside-down, watching them with onyx eyes.

"I guess we should go on," Marzi said, and they walked warily under the crocodile, Marzi wondering what it would feel like to have several hundred pounds of animate, biting stone fall on her head. It was easy to imagine, and for the first time Marzi was grateful that she didn't have much control over reality here.

"Now when you say 'hero,' " Ray began.

"He's writing a thesis about you," Lindsay said.

"You only get critical attention after you're dead. Or presumed dead," Ray said, but he sounded pleased.

"I think this is the inner chamber," Marzi said. There was a door at the end of the corridor—a very normal unfinished wooden door, like those inside any old house.

"That was easy," Ray said.

"I think once we got past the crocodile, everything else decided to leave us alone." Marzi turned and smiled at Lindsay. "That was brave, Linds."

"Yeah, well. I just wish hearing it was *us* had been enough to get rid of the crocodile."

"Don't be too hard on Jonathan. He's in a bad way." Marzi turned the doorknob—it was cheap, plastic painted gold—and pushed open the door into a fairly small room, dominated by a golden sarcophagus resting on a platform. A crystal chandelier hung overhead, filled with lit candles, making their torch unnecessary. The other details were more ordinary: filing cabinets on the walls, bookshelves, a desk, a few chairs, a liquor cabinet. Lindsay went to the shelves, touching the books. "These are made of stone! They're not real books!"

"They're replicas, I guess," Marzi said. "To serve him in

the afterlife." She shivered. "But I think they *should* be real books. The Outlaw filled Jonathan up with death. He's petrifying at the core."

"What's in the filing cabinets?" Ray asked, touching the handle on one of the drawers.

"At a guess? Everything. Everything Jonathan knows, everything he's done, everything he is."

Ray took his hand away from the handle. "This is heavy shit you've gotten us into, Marzi. We are *not* meant to be here."

"I know. But I bet the contents of those filing cabinets are turning to stone, too. We've got to wake Jonathan up."

"And how do we do that?" Ray asked.

Marzi shrugged. "Trial and error. And hope we don't err too much on the side of error." She looked at the sarcophagus. It was intricately carved, but not with the image of Jonathan—the bas-relief on the lid was actually that of a mummy, wrapped in cerements, robbed of identity.

Lindsay was still investigating the room, and when she got to the liquor cabinet she said, "Ew. Guys, come see this." Marzi went to her, and Lindsay pointed out the stone jars behind the row of liquor bottles. The lids of the jars were animal heads, familiar to Marzi from Ray's painting of the Teatime Room—there was an eagle's head, a jackal, an ibis. "I guess . . . his internal organs are in there?" Lindsay said.

"Ha," Ray said. "That'd be a trick, since *we're* inside Jonathan's internal organs."

"They're his internal something," Marzi said. "Things he doesn't need anymore, I guess, but that he's still holding on to." She looked around the small room, knowing it was filled with symbolic keys to Jonathan's mind, knowing she had an unprecedented opportunity to learn his deepest secrets, to uncover the answers to every mystery she might ever face in their relationship.

Also knowing that to take advantage of that opportunity would be nothing short of rape.

Marzi went to the sarcophagus and said, "Let's get this thing open, shall we?"

She slipped the pry bar under the lid and heaved. The lid moved a fraction. "Little help?"

Ray came over and added his considerable weight to the bar, and the lid groaned and rose a few inches. Lindsay shoved the lid, and though she didn't have much weight to put behind it, the push was enough. The lid slid off and hit the floor, ringing like a gong, a deafening sound in the small space.

The sarcophagus was filled to the brim with clean desert sand. Without hesitation—hesitation would have made her too afraid—Marzi began scooping out the sand with her bare hands. Ray swore, and joined in, and Lindsay started digging, too.

"I feel something!" Marzi cried, and started clearing sand away from the place where she expected Jonathan's face to be.

Instead she found his bare feet—but they weren't wrapped in sere cloth, and they weren't withered and dry. She rushed around to the foot end of the sarcophagus and started digging sand away from that end.

Marzi uncovered Jonathan's face. His eyes were closed, his face dirty, his lips slightly parted, sand between them. She wanted to cry, seeing him like this, buried—she hoped—alive.

"We're doing this ass-backward," Ray complained, and

reached into the sarcophagus. He lifted Jonathan out, sand streaming away from his limp, nude body, and set him down on the floor.

"Now what?" Ray said, and then Jonathan started to cough, a horrible, sand-choked sound, like a dying engine. Marzi knelt and turned him over, and sand poured out of his mouth in a disconcertingly long, steady stream.

"We need water!" Lindsay said.

"We'd better get back to the fucking Oasis, then," Ray snapped.

Jonathan was moving on his own now, and he crouched on hands and knees, coughing, spitting up sand, until he collapsed, facedown.

"Oh, Jonathan," Marzi said, brushing the sand from his hair. "Please be okay."

Then the pyramid collapsed. Not onto them, but outward, in a soundless slow-motion explosion. As the bricks fell, they faded, most disappearing before they hit the ground, and sunlight poured in on Marzi, Ray, Lindsay, and Jonathan. The crypts and pyramids around them faded, disappearing, replaced by trees and vines and bushes that sprang up everywhere around them. The stone under them became grassy earth, and the platform and sarcophagus faded away. The bookshelves and filing cabinets remained, but now all the objects were real again, not afterlife replicas carved in stone. Marzi noted that the new landscape wasn't totally lush— there were a few dead trees, and one that looked lightning-struck, and a few burned stumps—but she suspected those were ordinary traumas, wounds that the garden of Jonathan's heart had sustained in the course of his life. Still not good, but they weren't the work of the Outlaw. Jonathan turned over on the grass and blinked up at them. "What—" he said, but Marzi interrupted him.

"Join hands!" she said, grabbing Ray and Lindsay's hands. Lindsay reached for Jonathan, and Marzi said, "No, not him, just us!" She didn't want to think of what would happen if they tried to take Jonathan out of his own heart. The three linked hands, and Ray and Lindsay closed their eyes without being told. Marzi closed hers, too, and concentrated on getting *out*.

It was like being fired from a cannon. Ray was right; they weren't supposed to be there. Getting in had been difficult, but there was no resistance getting out.

They opened their eyes, back in The Oasis, and Jonathan sat up from the floor, holding his head in his hands. "What happened?" he said, looking at Marzi and Lindsay with bewilderment, and a little fear—but he was all there; that was Jonathan looking back at them, back with them, alive.

"We can do introductions," Marzi said, "and catch Jonathan up on . . . well, everything. But then we should get back through the door. I don't like to think of what the Outlaw is doing while the sheriff is away."

Made Wolf Meat

THE DUMP TRUCK looked hugely out of place on Ash Street, sticking out into the roadway even when parked right against the curb. Denis was embarrassed to be there, having followed the others in his car. He'd idly considered driving out of town, of course, but only as a sort of mental formality. He knew there was no such simple escape. At least Jane was hidden in the back of the dump truck, with the door, out of sight. Fortunately, there weren't many people around; it was, Denis real-ized dully, still quite early—not even ten A.M. yet. A lot of things had happened in a very small amount of time today. There should have been peo-ple at Genius Loci, but it was still closed, a hastily hand-lettered sign taped up in the window reading "Closed due to earthquake damage."

Denis, Beej, and the god-let stood on the sidewalk, looking at the café. "Aw, that ain't fair," the godlet drawled, standing on the deck with his thumbs hooked into his belt. "I wanted to kill the morning rush. And I hardly busted up anything when I got loose this morning, just a few bottles. Marzi spoils all my fun."

"So how do we get in?" Denis asked. "There are alarms, I think."

"Not if I don't want there to be alarms," the godlet said. "I'll just open the door. Not that I'd mind if the cops came—I do like killing lawmen—but at this point it would just be a distraction." The godlet strode toward the doors, took the doorknob in his hand, and twisted. He grunted, twisted harder, shook the knob, then stepped back.

"Huh. It seems I no longer enjoy the freedom of movement I once possessed. Not here, at least. The door won't open for me." A low, harsh noise emerged from his throat, like gears grinding.

"What happened?" Beej asked.

Denis knew what had happened, and it was all he could do not to laugh. "Cowboys can't magically open locked doors," he said. "Marzi must be getting better at imagining you."

"Yeah, well, her imagination's gonna be the death of her," the godlet said.

"If she did die, what would happen to you, I wonder?" Denis said.

"When she dies, I'll be free," the godlet said. "Once Marzi's dead, I can quit the costume party, and change back to what I was in the old days. But in the meantime . . . Jane! Come here, darlin'!"

Jane climbed out of the back of the truck and jumped lightly to the sidewalk, then came up the steps, smiling, eager to be of assistance.

The godlet thumped the door. "Can you get us in here with no fuss, Janey?"

Jane nodded. "Everyone step back, please. I need room. I've been wanting to try this."

They all dutifully retreated down the steps, Denis feeling freakshow-conspicuous. Maybe everyone saw the godlet differently, but it seemed unlikely that any of his forms were nondescript, and Beej was practically radiating madness. He hadn't been so bad when the godlet was away, while they were working on the door, but in the presence of the god, Beej took on a glassy-eyed fervor. And Jane . . . there were seven-car accidents that were less conspicuous than Jane.

Denis counted through multiples of nine, and hoped the process would speed up, that they'd get inside, out of view. He hunched his shoulders and tried to think invisible thoughts.

Jane began to melt. Her shoulders and arms ran like ice cream in the sun, and her face lost all shape. Her body sank to the deck, becoming a puddle of mud on the boards. Denis stared—there had been hints of this mutability before, but it was still astonishing to see how fully Jane had thrown off the tyranny of shape.

Denis never would have left her to die if he'd known she would subsequently become something like this.

Jane flowed through the crack under the door, oozing slowly but inexorably, and Denis was surprised that she didn't leave any mud on the deck when she departed, carrying every particle of her mud-body with her. He approved of her cleanliness.

Jane re-formed on the far side of the door. "It doesn't look like the alarm's on," she said.

"That was sloppy of Marzi," the godlet said.

"Maybe she just doesn't care if you come back," Denis

said. "Maybe it'll be easier for her to trap you again, if you're so close to your old prison."

"I can't be caught that way again," the godlet said. "You can't keep an outlaw in a jail cell, not in the kinds of stories Marzi favors. The bad guys always escape, or get busted out. The only way you can stop a real outlaw is in a mess of blood and bullets, or else swingin' at the end of a rope. Neither of those seems a likely end for me."

Jane opened the doors wide, and propped them open with doorstops.

"Go and fetch the door," the godlet said, and Jane trotted obediently away, to the rear of the dump truck. She clambered up the side with cockroachlike ease, disappeared from view, then climbed back out. She'd grown an extra pair of arms to carry the door over her head, making her look like a Hindu idol sculpted from mud. Denis wondered if the resemblance was deliberate on her part.

She brought the door up the steps, carried it into the café's front room, and set it down by the counter. Denis realized that Jane hadn't once commented on the door as an objet d'art. Normally, he and Jane would have enjoyed a spirited debate over its merits. She was, indeed, utterly changed, and not for the better. Jane closed the doors again, keeping her extra arms.

"What the fuck's going on?" Hendrix came from the Ocean Room, carrying an empty plastic trash can, his face red, his dreadlocks swaying. "Beej, Denis, Crazy Girl, you're banned for life! And who the hell's—" Hendrix squinted and frowned. "Is that Ozzy Osbourne?" he said, bewildered. "Why's he dressed like John Wayne?"

The godlet drew one of his guns and handed it to Beej, who took it automatically.

"No," Denis said. "This isn't necessary, it's just *Hendrix*, he—"

"Prove yourself to me, son," the godlet said, and put his hand on Beej's shoulder.

Beej raised the pistol in both hands, visibly trembling. He licked his lips. "Sorry," he whispered, and pulled the trigger.

Denis had never seen anyone shot before. It was louder than he would have expected. Hendrix flew backward, dropping his trash can, and fell. His arms and legs spasmed, and there was a great deal of blood—Beej had shot him in the chest—and then that was all. He stopped moving.

"Good boy," the godlet said, and took his gun from Beej's unresisting hand.

Jane put her arms around Denis from behind. "That's it, then," she said. "Now you're the only one of us who hasn't taken a life. I'm sure you'll get your chance soon."

"I think I'm going to be sick," Denis said.

"Pussy," the godlet said absentmindedly. "Come on, Beej. Now I have total faith in you. You deserve what you're about to receive. You'll be . . . exalted."

Beej stared at Hendrix for a moment, then looked up, and Denis could see the switch flip in his old friend's head. Beej just . . . shut Hendrix out. Made a little bypass in his mind that jumped over the experience of killing the man. It was a feat of repression that Denis almost admired. "I was thinking," Beej said. "Maybe I could do something with the murals?" He gestured toward the Ocean Room.

"You do whatever you think's best," the godlet said. "So long as you kill Marzi."

Beej nodded, but he looked unhappy. "I couldn't just . . . keep her there? Make sure she doesn't get out?"

"Hell, son, that's what she tried to do with me, and you see how well *that* worked. No, killing's the only way. Half measures won't do. You have to go, soon. I'm fond of you, boy. I'll miss you."

Beej nodded. "Yes, god. I'll miss you, too. I guess I should go in."

"Let's take the door to the Desert Room," the godlet said. "You should get a look at it first, you know."

"Of course," Beej said.

They went, Beej first, then the godlet and Jane, who carried the door in her extra arms, Denis last.

They approached the Desert Room, passing through the kitchen. The godlet seemed to grow smaller as they walked, until he hardly had to stoop to pass through the doorway. The Desert Room was much *less* than Denis had expected— the paintings water-stained, the room itself filthy and junk-strewn. But who said portals to the medicine lands had to be impressive? Denis stood off to one side, wrinkling his nose to spare himself any odors, trying not to touch anything. Jane set the metal door down in the middle of the room.

Beej looked around for a while, his forehead wrinkled in concentration, then sighed and nodded. "I'm ready." He stepped toward Denis and extended a sweaty hand.

Denis just stared at it. That hand had fired a pistol just moments ago. The godlet growled, faintly, and Denis decided he couldn't afford the luxury of horrified indignation. He shook Beej's hand. "Wish me luck," Beej said.

"Luck," Denis said.

Beej slid aside the bolt that held the metal door shut. The

door opened with a squeal of hinges, and Beej looked inside. "It's all . . . swirly," he said, dreamy and content.

"In you go, then," the godlet said.

Beej stepped through the doorway. He didn't pass through and emerge from the other side. He disappeared.

"Oh, fuck me," Denis said. He really hadn't believed it would work, but it had. They'd made a door to another place, a little primal pocket of unshaped void, and now Beej was there, presumably giving shape to the nothingness.

Jane shut the door slowly and slid the bolt closed.

"There," the godlet said. "Let's get a move on. We're burning daylight. Pick up the door, Janey. And you, Denis, open the other door. The one in the wall."

Denis looked at him for a moment. He was terrified, though he'd believed his capacity for fear to be burned out. Beej was gone. Say what you would about him, he was *human*, not like these creatures, one who loved him, one who suffered him for his usefulness. But if he wanted to live through the day, he had to attend to the matter at hand, and do as the godlet said.

At first, Denis couldn't even *see* the door, and then it popped into focus like an optical illusion resolving—just a door set into a painting of a building, so that the door looked like part of the painting. He touched the knob gingerly: It was strangely warm.

Denis hesitated, thinking. Could he shove this monster back through the door, into this prison? The godlet *was* smaller now, and seemed less powerful. That sense that the godlet's presence extended through unseen dimensions was no longer so overpowering. Still, the godlet was made of chrome, it was strong, and it had guns.

Denis gave in. This was not the moment, not his opportunity. He opened the door, which didn't even have the good grace to squeak ominously, and a hot wind blew into his face. There was a Western scene beyond the door, storefronts and hitching posts, and a sun like molten gold. It was stark, bleak, and strangely inviting. Beyond this door was a place that burned away complications, a place where Denis could hide, from himself as much as anyone else.

He could run there, and he knew the godlet wouldn't follow.

"Do it, then," the godlet said softly.

Denis stiffened, but didn't turn around. "I thought you couldn't read minds?"

The godlet snorted. "Don't have to read minds to know you're thinking of running away. So do it. Door's right there."

"I'd die, wouldn't I? You'd like that."

"Oh, I don't know. Your sort is well equipped to survive over there. Artists." He spat the word. "You're experts at seeing the world as it's not. Over there, the world becomes what you see, a little, anyway. Marzi's got as much of that kind of power as I've ever seen, even more than Garamond Ray. She shines like the sun. Beej is good, too; he's a bonfire, at least. And you . . . well, you're less than them, but I reckon you can muster a few dozen units of candlepower when your juices are flowing."

Denis turned slightly and looked at the godlet. "Talent isn't everything. There are contextual issues, learned skills, awareness of—"

"Not over there. Over there, talent is everything. Well, talent, and practice, and self-control. You think you're too good to bother with practice, and as for self-control . . .

you'd probably prefer it if I didn't go into that here." He inclined his head a fraction toward Jane. "Still, you could get by there. So why don't you go?"

Jane looked at him, her eyes pleading with him to stay.

Denis just looked at the godlet. This was his out, he realized. It was this, or stay with the monsters until the end. He looked through the door.

If the world over there responded to him, became the place he dreamed of . . . it would be all pure and unblemished, chrome and grinding wheels and whiteness. Denis would be the only imperfection there, and as such, he would have to be destroyed, stripped into clean, component molecules, ground away to nothing.

Denis shuddered. Better a dirty life than no life at all. Seeing Hendrix die had brought that point home. "No, I'll stay," he said. "I'm not ready to forsake this world yet."

Jane whooped in delight and rushed past the godlet, embracing Denis with one set of arms, while the other set held the weight of the metal door above their heads. "Oh, Denis!" she cried. "You stayed, you're staying with me!"

Denis began to regret his decision. Better a clean death, perhaps, than a messy life with Jane. But he'd made his choice.

"Yes, Jane. I'm staying."

The godlet growled. "Enough, Jane. Put the door in place."

Denis looked at the godlet and grinned. He *got* it—Why had it taken him so long? The godlet had wanted Denis to bugger off through the door, because he was afraid to kill Denis himself! Sure, Jane loved the god, but it was readily apparent that Jane loved *Denis,* too. The god needed Jane, and was afraid to excite her wrath by killing Denis! If the godlet told Jane now that Denis had murdered her, Jane might not even *believe* him. Denis was safe, as long as they didn't go back up into the hills, as long as the god couldn't show Jane her own corpse, the evidence of Denis's crime. Maybe he'd make it through this after all.

Jane let go of him, shooed him away, and set the metal sculpture in front of the open door to the medicine lands. She pushed the sculpture toward the door, against it—the door frames were sized to match exactly—and then the metal frame went *into* the wall, melted into the painted plaster, became part of the painting. The buffalo skull lost its three-dimensionality and became a flat painting. Jane kept pushing and grunting until the door disappeared entirely into the wall. Now it looked like a comic book illustration of the sculpture he and Beej had made, a metal door frame set into a wooden wall.

Jane closed the door, and now there were bars painted across it, to match the sculpture. The knob was gone, replaced by a sliding bolt.

"Amazing," Denis said, and meant it.

The godlet grunted. "It'll do. Now when Marzi tries to get out, she'll actually go someplace *else.*"

"Into a box canyon," Denis said. "Just like in her comic." In the issue Beej had given Denis to read, Marzi's protagonist—Denis didn't remember her name—had chased her enemy into a twisty box canyon and gotten lost there. Eventually she'd found her way out, and back to her own world—or at least, she *thought* she had, until her familiar home became surreal and monstrous, her friends treacherous, everything she knew twisted out of true. It turned out that she'd wandered into a *magical* box canyon, a place of illusions that mimicked whatever the victim expected to see. The heroine had eventually escaped, and dynamited the mouth of the box canyon closed.

Denis rather doubted that Marzi had access to dynamite, and even if she did, it wouldn't help her now. She'd be trapped in the box canyon, and she'd remain there forever, most likely. Her comic book protagonist may have been a wish-fulfillment doppelgänger, but Marzi herself was, after all, just a coffee jockey who drew comic books. She was doomed.

"Now that Marzi is out of the picture," the godlet said, "I can start getting my strength back without worrying about her interference. You know how you get strong, Denis? You *exercise*. And since you've decided to stay with us, let me ask you this: Have you ever made a Molotov cocktail?"

With a heart full of sand and a head full of mud, Denis shook his head.

"You're a quick study," the godlet said. "I'm sure you'll do fine. Let's go downtown. We'll take your car. Parallel parking that dump truck's got to be a bitch."

"WHAT THE HELL is this shit?" the godlet said, staring up at the clock tower near the north end of downtown, where Water Street met Pacific Avenue. Jane lurked by one of the four pillars that made up the base of the clock, her body at its most human-looking—she might have been mistaken for someone merely insane and filthy, rather than recognized as an inhuman monster.

"It's a clock," Denis said. "It's used to tell time."

"Shit," the godlet said. "This thing is *still* standing? It didn't fall in the last big quake?" Denis wondered what the tourists and passersby made of the godlet, if they thought he was a street performer of some sort, like the man who dressed up in a bee suit and declaimed Beat poetry a few blocks up the street.

"Apparently not," Denis said.

The godlet grunted. "I wouldn't have thought it was built to last. Damn it. At least nothing else looks the way it used to—I must have wrecked things pretty good. If it wasn't for that double-damned clock still standing there, I wouldn't even recognize the place."

"Yes," Denis said. "Downtown was pretty well destroyed. When people rebuilt, they didn't slavishly re-create the former appearance of the place. Hence your sense of *jamais vu.*"

"Sometimes when you talk, I want to punch your face," the godlet said matter-of-factly. He crossed his arms and stared at the tower, spikes turning deep in his eye sockets. "I can't believe they rebuilt after that quake," he muttered. "Those bastards. They can't take a hint." He turned to Denis. "This time, it's going to be different. Scorched earth, you get me? And this clock tower's going to be the first thing to fall. I can't knock it over on my own—not yet—so that means we need dynamite. Where can I get some?"

Denis blinked. "*Dynamite?* Are you kidding?"

The godlet stepped closer. "Cooperate, boy. You know what happens if you don't." He inclined his head fractionally toward Jane, who was fully occupied with thumping the bricks of the tower with her left hand.

"I'm not resisting," Denis said, holding up his hands.

Tim Pratt

"But I don't have even the vaguest idea of where to get dynamite. It's not something I've ever had a use for."

For a moment, the godlet looked lost. There was nothing in his expression, of course—that was as blank and robotic as ever—but there was something about his posture, something in the tilt of his head, that indicated a profound confusion. The sight filled Denis with glee.

Then the godlet sighed and said, "We'll have to stick with the firebombs, then. Go make up a few Molotov cocktails, Denis, like I showed you."

The car was parked in one of the slanted spaces in front of the post office. Several small gas cans sat in the back, covered with a blanket, and there were glass juice bottles to be emptied and refilled with gasoline. Denis had purchased those things, along with the cleaning rags that Jane had deftly torn into long strips to act as fuses. "But . . . here?" Denis said. "There are people everywhere, witnesses—"

"Don't worry," the godlet said. "We'll get around to firebombing the people, but I want to knock some buildings over first, get things burning, bring this place *down*. Now go make the bombs, unless you want to find out what it feels like to have your head twisted off by your own girlfriend."

Denis trudged to his car and opened the door, hoping a cop would notice what he was doing and arrest him. Beej had told him that the godlet had "taken care of" the police before breaking Beej out of jail. Denis didn't know what that meant, exactly, but it didn't sound good. If there were dead police officers in the station house, their surviving fellows would be looking for the killer, and maybe, if he was lucky, they'd look *here*.

But that wouldn't really be so lucky, he realized, not for the cops *or* Denis. The godlet was about to start chucking firebombs at the buildings in downtown Santa Cruz. He wouldn't be bothered by a few policemen. Denis, however, would very likely be killed in the crossfire.

He stopped hoping a cop would notice what he was doing. Denis poured a bottle of orange juice onto the pavement and filled the bottle with gasoline, willing his hands not to shake, pouring the fluid into a bright yellow funnel. When the bottle was two-thirds filled with gas, he shoved a piece of white cloth into the mouth. One end of the cloth submerged in the gas, and the fluid began to climb up the fuse. Denis carefully set the bottle on the ground and filled another, then carried both back across the street to the clock tower, where the godlet was deep in conversation with Jane.

"Ah, Denis," the godlet said. "Jane was just making some suggestions to me about where to go when we're finished here. I think we should take down the lighthouse, and then maybe wreck the boardwalk, but while we're over here we should tear down that footbridge over the river, and the Del Mar theater, maybe burn all the stock in the bookstores. Oh, and at some point we have to brew up some napalm or something and get rid of the monarch butterfly sanctuary." The godlet rubbed his hands together—honestly! The cliché!

"It sounds like you have quite a day planned," Denis said, carefully holding the Molotov cocktails by the necks. He wondered what would happen if he threw them at the godlet. Probably something very unpleasant, but he feared he would ultimately be the recipient of the unpleasantness, and so he refrained.

"Oh, I do. By the end of the day, after wreaking that much havoc, I should be able to do a few more spectacular things: spark wildfires by clapping my hands, cause tremors by stomping my boot, get a mudslide going by spitting on a hill."

"And then you won't need me anymore, I suppose," Denis said. "And you'll kill me."

"She won't hurt you," Jane said, but she sounded preoccupied. She'd moved beyond thumping the brick support arches of the clock tower, and was now punching them, hard, repetitively. Denis found himself counting her punches, nine at a time, and then tried to stop paying attention.

"That's right, Denis. You keep Janey happy. She's only going to get stronger. In fact, she's about to test her limits right now, isn't that right?"

"Yes," Jane said. "I'm going to tear this tower down with my bare hands." And with that, she began slamming her fists into the monument's base, arms moving so quickly that they blurred. Bits of brick and mortar flew where she struck, and with growing horror, Denis realized that she might be able to do what the godlet said.

"We'd better move out of the shadow of the tower, boy," the godlet said, and headed across the street toward the shops on Pacific, Denis reluctantly following. "Come on. There's a nice store here, with a nice open door to let the breeze in. We're going to light that bomb you've got, and you're going to chuck it inside. Agreed?"

"You want *me* to—"

"Spare me," the godlet said, and took a Zippo lighter from his vest and held it up for Denis to see. There was an insignia on the lighter, a shield with the words "To Protect and Serve."

"Got this off a cop," the godlet said. "After I stomped his head through the floor."

"You can't—" Denis began. He didn't know where the sentence was going, and it didn't get any farther than those two words, because the godlet flipped open the lighter and lit both Molotov cocktails in Denis's hands. Denis was so startled that he nearly dropped them, which would have been an incredibly painful mistake.

"Into a *store,* boy," the godlet shouted. "Don't throw them in the street, or I'll fill your belly with gasoline, shove a rag up your ass, and make a bomb out of *you.*"

Denis threw both bottles as hard and far as he could, into the gift shop with the open door. The bottles crashed inside, knocking over a rack of greeting cards and startling the shoppers. Gasoline splashed, flames leapt, and people screamed. Everywhere up and down the street people came out of shops and restaurants to see what was happening, but Denis barely sensed them on the periphery—he stared into the store, where an elderly woman was on fire, where fire was spreading across the carpet, where smoke was beginning to billow.

The godlet clapped him on the shoulder. "Good throw! You might be worth more than your weight in horseshit after all!"

Behind them, there was a horrible, grinding, crunching noise.

Jane had successfully smashed her way through one of the thick support columns, and the clock tower was beginning to fall. Jane ran from the square as the tower ponderously toppled, smashing into the street, crushing the hood of a silver sedan, brick and clockwork spraying everywhere, bell torn loose and bouncing on the asphalt. Such an improbable, huge act of destruction jarred Denis from his horrified fascination with what he'd done to the gift shop—what he'd been *forced* to do, what he'd had no *choice* but to do.

The godlet stomped his foot, and the ground trembled, only slightly, but noticeably; a few of the terrified people on the street fell down, and Denis nearly did so himself. "Happy trails ahead," the godlet said. "Let's go back to the car and make a few more bombs, what do you say? I can throw them out the windows while you drive."

Jane wrapped her hardened arms around Denis's waist. "We're tearing down everything," she said.

"Yes," Denis managed. They were. And it was horrible. This was not a clean, scouring act. This was chaos, and wreckage, and old women on fire.

He stepped away from Jane, bent at the waist, and vomited up bile onto the sidewalk.

"Greenhorn," the godlet said, almost affectionately. "Don't worry. A few more bombs, and you'll get used to it."

Box Canyon

"SO HE'S A SPIRIT of destruction, but he's *also* the Outlaw from Marzi's comics?" Jonathan said.

"Yes," Lindsay said.

"And . . . *that's* Garamond Ray?" If anything, he sounded more incredulous about that than about the other, more outrageous things he'd been told. Jonathan didn't remember much, he said, except feeling compelled to come downstairs and open the door—then it was just brightness, something monstrous brushing past him, and a sense of suffocation that lasted until they freed him.

"That's Ray. In all his glory," Lindsay said.

"Unbelievable," Jonathan said. "This is going to change my whole thesis."

"Yeah. You'll have to make something up, though, about where he's been all this time," Marzi said.

Ray still seemed taken aback by this turn of events. "I'll help you come up with something," Ray said. "Once . . . all this is resolved. And after I have a nice rare steak, and a few bottles of wine, and get laid, and take about a hundred showers. Not necessarily in that order. As close to concurrently as possible, actually. We can just say I was in the Middle East seeking inner truth for the past fifteen years, or something. And that I'm a youngish looking sixty-year-old, because of all that clean living I've been doing."

"Yes," Jonathan said. "We should definitely talk." He looked to Marzi, expression still a little dazed. "But in the meantime, what do we do?"

"I can't believe you're taking this so well," Marzi said.

Jonathan shrugged. "I'm here. I can look around. I remember you dragging me out of the sand. I remember the . . . thing . . . that passed me in the doorway. I don't think you're lying to me." He frowned. "I wish you'd told me about this stuff before, though. I never would have opened the door."

Marzi bowed her head. "I didn't think you'd believe me."

"Maybe I wouldn't have." He shivered. "I still can't get over the fact that you were all *inside* me. I feel like I've been turned inside out and rolled in the mud. I appreciate what you did, I do, but . . . I can't describe the feeling. It's not good."

Marzi nodded. She'd been inside Jonathan's soul—it was a profound violation, no matter how noble their intentions had been. She could feel his walls going back up, feel him pulling back. Marzi wanted to reach out and touch him, but she was afraid he'd flinch away.

"It's better than leaving you one of the living dead, kid," Ray said brusquely. "So, do we have a plan?"

"Yes," Marzi said. She couldn't worry about Jonathan, not

now—she'd brought him back, and facing the consequences of her method would just have to wait. "We're going to go through the door, back to Santa Cruz . . . and we're going to have a showdown with the Outlaw."

"Fuck," Ray said. "I was afraid the plan would be something like that."

"There's no point in trying to trap the Outlaw. He's not a djinn anymore. He's a gunslinger, and we have to defeat him the way you defeat a gunslinger." Marzi touched the gun at her hip. "That means I face him, and we fight."

"And what happens if you *die*?" Lindsay asked.

Marzi glanced at Ray.

"Well," he said slowly, "it's not like I'm an expert on these things, but I suspect that if Marzi isn't around anymore, imposing her perspective, the Outlaw will stop being an outlaw and become . . . whatever he was, originally. An earthquake with a mind. A wildfire that thinks. Right now, he's more limited than that—he can't fly, he can't walk through walls, he can't be in more than one place at once. Hell, he's less powerful as a gunslinger than he was as a djinn—though as Marzi has noted, he's harder to trap."

"If you put an outlaw in jail, he always escapes," Jonathan said. "In the stories."

"Yeah," Marzi said. "But in the stories, when the hero faces the villain in the final showdown, the hero usually wins."

"Usually," Lindsay said.

Marzi nodded. "Yes. Not always, it's true. I might lose. But I don't think I will. For one thing, I've got a better sense of how to control things, now. I think I can make the Outlaw more human, turn him into just a cunning, vicious wizard, instead of a god."

"A cunning, vicious wizard can still *kill* you," Lindsay said. "I do not support this plan, Marzi."

"And I'd like to note that, in the stories, if anyone dies, it's usually one of the hero's faithful sidekicks," Ray said, and looked at Lindsay and Jonathan.

Marzi wanted to tell them they had nothing to worry about—that unless she was very much mistaken, it would never come down to the Outlaw shooting at her. But if she told them her *real* plan, it might not work; she needed them to play their parts, to be her posse, and they would do that better if they didn't *know* they were only playing. She was the one in ultimate control of things, yes—she imposed the paradigm of her comic book on the situation—but Lindsay and Jonathan and, especially, Ray, could all change things slightly, create fluctuations, and she couldn't have that. It was imperative that she *be* Rangergirl, as far as they were concerned, that the spirit of the wasteland be the Outlaw from her comic—cruel, cunning, and powerful, but mortal—and that they stand facing one another, prepared to have the showdown that the story demanded. "We'll be okay," Marzi said. "You have to trust me. Okay?"

"I don't guess we have a choice," Ray said.

"I'm with you, Marzi," Jonathan said.

Lindsay frowned, then sighed. "I just don't want you to get hurt, Marzipan."

"I don't want me to get hurt, either," she said, managing a smile. "This will all be over soon. Let's get out of here."

They set out into the desert, away from The Oasis, through the sad little ghost town. There were figures in the distance, around the town, watching them: the Comanche, sitting tall on their chimera steeds; a stand of cactus people; a flock of humanoid vultures, their wings like cloaks.

"You sure stirred things up, Marzi. They've never paid so much attention to me," Ray said. "It's a good thing we're leaving."

"I don't ever plan on coming back, either," Marzi said.

They reached the door, in its freestanding fragment of wall.

"What's to stop the Outlaw from standing on the far side of the door with a shotgun?" Lindsay said. "Trying to get the drop on us?"

"Narrative imperative," Marzi said. "He doesn't want to win that way. He wants to face me, banter a little, and out-draw me. I *know* it." She worked hard at knowing it. If she doubted it, after all, it would become possible for the Outlaw to be standing on the other side of the door with a shotgun. "Besides, he's out raising hell, getting his strength back, so he can do some serious damage. He'll want to be strong when he faces me."

"How reassuring," Ray said.

Marzi opened the door, revealing the dimness of the Desert Room, enough light spilling in from this side to illuminate a little trash on the floor. "In we go," Marzi said, and ushered her friends in, keeping an eye on the things watching them; the Comanche in particular didn't seem happy, which was understandable, given the ass-whipping they'd received, but they seemed willing to just watch them go. Marzi backed through the door, still watching, and then slammed the door shut after her.

She turned around in the darkness. "Somebody turn on the light? It's by the other door, over on the right."

"Got it," Lindsay said. There was the sound of shuffling feet, then the light came on. Lindsay was standing by the door. "There. But it was on the left, actually."

Marzi frowned. "Oh. Sorry. Can't trust my memory, I guess."

"This is not what I painted," Ray said.

Marzi nodded. "I know. It's from my comic, mostly." The door was almost impossible to see now, blending in with the building it had been painted on.

"Ah, well," Ray said, sighing. "Who said art was immortal?"

"I wish I'd gotten some pictures of the old mural, before it changed," Jonathan said. "But you can tell me about it, at least."

"Can we get out of here?" Lindsay said. "Not to interrupt the art appreciation session or anything, but being near that door makes me *nervous*. Shouldn't we board it up or something?"

"The things over there can't open the door," Ray said. "They can slip through if someone else opens it, but they're stuck, on their own. If they weren't . . . well. Boards wouldn't stop them."

"Yes, but they'd stop someone else from opening the door, not knowing what could happen," Marzi said. "I should've boarded it up myself."

"I probably would've just gotten a hammer," Jonathan said. "Or even torn it off with my bare hands. I was pretty determined to open it."

"The Outlaw used to stand at the door and whisper," Ray said. "I've seen it. Most people resist pretty well, I think . . . but Jonathan wanted to see this room badly anyway. And the Outlaw's been pounding on the door for ages, making cracks in it, even projecting himself through it, in a limited way. I don't think he could affect physical things at all, then, but he could talk . . . and for some people, that's enough."

"Beej," Marzi said. "And Jane."

"And Alice," Lindsay said. "But she was strong enough to run away." Lindsay opened the door, violently, and left the Desert Room.

Marzi sighed and took Jonathan's hand. "She's been through a lot."

"Marzi!" Lindsay shouted, and there was a note of panic in her voice Marzi had never heard before, not even during their travails beyond the door. She ran through the kitchen, into the Space Room, and found Lindsay staring out the bay window. Marzi went to her, and looked. It was night outside, but the moon was bright enough to see by.

Santa Cruz was gone. Beyond the windows there was nothing but churned earth, bits of asphalt and wood protruding from the wrecked ground. No grass, trees, bushes, or buildings remained. Genius Loci seemed to be the only structure left standing.

Marzi was vaguely aware of Ray and Jonathan coming to stand with them, but mostly she was lost in her own mind. She'd failed. They were too late.

"Time moves differently over there," Ray said. "There's no telling how long we were gone." Lindsay was crying, and Jonathan was touching Marzi's shoulder, murmuring something meant to be reassuring. But Marzi could think of nothing but the wreckage out there, of the lives and places lost. Mostly she thought of what *she'd* lost—selfish, but true. Never to walk along West Cliff Drive again, watching the surfers and the bright sails of the boats. Never to see clouds of monarch butterflies, or eat a greasy slice at the newspaper-strewn counter in Pizza My Heart, or sit in the courtyard be-hind Javha House, or by the duck pond in the park across the river, or spend hours in Bookshop Santa Cruz. Never again to watch a midnight showing of *The Cat People* or *Nosferatu* at the Nick or the Del Mar Theater, or drink pints of Guinness at the Poet & Patriot. She'd never get her name on a plaque on the wall for drinking every kind of beer at 99 Bottles, or see the view of the bay from campus, or go to Shakespeare Santa Cruz in the summer, or watch kite surfing off High-way 1, or go looking for tide pools, or walk down Pacific Avenue while flowers fell from the trees and drifted in the air.

Gone, gone. Nothing left of her whole life here except the café.

If her gun were still real, not just a plastic toy again, she thought she might put it into her mouth and pull the trigger, rather than go on living in a place that was ruined because of her.

Suddenly there was a weight on her hip. She touched the gun's grip, and was only briefly surprised when she touched wood. It made sense, after all: This was the Outlaw's country now, saturated with the essence of a being from the medicine lands. Reality was flexible here, because Marzi had failed. But no amount of imagination on Marzi's part could bring back the dead or rebuild the lost places. They were gone forever. Even if she conjured illusions, there'd be no real life in them.

Maybe suicide was the best option. Or they could go back through the door, dwell in the lands beyond the lands under a tent of illusions, assaulted by monsters, living in fear of the scorpion oracle's frustrated wrath . . . No, that wasn't much of a choice, either.

"They rebuilt, after Loma Prieta," Lindsay said.

Ray laughed hollowly. "And I never got to see it. It couldn't have been this bad after Loma Prieta, anyway, and by then the Outlaw was locked away. It's still stomping around loose out there. What I don't understand is why it left the café standing."

"As a sort of memorial, maybe?" Jonathan said. "Something to gloat over?"

"No," Marzi and Ray said, simultaneously. Ray continued. "The Outlaw doesn't leave things. He *levels*."

Puzzlement was beginning to overcome shock in Marzi's mind. She looked around. Why *was* the café still standing?

And more importantly, what was *different* about it? Now that she really looked, the café was like one of those "What's wrong with this picture?" puzzles. It was basically the same . . . but the clock, made of a Fiesta dinner plate, was green now, instead of yellow. The pipes exposed on the ceiling over the counter didn't join up properly, and there were more of them than there should have been. The molding around the top of the walls wasn't chipped in the right places. The couch didn't have a hole on one armrest like it should have. They were minor things that no one else was likely to notice, but Marzi knew the details of this café better than she knew her own home. The murals were wrong, too, the stars and asteroids in slightly incorrect places. This wasn't Genius Loci. It was a good, but imperfect, copy.

And then she understood. Not the how, but the what, and the why, too—hell, even *how* was obvious, in its way: by magic.

Not just magic, but derivative magic, at that. Plagiarism made real.

They'd been lured into a box canyon.

"The Outlaw's fucking with us, guys, this is bullshit,"
Marzi said. She looked up, gestured at the ceiling. "There's
not even a trapdoor there, Jonathan, and you *know* there
should be. This isn't Genius Loci. That isn't Santa Cruz. It's
a trap, a tide pool, a pocket universe, and the Outlaw got
the idea from *me*, issue number seven, 'Box Canyon.' " She
laughed. "Did he think I wouldn't notice?"

"You're sure?" Ray said. "It's not just wishful thinking?"

"No, she's right," Lindsay said, no longer crying. "It's a
fake. I see it now."

"It's still a trap, though," Jonathan said.

"Then we'd better get out of it," Marzi said.

Their clothing had changed back to ordinary street garb
when they passed through the door, but now Marzi willed
them into their Western clothes—Ray in a serape and a battered brown hat, a rifle slung on his back; Jonathan in im-
maculate black, with a bolo tie and shiny silver guns; Lindsay
in her vest and bowler. With some effort, Marzi conjured a
tommy gun for Lindsay—it was hard, since she'd seen the
gun eaten by a giant flea earlier, but she managed to believe in
it enough.

"Do you think the Outlaw's here?" Lindsay asked.

"No," Marzi said. "He's out raising hell while the cat's
away. But I'm sure there's other nasty stuff in here with us."

They went into the Cloud Room, the paintings just foggy
swirls in the dimness. "*Fiat lux,*" Marzi said, and the lights
came on overhead. "I always wanted to do that," she said,
grinning. "They screwed up, sending us here. I can change
anything I want."

"I don't imagine they care what you imagine," Ray said,
"as long as we don't get out."

"Point," Marzi said, but the power still thrilled her. And she *would* get them out.

"Um," Lindsay said. "Is it me, or is it getting foggy in here?" Mist was swirling out of the walls, the clouds in the murals filling the room. A sound like paper tearing came from the Teatime Room, followed by a low growl.

"Shit," Marzi said. She hadn't written this, or even *thought* about it, though it was a hell of an idea. So who *had* come up with it? The Outlaw didn't have an imagination, so—

Marzi didn't have time to think about it, because Anubis was standing in the doorway, still holding a delicate teacup full of blood. Ra and Osiris stood behind him, and Sekhmet loomed in the deeper shadows, carrying a tea press with a heart inside. The murals were coming to life.

"Marzi," Ray said, "it's a neat idea, but stop it."

"I didn't start it," Marzi said. "Someone else is in here, changing things." She backed away, but the mural-gods seemed incapable of leaving the borders of their room. The Cloud Room was growing mistier by the moment, and Marzi could hear the distant wailing of ghosts. "Let's get out of here. Strategic retreat."

"The Space Room is . . . space, Marzi," Jonathan said. Marzi turned around, and saw a void of glittering stars and a hovering probe, armed with vicious pincers. She knew there would be no air beyond the doorway. Even if they made it across, there was the Ocean Room next, crush-depth blue water with a huge green serpent sliding endlessly past, and beyond *that* was the Circus Room, with Harlequin . . . No. They were better off here, in the mist, with the ghosts.

But how could they kill ghosts, how could they fight mist?

"We have to get outside," Marzi said. She looked at the windows, picked up a chair, and hurled it at the glass.

The chair just bounced off.

Lindsay fired her tommy gun at the glass, but her bullets were absorbed, as if she were firing into water. She shrugged, then glared at Ray. "Why'd you have to paint such nasty shit?"

"I should have painted puppies and flowers? Excuse me for not realizing my paintings would someday come to life and try to kill me!"

"Hey, that's enough. Focus, guys," Marzi said. The room became more misty, and the ghostly wailing increased in volume. "Try shooting the gods in the Teatime Room." She lifted her own pistol and took aim at Anubis's slavering head. She fired.

Anubis turned, and suddenly disappeared; the other gods did likewise. Marzi's bullet whizzed harmlessly by, and then Anubis was there again, grinning.

"They're two-dimensional," Jonathan said. "Look, they turned sideways, and it was like they disappeared! They're *flat*."

Marzi looked, and even through the thickening mist she could see what Jonathan meant: The gods weren't solid figures, more like sheets of paper cut into humanoid shapes, with images projected on them. "We're not going to be able to shoot them," Marzi said. She could barely see her friends, now, and she began to wonder what would happen when the mist completely filled the room—would they be lost in limbo, or fall through endless space?

"Ease up, Marzi!" Ray shouted. "Damn it, stop *thinking* for a minute!"

Startled, Marzi looked at him—and he flickered. His se-rape vanished, replaced by a Bedouin's flowing white robes and head scarf. The rifle slung over his back was gone, and he reached back and drew a wickedly curving scimitar. With a shout, he lunged for the doorway to the Teatime Room, and slashed at Anubis.

The jackal-headed god's face took on a comically shocked expression, and then the upper half of its body floated, like a sheet of paper, to land facedown on the floor. The lower half curled over and fell, too. Whooping, Ray went into the Teatime Room, slashing with his sword, cutting the gods down.

The floor beneath Marzi's feet became spongy and soft. Everything was turning to mist. "Come on!" she shouted, and grabbed for Lindsay's hand; she didn't see Jonathan, and feared he would get lost again, but there was nothing she could do about that, now. Marzi ran for the Teatime Room, where Ray stood grinning, chomping on a cigar that had appeared in his mouth without Marzi willing it. He *did* have the same powers she did, just not as strongly. She hadn't thought about him *using* his powers, but it made sense: Any artist, anyone with a well-trained imagination, could shape things to some extent in a place like this. Marzi was the strongest, so her vision overrode the others, but that didn't mean hers was the only voice.

The floor became more insubstantial, and Marzi *jumped,* dragging Lindsay with her. They passed the threshold into the Teatime Room. Jonathan came flying out of the mist a moment later, but he didn't quite make it—he fell, the Cloud Room having lost all physical substance. He grabbed onto the edge of the Teatime Room's floor, body dangling in the ghost-ridden mist. Lindsay and Marzi grabbed him by the wrists and hauled him up, so pumped with adrenaline that they lifted him with little effort. Jonathan lay for a moment on the floor, panting, then shook his head. "I'm okay. For a given value of 'okay.' Thanks."

"We all need to be rescued sometimes," Ray said. His Bedouin gear was gone now, replaced by the serape and rifle— but the scimitar still hung over his back, too, Marzi noticed. The Teatime Room was an island of calm, the gods nothing but strips of rough paper on the floor, the mural now depicting only chairs, tables, cups and saucers.

"There's someone here, controlling things," Marzi said. "At first I thought it was just a box trap we'd walked into, you know? But there's someone reacting to us. Making the murals come to life—that wasn't my idea. I didn't think of that at all, and I don't think Ray did, either."

"Nope," he agreed. "But it can't be the Outlaw. That guy's got all the imagination of a fence post."

"It's Beej," Lindsay said. She sighed and sat down in a chair. "Who else? It's not Jane; she doesn't have that turn of mind. But Beej . . ." She gestured at the murals. "He's always been interested in bringing two-dimensional images into a third dimension, with his photo collage and stuff. This is his kind of thing, and we know he works for the Outlaw. Or worships it, or whatever."

Marzi nodded. "Yeah. You could be right." She looked around. "Beej!" she shouted. "Come here! We need to talk!"

There was nothing, silence. Marzi frowned. "Listen, Beej, this is important, okay?"

"I'm supposed to kill you," Beej said from a dark corner of the room. He was sitting in the shadows now, but he hadn't been there a moment ago. "It's what I'm good for, it's how I can serve my god." He sounded even more unsure than usual. "But . . . things don't make as much sense, now that I'm here. Without the god's voice, I feel lost. Like I always used to feel."

"What happens if I cut your head off?" Ray said.

Beej looked startled. "Um. Everything here disappears, I guess. It's all mine."

"Not exactly," Marzi said. "It's a box canyon, right? Like from my comic."

Beej nodded. "I love that issue."

"But it's actually a little pocket of space, a bit of the medicine lands pinched off, a bubble. It's raw material. You were here first, you set it up, you controlled the parameters, but if you were gone, I think Ray and I would be able to create something new."

"Oh," Beej said. "I don't really know how all this stuff works. I didn't think you'd have swords and guns and stuff. I don't want to hurt you, Marzi. I was trying to *help*, even."

"With the floors turning to mist, and the killer space probe, and the dog-headed monster?" Lindsay said. "That was *help*?"

Beej ignored her, still speaking to Marzi. "I knew I couldn't kill you, Marzi. Your friends, maybe, but you . . . I knew I'd never be able to harm you. So I thought I'd do the next best thing, and keep you trapped here, where you couldn't bother my god anymore. That seemed like a good compromise. None of the things here actually hurt you, you know. I just wanted to keep you from leaving the Cloud Room. I was going to let you . . . float, in the mist. Sleep. Rest. See, you're *safe* in here, Marzi, that was the thing I finally figured out. I wanted the earthquake god to triumph, I wanted to serve a victorious master, but I didn't want you to die in the rubble and the fires. I . . . I *like* you. You've always been good to me. Sometimes, when it's all screaming and bright lights in my head, thinking about you is the only thing that calms me down. If you were out there, in Santa Cruz, you'd *die*. But in here, you're safe."

"In here I'm trapped, Beej. And you're not in charge of keeping me safe." She was having a hard time being angry with Beej. How could this be one of the faces of her enemy, this confused boy who just wanted to feel important, who thought he loved her and wanted to be in charge of the prison where she was locked away? "And your god . . . he's not nice, Beej."

"Oh, I know. But he's *important*. And he lets me be important, too."

"He's using you."

"I don't mind being used. It's better than being nothing at all. I made this place, me and Denis together—"

"Denis is involved in this, too? Why am I not surprised?"

"Well, he doesn't *want* to be," Beej said. "He hates our master, I think, he'd run away if he could, but he's scared, so he helped. We built a door . . ." Beej's voice was dreamy.

"A door, Beej? Can you show it to me?"

"If I showed it to you, you could walk through it," he said.

Marzi went to him. She knelt by his chair, and took his hand. "You've done a bad thing, Beej. I think you know that."

He nodded. "I always knew it. But it's an *important* thing, and that matters more."

Marzi nodded. "Well, now you've got the chance to do

another important thing. Me, my friends, we want to stop your master. We want to save all those people he's going to kill. You can help us do that. You can do something that's good *and* important."

Beej looked at her, his eyes bloodshot and watery. "You can really beat the earthquake god?"

"I think I can, yes."

"But you can only do it if I help?"

Marzi nodded.

"Okay," Beej said, and just like that, there was a door, standing in the center of the room, all black iron and spikes, pasted-on photographs, and a buffalo skull on top.

"Oh, Beej," Lindsay said. "That's beautiful." There was genuine reverence in her voice.

"It's a masterpiece," Ray said. "And I'd know. I'm a master."

"It belongs in a gallery," Jonathan said.

Marzi squeezed his hand. "You do good work, Beej." She stood up. "Come with us? Help us fight?"

Beej shook his head. "This is where I want to be. I'm the most important thing, here. I've never been any good at sculpture, but in this place . . . I can make anything."

He could, Marzi knew, but it wouldn't *mean* anything; there'd be no one real to share it with. But Beej had never been good at dealing with real people, anyway. Even now, he wasn't talking to Marzi. He was talking to his imagined, idealized version of her, same as always.

"Besides," Beej went on, "I did bad things over there, like you said. I'm happy here. I'd just get all twisted up again if I went back, I think."

"Whatever you did there, you've done us a great service here," she said.

"Go, then," Beej said. "Save the world or whatever."

The black metal door opened, and beyond it, Marzi could see the dusty Desert Room. Ray, Jonathan, and Lindsay passed through, their guns vanishing, their clothes changing from Western garb to their ordinary outfits again—Ray wore a Hawaiian shirt and khaki shorts. Marzi lingered at the door for a moment, looking at Beej, sitting in his dark corner. "Maybe you'll come out, someday, and visit us?"

"Maybe," he said, and he sounded saner than he ever had before. "But I think I like this world better."

Breaking the Medicine

"I LIKE IT UP HERE." the godlet said. "I can see *everything*."

Denis sat huddled miserably in the dirt. His clothes reeked of gasoline, and his hair smelled of smoke. They'd been setting things on fire all morning, throwing Molotov cocktails from overpasses, causing car accidents, attacking a strip mall, burning down beach houses. Jane had torn down the surfer statue on West Cliff Drive, and done serious damage to the lighthouse by Steamer Lane. They'd abandoned Denis's car near the wharf when they started to hear sirens. The cops the godlet hadn't killed were going crazy trying to respond to their activities, but the three of them moved too fast overground to be trapped—the godlet could run flat-out without getting tired, as could Jane, and she carried Denis. The cops couldn't follow them when they lit out on foot. Denis was exhausted. Destruction was incredibly tiring, and very messy, and not at all satisfying. He could still see the old woman, burning, in his mind.

They were up in the hills now, near campus, at a point where you could see the bay and much of the town. It was a gorgeous view, Denis supposed, if you liked landscapes, which he didn't. Smoke rose here and there from the town below, and the godlet looked at it, nodding in satisfaction. "That's a damn good start," he said. "From up here, it's easy to see the progress we've made. While we're up here, we'll burn down the redwoods and the university and all. Denis can siphon us some gas to splash around. We'll leave the hills on fire behind us when we go back to town."

Jane made a sound of agreement. She was barely recognizable as her old self, now. She had six arms, and she was nearly seven feet tall—she looked more and more like an animate statue of a Hindu goddess of destruction. The godlet, however, now looked almost human. His metal body had acquired a patina of flesh, though the chrome still showed through ragged patches here and there. He had eyes, too—black ones, without whites or irises, but still, they were recognizably eyes. Denis was reassured by these changes; the godlet was becoming less alien. If Beej succeeded in his task, however, and killed Marzi, that would change. The godlet would become something different. Wholly inhuman. Elemental, but still sentient. An earthquake with a mind. A process that could *think*.

The godlet grunted, stumbling, and fell to his knees. "Ah, *fuck*," he said, and when he turned his head, Denis saw that he had normal eyes, now, and he was all skin, no metal. "That little shit!" he shouted. "He let Marzi get out! And her stupid friends, her *posse*, too!"

Denis looked at the sky. It was almost noon. Only almost noon. What a day.

"We'll kill her," Jane said, her voice scarcely human.

"Oh, yes," the godlet said disdainfully. "Why didn't I think of that? It's not so easy, you know, especially now that Marzi's started to figure things out. Still . . . that's what you two are for. Killing on my behalf." He looked at the sky. "Hmm. You know, this might not be so bad. In fact, even if we *can't* kill her, I have an idea for how we can . . . keep her at bay." He frowned. "Then again, it's not exactly *my* idea—it's from her comic book, it's the way one of the bad guys saved himself from the good guy. . . ."

"This isn't a comic book," Denis said. "In case you hadn't noticed. There are more than four colors, here."

"You're right. And I bet *Marzi* knows it's not a comic book, too," the godlet said. "Huh. You know, this could work out well for us. See, she made me what I am, sort of, and part of what I am is *cunning*. And now I've got a cunning backup plan."

"How nice," Denis said. "Cunning backup plans always work."

"Let's go someplace where we can make a last stand," the godlet said. "I know just the place." He winked at Denis. "It's time we had a proper showdown, Old West style."

Just my luck, Denis thought, *to get stuck in a melodrama*.

THEY FOUND Hendrix's body, shot through the heart, and Marzi understood the bad thing Beej had done. She'd assumed he was speaking generally of his association with the Outlaw, but apparently not. Marzi wondered if there was even a real bullet in Hendrix's wound, or if an illusion with the velocity of total belief had blown his chest apart. Hendrix

was the first visible proof of Marzi's failure to keep the
Outlaw locked away, and she cried a little, looking down on
him. None of them went too close to his body, though; if the
Outlaw didn't destroy Santa Cruz, the cops would be inves-
tigating Hendrix's death. "They just killed him," Marzi said.
"For no reason."

"It's what the Outlaw does," Ray said. "That's why we
have to stop him."

Marzi nodded. They all went outside. There were sirens
in the distance, and smoke rising over the trees in the direction of downtown. Marzi swore.

"So where do we go?" Lindsay said, looking toward the
rising plume of smoke. Ray squinted around at everything, and
Jonathan leaned on a parking meter, his eyes half closed, his
breathing shallow. Marzi wondered when he'd eaten last, and
that reminded her that she was hungry, too. She hadn't felt
the need to eat, piss, or even rest in the West beyond the
West, but now that they'd returned, natural order was back
in force.

"Where the smoke is, that's where the Outlaw has already
been," she said. "He's had enough time to do some damage,
but he knows I'm free, now, and he's waiting for me. I say we
head for the hills. After all, that's where you run, if you're a
bad guy, and you're scared."

"Drop the pretense at logic, Marzi," Ray said. He turned
away from her, toward Lindsay. "Marzi and I can feel the
Outlaw, Lindsay. He's like a rotten tooth, throbbing, but in
my *skull* instead of my mouth. I can only imagine it's stronger
for Marzi."

Marzi nodded. "Sort of, but not so unpleasant. In my

comic, Rangergirl and the Outlaw are destined enemies, locked together in antagonism. She always knows which direction he's in, like a magnet knows north. She never knows how *close* he is, unfortunately. . . ." Marzi shrugged. "But I know he's up near campus, and I bet he's in the hills, someplace with lots of mud and rocks to pull down on top of us, lots of trees to burn."

"Do you really think you can face him, head-on like this?" Ray said.

"I didn't say I was going to face him head-on. I said I had a plan. And I do." Marzi didn't *like* the plan, but she couldn't think of anything else to do. It was either that or let the West Coast be razed. She didn't need to hesitate long over a question like that.

"Do we need to know anything about the plan?" Ray asked.

"When we get to the Outlaw, draw your guns, and cover him. Leave the rest to me." She paused. "And if I should die or something . . . use your best judgment."

"If you die, Marzi, we're going to be up against an earthquake with a score to settle," Ray said. "So don't die."

"She won't," Lindsay said.

"One question," Jonathan said. "What guns? I don't have guns."

"Your weapons will come back," Marzi said. "Don't worry." Her toy gun was tucked in her pocket, waiting to become real and lethal again. "Once we get close to the Outlaw, into his . . . charged field . . . our guns will reappear."

"And your pistol will be able to kill him," Ray said. "Jesus. You think you'll get a shot?"

Marzi knew she'd get a shot. She just didn't like thinking about what she'd have to do to get it. "Let me worry about that. We should get something to eat before we go."

"Last meal?" Ray said.

"They've got bagels just down the street," Lindsay said.

"Beats dirt sandwiches and date wine, I guess," Ray said.

They walked down the block to the Bagelry, Ray and Lindsay walking ahead and arguing about something, Jonathan and Marzi walking together. Inside, Lindsay and Ray went to the counter to order, and Marzi hung back with Jonathan. The people working behind the counter were talking about terrorists, fires, deaths. Marzi didn't want to hear that now. There was too much still undone for her to dwell on consequences. Jonathan touched her shoulder, lightly, and she turned to him.

"You saved me," he said, a little stiffly, and Marzi knew he was thinking about her wandering around loose in the halls of his soul. She wondered if the possibility of sweetness was spoiled, now—if a desert had spread out between them. Only time would tell. He was still here, standing with her, part of the posse. For now, that was all that mattered. Jonathan pinched the bridge of his nose with his thumb and forefinger. Marzi wasn't surprised he had a headache. She was a little surprised that she didn't. "I'm sorry for my part in this, for opening the door. I didn't know . . . that's no excuse. But I didn't."

"It's okay," Marzi said. "If you hadn't let the Outlaw escape, we wouldn't have freed Ray, I wouldn't have learned to use my powers, I wouldn't have met the oracle . . . my mind would still be fraying into a million pieces, and the Outlaw would still be hammering away, whispering through the door, trying to get free. This way . . . it's more decisive. I don't have to live with that gnawing fear that I'm going crazy. We can just get this done. One way or another." *By any means necessary,* she thought. "Let's get something to eat," she said. "Then we'll take Lindsay's car up into the hills. This will all be over by this afternoon, one way or another."

"WHY DON'T YOU STAY and keep watch by the road, Jane?" the godlet said. Jane nodded and took up a sentry position. The godlet was keeping her busy, for which Denis was grateful. After they firebombed the surfing museum, she'd taken him in two of her arms and embraced him, whispering in his ear about the palace of mud they'd dwell in forever, once the goddess transformed him into an avatar of Earth like herself. He didn't want to have another conversation like that.

"Walk with me, Denis," the godlet said. He was wholly a rugged gunslinger now, with battered boots, a leather vest, and a surprisingly pristine—but still misshapen—white hat. There was still a sense of *size* to him, as if he extended beyond the borders of his own body, but Denis had met ordinary people with that kind of charisma. It was remarkable, but not necessarily supernatural.

On the other hand, the ground cracked and split with dozens of tiny fissures with the godlet's every step, so his true nature wasn't *that* deeply suppressed.

"Do you know why I brought us here?" the godlet said. They entered the little clearing, where Jane's car was still parked, doors and hatchback open to the elements. The blanket, knife, and picnic basket were still inside the car, though some animal had carried off the loaf of bread. The godlet walked over to Jane's car and propped his boot on the bumper, looking thoughtfully into the back, where Jane had suffocated. "There's lots of reasons. Jane's strongest here, for one thing, and she's my ace in the hole, my hidden derringer, if I need her. I don't think I will—I think I've got a pretty good solution to this whole mess, actually. The only drawback is that it doesn't involve me getting violent and ripping Marzi to pieces, but I can show restraint. The other reason is . . . it's a good place for a last stand. Somebody else took her last stand here, didn't she?" He grinned at Denis, and his teeth were disgusting, the color of wet pine boards. "I want you to keep in mind who your *friends* are. I'm your friend, because I'm not telling your *other* friend that you left her to die under a heap of mud. And her body's here, Denis. I can show it to her any time—I can let her *see* it." He made a peculiar, delicate gesture with his fingers, and the mound of mud that covered Jane's body groaned and shifted, then settled again.

Denis didn't speak, though he wanted to shout, wanted to tell this one-time robot cowboy to shut *up;* he'd made his point. Denis had firebombed an old *woman;* didn't that prove his coerced loyalty well enough? Did the bullying and threats *have* to continue? But he knew such an outburst would be pointless. The godlet didn't have a lot of flexibility, really. He had to say the lines prepared for him.

"So be sure to do what you're told," the godlet went on. "You're going to suck a little gas out of the tank of Janey's car, take those empty bottles out of her floorboard, and make a couple more Molotov cocktails. When Marzi and her crew of merry miscreants arrive, I want you looking serious, like you're going to bomb them. But *don't* throw the bottles. We're not going for a massacre, here. Not by the direct route, anyway. You think you can handle that?"

"Yes," Denis said, his voice a dead monotone. This was tremendously stressful. Being so close to Jane's corpse, the reminder of the life-shattering break that had followed his first visit to this place . . . it was horrible. The godlet knew that, too. All the talk of last stands and giving Jane strength, it was *bullshit*—this was really all about hurting Denis, humiliating him, and probably killing him, in good time.

Denis stood by the hatchback while the godlet went back to the road to get Jane. Denis had been waiting for the right moment, for an opportunity to escape, strike back, *do* something . . . but it occurred to him that there weren't going to be any opportunities—not clear, unambiguous ones, anyway. You had to make your own opportunities. But would he be strong enough to do that?

"HERE," MARZI SAID, leaning out of the passenger window. "Pull over here." They were up in the hills, all trees and steep slopes and curving roads.

Lindsay pulled off to the shoulder. Her clothing flickered, from skirt and Mary Janes to jeans and boots and back again.

"We're close," Marzi said. "Is everyone ready?"

"No," Ray said. "But let's do it anyway."

"Just give me a minute to get my head straight," Marzi said. She thought about the Outlaw, about what it would do when confronted by Marzi—or by Rangergirl, rather—and her posse. The Outlaw would do just what its fictional counterpart had done, when the identical situation arose in issue number five of *The Strange Adventures of Rangergirl*, "Showdowns."

The Outlaw would surrender, throw down his guns, and give himself up. In the comic, Rangergirl had lowered her own weapon, confused. She'd expected things to end in a gunfight, after all, and instead the Outlaw was smiling and saying she'd won. Rangergirl escorted the company of Wild Rangers who took the Outlaw into custody, and she watched as the sorcerer was locked up. She knew it was a trick, but what choice did she have? The Outlaw had surrendered. She couldn't very well gun him down after that, could she? Rangergirl was a force for law, justice, order, mercy—everything the Outlaw was not. She had to play by the rules.

That first night in jail, the Outlaw's gang—a razor-wielding polyglot orangutan with a human brain, a mad scientific rainmaker, a woman with snake venom for blood—had busted their leader out, and killed all the Rangers. The Outlaw was no match for Rangergirl, and would have died in a showdown, so he'd surrendered instead, knowing Rangergirl wouldn't shoot, knowing no jail cell was secure enough to prevent his escape. Since then, Rangergirl had been trying to pursue the Outlaw into a situation where surrender wasn't an option.

Marzi was sure the Outlaw would pull that same trick again today, anticipating a similar result, sure that Marzi would escort him back to Genius Loci and lock him up again. Of *course* that would happen—the story demanded it.

But Marzi had other plans.

She *wasn't* Rangergirl. Marzi wasn't a hero, and she didn't have to play by a hero's rules. She was just Marzi, and even if she had trouble living with herself later, she would do what she had to; what Rangergirl was too honorable to do in the same situation.

"Mount up," she said, and the four of them got out of the car.

As soon as they stepped into the trees, their Western clothes and weapons returned, as substantial as they'd been beyond the door. Marzi stopped and turned to face her friends. "This is it. Your last chance to back out—"

"C'mon, Marzi," Lindsay said, rolling her eyes. "I don't think this is necessary."

"True," Ray said, checking to make sure his rifle was loaded.

Jonathan just nodded. There was a smudge of cream cheese on his chin. Marzi wondered if he was going to die like that.

"Good enough," Marzi said. She led them into the clearing, guns drawn and ready.

The Outlaw leaned against the side of Jane's mud-spattered car. The god looked like a grizzled character actor, all rotten teeth and menace, and the only trace of the supernatural left in the Outlaw was that long shadow, stretching out on the ground despite the high noonday sun. Marzi was gratified to see how human her enemy looked, how mortal. The Outlaw in her comic was a wily, long-lived sorcerer, but he *could* die, unlike an immortal spirit of destruction. Now the thing with the wasteland face *was* the Outlaw, and therefore mortal.

Jane, however, was no longer human at all: She was a multi-armed mud-monster with a ghost white clay face. She stood at the Outlaw's side, like a loyal attack dog. Denis stood on the Outlaw's other side, near the car's open hatchback, keeping himself a little apart, looking miserable and holding a bottle with a rag stuck in the top. Beej had said Denis didn't want to be here, and looking at him, Marzi believed it.

"So," she said, her gun pointed at the Outlaw. "Here we are."

"Yup," the Outlaw said, and spat. It grinned at her. "Guess you had to kill Beej to get out of the canyon."

"No," Marzi said. "He betrayed you."

The Outlaw sighed. "It's so hard to get decent help nowadays. I bet you didn't even reward him with a roll in the hay, poor bastard. Oh, well." The Outlaw tipped its ugly hat to Ray. "Garamond. I see a young hotshot came and took your badge away."

"No, friend," Ray said. "I passed it on. I'm just a deputy now."

"Moving down in the world. How nice. I see you got your mail-order cowboy back, too, Marzi. I'm impressed."

"Are we gonna jaw or slap leather?" Marzi said. It was exactly what Rangergirl said in issue number five. "I'm calling you out for the deaths you've caused."

The Outlaw looked at her for a long moment, and Marzi pushed with her mind, her imagination, exerting the full weight of her narrative imperative on the god.

"Reckon you found your fat manager's body, then," the Outlaw said. "And heard about the wild rumpus we threw downtown. We've killed lots of folks today, and I ain't hit my limit yet. I suppose I've got a lot to pay for." The last sentence was what the Outlaw said in the comic, and Marzi suppressed a grin. This was going to work.

"I reckon I know when I'm outgunned," the Outlaw said

meditatively. "Drop your weapons, boys." The god slowly took his long-barreled Colt .45 Warmakers from their holsters and tossed them at Marzi's feet. Denis gently set down his bottle, and Jane crossed all six of her arms.

"Pick up his guns," Marzi said to her friends, and Jonathan did so.

The Outlaw stepped forward, hands outspread. "I give myself up, Rangergirl. Let's start the rehabilitation process."

Marzi still had her gun pointed at the god. This was the point where fiction and reality would diverge, where it would become clear that life didn't imitate art, that this wasn't a comic book.

In the largely fictional code of the West, there was only one thing worse than shooting an armed man in the back . . . and that was shooting an unarmed man in the face.

That was exactly what Marzi intended to do.

Rangergirl would never do something so cowardly. Such an act would have violated everything she believed in, everything she stood for.

But Marzi wasn't Rangergirl, and she didn't have to play by Rangergirl's rules. She tightened her finger on the trigger.

Then she hesitated. Not out of mercy, but because a terrible thought had suddenly occurred to her. If she wasn't Rangergirl—more accurately, if she *stopped being* Rangergirl—would her enemy stop being the Outlaw? If she violated the laws of her own narrative, if she broke with her character so fundamentally, wouldn't that break *everything,* the whole elaborate framework that constrained the thing with the wasteland face? What if Marzi was about to set her enemy free, let it throw off the bounds of Marzi's Old West perceptions and become its true self, unencumbered, immaterial, unstoppable?

Marzi saw the Outlaw's smirk, and knew she was right—moreover, she knew that *the Outlaw* knew, that he had anticipated her plan and played along without resistance, knowing one dishonorable bullet from her would set him free.

She lowered her gun.

"Ah, fuck," the Outlaw said. "Well, plan B, then." He turned and hurried back to the car, and Jane stepped in front of her god, a living shield. She spread out her arms, and claws popped from her fingertips.

"Burn them, Denis!" the Outlaw shouted.

Marzi looked at Denis—and saw another possibility. In planning future plotlines for her comic, she'd had the idea of making the Outlaw's razor-wielding orangutan turn on his master; wouldn't Denis serve that function just as well? After all, outlaws weren't exclusively killed in showdowns. Sometimes they were betrayed, murdered by their own disgruntled henchmen, and Beej said that Denis had been recruited against his will. But Marzi couldn't just imagine a razor into Denis's hand—pure illusion wouldn't be enough to kill the Outlaw. For a weapon to kill the god, it had to have some spine of reality, even something as objectively harmless as Marzi's toy pistol.

Then she saw Denis drawing a butcher knife, a *real* knife, from his waistband. She stared at him, even as Jane roared and started toward them, Lindsay firing uselessly into Jane's clay body with the tommy gun. The Outlaw was grinning—he *loved* killing, he *loved* gunfire. Marzi watched Denis step forward, his face twisted with hate, and she thought, *Am I making him do this, or is he doing it on his own?*

Denis stabbed the Outlaw in the back, between the shoulder blades, then pulled out the knife and stabbed again, and again, hitting three times as the Outlaw fell, mouth open, expression stupid and stunned. Marzi wondered if the god had ever felt pain before, real physical pain, and she suspected not. Marzi concentrated hard on keeping the Outlaw mortal, and he fell, facedown. His long shadow snapped back into his body like a broken rubber band, and still Denis drove the knife down, kneeling on the Outlaw's back, ramming the blade in seven, eight, nine times. Then he stopped abruptly, as if deciding the Outlaw was finally dead enough. He remained kneeling on the god's back, his head hanging down, his breath ragged and loud.

Marzi turned, no time for relief, because Jane was still coming at them. Jonathan and Lindsay had stepped in front of Marzi, and they were shooting at Jane, but the bullets passed through her body, barely slowing her. Ray, standing back, fired one careful shot after another at Jane's head, but while chunks of clay flew away with each bullet, she didn't slow.

Then an engine growled, and a huge motorcycle roared into the clearing. Alice Belle was riding it, a Valkyrie in black leather and sunglasses, howling, whirling lit firepots on chains over her head with one hand, steering her bike with the other. Alice flung the firepots like a bolo, and they whirled straight for Jane, striking her near the throat. The chains wound around Jane's neck and spiraled down her body, severing her head, slicing through her arms, and then Alice's motorcycle struck Jane's falling body and drove *over* her, tires churning her into a pile of mud. The motorcycle stopped, miraculously still upright, and Alice cut the engine. The sudden silence was resounding.

"That was . . . improbable," Ray said. "The cavalry riding in."

"Damn, baby," Alice said to Lindsay. "That bitch nearly had you."

Lindsay dropped her tommy gun, which dissolved before it hit the ground. The medicine here was broken, the magic fading, and their old clothes were coming back. Jane was just mud, and Marzi supposed Jane was dying even before Alice stopped her—otherwise, she'd be re-forming now.

The Outlaw was still solid, though. Marzi had made him so mortal that he even left a corpse behind.

Lindsay ran to Alice, arms outstretched . . . and then Alice dissolved, faded into dust motes and airy spaces, her motorcycle ghosting away into nothing, until both bike and rider were entirely gone.

Lindsay stopped. "Alice? Alice!"

"She wasn't real," Ray said. "She was real *enough,* she was the cavalry, but Marzi made her."

"Not me," Marzi said. "I didn't. But Lindsay's an artist, too."

"I really believed she'd come back," Lindsay said, sitting on the ground, near where Alice had been. "That she'd come and save me."

"Good," Ray said. "If you hadn't really believed it, she wouldn't have."

"God," Lindsay said. "I miss her."

"I know," Marzi said.

Jonathan dropped his guns, and they vanished, too. "Now what? Are we done?"

"Almost. We should bury the Outlaw."

Denis stood up unsteadily and kicked the Outlaw in the head. Marzi winced. *Denis* wouldn't have hesitated to shoot the Outlaw in the face. "Don't bury him," Denis said. "Let the animals have him."

"No," Ray said. "Better to bury him. I'm sure his meat's poison, anyway. Do we have anything to dig with?"

"I've got a bucket in my car," Lindsay said.

"We could probably dig a grave in that heap of mud over there," Jonathan said. "It looks pretty soft."

"No!" Denis shouted. "Leave the mud alone!" He snatched up the butcher knife and brandished it at them.

They all stared at him, and he lowered the knife. "Shit." He looked away. "Do what you want. You could at least thank me. I saved your lives."

Marzi thought about it. Maybe she hadn't made Denis stab the Outlaw with the force of her narrative will. Maybe he'd done it on his own. She'd never know for sure. "Thanks," she said.

Denis grunted.

They dug into the drying mud, everyone taking turns except Denis, who sat by Jane's car, staring at the dirt. Lindsay, Marzi, and Jonathan were all sitting together on the ground, not talking, while Ray took his turn digging with the bucket.

"Uh, guys?" Ray said. "There's already somebody buried here. A woman."

Denis said "Fuck," loudly, distinctly, and nine times in a row.

Wallow in Velvet

"SO DENIS IS IN JAIL," Lindsay said, shaking her head. "Think he'll wind up in prison?" She sat on the couch beneath the bay window in Genius Loci, a week after the Outlaw's death. Bobby-O was behind the counter, trying to look cool, though Marzi knew he was terrified about his new position as night manager. The café owners had called from Florida and offered Marzi the job of day manager, and she'd accepted, deciding it might be nice to have her nights free for a while. Once Bobby-O was more secure in his position, they could trade off, if Marzi found that she missed nights. On her first day in Hendrix's old job, Marzi had blasted death metal all day long. It wasn't much of a memorial, but it was the best she could do.

"Maybe they'll put him in a mental hospital," Marzi said. Denis had confessed to burying Jane in a pile of mud, though the cops couldn't make much sense of his story, which involved ghosts and gods. He'd also confessed to the murder of an unidentified elderly cowboy, but he denied having killed Hendrix, claiming his friend Beej had done that. The police were looking for Beej anyway, since he'd escaped from jail on the same day that half a dozen cops were murdered and a group of mostly unknown terrorists blew up the clock tower and did significant damage to other local landmarks. The police understandably suspected Beej, and they knew Denis was involved—there were witnesses who'd seen him lob a firebomb. Marzi was worried about the investigation, of course, but she thought it would be okay. When the police did an autopsy on the Outlaw, he would be as human inside as anyone. She'd imagined him well enough for that. And if Denis had said anything about Marzi and her friends, the cops hadn't taken it seriously enough to follow up—Lindsay's friend Joey had enough inside information to let them know that. The police had questioned Marzi again about the night Denis and Beej and Jane tried to break into the café, but that was all the contact they'd had. Marzi wondered what story the cops would make up to explain everything. It would have to be pretty baroque, but she had faith in their ability to rationalize chaos.

Things had been ugly. Downtown and much of West Cliff Drive were wrecked, but it could have been much worse, and the townspeople were already rebuilding.

Everything was over, now. The door to the medicine lands was gone as if it had never been, and Ray's original mural was back. Marzi's cap gun was just a toy again, and she'd hung it up on the wall behind the counter in the café. Yesterday Marzi found the old man who'd sold her the gun in the first place, and she told him he could have free coffee at Genius Loci for the rest of his life. He'd nodded, as if such things were offered to him every day, and thanked her. Marzi hadn't heard from the scorpion oracle, but thought she wasn't the kind of creature that would bother with thanks—she'd expected Marzi to do her job, and Marzi had, and that was the end of their association.

Marzi sat snuggled deep in a velvet chair, a pint of Guinness in her hands. Ray sat at the far end of the couch, holding forth to Jonathan about his days in New York. Jonathan was taking notes.

"You and Jonathan have a nice time last night?" Lindsay waggled her eyebrows. She was back to normal, too, though there was a streak of melancholy in her still. Alice hadn't returned from wherever she'd gone.

The first few nights after the Outlaw's death, Lindsay, Marzi, and Jonathan had all stayed together, hesitant to be by themselves. Last night Lindsay had left them alone, saying she needed some time by herself to feel blue without bringing anyone else down. Marzi and Jonathan had finally had time together, to talk. His memories of his experiences beyond the Western Door were fading, and losing their horrible potency, and the distance between them was beginning to shrink. Things were still fragile, but after their time together talking last night she had hopes that, by the end of the summer, she and Jonathan could at least get back to the place they'd been when all this began—with possibilities stretched out ahead of them.

Ray, meanwhile, had spent every night with the avowed intention of "getting laid or getting drunk trying." Marzi didn't know if he'd succeeded in the former, but supposed he'd managed the latter. He even had some speaking engagements scheduled, and was honing a story about "travels in the desert" to explain his long absence. Ray was enjoying the real world—and after The Oasis, who wouldn't?

Lindsay nudged her. "Hello? Earth to Marzipan? Where are my sordid details?"

"Sorry," Marzi said. "My thoughts have been getting away with me lately. Yeah, last night was nice. He's still a little freaked out by the fact that we've been inside his soul . . ." She shook her head.

"He'll get past that," Lindsay said seriously, lowering her voice. "Don't get me wrong, I'm sure it was a weird and not very pleasant experience, but I think it's also partly an excuse for him to keep his distance. We've been through a lot these past few days. We all need some time to unwind."

"We'll see what happens," Marzi said. "And we might have more time. Jonathan is thinking about moving out here for a while, after he finishes his thesis defense. He wants to write a book about Ray, and Ray's agreed to let him."

Lindsay nodded. "You see? It's not all collapsing buildings and scorpion bites."

"Scorpions sting, they don't bite," Marzi said. "I don't even think they have teeth."

"Then how do they chew their food?" Lindsay asked. She grinned.

A motorcycle roared up outside, hardly an uncommon sound; bikers liked Genius Loci. Then a familiar voice said, "Lindsay?"

Alice Belle stood by the door, dressed in riding leathers, holding her helmet in one hand.

Lindsay looked at her for a long moment. "Are you real?" she said.

Alice cocked her head. "Last time I checked, yeah." Her eyes darted to Jonathan and Ray, back to Lindsay. "You know that . . . problem I was having? It cleared up. I'm not having those, ah, urges anymore. I don't want to do anything right now except sit and have a beer with you. I'm afraid that feeling will come back, but—"

"Don't," Lindsay said, springing from her chair. "Don't worry. It won't. I have a *lot* to tell you. Let's get you a beer. You'll need it." She led Alice toward the counter, shooting Marzi a grin over her shoulder.

Marzi settled back more deeply into the chair. Yes. It could have been worse. That was hardly an inspiring sentiment, but sometimes harsh optimism was the best you could do in the desert.

She'd decided to keep *Rangergirl* going—at the very least, the character deserved a good ending, rather than an abrupt termination. Marzi's best work was probably ahead of her anyway. In a year or two, she could do a different comic, something about connections rather than lonely wandering, something about love, and getting through the long nights. Ray had suggested they collaborate, which was an intriguing notion—associating her name with his would be a good career move, too, with publicity swirling around him because of his reappearance. He'd only been a minor figure in the art scene, but it was amazing what a miraculous resurrection could do for your image.

Marzi didn't know what was going to happen, but there were doors opening before her, and none of them led into the dead heart of the desert. Compared to the lonely desolation of her life before, every step she took now seemed to lead along a path strewn with flowers.

Marzi moved to the couch and settled down beside Jonathan, and listened to Ray talk about punching Andy Warhol in the face in Manhattan in the seventies.

It was probably bullshit, but it was a good story.

ACKNOWLEDGMENTS

It would be remiss of me to omit mention of the coffee shops that had a part in the creation of this novel. First and foremost, Caffe Pergolesi in Santa Cruz, which served (very loosely) as the model for Genius Loci; Café Au Coquelet in Berkeley, where I completed much of the major revision; and Café DiBartolo in Oakland, where I did most of the line-editing.

I listened to a lot of great bluegrass, insurgent country, and cowpunk while writing this, notably Ryan Adams, Caitlin Cary, the Old 97s, Paul Thorn, Son Volt, Todd Snider, the Two Dollar Pistols, Uncle Tupelo, Whiskeytown, Wilco, and, of course, all the good stuff they play on KPIG radio out of Freedom, California.

A lot of people made my life better during the course of writing this book. Thanks to Scott Seagroves and Lynne Raschke for their generous hospitality in Santa Cruz, when I first moved there and after I moved away; to Megan Parker, for listening early on, and to Marissa Lingen, for encouraging me when I wanted to stop; to the readers who gave me feedback on the raw first draft: Christopher Barzak, Jennifer A.

Hall, Melinda R. Himel, Michael J. Jasper, Jay Lake, David Moles, Jenn Reese, and Greg van Eekhout; to my coworkers at *Locus,* for giving me the best day job a writer could have; to my agent Ginger Clark, for taking a chance; and to my editor Juliet Ulman, for making this a far better book than it would have been otherwise. And finally, thanks to Heather Shaw, for everything.

ABOUT THE AUTHOR

TIM PRATT has been nominated for the Nebula Award and for the Campbell Best New Writer Award, and his fiction has appeared in *Best American Short Stories* and *The Year's Best Fantasy and Horror.* He lives in Oakland, California, where he co-edits a literary 'zine, *Flytrap,* with his fiancée Heather Shaw.